COLPO DI
FULMINE

DeVecchio

HARPER DALE

E-Book ISBN: 978-1-964011-10-3

Paperback ISBN: 978-1-964011-11-0

Trigger Warnings

DeVecchio: Colpo di fulmine is a Mafia Romance. Its content can be triggering for some individuals. This story contains explicit language, graphic violence, explicit sexual scenes, and contains mentions of drug abuse and human trafficking.

The Legend
Colpo di Fulmine

FOR MILLENNIA, the people of Italy have celebrated love at first sight—called Colpo di Fulmine, which is translated literally as lightning bolt, since it signifies an instant, overpowering connection between two people that strikes without warning.

Such love is said to occur when two souls recognize each other immediately, transcending time and space.

Colpo di fulmine is believed to be orchestrated by the gods themselves. Jupiter, King of the gods, symbolized by the sky and thunder—touches the hand of his mate, Juno, goddess of marriage and childbirth—and their electrifying spark forges an unbreakable bond uniting two souls.

Neither individual has power over it.

Playlist

Sherry... Frankie Valli & The Four Seasons

Isn't She Lovely... Stevie Wonder

Nel Blu Dipinto di Blu (Volare)... Dean Martin

Just My Imagination... The Temptations

Lay Lady Lay... Bob Dylan

Help Me... Joni Mitchell

Yesterdays Gone... Chad & Jeremy

Ain't No Sunshine... Bill Withers

Can't Get Enough of Your Love, Babe... Barry White

You've Lost That Lovin' Feelin'... Righteous Brothers

Heartbreaker... Dionne Warwick

How Long... Ace

Until You Come Back to Me... Aretha Franklin

I'm Not in Love... 10cc

Three Times A Lady... Commodores

You Are The Sunshine Of My Life... Stevie Wonder

You Belong to Me... Doobie Brothers

DeVecchio IMPORTS

Francesco DeVecchio
Capofamiglia

Matteo DeVecchio
Underboss

Christos Baka
Caporegime

Tommaso Ricci
Caporegime

Matteo

An Issue

Baltimore 1978

"**M**atty!" Tommaso approaches with urgency in his pace and an edge to his voice. "We've got an issue."

Issue is never good. My eyes widen and my chest tightens seeing the concern on my capo's face. The skin on my arms prickle. This is definitely—

"Matteo!" Before Tommy can explain our issue, he's interrupted by a high-pitched squeal. Our gazes arc toward the shriek to watch a strawberry blonde race across the room with open arms, her smile as wide as a slice of watermelon. "It's so good to see you!" The girl plasters a pink lipstick kiss on my cheek, tries to wipe its traces off with her thumb, and threads a well-tanned arm around mine, squeezing it tightly. "I'm so glad you're here."

I wish I could say the same. "Thank you, Miss..."

"Albright." Her big smile melts like ice cream in August. "You don't remember me?"

Sweetheart, I don't have a clue. "I'm sorry..."

"Adeline," she says with a pretty little pout. She's about to stomp her foot. "We went sailing in Charleston, remember?"

My mother, standing nearby, has the eyes and ears of a hawk. She nods with stern brows, and I respond quickly. "Why, yes, Adeline, I'm so sorry."

Adeline glows with relief.

Donna DeVecchio, always the consummate hostess, moves to wrap a supple arm around the girl's shoulder, drawing her close. "Thank you for coming, Adeline. Matteo and his father have spent weeks working in Europe and I wanted them to be surrounded by friends on their return." Mother shoots me a strained smile. "Adeline is Dr. Albright's daughter. You two met when we were in Charleston last spring."

"Of course, I remember."

The tall, shapely girl wears a navy blue polka-dot sundress that shows off her golden tan. Freckles dot her shoulders, cheeks, and nose.

I stroke her arm, and she beams brightly as Mother redirects this conversation. "Adeline, are you still studying at Columbia?"

"Yes, Mrs. DeVecchio, I'm a senior this year." She turns from Mother back to me, batting big eyes. "University of South Carolina."

My face must be blank, my mind having wandered to the issue. *Wandered my ass. It never left.*

Adeline's hazel eyes flash. "Matteo, you absolutely do not remember. I'm studying interior design." She may still stomp her foot.

"Oh, interior design." Mother claps her hands, determined to right this sinking ship. "I love it. Tell me all about it, dear."

Catching Tommy's impatient glare, I offer, "Adeline, would you like something to drink?"

Just like that, her smile is back. "Oh, please. A chardonnay?" Adeline Albright is as bubbly as Alka-Seltzer. Judging by that smile, I'm forgiven.

"I'll be right back."

Mother deflects. "Now, Adeline, remind me. What sorority are you in?"

I owe you, Mother.

Their voices trail off as Tommy and I head for the bar, my imagination swirling. "What's the issue?"

Before he can answer—"Matteo?"

I know that silky voice. And it doesn't belong here.

Turning, I see Sophia Gabicci wearing a mid-thigh, emerald-colored dress showing off a body that will make any swinging dick stand at attention. Hell. Sophia's curves could make a dead man's dick rise in the grave.

A teardrop diamond necklace accentuates her supple cleavage. At her elbow is a man I despise. I smile anyway.

"Sophia, sweetheart." I kiss her cheek and inhale her familiar fragrance, whispering in her ear. "You should have let me know you were coming."

Her dark eyes spark. She uses her thumb to wipe the smudge of Adeline's kiss from my cheek as she whispers with a hiss, "Your mother invited me, Matteo, not you."

"I didn't invite anyone, sweetheart. It's not my party. You brought Geno."

Her black eyes smolder behind long lashes.

Sophia kisses her fingertips and plants them on my lips. "I didn't want to attend unescorted. You don't mind, do you?"

Geno and I exchange our usual go-to-hell glares as I squeeze Sophia's soft hand.

He is a hard motherfucker to stomach with an eagle's beak that bears my imprint. I smirk every time I see the ugly mandible, which is a little askew. His granite jaw left me no choice but to go for the nose more than once.

We stand eye to eye. "How's the nose, Geno?"

If looks could kill, we'd both be dead.

His gaze narrows. "About like your ribs, I suspect."

Ribs and noses. Cartledge never heals back to its original shape.

Tommy clears his throat, reminding me we don't have time for this pissing contest.

"Sophia," I nod. "Excuse us. I've got something to attend to."

Geno polishes off his red wine and clomps the empty goblet on the side table, glaring from Tommy to me. "What's your rush, DeVecchio? Got a... *problem?*"

Our gazes cement together as I fight the urge to break his nose again, but my mother's party in my parents' house isn't the place for Geno and me to go at it again.

My ticker takes it up a notch as I turn my back on the fucker, and Tommy and I thread through the crowded room.

"What are they doing here?" Tommy asks.

"Beats me. What's the fucking issue?"

"The shipment."

I was afraid of that.

"Chardonnay," I bark at the bartender. "Allesandro." I summon my cousin, standing at the end of the bar. His mother is my mother's sister. He draws girls to his side like a vacuum cleaner sucks dust.

Alessandro looks up from his cadre of admirers, all versions of Adeline—young and coiffed, showing off their tits, which, even if they're not, are pushed up and pinched together in an effort to make them look enticing.

"A favor, please," I say to my young cousin. "Carry this to Adeline over there with Mother. Tell them something came up that I have to deal with. And while you're there, make nice with Adeline."

Allesandro takes the wine glass with a suspicious gaze, followed by a nod. "I like Adeline."

"Good, let her know it. Excuse us. Tommaso?"

As we continue toward the office, I try again to get answers. "What happened?"

"I'll let Christos explain."

Internally, I groan.

Opening the office door and striding to the telephone on the desk, I furiously dial the warehouse.

On the first ring, my other capo answers. "Baka."

"What happened?"

Chris covers the mouthpiece as he clears his throat. "I gave him thirty minutes leeway, considering traffic. When he was thirty-one minutes late, I sent a crew to backtrack the route. Sal just called."

He clears his throat again, this time louder. "Looks like the highway patrol pulled the truck over—"

Fuck!

"Where?" Covering the mouthpiece with my hand, I whisper to Tommy, "Get Pop."

Breathe.

We pay through the nose to make sure things like this don't happen. Feeling my pulse in my fingertips as I press them to my eyelids, I ask calmly, "Exactly, where is the truck?"

"Just south of the city limits on I-95."

Anne Arundel County. My heart drums like 'Wipeout.' "Is the driver in custody?"

"He's in the back of the trooper's patrol unit, in bracelets, as we speak. Guess they're waiting on a tow truck."

Already handcuffed. It wasn't a random traffic stop.

Now my scalp tingles.

Don't lose your cool. When you lose your temper, you lose control of the situation.

I'm pouring a drink from the heavy decanter on the antique credenza as the office door swings open. Pop and our consigliere enter, their faces weighted with concern. I signal for them to sit as Tommy closes the solid wood door behind them.

This room is all but soundproof. For good reason.

Pop and Antonio sink into stuffed chairs in front of the desk, two sets of eyes locked on me as I put Chris on speakerphone, asking, "Do you trust this driver?"

Chris replies in a hushed tone as if he doesn't want to be overheard. "He's a new kid, Matty, but he was vetted, and he took the oath."

Pop and I exchange glances. Omerta. The oath of loyalty. Dates back to the Middle Ages. But I don't know—with some young kids, omerta doesn't mean what it used to.

"What's his name?" I ask.

"It's Joey. Joey Carbona, Leo's kid."

Pop tweaks his mouth to the side and nods.

Leo Carbona is a trusted soldier who has been with the family for decades. This kid was born into the De-Vecchio regime.

"You say the tow truck isn't there?"

"Not yet," Chris answers. "Sal's on a payphone down the road. He can see everything. The tow truck isn't there and the troopers aren't searching. Says they're just standing around bullshitting with some big guy in plainclothes like it's party time."

"A narc."

"Would appear."

"Get on the phone with that public defender you're so fond of. Head her that way. She needs to get Joey released ASAP. I'll call you back."

I dig in my jacket pocket, find my black book, and dial another number.

A woman answers, "Rhinehart residence."

"Good evening, Mrs. Rhinehart. Is your husband available?"

"He's in the backyard." Her voice is distinctly Southern. There is no 'r' in her yawd.

"May I speak with him, please? This is John Smythe. That's Smythe, with a Y. I have an urgent matter."

"He's barbecuing." Again, the r is missing. Rhinehart is bobby-cuin'.

"Please, if you tell him who's calling, he'll want to take the call. I promise. John Smythe. Be sure to tell him Smythe with a Y."

She clunks her phone receiver onto wood, and we listen to her plod across a hardwood floor. A heavy woman. From a distance, she calls, "Alan!"

I refill my two fingers of Glen Livet neat, the telephone still on speaker as we wait.

I would offer Pop and Antonio a drink, but they each have one in hand, and Tommy, leaning his back against the office door with his arms crossed over his thick chest, won't drink on duty.

Other than the noises from the Rhinehart house, silence blankets Pop's office. Too much is at stake for small talk. My hair stands on end. I'm sure theirs is, too.

"Mr. Smythe." It's Rhinehart's gravelly voice. "I understand you have a problem."

My eyes are on Pop as I speak. "Troopers pulled over our eighteen-wheeler in your county."

Sheriff Rhinehart is slow to respond. When he does, we can barely hear him, like he's speaking into his cupped hand over the mouthpiece. "I can't control state troopers."

"Then why do we pay you!" My father roars as he stands and joins me at the desk.

Francesco DeVecchio is not known for his patience.

The sheriff clears his throat. "Mr. Smythe—"

Pop doesn't let him finish. "Rhinehart, do you need to be reminded—?"

Silence. Tommy and I exchange glances.

"Do you?" Pop demands.

"No." Rhinehart answers, his voice lifeless.

Pop sits back in his chair, nods at me, and I give Rhinehart instructions. "Hang up and call dispatch. Tell them whatever tow truck company they called—call them off. They made a mistake. It's another company's turn in rotation. Then you call Jeremiah's Tow Truck Service. Make sure no one touches that truck but Jeremiah. Understood?"

"Yes."

"You've got the number?"

"Yes."

"Make it happen. Next week, Rhinehart, we'll visit. You, me, and my father."

That'll have him pissing his pants. My father is Capo-famiglia. Nobody wants to be summoned to a meeting with Francesco Matteo DeVecchio. Not even me, and I'm his underboss.

Tommy and Chris—Tommaso Ricci and Christos Baka—are my capos. I run the day-to-day business, delegating to them. They answer to me, and I answer to Pop.

Ours is a tricky business.

The pezzo da novanta are all alike—always with their hands out, wanting us to pay them more for doing less. Politicians and bureaucrats are loyal only to money. But we need them. So, we do the dance.

Rhinehart wouldn't be in office were it not for the DeVecchio family.

He knew what he signed up for when he accepted my father's campaign contributions and what was expected of him: a warning if any law enforcement agent in his county was after us.

The problem is that Rhinehart is as lazy as he is greedy.

Hanging up from Rhinehart, I call Chris. Learning Jeremiah's on the way, he knows what to do.

This has never happened, but it's a drill the men have practiced.

Our imports and exports are stamped with the family crest, an ancient Roman warrior emblem—an eagle with its wings spread wide, holding a banner with the family name.

Legal cargo is carried in boxes stamped with the green logo.

Our men must remove everything not stamped in green before the truck reaches impound.

"Have Sal use the payphone to report a robbery in progress when he sees Jeremiah pull up. Get dispatch to divert those troopers so they won't follow Jeremiah."

"Got it."

If everything goes as planned, our driver will be released after the truck is searched and nothing is found.

One slip-up and We. Are. Screwed.

Sherry
THE RUNNER

"**Y**ou are such a badass." My best friend Tina high-fives me as she clicks the stopwatch. "I can't believe you're that fast."

Bent at the waist, hands resting on my thighs, I suck in badly needed air.

"I still didn't beat Marguerite's time." I don't have to look to know. Marguerite Guerrero, my co-worker and racing arch-nemesis, is lightning fast. I'm more of a sound wave.

"Marguerite's won the two-hundred-meter every year since they started the office Olympics." I don't like losing. I really don't want to lose two years in a row.

"It's not like you're trying for the real Olympics, Sherry Baby. It's a friendly office competition."

I snatch the towel from Tina's hands to blot sweat from my face. "You know I hate it when you call me that."

She flashes her taunting smile. "And that's why I do it. Do you want one more run?"

"No, I've got to shower and dress. I'm meeting Scott for dinner."

My best friend blows out a loud puff of disgust. "He never picks you up."

"I don't mind."

"Your date should pick you up, Sherry."

"I don't need a man to hover over me. I don't like someone trying to control me. If I meet a guy for dinner, I can leave when I want."

"If you had the right man, you wouldn't want to leave." Tina knows she won't win this argument. I like my independence. "See you back here Monday?" she asks.

I nod. "Same time." Giving her shoulder a squeeze, I smell my stinky self. *Ugh.*

Tina is tiny, so the poor girl got an overwhelming whiff of my sweaty armpit. "I'm sorry, Tina, I didn't think. Thanks for helping me train."

She smiles. "You know I don't mind." She glances at her watch. "Besides, I've got to get ready for my Saturday night date, too."

Tina has been married for several years and still gets ooey-gooey over her husband. She can't understand why I'm still single.

I cup my hands, yelling through them as she heads for her car. "Make Adam take you some place nice! You deserve it!"

I have no desire to let one man control me. If I want to pick up and move to San Francesco tomorrow, I can. Well, technically, not tomorrow-tomorrow. I have a debt to pay off first, but then I'm free as a bird.

I train at a high school track a few blocks from my apartment building. I give myself a pep talk as I get my wind back. "Okay, one more run."

I jog for home.

The phone is trilling impatiently as I unlock my front door.

Making a flying lunge across my tiny apartment, I grab the receiver, but before I can even say hello, I hear, "Where the fuck have you been? I needed you thirty minutes ago."

My cousin is six years my senior, and he thinks he's my boss. Well, technically, he kind of is.

"Jesus, Chris. It's Saturday night."

"I'm going to buy you a damned beeper. Anne Arundel County Jail. Meet Joey Carbona. And I mean step on it."

"I have a date."

His voice quietens. It's his professional, threatening tone. "You going to make me repeat it?" That tone would scare me to death if I weren't family, but Christos Baka is a teddy bear to me. Thanks to him, I'm indebted to the DeVecchio family until I pay back their college loan. How can I complain?

They put me through law school. While my friends pay off grad school loans to the bank, I pay in discreet services. I guess you could say I'm a modern-day indentured servant.

Hum.

So much for my liberation. But I have a law degree. That's worth a lot, right?

"Fine. I'll call off my date. Joey Cardona. A.A. County Jail. It'll take me an hour to get there. I need to shower first."

"Carbona with a B and skip the shower. Haul ass. I mean it."

I roll my eyes. "What did Mr. Carbona with a B do?"

"Not a goddamned thing. Remember that, kiddo. Get him out and bring his ass straight to me."

I aim to please the people who paid for my law degree. They don't call on me often. I may not look much like an attorney with my wet hair pulled back in a ponytail, wearing a T-shirt and jeans, but at least I don't stink as I walk into the Anne Arundel County Jail.

I took the time for a quick shower.

"What can I do for you?" the desk sergeant asks. He's a tall, slender, white-haired man.

I show the man with gentle gray eyes my driver's license and public defender badge. "I believe you have a young man named Joey Carbona in lockup." I glance around at the gray tile lobby. This place hasn't been updated since Lucky Luciano was a guest. "I'm Sherry Drakos with the Maryland Office of the Public Defender. I'm here to see Mr. Carbona."

The desk sergeant harrumphs. "That's record time." He chews his lips as he scans the roster. "We'll bring him to Room B. You can wait there."

Like I know where Room B is.

My head is on a swivel. "I'm sorry. I've never been here. Which way?"

With his brow hiked, the sergeant aims his left arm like an arrow, indicating a long corridor. "Second door on the right."

"Thanks."

The room isn't much larger than a walk-in closet. In the middle is a small metal table with a chair on either side. No windows other than the glass in the steel door.

Gray tile floors. Cinder block walls.

Waiting for Mr. Carbona with a B, I've got time to ponder.

I don't know much about the DeVecchios other than their scary reputation, but Chris has been best friends with Matteo DeVecchio for as long as I can remember. I don't recall the last time I saw Matteo. Maybe in middle school at a birthday party? But I've heard the man is as gorgeous as he is dangerous.

Chris is a handsome man, too. Growing up, all of my girlfriends drooled over my big, blonde older cousin who has crisp blue eyes and a dimple to die for.

I'm not afraid of Chris. How scary can Matteo DeVecchio be, being so close to my teddy bear cousin all of his life?

The door opens, and a small young man is escorted in wearing an orange jumpsuit. He shuffles in ankle shackles, and his wrists are cuffed in front of him. A little overboard. "He can lose the cuffs."

The jailer gives a lopsided grin. "Not in Sheriff Rhinehart's jail." The jailer, who is a head taller than my client, says, "You've got fifteen minutes."

As he stands guard on the other side of the door, I slip the incarcerated driver my card and whisper, "I'm Sherry Drakos. Mr. Baka wants you to know you have nothing to worry about."

It's against the law for these rooms to be bugged, but I don't trust the law. I've never known a cop who was above bending the rules.

The kid leans across the desk, his shackled hands in his lap as he whispers, "You tell him he has nothing to worry about. I swore Omerta."

"Omerta? Sorry. Never heard of it."

Joey nods. "Our oath of loyalty."

"O... kay. I will. First, tell me what happened."

Joey glances over his shoulder, still whispering. "I look in my side mirrors and see flashing lights. I pull over. They jerk me out all rough-like, slap cuffs on me—no one says a fucking word about anything except 'you're under arrest.'"

My brows quirk. "Did they give you a ticket for speeding? Anything?"

Joey shakes his head.

"Did they read you your rights? Tell you why they were pulling you over?"

He scrunches his mouth and shakes his head. "Not a fucking word, ma'am."

The arrest won't hold up.

"You didn't speed? Change lanes without using a blinker? Run a stop sign or redlight?"

"Ma'am, I'm driving down the highway right on the speed limit when I see flashing lights. Soon as I see them, I pull over. I've been schooled all about not resisting and doing what they tell me to do. I knew Mr. Baka would send someone when he heard."

I look beyond Joey Carbona at the jailer's back and raise my voice. "Officer, can you come in here?"

The big guy opens the door and pokes his head in.

"He doesn't know what he's charged with and neither do I. What am I defending here?"

"Lady, I'm a guard." He has an unusually square face. Kind of bulldoggish minus the underbite.

"Can we find out?"

The guard closes the door and disappears down the hallway.

"I don't understand." I'm still speaking just above a whisper. "Were you transporting something... you shouldn't?"

Joey stares for a moment, his face a blank slate. He blinks. "I can't answer that."

I lean back in my chair. Okay. So, the cops pull him over because they think he's transporting drugs or something illegal—but they still need probable cause to stop him. If they don't, it's the fruit of the poisoned vine. No matter what they find, it will be tossed. Inadmissible.

But knowing how cops work, they'll make up an excuse, so even if Joey didn't, they'll say he changed lanes illegally or they clocked him speeding. It's his word against the cops.

If they want you, they will get you. To them, the end justifies the means.

The guard sticks his head back in the doorway. "Ma'am, he was pulled over on suspicion of interstate trafficking of illegal drugs."

The feds?

I stand. "Let me say this slowly. What was the probable cause to stop him? Some fed's suspicion isn't enough."

The guard lifts his hands high. "Lady, I told you. I'm a jail guard." He has green eyes. Green eyes are a Scottish thing.

"What's your name?" I ask.

He glowers. "Price Morgan. Corporal Price Morgan."

"Corporal Morgan, you know as well as I do, even if an investigator's gut or his snitch tells him someone is a bad man, they still need a legal reason to detain him. What was the reason for Joey Carbona's arrest this evening?"

His thick blonde brows draw together. "What'd you say your name is?"

"Sherry Drakos."

The guard cocks his head with a sneer as he crosses his arms over his thick chest. "Ms. Drakos, let me say this slowly. I'm not a lawyer or an investigator. You'll have to ask them those questions."

I close my eyes and inhale deeply. "Can you please get someone in here who can shed light on this arrest?"

Corporal Morgan leaves the room, muttering swear words under his breath as if I can't hear him.

I sit back down across from Joey. "We don't have time for anything but the truth. Have you been arrested before? Now's the time for honesty."

"Not once."

Joey is a handsome man about my age or younger and not much taller, but he has the trademark dark Italian eyes, complexion, and hair. Those eyes are quick. He's intelligent, and I don't see panic on his face; he's just concerned. He'd be a fool if he wasn't.

This kid isn't a fool.

My head down, I jot notes on my yellow paper notepad. "The truck you're driving. Who is it registered to?"

"DeVecchio Imports."

"So, you work for DeVecchio Imports?"

His brows twist. "You know I do. Got my CDL and everything. I'm taking classes at community college." He grins. "I'll be a lawyer someday, too."

I like Joey.

The door swings wide as a guy the size of Rhode Island bursts in, making the windowless room shrink. He's burly with dirty blonde hair cut short over the ears, full on top. His gray T-shirt hugs his muscular torso, and those eyes are the blue flame of a welder's torch.

They slice through me as he snarls, "Who the hell are you to question my investigation?" The tendons in the man's thick neck bulge as he tries to reign in his rage.

He thinks I'm going to cower in the corner.

Instead, I hold his gaze, stand, and offer my hand. "I'm Sherry Drakos with the Maryland Public Defender's office."

He ignores my hand as his eyes scour me from head to toe and climb back to my eyes. "Public defender my ass." He rests his hands on his waist, elbows out—a trademark territorial stance, his legs braced. "No public defender ever got here this fast. And public defenders don't wear Rolex watches."

I glance at my wristwatch with pride. "A graduation gift." I offer him my card and smile. "Listen, jackass investigator whatever your name is, I am a public defender, and I want to know what my client is charged with."

The gargantuan man snarls first at Joey and then at me. "Nothing. He's free to go."

Joey and I exchange stunned glances.

"Free?" I ask.

"Yeah." Rhode Island leans against the door, holding it to the wall with his back, and sweeps his arm to the open doorway. "Get the fuck out."

He'll break a tooth if he keeps grinding his teeth with that much force.

"If you don't want to get sued for wrongful arrest, tell me why my client was brought here in the first place. You know it's degrading for an innocent person to be hauled to jail in handcuffs. I'm thinking my client suffered emotional stress and loss of reputation."

This is when being a woman pays off. If I were a man, Rhode Island would have taken one step and snatched me up by the scruff of my neck.

Instead, he glares. "He's here under suspicion of transporting illegal goods."

Rhode Island is tall enough that I have to crane my neck back to meet his gaze, and I'm not a shorty. "May I get your name?"

Those blue eyes still simmer as he squints. "Special Agent Viggo Johansen. I thought you wanted out of here."

Viggo. Never heard of anyone named Viggo. I pick up my notepad and pen. "Spell that, please."

You couldn't pry his mouth open with a jackhammer. It's welded shut as he glowers.

"Is that Johansen with an E, an A, or an O?" I ask.

"J.O.H.A.N.S.E.N."

"Thank you. Now, Special Agent Johansen with an E, are you special with the DEA? FBI? What initials accompany your title?"

"D... E... A..." He snarls through clenched teeth.

I nod with pursed lips, lifting my brows for show. Pissing him off is pure pleasure.

"Very well, DEA Special Agent Johansen, you realize suspicion alone doesn't warrant pulling him over on the highway and dragging him to jail. One last time: Why?"

"W... H... Y... was my client stopped by the Maryland Highway Patrol and slapped into handcuffs? Last chance to answer this right before I file a wrongful arrest complaint."

Viggo flashes a full-frontal smile as his eyes soften a degree of two. "You've got a fine color when you're mad."

My fine color, as he calls it, is crimson. I feel the heat in my neck and cheeks, but it's not all fueled by temper. Some of it has to do with him. Viggo is one fine-looking, intimidating man.

I'm in a fight or flight mode, and flight is not an option.

As I stuff my notepad and pen into my briefcase, it occurs to me as if a frisbee thunks me in the head: Viggo had intelligence on the DeVecchio truck so he had every right to pull it over merely on his intelligence. But admitting it means, sooner or later, he will have to give up his snitch.

Lie to me, Viggo, or burn your snitch. "I'll file my complaint in the morning."

"Highway patrol said he changed lanes illegally. And he was speeding."

Our gazes align. "We both know that's bullshit."

Viggo lifts his hands with a cocky grin. "I wasn't there. I'm not about to call a highway patrol officer a liar. Are you?"

In a heartbeat.

"Get the cuffs off my client and let him get into his street clothes. I'm taking him out of here."

"About fucking time." Viggo nods at me with an entertaining smile, then gives Joey a two-finger salute. "Kid, you tell your boss he won this round but I'm a patient man. I'll tack his ass to the wall sooner or later."

He glares at me. "And you? If you're a public defender, I'm—"

"A horse's ass. Feel free to call the Maryland Office of the Public Defender, Special Agent Viggo Johansen. Ask for Sherry Drakos."

Matteo
Lake Bolsena

My mind races as I head to Chris's office. I'm not back twenty-four hours, and this happens. Pulling up and parking, my heart still pounds in my ears. Too much is at risk to breathe easily.

Exiting my car, I shuck off my jacket and lay it in the backseat, unbuttoning the top two buttons of this starched dress shirt Mother insisted I wear to her party.

I breathe in the humid summer air as I roll up my shirt sleeves and survey our main warehouse. It's a three-story red brick building in the Port of Baltimore that Pop bought during the Depression.

No telling how old it is.

This is where Pop and Angel and their troops went to the mattresses back in the day. The top two floors are reserved for family business.

The parking lot is illuminated.

A light shines through the front office windows, the wooden blinds drawn.

We import and distribute goods from the eastern Mediterranean, Aegean, and Baltic seas, everything from calamari to pearls to wine, olives, and olive oil.

We export American tobacco products and whiskey.

The ground floor warehouses our products, domestic and foreign.

Among other things, it's my job to negotiate contracts. The task kept me in Europe for much of the summer while Chris and Tommy handled business here.

It feels good to be home.

As I enter his office, Chris is on the telephone, which he puts on speaker when he sees me enter. A woman's voice is saying, "They decided they had no reason to hold Joey Carbona with a B. I'm bringing him to you."

I close my eyes and blow a breath of relief, giving Chris a thumbs up. This was too close. After tonight's fiasco, future shipments will be delivered here via ship, like everything else. We'll bypass the narcs and highway patrol.

Chris says, "Good job, Sherry Baby."

The woman snaps over the speaker. "You know I hate that."

Chris chuckles. "I do. See you in a few."

As he hangs up the phone I mimic. "Sherry Baby?"

"Yeah, we've called her that since she was a kid, you know, like the song."

I sink into a chair. "Who doesn't know that song?" We were in high school when Frankie Vallie and the Four Seasons rocked our worlds with Sherry Baby. "What's the trawler doing here?"

Chris smirks. "Disposing of trash."

"Anything I need to know about?"

His lips pinch down as he wags his head slightly. "Usual shit, Matty. Punks thought we wouldn't notice them trying to set up shop in Cherry Hill." He clears his throat. "Tommy and I tried to explain the... terrain." He hikes his shoulder before leaning back, getting comfortable in his chair. His gaze is steely. "They wouldn't listen to reason. Got a little messy."

I nod slightly. It's an on-again, off-again thing. One of Pop's favorite sayings plays in my mind, and it's clear Chris is sticking to it: *They won't listen to reason, take 'em deep sea fishing.* I refocus. "About your cousin—her name's Sherry, right?"

"Sherry Drakos. Her mana and my mana are sisters. You met her when we were kids. You paid her way through law school."

I relax in the stuffed chair nearest the bar cart and lean my head back, staring at the ceiling. "We've paid for several to go through law school. Sorry. No memory of your cousin."

"She's starting her second year with the public defender's office."

I do the quick mental math. "That means she would have started law school about the time…"

"Yeah." Chris sighs heavily. "I guess you wouldn't remember her. How is your leg?"

"It aches when the weather changes. By all indications, it will soon." Pain is something I've learned to live with. It's okay. Pain lets you know you're alive. "I just wish Pio was still here."

"Me, too."

We look at our friend's picture on the bookshelf behind Chris's desk. Beside it sits a framed snapshot of the four of us taken our senior year in high school. Pio and Chris, both of Greek ancestry, have thick, curly hair. Tommy and I are one hundred percent Italian.

We were tight, the four of us. We've had each other's backs all of our lives. Now, it's just the three of us.

My right leg was broken in three places. Tommy's hip was broken and his ribs punctured. But Pio—his real name was Petros Vassiliou, but we called him Pio—he didn't survive. Pio was crushed when a construction crane overturned on top of a restaurant that we were in several years earlier. It was a freak accident that changed our lives. Any time that day comes to mind, I get up and move.

Heading for the bar cart I ask, "Drink?"

"Yeah." With his gaze glued to the high school photograph, Chris runs the palm of his hand over his face, maybe trying to erase the same miserable memory I have. Chris wasn't there. It happened in Richmond. But he suffered along with the rest of us.

He forces a smile to shove one bad memory away and toast tonight's happy ending. "Let's celebrate. What a shit show. That could have been a freaking disaster."

"Scary."

"No shit."

I pour two fingers of whiskey into the first glass. "Speaking of shit-shows, I ran into Geno-fucking-Gabicci earlier."

Chris growls. "Where?"

Pouring two fingers of the golden-brown liquid into the second glass, I answer, "My parents'."

He scoffs as he leans back in his desk chair, which creaks with old age, and folds his thick arms behind his head. "Damn, man. He's got a hell of a pair. What was he doing there?"

I hand Chris his drink and hold mine high. "Salute." We clink glasses. "To Pio."

"To Pio."

"Sophia brought him. She said she didn't want to attend my mother's party un-escorted."

"So why didn't you escort her yourself?"

He knows why. He's fucking with me like he does his cousin. It is one of Christos Baka's favorite things in life: gigging people. He wants to hear me say it.

I might as well. "You know Sophia and I... we're not a 'take her home to meet mom and dad' kind of thing. But that's not the point. Tommy and I were headed to the office to call you back when Sophia caught me, and Geno said something that crawled up my ass."

Chris tilts his head.

"He asked why I was in a rush. Asked if I had a problem."

My blonde capo tucks his chin. "You think he knew?"

"Why'd he ask?"

He leans his forearms on the desk with a scowl that would frighten someone else. "How the fuck would Geno Gabicci know about our business?"

"I don't know. I just know tonight doesn't add up. Geno in my parent's house while the cops stop our truck. I talked to Rhinehart. The way I read him? He didn't have a clue."

Chris chokes on his swallow and sputters. "That simple son of a bitch doesn't have a clue about much of anything, does he?" Chris's smile exposes a deep dimple in his left cheek that women can't seem to resist. I've watched him use it like a fishing lure at many a bar.

"You think we have a traitor?" If anyone would have a gut for it, it's Chris. He's close with the troops.

He runs his hand over his jaw, then tweaks his mouth to the side with a penetrating gaze. "Anything's possible, Matty, but I don't see it. Not within our ranks." Chris sets his empty glass on the desk. "It's none of my business, but I've always wondered, what's the old man got on Rhinehart?"

"Something besides Geno that makes my flesh crawl. Pictures."

Chris responds by raising his palms in a question.

"Sheriff Rhinehart has an affinity for young men. Very young men."

"Oh, fuck." He spits into the trash can at his desk.

"Yeah, caught on camera. Rhinehart will do anything to keep those pictures from seeing the light of day."

My father has a unique talent for knowing how to make public officials beholding to him.

Thinking about those pictures of Rhinehart, on top of this fucked-up night, I crave another drink. "You ready?"

"Sure." Chris looks at his watch. "They should be here. She said she was at a payphone not far. After we get the lowdown from Sherry and Joey, we can call it a night."

"Want to have a drink at Angelo's first? It's been a long time."

"Yeah, I was going to hit it on the way home anyway."

"I won't be able to sleep until I know how this happened." I'm refilling our glasses when I hear the office door open behind me.

"Sherry Baby!" With that tone, Chris is on his feet with open arms to greet his cousin.

I turn to meet her and stop cold, a glass in each hand, as our eyes meet.

The woman's eyes are like the water of Lake Bolsena, high in the Italian Alps. That icy water takes your breath as her eyes take mine.

Her hair is thick and rebelliously wavy like Chris's, but while Chris is blonde, her hair is the color of chocolate fudge, long enough to be pulled up in a high ponytail that falls below her shoulders. Long black lashes fringe those big fucking ice-blue eyes. Shit.

Chris looks from the woman to me as we each stand motionless, staring.

"What's going on?" His arms are still spread wide, waiting for a hug from her that doesn't come as she gawks at me with her mouth open slightly.

A young man sidesteps the woman and enters the room. "Sorry, Mr. Baka."

Must be Joey. He's a small kid, like his father, just slightly taller than the woman. But Joey is thick through his arms and chest. A weightlifter if I ever saw one.

"Joey, sit down and tell us what happened." Chris responds to his driver with his gaze bouncing between me and his cousin. "Sherry. What the—"

Breaking away from her hypnotizing eyes, I meet Chris's inquisitive stare and hand him his drink, sculling mine. "I'll catch up with you later."

God, I'm a sucker for ice-blue eyes.

Not this time. I nod at the woman. "Excuse me. I've got some place to be."

As I move past her to leave the office, my shoulder grazes her arm, and my skin feels warm.

No. I will not go through that again.

Sherry
Onyx Eyes

Staring at his back, watching him disappear into the darkness of the warehouse, I wonder where, along the drive from Anne Arundel County, I lost my sanity.

"That was odd," tumbles out of my mouth.

"No shit." Chris points to the empty warehouse, where the man disappeared. "What was that about?"

"I don't know." I'm still bumfuzzled. A little dizzy. Or ditzy.

"Then why were you drooling? Don't embarrass yourself, Sherry. Don't embarrass me." Chris hasn't been this irritated with me since I wrecked his bicycle in the sixth grade.

"I wasn't drooling." *Was I?*

"Yeah, you were." Chris downs the drink the man handed him, tromps to the bar, and pours another.

I notice Joey's taken a seat in front of Chris's desk—I guess while I was drooling.

Joey aims his thumb at me. "Sorry, Mr. Baka. Looked to me like that guy was gaga over her."

Chris whips around to face him. "Kid, you won't live long insulting Matteo DeVecchio."

"That was him?" Joey and I ask together.

"Who the fuck did you think it was?"

Joey hikes a nonchalant shoulder. "I never met him."

"You still haven't." Chris plops into his desk chair. He is one hundred percent pissed. "Tell me what went down tonight."

I interrupt. "Where's the girls' room?"

Chris points across the warehouse, still glowering at me.

"I'll be right back. Joey can fill you in."

I need fresh air. I heard Matteo DeVecchio was handsome, but I had no idea. I never expected that.

Shit, shit, shit.

Seeing him—I couldn't breathe. The man's eyes are mesmerizing, like polished onyx or shiny granite. No one has eyes like that.

And men who are powerful through the chest, with sculpted bodies—they don't have faces like his. *Oh, Lord,* he is chiseled from bronze marble, a Roman god brought to life.

His black hair is thick and wavy, cut neatly above the ears. And those lips. For a second, I could feel his mouth on mine, his hands across my back pressing me to him.

In the privacy of the restroom, I bury my face in my hands.

I made a fool of myself.

But he stared at me, too. It wasn't my imagination. Even Joey noticed.

Only Matteo DeVecchio looked at me like I was a ghost.

Returning to Chris' office, I find my cousin has morphed into Attila the Hun. "Why didn't you say something about the DEA agent while Matteo was here? That's something he needs to know."

The best I can offer is a shoulder shrug. "It happened too fast. I intended to. He just up and left before I had a chance."

"Give me your version."

"Am I in good enough graces to have a drink? I did get Joey out, you know." Between Viggo and Matteo—and now Attila the Hun, I need something to take the edge off.

Still demonstrating his irritation with an exaggerated growl, Chris walks to the bar cart.

"You should've seen her, Mr. Baka. Ms. Drakos was a tiger. She threatened to file a wrongful arrest complaint against the jail and that fed." His smile shows me Joey was proud of the representation he got. At least that makes me feel good.

Chris glances over his shoulder at me. "Go girl." He offers me two fingers of something neat.

I shove it back. "Nice try. A little ice and a splash of soda. Please?"

He rolls his eyes and scoffs. "This isn't a sorority house. You want a drink or not?" Reluctantly, I take the glass he's holding out as Chris prods, "Joey wasn't sure of the agent's name."

That name is etched into my brain. "Viggo Johansen. With an E."

Chris's jaw sags slowly. He closes his eyes and shakes his head. "Fuck. Me." He kicks the metal trash, which, luckily, is empty, as it clangs and rolls across the hardwood floor. "Son of a bitch!"

Anyone within a quarter mile heard that. My cousin needs to work on his anger management skills.

"What's the big deal?"

His eyes slice through me. "Viggo Johansen put Colosimo behind bars for life." My stomach does a summersault as Chris barks at me. "Tell me everything."

"Viggo had the highway patrol pull Joey over on suspicion of interstate trafficking of drugs. He claims the highway patrol said Joey changed lanes without a signal, but we all know that was just an excuse so Viggo could protect his snitch. Where they screwed up was not telling Joey why they pulled him over. The cops didn't even write him a ticket."

"Motherfucking son of a bitch." My cousin pounds his desk with his fist and aims his index finger at Joey with a murderous glare. "Did you talk to anyone about anything?" Loud. Still loud.

Joey's eyes are big as he shakes his head. "No sir, I swear."

I hold up one finger as I polish off the whiskey. It burns going down. "First let me finish so you know everything. Johansen told Joey, and I quote, 'Tell your boss he won this round but I'm a patient man. Sooner or later, I'll tack his ass to the wall.' Then, he insisted I'm not a public defender, which tells me, he'll try to tie me to the DeVecchios."

Chris snaps his fingers like he's trying to wake me up. "Sherry, Baby, remember. You went to law school on a scholarship from the National Hellenic Society. Greeks. No ties to DeVecchios. I'm not worried about you. I'm worried about Johansen getting tunnel-focused on us."

"I got the impression he and Matteo were old adversaries."

Rubbing his hand over his jaw, his blue eyes darting high in the room, Chris says, "No. This the first we've heard of Johansen coming for us. Why's he got a hard on for us all of a sudden?"

He dials a number, waits while it rings and rings, and finally slams down the receiver.

He dials another number. "Yeah, it's Chris. Is Matteo in there?"

In the background, I can hear a lot of noise. Maybe a nightclub. A moment later, Chris says, "Okay, if he comes in, have him call me."

He dials a third number. "Hey, do you know where Matty is?"

He listens a moment. "Dammit. Okay. I'll catch him in the morning."

"Where did he go?" I ask.

"Fuck if I know. Maybe a bar. Maybe Sophia's."

That feels like a knife to the heart. "His girlfriend?" I can picture her, all shapely and sophisticated and beautiful, like him.

Chris shrugs. "I don't know if I'd call it that." He turns to Joey. "You can go."

When Joey leaves, Chris sinks back into his desk chair and stares at the ceiling. "Fuck. Johansen."

I watch as his muscles tense. Johansen frightens my cousin terribly.

He cracks his knuckles and peers at me. "You did good, kid. You want to work for us? Like directly? No public defender bullshit in between?"

"Work for the mob? That's scary."

"Don't call us the mob. And Matty likes bulldog lawyers. Based on what Joey said, you are. DeVecchios pay a hell of a lot better than the public defender's office."

Okay, that's tempting.

My meager salary has me living in a one-bedroom efficiency in Greektown. "Let me think about it."

"Done."

When I get back to my apartment, I call Scott. I didn't know how long it would take when I'd called off the date earlier.

We've been seeing each other for several months. "Do you want to come over?"

"Why'd you stand me up again?" Not his happy voice.

"I told you. I had an emergency with a client. I'm home now if you want to get together. Too late to go out."

"You come over here. My place is better than yours."

It should be.

Scott Buchanan is an assistant district attorney. He's ambitious. He wants the DA's office someday. We met across the aisle from each other.

Scott is several years older, probably Chris's age. Divorced. No kids. He's athletic, like me. We run, golf, play tennis. Plus, he's easy on the eyes.

I slip off my shoes as we talk. "Say what you really mean, Scott. Your bed is bigger."

"It is. Here we can have some fun, unlike your almost-twin sized bed we roll out of."

"You're such a romantic."

"We're not in love."

He's right. I'm not. "I'll pass."

After running in the heat, driving to Anne Arundel County, arm-wrestling with an intimidating narcotics officer, and then encountering Matteo DeVecchio's knee-weakening eyes—I'm not even sure why I called Scott in the first place.

Courtesy, I guess.

Scott's tone takes on an edge. "You know, Sherry, I'm tired of this. How many dates have you canceled on me at the last minute?"

"Like you just said, Scott. We're not in love. Good night."

He's not just a smart, good-looking athlete; Scott is a sexaholic, and the last time we were together, his desires felt... a little kinky. I'm not up for him right now.

Besides, I'm pretty sure I'll go to sleep dreaming about someone else's eyes.

Matteo
What Sophia Wants

"**M**atteo." Sophia mumbles sleepily beside me, stroking her hand softly across my chest. "I want you."

Her warm breath teases my neck just before her tongue does the same.

My eyes open to see it's still dark.

Outside her second-floor bedroom window, a streetlight glows yellowy gold in the morning mist. "Sweetheart, you've had me all night."

She purrs, nuzzling and nibbling my neck, wrapping a long leg over me. "So what?"

Her fingernails trail slowly down my abdomen, finding my sleeping cock. In her warm hand, it stiffens immediately.

She notices, gripping me, stroking, pressing her breasts against me. "Satisfy me again, Matteo. Please."

Part of me wants to groan and go back to sleep. How can she want more?

But the part of me she's kneading—the part of me that's swollen and beginning to throb—says you can always sleep when you're old.

I guess I don't move fast enough because Sophia takes me into her mouth, swirling her tongue, as she squeezes and sucks my cock, determined to have her way.

My eyes roll back as she takes me deep into her throat, sucking while she pulls out and slides back down again. She works her tongue around my sensitive tip.

Shit. She can do magic with that tongue of hers.

"Now." She whispers her demand.

Her taught nipples rub my chest as she straddles me, placing me at her entrance. "I'm ready."

She's dripping.

"Yes, you are," I mutter into her mouth. "Wait." I reach for the bedside table, where she keeps condoms in the drawer.

"Dammit, Matteo, I'm on birth control. You don't have to—"

Not this conversation again. "Yes, we do."

"Why?" She lifts those heavy breasts to my face.

Because you say you're on birth control, but I can't be sure, and I don't want a bastard child. For starters.

Gripping her breast, I take it in my mouth, suckling that hard nipple. "We just do."

"Fine." She crawls off of me, showing her disgust. Waiting impatiently.

Not the most dick-hardening way to go about things, sweetheart.

But it's her way. We've been through this before.

What Sophia wants, she usually gets.

But not on this. "No glove, no love."

She huffs. "You can't get me pregnant if you fuck me in the ass. You know I'd let you."

"Shit, Sophia. We've been through this. I don't have any desire to put my dick in anyone's ass. Personal preference."

We're getting this round off to a bad start. My dick is shriveling.

Sophia notices... slides on her stomach and takes my withering cock into her mouth, stroking my balls. "Come back to me, big boy," she mutters as she sucks and strokes.

Okay. That's better.

The condom in place, Sophia positions herself on my cock, and I give her what she wants—thrusting hard.

She moans, arches her back, and tilts her neck so that her long hair tickles my hands around her waist.

Good girl.

Her pussy is slick and warm as she rolls her hips on top of me, making almost animalistic sounds of pleasure.

I grip her waist and pull her down as I thrust deep.

"Harder," she commands.

I have to grin. "Not hard enough, sweetheart?"

Sophia licks her lips, watching me in the glow of the streetlight that shines through thin bedroom curtains.

Her eyes drift from my face, down my abdomen to my shaft pumping into her. She likes to watch. "Don't be gentle, Matteo. Give me your beast."

Maybe if we did this more often, her appetite wouldn't be so insatiable.

I flip her onto her back, never pulling out. Gripping, lifting her ass, I ram her cervix once... twice... then pull out, slowing my pace, watching her eyes as I tease her slick, swollen clit with my tip.

I slide back inside of her slowly, and our gazes lock as I plunge deep with a deliberately hard thrust. The way she likes it.

She closes her eyes in pleasure.

I pick up speed, fucking her balls deep... keeping my weight off of her with one arm, the other gripping her ass—pumping fiercely again... and again... and again... as Sophia takes all of me. I know what she wants.

"Matteo," she says breathlessly.

Sweat glistens on her tits as she grips my ass, her chocolate-colored eyes locked with mine. "Oh, my God..."

She catches her breath, arches her back, and throws her arms over her head, exposing those voluptuous breasts. Her nipples pebble as I stare down at her, slowing my pace again.

I like to toy with her. Get her right there—and stop.

Wait for it, Sophia. Learn to savor it when it comes.

"Matt—" She doesn't appreciate the tease. "Dammit..." She wraps her long legs around my waist, hiking her hips. With one hand, she digs her fingertips into my ass; with the other hand, she strokes my balls.

Oh, shit.

"I'm almost..." I drive in hard and fast as her body trembles and her walls pulse around me.

"Oh—Matteo!" She wails so loudly she's bound to have awoken her neighbors.

As her legs squeeze me like a python, I pump her through her orgasm—and spill inside of her as I feel her coming down from the high.

We both collapse on the bed, our sweaty skin sticking together.

Sophia kisses my neck and takes a deep breath. "I like your morning stubble."

I pull her to me, cup her breast, and take it into my mouth, teasing her nipple with my tongue. "You didn't give me time to do that properly."

"You can keep doing that, you know."

I smile back. "I would. But I've got to go."

"No. You can't leave now."

Glancing at the bedside clock, I disagree. "I have to go."

If I stay here, in her bed, we'll go again—she just made that clear—and then I'll be so fucking exhausted—no pun intended—I'll be worthless.

I've got too much to do. I give her a quick kiss and head for the adjoining bathroom.

Sophia twists, reaches, and turns on the bedside lamp. "You came late, and now you're leaving early."

"Business, sweetheart." I splash cold water on my face and grab a hand towel.

"What is so important you have to leave before daylight?"

She knows I'm not going to discuss my business with her, which makes me remember last night. I move to the doorway, asking, "Why would you bring Geno to my parents' house?"

She shrugs dismissively. "I thought you two were over all of that."

"We'll never be over all of that."

Sophia bats her eyes at me, and her lips quake. "He thinks you're awful."

"He's a soulless fucker. Don't ever bring him near us again." I step closer. "You and your father are the only

Gabiccis allowed near the DeVecchios, and that's only because you're sexy and beautiful and your father's a decent man. Geno is wasted space. He uses oxygen the snails need."

Sophia sits straight in the bed, her covers falling to expose her full breasts, trim waist, and stomach. That smooth olive skin. She is a vision.

But now she's mad. "Why do you hate my cousin so badly?"

Geno Gabicci once sliced the skin off of a man's chest—skinned him—to get him to talk. They say he tanned the hide.

People think slavery doesn't exist in America? Geno doesn't import slaves from Africa like they did centuries earlier, he gets his sex slaves from Asia. Women and girls. His people offer the poor souls a free trip to America in exchange for years of forced labor. They have no idea what kind of labor they're signing up for.

I've heard, I can't prove, he's a major player in the porn industry, and many of his Asian stars are of questionable age.

The DeVecchio family doesn't do any of that shit. In our world, they call us old school, because as much of our income is from legitimate business as not.

We don't traffic women, run whores, or sweatshops or make pornographic films.

We sell our goods to middlemen with instructions that our product is never sold to kids.

We damned sure don't skin people alive.

I spare Sophia the details. "What's between me and Geno is between me and Geno."

Her gaze wanders out the window. When it comes back to meet mine, she surprises me with a look of hurt and lets out a puff of exasperation. "Why didn't you invite me to your party, Matteo?"

"Sweetheart, I just got home. I didn't know about Mother's party."

"Why don't you ever take me out? To dinner or a movie or a play? All we do is this."

I feel my face fall flat.

"Matteo, I thought... someday..."

"Someday what?" I snatch my pants, folded across the back of the bedroom chair, and slip into them, watching her closely.

She fidgets with her covers, ducking her head.

Stepping closer, donning my shirt, I ask her pointedly, "Someday what, Sophia?"

She tosses her dark hair, her chin high, the look in her eyes defiant. "I just thought..." She sighs heavily. "Someday."

I was afraid this day would come. She wants an official relationship.

I take her face into my hand, her chin resting in my palm as I stroke her cheek with my thumb. "Sweetheart, if your family knew you were fucking me—if my family knew about this—we might both be dead. We can't be open. Secondly, even though you are a goddess, even if our families didn't oppose our relationship, I'm not ready."

"Not ready for what?"

I'm surprised again, seeing pain in her eyes, and I soften my tone. "For a commitment, Sophia. Sweetheart, you wonder why I use the condoms even though you're on birth control? I haven't made any demands. We haven't made this exclusive. I thought we were just having fun."

Her cheeks flush the color of strawberries. Her gaze narrows. "You see other women?"

I take my time to answer. That is a dangerous look in her eyes. I'm not a liar. "I have, yes."

Fire flashes in her eyes. "So, I'm just the fuck du jour."

Another surprise.

"You expect me to believe you don't see other men?" Impossible with her looks and sexual appetite.

She throws her covers back and gets out of bed. She stands before me, her hourglass figure bare. She doesn't try to cover herself. The hurt in her voice is gone. "I actually thought you loved me, Matteo, and you were afraid to let our families know. I thought, with time, we'd be open and become..."

If it wasn't such an inappropriate time, I'd laugh. She doesn't know me at all. If I loved a woman, I wouldn't give a fuck what anybody thought.

I felt love once. It was briefly the most exhilarating feeling I'd ever experienced but the pain love brought lasted a hell of a lot longer than the ecstasy. I don't want the fucking L-word in my vocabulary.

My tone changes to match hers. "Love is for fools, Sophia."

"So, then, take love out of it. Matteo, if we married, if we combined the DeVecchio and Gabicci families, no one would challenge us."

"No one's challenging us now."

Sophia grabs her gown off the back of the chair and slips it over her head. "I want more than this. I'm not someone to be ashamed of."

I see it cross her eyes—she's about to try and slap me. I take a step back. "You don't want to do that, Sophia."

After a drawn-out, mutual glare, I tell her, "I'm not ashamed of you. I've said, you're a goddess. But I can't give you more."

"Ever?"

I shake my head.

She slips on a robe, tying the sash. "Can't or won't?"

A snicker slips from my throat.

Her face flushes as I let the silence linger. "I'd as soon be strung up by the balls as marry anyone."

She grabs my bicep, her tone pleading. "Listen to me, Matteo. I can give you an heir to two families. Think how beautiful our children would be. How powerful you would be."

Has she been listening?

I never thought I'd see Sophia Gabicci beg. "Where's this coming from? We've never had a real date, and you suddenly want to get married?"

The woman is almost as tall as I am. She steps forward, our faces not a foot apart. The fire in her eyes is scorching. "I think what we've shared for the past six months is a little bit more than dating."

I take a deep breath and feel my jaw flex involuntarily. Enough.

Our gazes hold steady as I nod. "It's been nice, Sophia."

I parked a block from her downtown loft. Saturday night—the neighborhood was packed when I got here. Boutiques, restaurants, and bars line the old brick street, with condominiums and apartments filling the higher floors.

It's an old part of Baltimore that is being gentrified; I think they call it. Developers buy dilapidated buildings for pennies on the dollar, renovate them to appeal to a young, affluent crowd, and make a fortune in the process. People like Sophia live above fashionable night spots.

In the early morning darkness, the sidewalk and street are empty and damp. The air is cool for this time of year, and it brings with it a fog from the harbor.

She wants to know what I have to do? Find out what happened with last night's shipment. I'm betting her fucking cousin had something to do with it. First step, meet with Rhinehart. He owes us ears on the ground.

And I'm still fending off the second surprise of last night—those beautiful eyes. Shit.

Not even hours in bed with Sophia erased Chris's cousin from my mind. Her oval face with soft, supple lips, a small nose, the long, wild, curly hair, the clear intelligence in her mesmerizing blue eyes. I imagine her legs wrapped around me the way Sophia's were. I want her to call out my name when I drive her to the edge with my dick buried deep inside of her.

Dammit. Blue eyes. Again.

And now a third surprise—Sophia wanting to get married. That came out of nowhere.

My body jolts as fire shoots into my back. I stumble against the car.

A meat cleaver slams into my shoulder, spinning me around. My knees buckle.

My chest. It's... too dark... to see.

Sherry
ORANGE. UGH.

"**O**oh-wee, girl." Cedric, I don't know his last name, beams seeing me walk into Blue Parrot Java. His big smile displays a mouth full of bright, white teeth with one glistening gold cap.

It's the kind of genuine smile that prompts one from me. "Cedric, my favorite barista."

I'm not sure if Cedric owns the Blue Parrot or if he's a manager or just a barista, but I've never been here when Cedric wasn't.

He flicks his brows. "My favorite public defender." Cedric's eyes trail over me. "Girl, you realize that skirt split up the side like that—um, um, um. Are you hoping to distract the judge or impress the jury?"

I twirl around and curtsy. "Neither. I just like to look nice."

"Sherry, Baby, I have never seen you not look nice. What are you having today?"

I give him a flirtatious wink. "The usual. Strong and black, like you."

Cedric and I play this way all the time.

"You got it. See you changed your hair, too." That wide smile brings out a little dimple in each cheek.

I toss my hair. "Thanks for noticing."

I'm ready for something different. Something new. After hanging up on Scott last night, I made up my mind.

He's archives. Done and dusted. I'm moving on.

Thus, the new look.

Someone rasps behind me. "Now you look like a lawyer."

Ugh. I recognize that slow, deep voice.

Special Agent Viggo Johansen stands just inside the entry of the small café, staring a hole through me. I've never seen him here.

My brows twist. "Are you following me?"

"You wish." The big guy moves forward.

With those piercing blue eyes, he is obnoxiously handsome. Agent Johansen is—I don't know how many inches over six feet tall—and weighs Lord-knows-what, but every single ounce of that man is muscle.

Last night's gray T-shirt is replaced with a white dress shirt and tie. Instead of the faded jeans, he's wearing black slacks and black leather shoes. And he shaved.

He is undeniably hot. Really hot when he smiles—when his blue eyes aren't eviscerating me.

He spoils the delicious image by opening his mouth. "Did you give my regards to DeVecchio?"

My fists flounce to my hips. "Why would you ask that?"

"Here you go, Sherry." Cedric hands my coffee over the counter, and I turn my back on the glaring federal agent to pay.

"Thanks, Cedric." He knows to keep the change.

I turn back to face Viggo, waiting for his answer.

He doesn't give one.

So, I repeat myself, "Why would you ask that?"

He steps around me to the counter. "I'll take a large coffee to go, please. Black."

When his eyes meet mine, Viggo gives my body another once-over. "Like I said, public defenders don't dress the way you dress."

"My job pays enough to buy decent clothing, thank you."

Here comes that slow, sly grin that I saw last night. His eyes light up when he smiles. "Not for Rolex watches."

"I told you it was a graduation gift. From my parents. Jerk."

Viggo purses his mouth and scratches his heavy brow, studying me. "Naw. You're not a public defender."

I aim my arm at the limestone building behind me. "My office is across the street. Would you like to accompany me? You can see my office. I'll put your teensy but suspicious mind at ease."

"Maybe you do work for the public defender's office, but you also work for DeVecchio." He leans down so his mouth is near my ear and speaks just above a whisper. "You got to that little dirtbag too fast last night. It was a dead giveaway."

My gaze doesn't falter. "What if I told you Joey Carbona was a family friend?"

One brow shifts high as he grins smugly. "I'd tell you Joey Carbona hadn't even made a phone call when you showed up."

Oh, shit.

"Why are you here, Viggo? I've never seen you at the Blue Parrot before. Where's your office?"

He snickers. "Why? So, you can tell your cousin and have me offed?"

How would you know who my cousin is? And who says he offs anyone?

My heart begins to race.

I play it cool. "Sometimes you seem to have trouble hearing or understanding, Agent Johansen with an E. Why...Are... You... in Blue Parrot Java this morning?"

Cedric interrupts before Viggo can reply. "Here you go."

Viggo pays and takes his coffee, then turns back to me, blowing softly on the steaming brew.

"It so happens I'm on my way to court. A word of advice, Ms. Drakos. Cut ties with the Butcher of Baltimore or go down with him."

An audible gasp slips out. "What? What did you call him?"

Viggo lifts one shoulder with a steely stare. "The Butcher of Baltimore. That's what they call your boss. You didn't know?"

"Why would you care what happens to me? You don't know me."

Viggo takes a deep breath and blows it out slowly. "Tell you the truth, I don't know." His gaze roams the room over my head as I wait for him to finish. His topaz eyes finally join mine. "You shouldn't be in prison. And that's where you're going to be if you keep working for DeVecchio."

Our gazes lock, and I feel the heat of my own glare. "What have you got against them anyway? I mean, versus other families?"

Viggo takes a sip of his hot coffee, those eyes studying me. "Ms. Drakos, I'm an equal-opportunity cop. You break the law—no matter what your color or your creed—black, white, Mexican, Italian, German—Catholic, Baptist or

Buddhist—male, female, short, tall, fat or skinny—doesn't make a flying fuck to me." He steps closer. "If you make a mockery of the law, I will bring you down. DeVecchios thumb their noses at the law."

I step into him, invading his space. Our toes almost touch, and my neck cranes back miserably to meet his gaze. "You may be an equal opportunity cop, but for some reason you seem tunnel-focused on one family. Why?"

He tucks his chin to peer down at me. "None of your business."

"You just said it is my business."

"Distance yourself, darlin,' or go down with a sinking ship."

"Well, like I said. I don't work for the DeVecchios. I'm paid by the Maryland Office of the Public Defender and if you don't mind, I have to get to my office, gather my files and meet with a client at the county jail."

As I leave the café, I make a point to hold my shoulders back and my head high. Fuck him and his threats. I'm telling Chris.

And what's this about Matteo being a butcher?

Viggo follows me outside, watching.

Feeling his eyes on my back, I turn and ask, "Something else?"

He lifts his coffee cup high. "You won't look good in orange."

Every now and then, I defend an innocent person. But not often. And not today.

This guy is a sleaze. A john sitting in Baltimore City Jail charged with statutory rape for having sex with a minor.

This guy can find the money to pay a prostitute, but he's poor enough to qualify for a public defender. One of those, 'Sorry, can't pay the electric bill because I paid for sex' kind of guys.

He makes my skin crawl.

But it's my job to give him a proper defense. And I will. Thumbing through his arrest sheet, I ask, "So, this girl…"

"Monica," he mumbles.

His cheek twitches just below his left eye. Very distracting.

I take a moment to study my new client. Johnathan James Jenkins, age thirty-six. Pale skin. Listless eyes. He looks like someone who knocks doors for a living, trying to sell you insurance. Or encyclopedias. Or Fuller brushes.

"Does Monica have a last name?" I ask.

She's a juvenile. Her name isn't on the arrest record.

Johnathan snickers, his gaze meeting mine directly for the first time. "I didn't ask."

He rubs his hand over his mouth and squeezes his narrow chin. The movement makes me notice his measly mustache.

"Okay, Monica." I jot my notes. "How old is she?"

"Cop said she's fifteen, but I swear, she told me she was twenty. You look at her and you'll think she's twenty, too."

"You paid for her... services?"

He hangs his head and nods.

"Anything specific?"

He shakes his head.

"And where were you when... her services were performed?"

"In my car."

I'm thumbing through his case file. "Where was your car?"

"Sanderson Park."

It's all in the report. I just need to hear him say it. I've got to make sure what the cop wrote is what my client recalls. Make sure he's aware of his charges. I like to keep my client and the cops honest.

"And how, exactly, did you happen to get arrested, Johnathan?"

I'm casting a wide net. The easiest way to get a case dismissed is to catch the arresting officer not following procedure.

"A cop knocked on the window right in the middle of—"

I cut him off, showing him my palm. Caught in the act. This guy has no defense.

"I get the picture. Did he apprise you of your rights?"

"Yeah."

"How much did Monica charge you?"

"Thirty bucks. Enough for a fix, I figure. And she's hot as hell."

I thumb through his records. "This is your first offense?"

"Yes."

Our gazes latch again. He's not the first one I've dealt with.

I lean my forearms on the desk. "This is the first time you've been caught. Not the first time you've done this, right?" No one gets caught the first time.

He's been paying women to suck his dick for years. Why did he go for a juvenile this time?

"Johnathan. There are lots of women who will service you. Why a fifteen-year-old?"

He hikes a shoulder. No answer.

I've got a gut about this one. He's gravitating to younger and younger girls. It's a sickness.

When he doesn't answer my question, I prod. "I'm your lawyer. It's in your best interest to answer me. Nothing you tell me can go any farther. I'd be disbarred."

"I don't know." He picks at his fingernails.

I fold up the case file. "You have no defense. Caught in the act and she is legally underage. But, if you agree to enter a program for therapy, I may be able to get this reduced to a misdemeanor indecency. I can't promise, but I think I can get the judge to approve that. You'd still have to do thirty days minus time served. And be on probation. Does that interest you?"

Angry surprise flashes across those normally dull gray eyes. "Therapy? For what? I'm not a druggie."

"Sex can be an addiction just like drugs or gambling or over-eating. You need help to kick it, especially if you feel pulled to young girls."

He won't look at me anymore.

"Johnathan!" I whisper-shout at him.

"I told you she said she was twenty."

"If you aren't honest with anyone else, be honest with yourself. If you keep being drawn to young girls—pretty soon you won't be paying them, you'll be forcing them. At that point, you'll spend the rest of your life in prison, and you don't want to know what happens to a child molester in prison."

He mumbles and shakes his bowed head. "I don't know..."

Sizing Johnathan up, I'm willing to bet he's married. Maybe with kids.

"You're looking at statutory rape. That could mean life in prison. Life, Johnathan. Life."

He whines with those gray eyes, begging for sympathy. "But she offered." Johnathan sinks his balding head into his hands, his elbows propped on the desk.

This numbskull isn't picking up what I'm putting down.

"She's a minor. Fifteen years old. The law takes that very seriously."

His eyes meet mine. "She looked like an adult."

I close my eyes and shake my head.

He snatches my wrist. "Can you get my bond lowered?"

I see hope in his eyes, like the flicker of a candle.

I yank my wrist free.

"Again. Your bond is set high because the victim is a juvenile. I will ask for a bond reduction hearing. In the meantime—think about treatment."

He looks over his shoulder and around the room. "Another night in this shithole?"

The hope I detected in his eyes a moment earlier is replaced by sheer panic. "What will I tell my wife?"

"I'm sorry, Johnathan. It's the system." As I start to leave, I turn back, hoping I might get through his hard head. "Johnathan, if you don't agree to treatment, this may be the beginning of the next five to ten years of your life."

Leaving the facility, I want to step into a hot shower. With lots of soap. I want to feel clean again.

I'm thinking more and more about Chris's offer.

Yes, they're the mob. But are they really that much guiltier than guys like Johnathan James Jenkins? The man has no remorse for having sex with a girl less than half his age, knowing she's just doing it for money to get high, knowing he's got a wife at home.

No guilt. No shame. He's just mad that he got caught. I wonder, sometimes, why I defend people like him.

I know the answer—because once in a while, the cops get the wrong person. I'm here for them. The innocent who can't afford a defense.

My inner voice chides, 'DeVecchios aren't innocent.'

My gut answers, 'But they're not sleazy.' They don't have sex with children.

To my cousin Chris and the DeVecchios, it's all about family. Loyalty. Survival.

They seem cleaner than a lot of the scumbags I defend.

When you look at them, you know exactly what you get.

Looking into Matteo DeVecchio's eyes last night—Lord. He is all man.

A black panther with brooding eyes. Fierce. I can only imagine the passion that man is capable of if what simmers beneath the surface is unleashed as hate or love.

I know it. I feel it.

That man will do whatever it takes to protect his family. He wouldn't be out on the street paying a girl for a blow job.

I have never wanted to know anyone the way I want to know Matteo DeVecchio.

Viggo's warning starts rattling around in my brain. He's right about one thing. I don't look good in orange.

Neither would Matteo or Chris.

I need to warn them.

I need to get past the whole eye issue, the staring at each other, the tingly feelings in my gut, and talk to him. Matteo needs to know how serious Viggo Johansen is about bringing him down.

Stepping out of the Baltimore City Jail, my mind on those onyx eyes that captivated me Saturday night, who do I bump into but Scott Buchanan?

"Sherry. Why are you here?" he asks, peering over my shoulder.

He makes me smile because I know if I asked him the same question, he'd tell me what I'm about to tell him. "That's none of your business."

Scott looks good in his blue Oxford cloth shirt, which makes his light blue eyes pop. Right now, they're hungry as they take me in. I've seen that look in his eyes before. "Try again tonight?" he asks.

I give him a sad smile. I was fond of him, but... "Scott, we don't work. You said as much last night."

He lifts a shoulder with a grin. "Can't blame a guy for trying."

I stand on tiptoes and kiss his smooth cheek. "It's been nice, but we want different things."

Scott nods with a grin. "See you around, Sherry Baby."

Reaching my office, I put the job first, making the call to schedule a bond reduction hearing for Johnathan Jenkins. Done.

I make the second call to be sure I can get Johnathan into a treatment program to facilitate a plea deal. Success.

Family next.

I call Chris. He has to be warned.

Another man answers his office desk phone with a deep, gruff voice. "DeVecchio Imports."

I ask for my cousin.

"He's not here. I'll take a message."

"This is his cousin, Sherry Drakos. Will you tell Chris I need to speak with him as soon as possible? It's... pretty important."

"I don't expect Baka back for a while."

Maybe it's the way the guy said it. I don't know. But my skin tingles.

"Why? What happened?" I hear the alarm in my own voice.

A hesitant response. "You say Christos is your cousin?"

"Yes, I'm Sherry Drakos. Look on the bookshelf behind his desk. That's a picture of me and Chris when I graduated college. I've got long, dark, curly hair. His arm is around me."

A second later, the man replies, "Christos is at Baltimore General."

My pounding heart clogs my throat. The words squeak out. "What happened to him?"

"Nothing happened to Christos, but Mr. DeVecchio was shot."

My mind freezes on that vision of Matteo Saturday night—our gazes locked together—his sculptured face, his hypnotizing eyes. "Matteo? Or his father?"

My pounding heart has moved from my throat into my ears.

"Matty," the man says.

Bile scalds my throat. I can barely whisper, "Tell me he's alive."

"That's what we're waiting to hear."

Matteo
TENDER MERCY

Something squeezes tightly around my left arm. How is it that my chest is on fire, but I'm shivering?

My eyes startle open to the sight and sounds of machines beeping. Tubes. White walls.

A quiet voice... a woman's voice.

My gaze moves from the machine to the mumbling.

My mother stands beside my bed, her murmur barely audible above the machines' beeping. "Please look upon my son with your tender mercy." A familiar prayer.

My eyes open wide. My ears, my senses are working. Mother's warm hand rests on my forearm, her head bowed as she pleads with God, "Holy Spirit, fill Matteo Dante DeVecchio with your peace and presence."

"Mother," I rasp. My voice is hoarse.

"Oh, Matty, Matty! My son!" Tears flush her swollen eyes as she raises my hand to her lips and kisses it. She lifts her bloodshot eyes to heaven and whispers, "Father God, thank you."

The memory washes over me.

Reaching my car, fire pierced my back. It felt like a knife plunged into my shoulder. My knees buckled as my body spun around, and another fiery bolt slammed my chest. How am I alive?

"They shot you in the back." Pop spits his words.

My gaze leaves Mother to see him standing at the foot of the bed, Antonio at his side.

My father's face is distorted with anger. "Cowards shot my son in the back." He pounds his chest with his fist as he repeats with loud indignation, "My son."

It's murder I see in my father's eyes as he snarls, "He is as good as dead."

My gaze roams the dimly lit room. Chris leans his shoulder against the wall behind Mother, his weight on one leg, arms folded across his broad chest. Studying me with his piercing blue eyes.

Tommy is beside Chris, sitting in a straight-backed chair, running his palms over his thick thighs back and forth, back and forth. He senses me looking at him. Our gazes meet.

Mother squeezes my hand. "Son, who did this to you?"

I shake my head.

She glances over her shoulder at Chris and Tommy before asking, "What were you doing downtown at that hour?"

It pains me to see my mother's eyes so red and swollen. Seeing what my being wounded has done to her, I hold nothing back. "I was with Sophia."

"Gabicci!" Pop roars as he shakes the foot of the bed. "That slut set you up."

"Who knew you were there, besides her?" It's Tommy asking. He moved to stand beside Mother, looming over me, dwarfing her.

"No one." My gaze drifts to Chris. "I drove to Sophia's when I left your office."

Chris nods, his arms still folded. "Someone was hiding in the entrance to a shop where you parked."

"I parked around the corner from her loft."

"Well, they were waiting for you, brother." Chris pushes off the wall he's been leaning against.

One big step, and he's hovering over me, too. My tiny mother is a little doll wedged between the two capos. "This was an assassination attempt."

Chris looks from me to Pops. "First our truck. Then Matty. Francesco, that means you're next. This is war. We just don't know who we're fighting."

His gaze on Chris, Pop's right arm swings wide. "We know damned good and well who we're fighting. The fucking Gabiccis!" His eyes meet mine. "Geno wants to expand his territory while his uncle lies dying. What was Geno Gabicci doing in my house, Matty?"

I blink, pulling memories. "Sophia brought him."

"How dare she," my mother hisses.

"She said you invited her, and she didn't want to attend un-escorted."

My mother's mouth sags before she turns her head and fake spits. "I would never invite a Gabicci into my house. You should know that." Her hand flails high. "I thought you invited her. I knew you had been slipping around seeing her. I kept my mouth shut out of respect to you, but my son and a Gabicci woman?" She turns her head and fake spits again.

I've got one hand with no tubes stuck in it. I use it to rub my eyes. *Did I let Sophia play me?*

"Tommy heard her say you invited her."

Tommy looks at Mother and nods.

"Never. I was only courteous to her because of you."

That makes my eyelids feel like they weigh a thousand pounds. "I need to think."

What does this have to do with her marriage talk that came out of the clear blue? I left there feeling like a callous ass who broke Sophia's heart. Now, I have to wonder if she was setting me up all along.

The men all stare at me, waiting for an answer I don't have.

My free hand lifts high. "I don't know how anybody could have known where I was. I had no plans to be there. My car just kind of steered itself to her place when I left the warehouse."

Chris and Tommy exchange looks again.

"What are you thinking?" I ask.

"Did you fall asleep while you were inside?" Tommy asks.

Well, fuck, yeah. I nod.

"She called them while you were asleep."

"But why would she do that? She brought up marriage."

"Oh, my Lord, never!" Mother shrieks. "Never will my son marry a Gabicci."

My eyes meet Mother's. "I made that clear."

Pop presses. "Think. Did you see anyone, anything?"

I shuffle through more memories, like cards in a deck. No one followed me from Pop's to the warehouse, I'm sure of that. I don't remember being followed when I drove downtown.

I was inside for hours.

Sophia and I went several rounds. I'd drifted to sleep. Tommy's right. She could have used the telephone while I slept. But why, if she wanted to marry?

I tried to kiss her goodbye, but she turned her head. She slammed the apartment door behind me. I waited to hear her lock and latch her door like I always do to make sure she was safe.

I took the stairwell down one floor. Why wait on an elevator? The lobby, lined with mailboxes embedded in the walls, was empty.

So was the street.

The sidewalk was damp. The early morning air was cool. A fog had rolled in from the harbor, hanging like thin gauze over everything. With the storefronts veiled in shadows, the only light illuminating the street came from streetlights that glowed in the humid air.

I walked to the end of the block and turned right.

"The shots came from behind me. That's her building. Sophia's loft is on the second floor, on the opposite side."

Tommy exchanges some kind of knowing glance with Pop, who nods.

"What?" I ask with irritation. Their little knowing eye exchanges grate on my nerves.

"We'll find out who's in every apartment in that building and who owns every shop on the street," Chris says.

"What day is it? How long have I been out?"

"You were shot yesterday morning," Pop says. "This is Monday afternoon."

"Let me sleep."

Matteo

BUGGING ME

Chris and Tommy are in my room. My guards.

Neither notices me open my eyes. Chris sits in a straight-backed chair against the door. He seems to be dozing with his arms folded over his chest and his chin tucked into his neck, but I can rest assured not even a nurse will get in my room without waking Christos Baka. Who wants to wake a sleeping bear?

That looks uncomfortable as hell. He'll have a crick in his neck when he wakes up.

Tommy sits in a nearby chair, working on a crossword puzzle. He saves them from the Sunday paper, folds the page, and works on them all week. No one would ever suspect Tommaso Ricci of working crossword puzzles. But he does.

They're doing what we've done for each other since grade school. Being here.

Glancing around the room, I see they're alone.

My parents were here earlier in the day. I guess they left while I slept.

I draw a deep breath and turn my head. I don't even want to deal with my closest friends, shame seeping into every pore. I've prided myself on being educated, intelligent, and intuitive. In reality, I'm a fool.

My mind is dull.

I can't believe I let Sophia play me. I keep hearing her silky voice saying through tears, *I thought someday... I want more than this...* Her tears elicited exactly what she wanted: my empathy. I left her feeling like a prick—and she set me up to be killed?

I don't know. It doesn't make sense.

She hadn't expected me. She didn't ask me to come over. I just showed up at her door. She always lets me in.

And again, she wanted to get married.

In the length of time from our parting until I got shot, Sophia couldn't possibly have gotten an assassin in place.

But this has to be Geno. The question is—was Sophia part of it?

Lightning flashes and rain slides down the windows.

Rain. Water. Lake Bolsena. Out of nowhere, I see Chris's cousin, with her crystal blue eyes frozen wide, staring at me in his office. She was too much. *Damn her eyes.*

Everything about her put me back in Austin in 1969 when a little girl with big blue eyes rocked my world for the first time. Patsy did it again in Richmond in 1974. That blue-eyed girl ripped my fucking heart out of my chest.

As I locked eyes with Chris's cousin, Sherry—my heart stopped for a second—just as it had when my eyes met Patsy's.

Then it pounded in my ears. I was suffocating. I had to get away. I knew Sophia would make me forget Sherry and Patsy.

And she did, for a while.

I scoff at myself, dragging my fingers through my hair. "Fuck." That's what comes to mind first thing when I wake up. Pussy. Not the holes in me or the man who put them there.

"What?" Tommy peers at me from his crossword.

"Nothing. It's raining." I knew the weather was changing. "What day is today?" You lose track, lying in bed. Drugged.

"It's almost Wednesday. How do you feel?" Chris asks.

It's such a dumb question I can't suppress a nasty laugh. Laughing hurts. That pisses me off. "How do you think I feel?"

"You're going to live, brother. You don't have time to wallow in self-pity." Tommy's voice carries a rare edge. "We've got bigger problems."

Bigger than being shot in the back?

Okay. That yanks my attention away from the women.

"The warehouse is bugged." Chris is standing over me.

"What?"

"You heard me right."

"What the fuck?" When I struggle to sit up, the bed begins to lift on its own. Chris is on the controller.

"How do you know?"

Tommy replies, "After the cops knew to stop our truck and a few hours later, you got shot, we got busy. There had to be a leak. We found a bug in Chris's desk phone and another in the lampshade on the bookshelf."

Chris interrupts. "Matty, they're not just listening to the phone calls. They've heard every fucking thing said inside my office. That means they heard us talking about Sherry the other night. And they heard me say, maybe you were going to Sophia's. If Geno's listening, he could have called her."

I close my eyes, feeling the weight of the world.

This is the most serious breach the family has ever suffered, and it happened on my watch. I'm already seeing handcuffs. Pops will lose faith in his son.

We have influence with the courts, but no DeVecchio has ever been arrested.

"You think it's Geno? Not the cops?"

"I'm pretty sure it's not cops." Tommy sounds adamant. "The law can't listen without a warrant. No, this is all Geno."

I inhale another long, deep breath. It's like I need oxygen with my heart throbbing the way it is. "We have people who would have given us a heads up if the law applied for a wiretap."

"Plus, cops tap the lines going into and coming out of buildings," Tommy says. "I checked. Our lines in and out are clean."

I close my eyes and breathe relief. Good. We can deal with Geno more easily than the law.

All I want is to get my hands on a gun, but I hear Pop in my head. 'Keep emotions out of our business.'

"Does Pop know?"

"He's been briefed on everything," Chris answers.

"How did they plant bugs inside your office?"

They do their obnoxious eye exchange again. It makes me feel like they're keeping secrets, deciding together what to tell me. I'm not in the mood. "How?" I demand.

Chris drags his fingers through his thick blonde hair and meets my gaze with a sheepish but direct look. "I fucked up."

This is going to be bad.

He holds up both palms in self-defense. "Keep in mind, you've been gone. Until Saturday night, I hadn't seen you in weeks. It didn't cross my mind until you got shot but..."

"Fuck, Chris, spit it out."

"You've never talked about your relationship with Sophia."

"My past relationship."

"Whatever. She's the only person who's been in my office without me, who's not one of us."

"When? How?"

"While you were in Italy, she pulled up one day with a girlfriend saying she wanted to throw you a surprise birthday party in the warehouse, because you'd never expect it there and she really wanted to surprise you."

"My birthday isn't until the end of August."

He lifts a shoulder in resignation. "She said she had lots of planning to do."

"How would she even know about the warehouse? Trust me, Sophia and I never talked business. That's not how we spent our time."

The two snicker.

Now, I don't care.

I shift in the bed, fueled by anger. "And we were never officially seeing each other in the first place, so why would she invite people to a party for me?"

Chris's hands rise high. "I didn't know." He glances at Tommy. "I knew you were seeing her. I didn't know how tight you two were."

"You're an idiot if you let her into our warehouse."

"Piss off, Matty. I didn't let her in. She walked in like she'd been there before. For all I knew, she had been. I didn't want to insult the woman I knew you were seeing so I damned sure wasn't going to throw her out, and it wasn't like I could pick up the phone and call you or the old man."

I interrupt, holding up my hand. "For future reference, no one comes into our place of business who you haven't personally vetted."

"Fine with me," he responds. "Like I was saying, Sophia comes into my office with a girlfriend and says they want to get ideas for decorations. They step into the warehouse for a minute, just outside my door. They can't see anything the public can't see.

"Then Sophia comes back in and asks if she can use the phone to ask another friend about decorations, and at the same time, her girlfriend asks if she can use the restroom. It's not like we have men's and women's, and I didn't want this woman, who I didn't know, wandering the warehouse unescorted—so, I show her the way to the restroom, make sure no one is in there and wait and escort her back."

"Son of a bitch." I pound the right bed safety rail with my fist and it rattles.

Christos Baka isn't a nice guy. He should've thrown Sophia Gabicci out on her ass when she walked in unannounced.

He lifts his hands high. "I'm sorry, Matty."

I love him like a brother. But that screwup makes me want to pound the shit out of him.

Tommy jumps in. "I'd have done the same thing. Your secret wasn't as secret as you thought. Your little stolen moments in dark corners of Angelo's, you sneaking out the back a few minutes after she leaves out the front door? Shit, Matty. You didn't trust us enough to tell us anything so how were we to know you hadn't had her in the warehouse before?"

"Fuck. No. I never saw Sophia anywhere but her apartment."

A chuckle escapes Chris's throat. "And Angelo's."

"And Studio 55." Tommy's shoulders shake as he tries to bottle his fucking giggle.

Chris hits his shoulder and snorts. "What about Limelight?"

"Fuck off, both of you. I never actually dated her."

"We know," they say together.

I shake my head, disgusted with them and myself, as Tommy says, "It doesn't take long to slip a bug in a phone and lamp. Chris says she's the only person who's had a chance to do it. And you had just left her apartment when you got shot. They were listening, Matty. They warned her you were coming. One and one equals two."

"Any other bugs?"

Chris sinks back into his chair against the wall, tilts his head back, and stares at the ceiling. "In the meeting room and bathroom."

"Dammit!" I explode. "Shit!"

A nurse opens the door with a terse scowl. "Is everything alright in here?" She's an older woman who wears an almost frightening frown.

Do Not Disturb has been stamped on her forehead.

I offer a smile. "I apologize. It won't happen again."

"Do I need to—"

I show her my palm. "No. I'm fine. Again, I apologize for my outburst."

She wags her finger. "Don't let it happen again."

As the nurse leaves, I peer at Chris. "How'd she get bugs in those other rooms?"

"She didn't. I hired a construction company to do some repairs while you were gone. Fuck, man. The roof was leaking. We found out yesterday, that company is a blind holding of—"

"Let me guess."

He doesn't. "Yeah. Gabicci Enterprises."

Tommy says, "Here's what we think." The two men exchange glances. "We don't know, but it makes sense. The listening devices have a short transmission range so whoever is listening is nearby. I scouted around and got pictures a block from the warehouse."

He hands me several black and white photographs. I sift through wide, medium, and zoom-in shots of men getting out of vehicles and going into a metal building. "I don't recognize these people. What makes you think they're listening to us?"

"Gut," Chris says. "But in the meantime, my office is off limits for everything but legitimate business."

"Fine." An idea occurs. "Feed them bullshit."

The obnoxious eye exchange between my capos.

"Have you said anything on the phone or in the warehouse that lets them know you found the bugs?"

"Nothing."

"Then arrange for another shipment. Same route as last time. Make sure there's nothing in this run but legit goods. No need for Jeremiah. When our driver is pulled over a second time, we'll know what cop we're dealing with. See who he associates with. Watch him twenty-four seven until he leads us to someone. Geno's got a dirty cop on his payroll."

"Speaking of dirty cops—Sherry wants to talk to you."

"No."

Chris raises a hand in exasperation.

"Not now, Christos. Find out who owns that building. Just keep your office conversations vague, talk about a next shipment, no dates."

They nod.

"I don't suppose there's a chance one of you snuck in some booze."

"Is that safe?" Tommy asks.

"Safer than what they're giving me for pain."

He reaches into his jacket and pulls out a small silver flask, handing it over with a rare grin. Tommy always wears a jacket to conceal his shoulder holster, which I notice is empty.

He notices that I see the empty holster. "They won't let us bring them in."

He's got one tucked in a holster on his leg. They both do.

With a nod, I take a long chug, savoring the warmth as it slides down my throat. Not to mention the taste. "Thanks. Now tell me what you think."

"You know what we think. Everything ties to Geno. The contractors work for him and Sophia is his cousin."

This puzzle is coming together.

"Okay, so Geno has a dirty cop. Taking us down would be a feather in the cop's cap, but he doesn't have enough evidence to go to a judge and get a warrant for a wiretap. Geno's only too happy to assist."

My gaze lands on Chris. "He lucks into you hiring his construction crew. They plant bugs in the warehouse, but that's a waste of time since we don't talk business outside of the office. He turns to Sophia to get ears inside the office. That's how they knew to stop Joey's truck."

Chris interrupts. "And that you might be headed to Sophia's."

Tommy runs his hands over his face. "If Geno's working with law enforcement to bring us down, he's violating his oath. That's punishable by death."

"So is their assassination attempt," Chris says. "But why would Sophia help him? That's the part that doesn't make sense to me, especially if she's in love with you. If you married her, she'd be queen of two families."

I take another long draw on Tommy's bottle, wipe my mouth with the back of my hand, and offer it back.

"Keep it. I brought it for you."

"Thanks," I answer Chris. "Because Sophia realized, we'd never marry. And she knows she can't run her family alone when her old man dies, which won't be long. She and Geno know they need to hang tight."

"Geno's not the only one with a cop in his pocket," Tommy says.

Rhinehart. There are others. "Yeah."

"Need to find out what they know," the big guy grumbles. Time to act.

Three days in this bed. I'm stronger. The doctor said I was lucky. The cowardly fucker who shot me in the back was nervous. His aim was off. Didn't hit anything vital.

I throw my covers back. "I'm getting out of here."

Chris shows me his palm. "Slow down, tiger. Your Pop is on top of everything, and you have us."

"I won't lie here in bed while Pop is a target. Does he have guards at the house?"

They both nod.

"Call him. Get me released. Hell, for all I know, Gabicci will get someone in the hospital to poison me."

As Tommy reaches for the room phone, my mind does a U-turn, and I peer at Chris. "You need to get your cousin out of the public defender's office."

"Why?"

"That cop in Ann Arundel is probably Geno's man. He can ruin her career."

"About that cop. She wants to talk to you. She has some important information."

"Then you tell me."

"No. It's hers to tell."

Chris gets a headshake. "I already told you. I don't want to talk to her. But I also don't want her harmed because of her association with us. You have to protect her."

"Protect her from what?"

"Damn, Chris. The public defenders' office didn't send her to represent Joey. We did. If her boss finds out she was in Anne Arundel County saying she was there on behalf of his office when she wasn't, she could be fired or disbarred.

The law will squeeze her to get to us and they'll show no mercy. Get her out of the public defender's office. And let's find the dirty cop."

"Pull your head out of your ass and she'll tell you who your dirty cop is."

Sherry
REJECTION STINGS

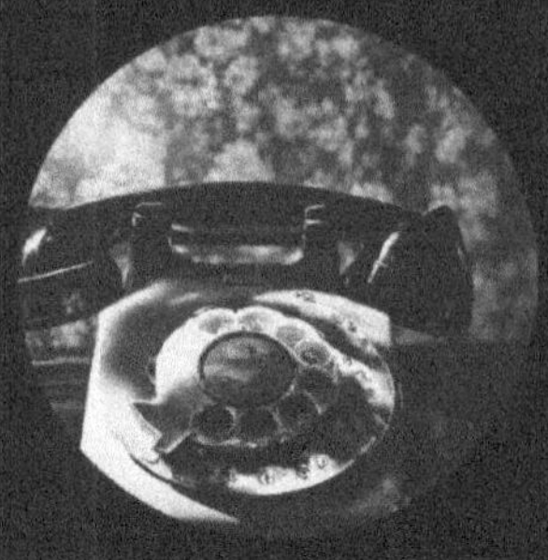

I have been pacing like a trapped cat since I got home from work, waiting to hear from Chris. I haven't even practiced running since Saturday, putting Tina off.

The ten o'clock news said no arrests had been made in the gangland shooting of Matteo DeVecchio in downtown Baltimore Sunday morning. They called him a mob boss.

I didn't like that. Now I understand how Chris feels.

When I finally spoke to my cousin Monday night, he gave me the details. Matteo was shot twice in the back, once in the chest.

I told him about my run-in with Viggo in the coffee shop and that Matteo should be warned. I haven't heard whether they want to hear what I have to tell them.

The phone rings, and I snatch it before it rings a second time. Chris speaks before I can say hello. "He won't see you."

My heart crashes onto the apartment floor. It shatters like glass. I made such a fool of myself when I saw Matteo DeVecchio, the man never wants to see me again. Even for business.

As I scrape my broken heart into a dustpan, I clear my throat to ask, "Is he going to be alright?"

"Yeah, he's tough."

I can't explain the effect he has on me. Why I want to be beside him. A man I saw one time, for a few minutes. Yet I want to stroke that handsome face and take away his pain.

Chris pauses for a beat. It sounds like he's dropping ice cubes into a glass. "They were sure he was dead, or they'd have shot him again. They're going to be pissed off motherfuckers when they find out he's not."

"I'm so sorry. But he or his father needs to know Viggo Johansen is hellbent and determined to put them in prison."

"Why's Johansen suddenly after us?"

"I have no idea."

"Your time at the public defender's office has come to an end."

It feels like Chris backhanded me. This is the first time I understand why people fear Christos Baka. My cousin's normally warm voice feels like the edge of a sword. This conversation is all business. There is no Sherry Baby in it.

"What do you mean?" I ask.

I hear something fizzing over ice. "It's for your own good. Give your notice. We want you out." When I don't respond, Chris says, "Matty's orders. You're out."

My mind is blank. I'm fired, even though I owe them money.

All that comes to mind is, "So I'm free to move to San Francisco?"

I always wanted to go there. Now, I want to get to the other side of the country as fast as I can. I wish the world would open up and swallow me. I'll gladly slide through a hole all the way to China.

Chris snickers. "I didn't say that. You're family. I'll explain later. Tomorrow, you need to relay your cop information to Matty's father."

Despite the relief of learning that I'm not being fired, I draw a sharp breath. "You want me to talk to Francesco DeVecchio?"

Everything I've heard of him terrifies me.

"He's the capofamiglia. Matty is his underboss. Tommy and I are the capos. For whatever reason, Matty won't see you right now, so this is my call. You need to tell Francesco about Viggo. Get over it, kid. It is what it is."

I'm too stunned to respond.

Chris's tone changes again. "Sherry, you're not playing with pimps and wife beaters like you get in the public defender's office. This is a different world."

I've got nothing.

"Do you understand?" It is his hard voice again.

Do I?

"Yes," I squeak. It doesn't sound convincing.

"Call into work tomorrow. You can't come in. I'll pick you up and take you to Francesco. The next day, you'll resign."

"I have to give notice. I have cases—"

He cuts me off. "We'll handle everything. Go in and resign."

"What do you mean, you'll handle everything?"

Now, he's irritated. "I mean, we have the resources to smooth things over." My cousin lacks patience. His voice bites. "There won't be any backlash for a short notice, Sherry. Don't argue. Just do it."

My mind is spinning. My cases... *What's happening?*

He barks. "Understood?"

I'm glad I'm not a trash can. I'd be tumbling across the room.

"Yes."

"I'll pick you up first thing in the morning. Get some sleep."

Did I sleep well? Of course not. My mind wouldn't rest. Thinking about him. Trying to figure out why they want me out of the public defender's office. Wondering what my new assignment might be.

And, of course, Viking Viggo and his threats.

I brew my morning coffee double-strength, preparing for the unknown, and dress as if I were going to court. A peach-colored suit with a white silk blouse and a single strand of pearls. Matching heels.

Professional make-up: not too much, but enough. I tame my hair with hot rollers, noticing it's gotten awfully long. Time for a trim. Or maybe a new do, since my life is changing.

Scott. Out.

Public Defender's Office. Bye-bye.

New style, maybe.

I don't know. I've always worn my hair long. The weight helps subdue the curls. And as someone who loves to run, I can pull it back and tie it up. Long hair is more manageable than medium length, and I'm not going for short.

Yeah, that's where my mind is—on my looks—driving to the house where Matteo DeVecchio lives. Or his parents live.

Where does he live?

Francesco DeVecchio is the most feared name I know, but he did, after all, put me through law school. I want to look professional to meet him.

I want to look like an attorney because I am, although I've been told on more than one occasion that I don't look like an attorney.

I have no idea why.

I never ask.

College, my parents and I paid for ourselves. I was applying for scholarships and loans for law school when Chris intervened.

I never told them thank you. I'd never seen them to thank them until that night in Chris's office.

I hope Mr. DeVecchio's eyes don't paralyze me like his son's.

I hope Matteo recovers. I don't know him. I can't explain how seeing him made me feel. It was a paralyzing electrical pulse coursing through me like I'd never felt before.

Chris is mono-syllabic on the drive, making me more nervous by the mile.

Pulling up to the gates of the DeVecchio home, which is surrounded by a tall iron fence, a truck is parked across the road, barricading the tall gate. On the other side of the gate, a second truck is parked facing the opposite direction.

Men in both vehicles wear shoulder holsters and carry automatic rifles.

Before getting out to speak to the men, Chris pats my hand. "Relax, kiddo. This isn't an execution. Francesco wants to hear what you have to say."

Chris meets with the men at the trucks and gets back in.

Both trucks move to let us drive through, then they close the gates, and the trucks resume their guard positions.

As we travel the long driveway lined with ancient trees, I feel a charge of excitement ripple through me. "What's my new assignment?"

"Not for me to say."

His words from last night come back to me. You're stepping into a whole new world.

I never imagined being here. A place like this.

My Dad operates a crane on the docks in the Port of Baltimore. My mother is a secretary. My dream of law school was the grandest dream any Drakos ever had. I've never traveled across America, much less seen Europe like some of my friends.

Now, I feel like I'm there as we walk up the rock path to the sprawling old brownstone home with its red tile roof. Ivy grows over the rock walls to the windowsills. It feels Old World. How I imagine the Old World, anyway.

The bigger surprise is being greeted at the front door by Francesco DeVecchio himself. Hugging Chris and patting his back, Mr. DeVecchio takes me in as Chris makes the introduction. "Francesco DeVecchio, this is my cousin Sherry Drakos."

Francesco shakes my hand with a smile that lights up his eyes. "Welcome to our home, young lady."

Chris glances at me, then Francesco. "I'll wait in the office."

Mr. DeVecchio smiles and offers his hand. "I want you to feel at home. Come, I'll show you around."

I never expected a tour of the first floor of the De-Vecchio home. It is spacious, warm, and refined. High ceilings. Hardwood floors.

The man is soft-spoken. Composed. Dignified. Nothing like his public image.

As I follow him and listen to him, I can't help but notice his family resemblance to his son, with his black eyes, bronzed skin, and thick salt-and-pepper hair. He is not powerfully built like his son but a handsome older version of Matteo.

Finally, in his large office, Mr. DeVecchio spreads his arm, ushering me to a stuffed chair in front of his desk. "Please, have a seat."

Getting comfortable in his own chair, Francesco faces me, his hands folded on his lap. "Now, Christos says you have information you feel is vital."

His dark eyes bore into mine, listening intently as I relay my exchange with Viggo Johansen at the jail and again at the coffee shop.

As I speak, Mr. DeVecchio occasionally cuts his eyes at Chris as if they share a secret.

"I'm sorry to be the bearer of bad news, sir. But I thought you should know. I can't imagine how he knows Chris is my cousin."

Mr. DeVecchio nods, his gaze locked onto mine with his mouth tweaked to the side. No doubt, his son inherited his father's intense stare. He cuts his eyes at Chris again. "She doesn't know?"

"Didn't want to say anything until I had the go-ahead."

"She should know," the older man prompts.

Chris turns in his chair beside me and folds his hands together, his knuckles locked. He takes a breath and leans toward me, letting it out. "Sherry, my office was bugged."

My hand covers my gaping mouth as I feel my eyes stretch wide. "They heard us talking the other night. That's how he knows."

"He, being Viggo Johansen?" I ask.

Mr. DeVecchio leans his forearms on his desk. "If Viggo Johansen is listening to us, he's a dirty cop. The men checked. The lines going into and out of our warehouse are all clean."

My mind is regurgitating law books. "Law enforcement officers have to obtain a warrant from the court to listen legally."

Francesco goes on. "And we have friendly ears inside courthouses. This isn't law enforcement. We think we know who's responsible. We think that person has a dirty cop on his payroll. We assume it's your boy, Viggo Johansen."

It's hard to comprehend. "If Viggo is dirty, he's one hell of a good actor. I told you about his whole, 'I'm an equal opportunity cop' speech. Viggo Johansen thinks he's the Lone Ranger. Could it be someone else?"

The men exchange their knowing looks. They're parceling out information as they feel I can process it, like feeding a baby bird. "Finding the dirty cop is right behind finding out who shot my son," Francesco says. He leans back in his chair, his gaze on Chris again as his brows bunch together. "You said Matteo did not want to speak with her?"

My head dips. My focus is on my lap, twiddling with my fingers. I still haven't recovered from embarrassing myself. Rejection doesn't play well with anyone, especially not when the feelings are so one-sided.

I notice Chris shrug. "No sir. I've asked him twice. He refuses."

Just plunge the fucking knife in my heart.

Francesco DeVecchio nods, his mouth still doing that odd thing. "I will speak with him."

He stands and offers me his hand. "Thank you, Sherry. We will take appropriate precautions." His eyes smile softly.

"May I share one other thought?" I ask.

A cursory head nod answers me.

"Mr. DeVecchio, the people who did this won't stop until Matteo is dead. They will find a nurse who needs money or who has a dark past and they will get that nurse to give your son something that will kill him."

One more time, I see their quick glances. "We have guards inside and outside the room."

"Would your guards know what a nurse is giving him? She could inject him with a lethal dose right in front of your men. They wouldn't know. Get him out of that hospital as soon as you can. Please."

"She's smart."

My head turns to the voice. The man is larger even than Chris, with Sicilian features.

Francesco spreads his arm, aiming at the man who just entered the office. "Ms. Drakos, this is Tommaso Ricci. He and Christos grew up with my son. I trust them as my own."

Chris mentioned him earlier. The other capo.

"Pleasure to meet you." Standing, I offer my hand to the big man, who takes it and doesn't let go. After a long beat, Tommaso says, "Now I understand."

"Excuse me?" I draw my hand back.

Tommaso's gaze travels to the elder DeVecchio as he nudges his head toward me. "The girl in Texas. Dead ringer. This one's a little taller, but the same color hair. Exact same eyes."

"I never met her." Chris stares at me like I'm a three-headed snake.

"Nor did I, but he told me about those eyes years ago. I wondered earlier." Francesco smiles softly. "My dear, your eyes frighten my son. And he's not a man who frightens easily. Maybe someday you will understand. Until then, do not take his rejection personally. It is a means of self-protection."

I have no idea what they're talking about, nor do I know how to respond.

Chris clears his throat, talking to Tommaso. "That's why he ran to Sophia."

Tommaso plops his enormous frame into an empty chair. "Yeah. It's coming together now."

Looking from one man to the next, I tell them, "I'm sorry, I'm lost."

Chris chuckles and shakes his head.

No one responds.

"Well, are you going to get Matteo out of the hospital?" I ask.

Francesco steps around his desk. "Would you like a formal introduction?"

I really don't know what to say to that.

"Follow me."

"He's not in the hospital?" My heart races.

"No."

I plant my feet as my stomach climbs toward my throat. "He's made it clear. He doesn't want to see me." I may throw up. "I don't want to see him."

Francesco chuckles and wiggles his fingers in a summons. "Nonsense. Come."

I am sure my eyes are the size of dinner plates as I look at my cousin for help.

Chris twists his neck with what I'd call a wicked grin. His dimple shows. "Not wise to tell Francesco DeVecchio no."

Francesco summons me with his hand. "Come, come. Let's get this behind us. You've proven to be a valuable asset. My son is an intelligent man. You two will work together, like it or not."

Matteo
Face Your Fears

"Come in." I respond to my father's knuckles rapping on my bedroom door. I know his terse knock.

Sitting straighter against the bed pillows, wearing pajamas, I don't bother pulling up the sheet to cover myself. It's my father.

He steps in, steps aside, and those haunting blue eyes stare back at me.

One more time, her beautiful pink lips part.

What a vision, dressed in a suit the color of tulips in spring, her hair hanging in waves around her face, falling below her shoulders.

One more time, neither of us can speak. Our gazes lock magnetically.

Pop harrumphs. "Son, I don't think you've been formally introduced to Sherry Drakos, Christos's cousin. It's time. Sherry, my son Matteo Dante DeVecchio."

The room suffers a few seconds of silence before the woman steps forward, her hand extended. "Matteo, it's nice to meet you."

The cat's got my tongue for another second before I answer, not moving for the extended hand. "What can I do for you, Miss Drakos?"

She drops her hand to her side as Pop steps forward. "It's not what you can do for her, son. It's what she can do for you. Sherry, have a seat and tell him."

Fuck.

"Wait. Let me get dressed."

"If you insist. You've got five minutes," Pop says. "I'm not playing games. Sherry? Come with me."

She follows dutifully.

"Pop. Wait."

He shakes his head. "Time to move on son. Our ox is in the ditch."

"Maybe so, but I need help getting dressed."

Dammit.

The bedroom they turned into my recuperation room has a sitting area tucked in front of a bay window that overlooks the back of the estate. From here, I can see my house, a few acres away from my parents' home.

I quit living with them when I graduated college, but Pop insisted, for safety, that I live within the compound. I chose a place near a small creek running through the property.

"You can show them in," I tell the nurse once I'm fully dressed.

Maria, a portly, older woman, shuffles to the door. She is the sister of my mother's housekeeper, Bettina. Maria's not here to medicate me; she just changes bandages and assists me until I can dress myself.

Opening the bedroom door, Maria says, "He's ready." She glances over her shoulder. "Anything else, Mr. DeVecchio?"

"Not unless Pop needs something."

Maria swings the door wide for Pop and Sherry to enter.

Pops says, "Maria, will you have Bettina send up some coffee? Three cups."

"Yessir."

I'm listening. Not looking. Pop laid down the law with that one sentence. Our ox is in the ditch. I've got to deal with this woman. Turning to face her, ignoring the eyes, I nod. "What is so important that you need to tell me?"

"A Drug Enforcement Agency officer has set his sights on you, personally," she says matter-of-factly. "His name is Viggo Johansen."

My gut tightens as I feel my face solidify. We all know the name.

My gaze fixes on Pop as the woman continues. "He was at the Anne Arundel County Jail. He's the one who had the highway patrol stop your truck and he told me and Joey that he intends, and I quote, to 'tack your ass to the wall.'"

She's direct. Well-spoken. I like that. "Have a seat." I extend my hand to a chair.

She stands primly. "Thank you, I'll stand."

Our gazes lock together. "I said, have a seat."

Pop is behind her, smirking.

She nods and sits in the chair across from me, slipping her hand beneath her thigh as she does. She tugs on her pencil skirt, smooths it over her knees, and crosses her ankles. "I saw Viggo the next day at the coffee shop across from my office. I've never seen him there on any other occasion, so I immediately wondered if he followed me.

"Anyway, he said he was just on his way to court, but he told me to distance myself from the DeVecchios or go to prison with you. It was a very odd conversation. The bottom line is, he is tunnel-focused on this family for some reason. And, he said I showed up at the jail too fast that night and that he knows I work for your family. I assured him I was with the defender's office, but he refused to believe me. I wanted you to know. He even knew Chris is my cousin. He asked if Chris was going to 'off' him."

Damn. Shit. Hell.

Fuck. We know what Viggo Johansen is capable of.

I divert my attention to the window. "Thank you. We'll take it from here."

"Chris said you want me to resign my position with the public defender's office. I don't understand."

I meet her questioning eyes. "If Johansen calls your boss and asks if they sent you to Anne Arundel County Saturday night and your boss says no, and Johansen tells him you said you were there as a public defender, you could be fired. Maybe even disbarred. I want no harm to come to you."

Her delicate brows draw down. "Public defenders have the right to take on private clients."

I lean forward. "But you told them you were there with the public defender's office."

"They can interpret it any way they want. I am a public defender. I was at that jail. I don't think they can fire or disbar me." She glances at Pop, who has taken the chair beside her, wearing a look of amusement. "But I owe both of you for my law degree. If you want to send me to Alaska for the next year, I'll go."

"We have other uses for a brain like hers," Pop says.

"Yes, we do. I assume you're somewhat of an investigator. I'd like for you to start digging up anything you can on Sophia Marie Gabicci."

Her mesmerizing eyes fix on mine. "Your girlfriend?" The light coming from the window makes those eyes a reflecting pool.

"She's not my girlfriend."

She blinks. "I'm sorry. I thought you were with—"

I cut her off, showing her my palm. "Just find out what you can. I don't really know what I'm looking for. But I realize, I don't know much about what Sophia does during the day. I want to know who she hangs out with. I know she brought a girlfriend to the warehouse while I was in Italy. Get her description from Chris. I just need to know everything and anything about Sophia Marie Gabicci."

"Yessir."

"Don't call me sir."

She dips her head. "Yes, Mr. DeVecchio."

I snicker. "Don't call me Mr. DeVecchio either. I'm Matteo."

"Yessir. Matteo." She glances at Pop. "When I resign, do I work from home?"

I answer. "No. We'll either give you an office at the warehouse or get you a storefront where you can hang your shingle as a private practice. I'll let you know."

"She can work from here in the meantime." Pop slaps his thighs and stands. "You two need to work together. I have a feeling the minds will be effective together."

With Sherry out of the room, Tommy joins Pop and me in the bedroom. I give instructions, running my hand over my forehead. "Pop, have Rhinehart run a nation-wide background on Sophia and Geno."

"What are you looking for?"

"Like I told Sherry, I don't know. But them ambushing us at your house, saying Mother invited her—then our truck being pulled over and me being backshot, bugs in the warehouse. We're missing something. Tommy? Do me a favor. Go to my house. Play my phone messages. See if Sophia has shown any concern. Pop, did you ask Mother? Has Sophia called here asking about me?"

He grins and scratches the back of his neck. "I know what your mother would say if she did."

"Maybe someone else took the call. I just want to know."

"For God's sake, you're not fucking worried about her, are you?"

I have to love Tommy's righteous indignation. "No. I just want to know."

"Okay. I'll be back."

When Tommy leaves my room, Pop and I are alone. "Why are you pushing this girl on me?"

"Because you're afraid of her. Face your fears, Matty."

"I'm not afraid—"

"Yes. You. Are."

I glance out the window. "It's not fear. It's humiliation. The memories those eyes stir."

He takes a step closer and aims his arm at the door. "Those eyes adore you. They are not the eyes of the other girl. Sherry sat in my office and insisted that I get you out of the hospital, that some nurse could poison you. She was trying to warn you about Johansen before she learned you were shot. I'm telling you, son, those are the blue eyes that will love you as you should be loved."

"I never pegged you for a romantic."

His brows bunch together. "Did you see how she looks at you?"

"Yeah, well, Patsy looked at me the same way. I'm not falling for it again."

"The girl in Texas looked at you like that?" He's still pointing at the door.

"Yes, Pop. She did."

"Well, no wonder you thought she loved you. Maybe she did, she just had prior obligations."

"I told myself that. Didn't get me anywhere. Let's just drop it."

"Fear can distort your perception of life. Buck it up. Face your fears." He leaves my room, shaking his head.

Sherry and her blue eyes were nowhere around when the thunderbolt struck me. It only happens once in a lifetime. I'm just a sucker for blue eyes.

"You've got half a dozen messages on your answering machine from Sophia," Tommy announces. "Each time it's, 'Matty please let me know you're alright.'" He mimics a female voice. "'I tried your mother's. They hang up when I say my name.' Blah blah. 'I just want to know you are alright.' Fuckin' bitch."

His performance prompts a laugh strong enough to make my chest hurt.

Of course, Donna DeVecchio guards her son like a pit bulldog. And it makes me feel warm to hear Tommy so disgusted.

But my logic argues. "We still don't know she had anything to do with it."

Tommy tilts his head back and snorts. "The fuck we don't."

Sherry
NEW ASSIGNMENT

"This is pretty unbelievable," I admit as Chris drives me back to my apartment. My head is churning with everything that happened this morning. A part of me is terrified.

Another part of me is soaring on the wings of an eagle.

Francesco DeVecchio was nothing like I imagined.

His son? Professional like his father, but not as friendly. He didn't look at me the way he did at the warehouse. Reservedly cordial.

"Why don't you go ahead and call work? Give notice today?" My cousin asks, his focus on the traffic.

"What's the rush?"

"We told you."

Repositioning in the bucket seat, I take a long look at my cousin. His profile is impressive. That thick head of wavy blonde hair is neatly trimmed. A strong brow line and jaw, a perfect not-too-big or too-small nose. Full lips. Chris keeps a closely trimmed blonde beard.

"Even if I get called in and they say, 'Why were you in Ann Arundel County saying you're there as a public defender?' I'll just say, Joey's a friend and his parents called me."

Chris cuts his eyes at me. "You said, Viggo said Joey hadn't made a phone call when you showed up."

"That can always be disputed." I hold up my hands in a defensive stance. "But I'm quitting, don't worry. I'm excited about this new adventure."

I get a narrow squint from my cousin. "You and Matty. Is that happening?"

A sad laugh seeps from my throat. "Are you kidding me? The man loathes me."

Holding the steering wheel with one hand, Chris leans his forearm on his window as he peers at me. "No, kiddo. That's not loathing. There was a girl years ago who tore his heart to shreds. He's afraid you could do the same. He looks at you and sees her."

Another slap in the face. My hackles rise. "Do you know how belittling that is? That someone doesn't see you? He looks at me and sees someone else? Step into those shoes, Chris, and tell me how that feels to you." And suddenly, I wonder, "Have you ever been inexplicably drawn to any-one?"

He scoffs. "Lust? Sure. I don't have time for love."

"What about Tommy?"

"Married out of high school. Has kids. He makes his job work with his family."

"You know, love isn't something you schedule on your calendar, doofus. When it hits, it hits."

"Like most people, you're confusing infatuation with love. Love is a deep commitment fueled by passion. No, I haven't felt that. Yet."

"I'm glad to know some men feel that way. I met a client in Baltimore City Jail yesterday." Chris glances my way, all ears. "A john charged with statutory rape. His prost was a fifteen-year-old junkie. That man has a wife and kids at home." I sigh heavily, glancing out the window at the traffic. "I get guys like him all the time. I'd rather defend the DeVecchios all day long than one more guy like him. He thinks fucking teenage girls and cheating on his wife is his privilege."

That wins me the warmest smile Chris has shown me in days.

Reaching across the truck, he shakes my shoulder. "Welcome aboard, Sherry Baby."

"What do I need to know about this Sophia Gabicci?"

"She is the only child of Alfonso Gabicci, head of the Gabicci family. The Gabiccis are based in Jersey and Delaware. We have Maryland and Virginia. Families are like little countries. Territorial. Kind of like Hitler forty years ago. Every now and then, some fucked up son of a bitch like Geno Gabicci looks around and decides he wants more territory than he's allotted and decides to take it."

He lifts one shoulder. "Besides, he and Matty have hated each other since they turned fifteen. This fight has been brewing a while."

"Why?"

He tilts his head, his eyes on the road. "That's Matty's to share if he wants to."

I play with the hem of my skirt, afraid to broach the subject. But I must. "Viggo said they call him the Butcher of Baltimore."

He cuts his eyes at me. "That nickname's got nothing to do with business."

I look at him with surprise.

"That goes back to his boxing days. Matty slaughtered every opponent who came after him in the ring. Some sportswriter coined him the Butcher of Baltimore. In the ring, Sherry. Viggo knows that. He was just trying to get under your skin."

"He succeeded." I feel the relief. "Is he in love with Sophia? Did she betray him?"

Chris chuckles again, showing his adorable dimple. "Geez, you're such a kid. Sex doesn't have to have anything to do with love."

"I'm an adult. I know that." Scott Buchanan being a perfect example.

I'm still jealous of him being with her. I can't help it. I know jealousy when I feel it. "If the Gabicci's have New Jersey and Delaware, why does Sophia live here?"

"I've wondered that myself. I think she wants a future with Matty so she moved closer. He pretty much uses her."

"That's not nice." Maybe I don't like him as much as I thought.

"Don't get me wrong. I think Matty's had feelings for her, but he was never going to marry her. Certainly not now."

"And you know that how?"

"He told me. He ended it the night he was shot. Right before he was shot, as a matter of fact."

"Did she do it?"

"Tommy thinks she had it done."

I sigh. "I'm sure she's beautiful."

My cousin lets out a wolf whistle. "That she is. Hell of a body." He glances at me and does the hourglass figure thing with his hands.

"Keep your hands on the steering wheel!"

I look away, out my window. Jealousy burns my cheeks. "Well, then, he won't look at me twice. No hourglass going on here."

"Shut up, Sherry. You know you're a looker. Don't be self-deprecating."

"Didn't know you had a word like self-deprecating in that pretty blonde head of yours." I nudge him with my elbow and wink. "Teasing."

Chris gives me a hard look. He holds it long enough that I want to tell him again to watch the road. "I was there, remember? You knocked Matty off his feet. He went to Sophia to get a fix. That's all that was."

"Wrong. He didn't see me. He saw her. He saw someone who made him think of her, whoever she was, and he had to get a quick fix of... whatever."

He shrugs. "Same thing."

"Not in the least." Fine. I won't argue with him. But me, Sherry Drakos. I don't exist to Matteo DeVecchio. I change the subject. "Give me the ground rules going in."

"The rules of engagement," he says. "First, honesty. Don't hide anything. Don't lie about anything. Just tell the truth and take the consequences. Two, don't dishonor the family. Never talk about our business to anyone else. Never ever publicly criticize anything we do. If you disagree, do it in private. If you have the DeVecchios' backs, I can promise you, they'll have yours."

"If the ship sinks, we all go down together?" I ponder aloud. Viggo Johansen is rattling around my brain again.

"That's just how it is." Chris's face morphs to stone, along with his voice. His gaze grabs mine. "If you have any doubts. If you can't handle it, tell them now. Not later."

"I said, I'm in."
"You're sure? No doubts?"
"I've never been surer of anything."

Sherry
DIGGING

Finding out about people isn't as easy as it sounds.

Per Matteo's instructions, I immersed myself in public records, starting at the Baltimore County Courthouse.

Then, I waded through weeks' worth of courthouse records in Wilmington, Trenton, and Newark before returning to Baltimore.

Gabicci Enterprises is all over Jersey and Delaware, as would be expected. But they also have holdings inside Baltimore proper, all recent acquisitions.

If I understood Chris correctly, the Gabicci family shouldn't be doing business in Maryland or Virginia. Yet here they are. Maybe Sophia's move here wasn't coincidental.

Among their holdings are Ace Construction, Blackstone International, a real estate investment firm, and Apice Productions. Whatever that is.

All on DeVecchio turf.

According to the county clerk's office, Sophia Maria Gabicci owns no property individually in Baltimore, and she is not listed as a partner or officer in any of the three companies.

Maybe Blackstone buys properties, Ace Construction renovates them, and they sell for big profits. Or they buy, renovate, and manage the properties.

For all I know, Blackstone owns the downtown building where Sophia lives. Maybe she and Geno both have apartments there.

Right now, it's all conjecture because no documents list the names of officers or their percentage of holdings of any of the companies. Nor, can I find addresses for properties owned by Blackstone International.

But I'm just getting started.

My background is in criminal law, not civil law. I have no foundation in real estate or financial holdings, so I'm out of my element, but I'm a fast learner. I'll get the information Matteo asked for.

"Sherry Baby, what are you doing here?" It's a familiar voice.

I look up from my stack of papers to meet crisp, light blue eyes. "I could ask you the same, Scott."

He smiles. "I hear you quit the public defender's office."

"I did."

"So why are you here?"

I throw him a smirk. "I quit the defender's office. I didn't quit law."

Scott moves closer. "I told you for months to quit that cheap outfit. What made you finally do it?"

A caution light flashes in my head. "I just decided to, that's all."

His gaze narrows. "So, what are you doing now? Private practice?"

"Yeah."

His focus is trained on the copies of real estate documents in front of me.

"In civil law?" he asks.

I gather my papers and turn them face down. "Yes and no. And none of your business, remember?"

He scratches his brow, studying me. "We've got openings in the prosecutor's office."

"No. Thanks, though."

He glances left and right in the busy clerk's office, then peers over my shoulder at my pile of documents. "Why are you interested in Blackstone International?"

Our gazes catch. "What do you know about Blackstone?"

He gives an exaggerated shrug. "Nothing. Should I?"

I'm not sure why, but I don't believe him. "Convince me, counselor."

He scowls defensively. "Nothing, I just see the letterhead on the papers. Geez, Sherry. Lunch someday?"

"Maybe."

"Same number?"

"Yep."

He glances at his watch. "Heading to Judge Hildebrand's court. Catch you later." He aims his finger at me before he walks away. "And think about that job offer. We're short-handed."

Not on your life.

Leaving the courthouse, I swing by DeVecchio Imports to find Tommy and Chris in the office. "My two favorite—"

An astonished Chris looks up from his work, eyes wide, and puts his index finger to his lips, shaking his head. "Mrs. Jones!" He interrupts me loudly. "Glad you dropped by. Let me show you what we got in today." He leaves his desk to usher me out the office door, through the warehouse, onto the parking lot.

Tommy follows.

Even in the parking lot, my cousin speaks in a hushed voice. "I wasn't expecting you. I haven't had a chance to tell you—we're not talking business inside my office. And no names."

"You mean you haven't removed the bugs? Why not?"

No answer. Two stone faces peer back at me.

"Well, the reason I'm here is because you told me Gabiccis don't operate in Maryland. But they do. I just found out they've got three businesses in Baltimore proper."

Surprisingly, those stone faces get even harder. I had no idea it was possible.

"No telling what they hold in the rest of the state, and I haven't gotten to Virginia yet."

Their eyes angle to each other. Chris and Tommy have been together for so long that they communicate telepathically.

"A construction company—"

Chris shows me his palm with a sheepish shrug. "Yeah, I know about Ace Construction. Didn't know about the others."

"Well, there's also Blackstone International. It looks like a real estate investment firm."

The eye exchange between the capos.

"Okay that's two," Tommy says. "What's the third?"

"Apice Productions."

The capos stare blank-faced again. These guys must be hellacious poker players.

Finally, "A production company?" Chris asks.

"I guess. I don't know what they produce."

"Interesting," Tommy muses aloud.

Chris turns to Tommy. "Apice... isn't that Italian for—"

"Yeah."

The two snicker.

"I don't get it."

Tommy hits my back with a hand that covers half of it. "You don't need to."

I think it was his attempt at a pat. "Geez, Tommy. I'm not one of the guys. That hurt." I rub my shoulder.

"Sorry, kid."

"You don't know your own strength."

"So, I've been told. Have you told all of this to Matty? He's the one who needs to know."

I feel an unwelcome flush in my cheeks. "He doesn't really want to see me, so I decided I'll report in once a week."

Chris cocks a brow and crosses his thick, hairy arms over his chest. "I heard you didn't report in at all last week."

"I did so. I report to Francesco every day. He knows what I'm doing."

"Matty doesn't."

"How do you know?"

"Because he told me."

"Is he mad?"

Chris hikes his shoulders. "I asked how you were doing in your new position, and he said he hasn't seen you. That's all."

I nod.

"So, you two are avoiding each other." Tommy flashes a mischievous smirk and winks at Chris. "Wonder how much longer that will go on?"

Blood rushes up my throat to my cheeks. Crimson again.

Dammit. I clear my throat. "It's been established. Matteo doesn't want to see me. So, I deal with Francesco."

They do the eye thing again, and Tommy asks, "What *have* you been doing all this time?"

My hands meet my hips, my elbows wide. "Now how the hell do you think I got all that information? Research takes time. I've been buried under paperwork in courthouses from here to Trenton, combing through records of property and business ownership. I didn't go to college to study real estate and investment."

Digging through boring courthouse documents, I'd felt a surprising twang for the familiarity of the perps and criminal courts. "Right now, you could give me a good old crook any day."

"You don't mean that," Chris says.

"No. I don't. Not really. But digging into the backgrounds of people is... different. It's not like I have access to law enforcement databases. I've combed through every district clerk's office. I can't find where Sophia or Genovese Gabicci have ever been charged with a crime."

Chris leans his back against my little car with a smug smile. "The man you need to tell this to is named Matteo Dante DeVecchio. Maybe you know him. He's about six feet tall, with black hair and black eyes."

I open my door to get in my car. "Okay. I just thought you'd want to know, since you told me the Gabiccis were supposed to stay in Jersey and Delaware and they're clearly in Maryland." *Talk about unappreciative.*

"I do. Thanks. Now go tell Matty." My cousin's dimple shows as his eyes glimmer with the same mischief I saw in Tommy earlier.

"Maybe tomorrow afternoon. I've got something I need to do in the morning."

He leans in, his giant hand on the top of my door as I slide into my seat. "Like what?" he asks.

I flash a snide grin. "That's need-to-know. And you don't need to know."

Matteo
SHOT OF
PENICILLIN

"**T**alk about what happened in your county." I roll my wrist, a glass of soda in hand.

Sheriff Rhinehart squirms, glancing around the little café, avoiding eye contact. I've been around him a few times, and in each instance, he acts like this. Paranoid. Like he's terrified that he's being followed.

He is. By us. I don't trust the fat fuck. Any married man who would do that—he's got no soul.

"Relax." Pop reaches across the booth and pats Rhinehart's pudgy hand.

I don't know how he stands to touch it. I can't figure out how this guy got elected dog catcher, much less sheriff. I remind myself our money put him in office. "You're safe here." Pop manages a smile, trying to put the sheriff at ease.

We're meeting in a small family café in rural Virginia. For all appearances, Pop and I are passing through, stopping for a late lunch, running into an old friend who is fishing in town.

Rhinehart studies me from across the booth, his gaze falling on my chest. "How are you feeling?" he asks. It sounds sincere.

"It's more than a month. I'm stronger. Thank you for asking."

"Shot three times in the torso, and you're sitting here a few weeks later. You have the constitution of a horse."

I nod my appreciation. "My immediate worry is what happened with our truck. What have you learned?"

The sheriff pulls a folded piece of paper from his fishing vest and slides it across the tabletop. "Johansen filed that with the federal district clerk's office. He bypassed my county, working with state troopers."

Unfolding it, Pop and I study the paper, sitting shoulder to shoulder.

"He used this to get his warrant?" I ask.

The sheriff nods. "Reading between the lines, I'd say his informant is someone in law enforcement." He tilts his chin toward the document in my hand. "That's why it's so redacted. Someone who works in a different agency is his informant. Viggo's guy just passes information to him since the DEA has a broader jurisdiction."

Rhinehart takes a long drink of his soda and sets his glass down. "I'd say his guy is another fed, or maybe even a prosecutor who feeds Johansen information he gets that is over his head."

Pop's gaze moves from the paper to the sheriff. "So, you don't think Johansen is dirty?"

Rhinehart shakes his head with a doubting scowl. "The guy's got one hell of a reputation to be dirty. The state troopers were in awe making the stop for Johansen. I guarantee they went home dend told their wives, 'You won't believe who I helped today.' You know he—"

"We know." I've heard enough, especially knowing Johansen now has us under his microscope. I don't need to hear what a hero he is to law enforcement.

I'm still not convinced Johansen is clean. Everything of importance has been blacked out with a magic marker.

The affidavit says something about a shipment of cocaine arriving at the Port of Baltimore from Florida that Saturday, the route taking the truck through Anne Arundel.

I hold up the paper to the window, hoping maybe I could read it through the markings.

I can't. "This is bogus. It doesn't even identify the truck or its plates. None of our trucks carry our name or emblem. He had to have at least a license plate number to know what truck to stop."

"That's all I've got," the sheriff replies. "This is deep shit."

I glance away. This is taking too much time.

No telling what damage Geno is about to unleash.

"What did your national search find on Sophia and Geno Gabicci?" Pop asks.

Rhinehart shakes his head. "Neither has had anything more than traffic tickets."

"I'm going to rest," I tell Pop when we near his house.

I'm not tired. I'm frustrated. We haven't gotten anywhere. "It's time for me to go back home. There's no need for me to stay here any longer. I can dress myself." Once you leave your parent's home, you can never really go back. Not to stay.

"Nonsense," Pops says. "Wait another week at least. You feel strong because you are strong, but the meat inside has not fully healed. It takes time."

I notice the little red Volkswagen convertible parked in front of the house.

"Sherry hasn't been here in weeks. Is she worth her pay? I haven't heard anything from her."

"Maybe if you weren't hiding upstairs, you'd see. She's smart. A good worker. She's not a cop. She can't run background checks on people like Rhinehart. She is doing it the old-fashioned way. You can't avoid her forever."

"I'm not avoiding her. I have a private line in my bedroom. I'm working from there. It's more comfortable."

Pop hikes a brow. "You've made yourself as scarce as summer snow, son."

He gets a glare. "I'm not avoiding her."

Pop snickers. "A rose by any other name..."

Sherry and I have given each other a wide berth. She's had an effect on me both times I've seen her. Not just the eyes. She is very professional. Very ladylike. A heart-stopping knockout.

A part of me doesn't like that she avoids me.

Early on, when I walked into Pop's office, she suddenly had somewhere else to be. "I just need to go... wherever." It happened a few times before I decided if she was so uncomfortable with me, I'd make it easier on her.

Not today.

When Pop and I walk into the kitchen from the garage, Sherry is waiting, beaming like the August sun.

That big smile—it's the first time I've seen she has a dimple exactly like Chris's.

"I have news for you!" She almost squeals. I think she's about to jump up and down.

"And what is that?" Pop wraps his arm around her shoulder and guides her into the kitchen. He treats her like she's one of his kids. My sisters would be jealous if they were in the country. Both are still in Europe with their families until after Labor Day.

Sherry cuts her eyes at me. "I got pictures of Sophia meeting with a man."

Pop and I look at each other, asking in unison, "Where?"

"The Shangri-La, in D.C."

"You followed her?" Pop asks, surprise evident in his tone and lifted brows.

Sherry draws back. "Why not? She doesn't know me."

"She's a Gabicci, sweetheart. Sophia carries a snub nose pistol and a knife in her purse."

Sherry's face falls. "You've got to be kidding me."

This beautiful woman should never play poker. She is such an innocent. I try but can't hold back a smile. "I just said, Sophia is a Gabicci." My gaze darts to Pop. "She's got a lot to learn."

His hand goes high as he heads for the refrigerator. "So, quit avoiding her and teach her." Sticking his head in the freezer, he says over his shoulder, "She's your pupil."

There goes my nap.

He draws out a bottle of scotch and wags it at us. "Time for my afternoon Penicillin."

Sherry looks at me with inquisitive eyes, and I cannot stop the grin that hijacks my face. It's pure Pop.

"Scotch, lemon juice and honey-ginger syrup," I explain to her in a hushed voice.

She squinches her little nose. "Ugh. He keeps the scotch in the freezer?"

"We like it cold. I'm not a fan of their Penicillins, though. Tell me about your photographs."

Her face lights up. "You want to see?"

"You already have them processed?"

"Yes, at one of those quickie places. They're just snapshots." She leads me into Pop's office, where she has a small desk beside the window facing the grounds. Paperwork organized in neat little stacks shows she's been doing something.

How have I not noticed this earlier?

She catches me staring at her workstation and apparently feels obligated to explain. "I didn't feel comfortable working at your father's desk. It wouldn't be appropriate. So, he had this brought in for me. I haven't been here a lot. I've been doing research in different courthouses." She has files, a typewriter, and a telephone. Unbelievable.

So is she, wearing a white above-the-knee sundress with big daisies on it. It has a square neckline, and the fitted waist tells me hers is tiny. With the sleeves cut in, the outfit shows her nice shoulders, toned arms, and tan. Not to mention the legs.

Fuck, those legs. What they could do wrapped around my waist.

I hold out my hand. "Show me the photos."

"First, I should tell you. I found out the Gabiccis have several businesses right here in Baltimore."

Cockroaches.

I feel my brow crease. "Do tell."

Sherry lays out her findings along with her explanation of scouring through records in courthouses all along the Mid-Atlantic.

She retrieves an envelope on her desk and hands it to me. "I got these today."

Opening it, I thumb through the distant shots. I know that's Sophia because I know her so well—the hair, the figure. She is dressed conservatively, but in true Sophia fashion, her dress has a wide belt that accentuates her hourglass figure.

They aren't holding hands or showing any affection. Just a man and woman walking into a restaurant. "Looks like a business meeting to me."

My gaze moves from the pictures to meet Sherry's eyes, finding them laser-focused, studying me. She blushes and looks away.

"Do you know who this man is?" I ask.

Her smile comes back. "I didn't, but I do. When they left together, I went inside and told the maître de I was sent to get a message to Ms. Gabicci, and he said, 'You just missed her.' I looked shocked and distressed and asked if he knew who she was with or where they went so I could find them and get the message to her."

That dimple deepens as her shoulders sway. "Frankly, I think I did a good job of acting because the maître de volunteered that she left with Senator Mulholland's aide, Bob Kerrigan."

I swear under my breath.

"Is that bad?" Sherry asks with wide eyes.

"Mulholland. He's in Geno's pocket. Somewhere along the way, Geno got something on him. Your pictures tell me money and messages go from Geno to Sophia to Kerrigan, from Kerrigan to the senator. And visa-versa. No doubt, Kerrigan gets his cut."

"So does Sophia," Sherry adds.

No senator can be seen with any member of any family. "Did you notice where they went when they left?"

Sherry smiles again. "They parted ways on the sidewalk outside the restaurant. Sophia," she cuts her eyes up at me, "who really is beautiful. I'm not butch or anything, but the woman should be a movie star... walked to her car, and Mr. Kerrigan took off down the sidewalk.

"I was going to follow her, but she never went anywhere. She just started her car and waited in it. I guess she ran the engine for the air conditioner. I saw her check her watch. Fifteen minutes later, she turns it off, gets out and goes into the Radisson Hotel on the other side of the street. I had a hunch, so I waited. Another fifteen minutes later, Kerrigan goes inside, too."

A hearty laugh rumbles from my chest. "I don't guess you waited them out?"

Here comes that wonderful little dimple and a timid girly giggle. "No, I didn't figure that would be a quickie."

I tilt my head back and guffaw. It's the best laugh I've had since I left Italy. I use my knuckle to wipe a laugh tear from my eye. Knowing Sophia, she would wear Kerrigan out.

Judging from the photos, I'd put him fifty-ish. Not a bad-looking guy. Medium height and build, light brown hair. Nice, tailored, dark blue suit. Of course. He's a Senator's aide. He would wear a tailored suit. Kerrigan is in good enough shape to keep up with Sophia for the afternoon, but his wife won't get much attention when he gets home.

Holding up her photographs, I smile involuntarily. This woman seems to bring that out in me. Smiles. "You did very good."

"Thank you." She looks like a schoolgirl who just got a gold sticker from her teacher. Heartwarming, that's what she is.

She took the initiative following Sophia. She's worked hard, uncovering valuable information. Sherry has given us fresh insights into what our enemy is doing.

I make her the same offer I'd give one of the guys. "Would you like to join Pop for his afternoon drink?"

"Would you?" The expression on her face—she looks almost afraid.

She is entertaining.

"Don't answer a question with a question."

Her shoulders shift high. "I guess."

This woman is an attorney who just followed Sophia Gabicci fearlessly. She went to battle with a D.E.A. agent for us. I don't get the impression she is normally timid, but the way she looks at me? She is.

I extend my hand. "This way."

I guide Sherry back to the kitchen, finding Mother mixing a second Penicillin for Pop and one for herself. He's in the sunroom, just off the kitchen, with his feet propped on a footstool. "Mother, I assume you know Sherry Drakos?"

She smiles. "Of course. Sherry, would you like to join us for a drink?"

"Thank you, Mrs. DeVecchio. Matteo just asked."

Mother cocks her head with amusement, staring at me. "He did, did he?" She turns her attention to Sherry. "You've been here long enough, you can drop the Mr. and Mrs.

I'm Donna. My husband is Francesco. And the man at your side, inside this house, is Matty."

Sherry remains speechless. From what little I know of her already, she will not call me Matty—not until I tell her to.

"Yes ma'am," she says.

"What's your pleasure?" Mother asks Sherry.

"You join Pop," I tell her. "I'll fix our drinks, and we'll join you."

As Mother takes their drinks into the sunroom, I ask Sherry, "What would you like?"

"I don't drink much."

More often than not, women come on to me, but this beautiful woman is charmingly bashful. Standoffish.

I can feel another grin spread across my face. I didn't realize how afraid of her I'd been. How relieved I am to not be. I was wrong. Patsy never looked at me that way.

"When you do drink, what do you like?"

It's not a familiar feeling, so much smiling. It's beginning to strain my face.

Sherry purses her lips, contemplating. "Hum." Her eyes meet mine. "Wine? Whiskey and Coke, with less whiskey than Coke?" She holds her thumb and index finger, indicating a tiny splash of whiskey. "I don't want to get tipsy in the afternoon."

I chuckle and nod. "Join Mother and Pop. I'll be in with our drinks."

She obeys.

This is... nice. I've never, in all my years, had a woman join me, visiting with my mother and father.

I pour myself a stiff one. I feel like it. Sherry gets a sissy whiskey and Coke.

Moving to the sunroom, I find them clustered together on wicker furniture at the windows.

"Here is your baby girl whiskey and Coke."

"Thank you." She smiles graciously. As she takes her drink, I sit beside her on the couch.

My parents are in the two chairs to our side, a table between them.

Pop snorts. "Baby girl whiskey?"

"More Coke than whiskey," I clarify. "Unlike her cousin, Sherry is not much of a drinker."

"Good for you, dear." Mother holds up her Penicillin. "Wait until you've been with this bunch for a few years. You'll be right here with me." Mother finishes off her first drink. "Bettina?" She wags her glass, rattling the ice.

It is surprisingly pleasant sitting in the lush sunroom, which is filled with banana trees and tropical plants. I never do this. From our vantage point, we have a view of our pool and back lawn.

Mother has had one drink, and she's beginning to gab. "We did this room to remind us of Havana before the communists took over."

I watch Sherry's eyes twinkle as Mother tells her story.

"Our families, Francesco's and mine, had vacation homes in Cuba when we were young. We had our own when Matteo and the girls were growing up. Then Castro came to power." She turns her head to fake spit. "The communists took everything. This is as close as we can get anymore." Mother's eyes are wistful.

"I'm sorry," Sherry offers. "But you have certainly made a beautiful home here."

"Thank you, dear."

Bettina enters, and Mother holds out her drink. "Will you, Betti?" She peers at Sherry, sitting beside me on the wicker couch. "Sherry? Join me in another?"

Sherry's drink has very little alcohol. She gulps it down and holds out her glass. "Yes, thank you."

I have to chuckle on the inside. Bettina doesn't have my recipe. "Light on the whiskey," I warn her.

Bettina nods, but she has no idea how light I went on the whiskey. Bettina peers at Pop. "One more, sir?"

"One more, Betti and we will be done."

I throw mine back and hold my glass for her, too.

Mother has only just begun talking. Whiskey loosens her tongue. "So, Sherry. I've been talking about us. What about you? Tell us about yourself."

I'm all ears as I turn to her.

Sherry is modest. "There's not much to tell, Mrs.—"

"Donna." Mother interrupts.

"Donna, my mother is a legal secretary in a small private practice. Dad is a crane operator in the Port of Baltimore. We're just working people. I guess I got the dream of becoming a lawyer from Mom talking about their different cases. I have an older sister and a younger brother."

"Ah, the middle child." Mother peers at me with a smile I find embarrassing. "She's an appeaser, Matty. A peacemaker. Mediator. Driven. Half of the presidents of this country were middle children. They are over-achievers."

Exchanging glances, Sherry and I both blush.

It adds up. Chris told me Sherry pushed herself to run track, hoping for a college scholarship. She was successful in high school competitions but not fast enough to earn a scholarship, so she and her parents paid for her first four years—no loans. We helped with law school.

She is willing to pay us back, even if it means living in Alaska.

I am drawn like a moth to a flame. I have a sudden urge to get her alone.

Before I can open my mouth, Mother chirps. "Sherry, Saturday is Matty's birthday. Join us, please. We will go to dinner wherever our son chooses."

"Jesus, Mother."

Sherry's skin takes on the color of watermelon. "Oh, Mrs.—"

Donna DeVecchio wags her finger. "Uh-uh. I've told you, call me Donna. And I won't take no for an answer."

I'll spare her arguing with my mother. "I'm sorry, Sherry, but she doesn't. I can invite Chris and Tommy, too. Will that make you feel more comfortable?"

"I don't feel uncomfortable, I just don't want to intrude on your birthday."

"It's not an intrusion," Mother snaps. "After everything that has happened, we need a party." She is adamant.

How stiff was her drink?

Bettina is here with the second round, handing the first to Pop, who says, "Donna, we still have guards at the gate and around the warehouse. I'm not sure we need a public party." My father is flexing his head of the family authority, but I'm betting on Mother.

She flashes those big dark eyes at him. "Francesco, I am not taking no for an answer. We can book the whole place and post guards outside if we have to, but we are getting out of this house, and we are enjoying our son's birthday."

 Sherry
RING OF TRUTH

"**G**uess what. I'm going out with Matteo DeVecchio Saturday night." I squeal like a schoolgirl over the telephone. I couldn't wait to get home and tell Tina, even if Donna invited me, not him.

To my disappointment, she doesn't share my enthusiasm. Instead, Tina whispers, "The mob guy?"

"Dammit, Tina, why is that the first thing you say? He's the most wonderful man I've ever met. The first time I laid eyes on him, I could not speak."

"You told me." Her voice is flat and cold.

"Why aren't you excited for me?" This isn't like Tina.

"Matteo is a black-headed version of Chris, right?"

"What's Chris got to do with anything?"

She lapses into silence before finally answering. "Chris broke my heart."

I hold my receiver away, looking at it in disbelief. Did I hear her right? "Chris? I had no idea. When?"

"When you were in college. We dated for a while. Chris used me and tossed me aside. I don't want to see that happen to you. They're players, Sherry. Neither one of them has ever had a committed relationship."

My mind is stalled on the railroad tracks of her and Chris. The two people I'm closest to in life—and I never knew.

I slump onto the couch. "I knew you had a crush on Chris in school, but you never told me you dated him. He never said anything."

"He wouldn't. He's your cousin. I didn't want to—"

My surprise and hurt erupt, cutting her off. "He's my cousin and I love him, but you're my best friend of life, Tina. You should have told me."

More silence.

"I didn't want to put you in between your best friend and cousin. It was for the best. I met Adam not long after that. The rest is history."

"All this time and you never said a word."

Nothing from my best friend.

I lose patience. "Tell me you didn't settle for Adam because Chris broke your heart."

She snickers. "Don't insult me or Adam, please."

"Okay. I'm sorry. But I had no idea. How is Adam, anyway? You haven't mentioned him in a while."

My question is met with another long silence.

"Tina?"

"Honestly? I don't know. He's been working a lot."

Something is going on. What is she not telling me? "Do we need to talk?"

"Not now."

"Will you fix my hair Saturday? It's his birthday and we're going someplace swanky." My best friend is a beautician.

"Of course. What time?" That's not enthusiasm I hear in her voice. But I know she will. She would fix my hair if I was going out with Attila the Hun, if I asked.

"I'll let you know."

"Wait—Sherry, don't let him break your heart." My best friend is over-protective.

"It's one date."

"Yeah, but you better stop and think. If it does turn out to be more, are you ready for that life?"

"What life?" She's beginning to piss me off.

"*The* life. Where bodies disappear. You think Chris and Matteo don't have blood on their hands, Sherry? Honestly? How naïve can you be? Do you want that on your conscience?"

I ponder, my brows shifting high as I see Lady MacBeth scrubbing her hands. "Out, out damned spot?"

"Exactly," she mutters.

My heart hitches. A life spent in the Greek Orthodox Church, the commandments drilled into our heads. *Though shalt not kill.*

"I don't know," I say with all honesty. "I'll think about it. *If* it's more than one date. See you Saturday." Hanging up the phone, I stare at the wall. Are you ready for that life?

I argue with myself. First of all, it won't come to that. Like Tina said, Matteo's a player. He wants me for a date. Not life. Besides, he didn't even invite me. His mother did.

I groan, my inner demons battling. I cannot lie to myself. I want it to be more than one date.

I grab a half-finished bottle of wine from the fridge. Let's be analytical. *Thou shalt not lie. Thou shalt not steal. Though shalt not commit adultery.*

Is he really that different than prosecutors who send the wrong person to prison for life? They steal lives, without spilling blood, in their own self-righteous way. What about priests who molest kids and hide their sins inside their robes? Sanctimonious jerks who steal from their parishioners?

Is Matteo worse than cops who let prostitutes service them sexually in order to stay out of jail? Professors who coerce students into relations for grades? There is corruption in every corner of every level of society. Just because a person doesn't bleed doesn't mean their life wasn't ruined.

At least the DeVecchios look the world in the eye, hold their heads high, and say, "This is who we are." They don't hide behind masks of hypocrisy.

But they kill people. I guess. Everyone says.

Dammit. I don't know.

I'll deal with it—if and when the time comes.

My instincts are paying off. After seeing Sophia with Bob Kerrigan—Robert Edward Kerrigan, aide to Congressman Donald Mulholland, I drove into D.C. and did a deep dive to find something that might interest the DeVecchios, which I present at our afternoon meeting a few days later.

For the first time, Matteo joins us.

Passing copies of the bill to both men, I explain. "Mulholland has introduced a bill. It hasn't gone anywhere yet, but if it does, it will lessen the requirements for immigrants to gain their green cards so they can work."

Matteo runs his hand over his face, pressing his thumb and forefinger on his eyelids. "That adds up."

He is sitting in front of his father's desk, in the chair beside me, reading the bill. After a moment, he sets it aside. "We suspect Geno of trafficking immigrants. We understand his people promise Asians a free trip to America in exchange for so many years of labor."

His gaze darts to Francesco. "They don't have many options once they get here." He clears his throat and turns to face me with those beautiful black eyes, but he is all businessman as he speaks. "We know the Gabiccis have interests in the adult entertainment industry. Films and photographs. We suspect some of his talent is..."

Matteo pauses and tweaks his mouth to the side, the same way Francesco does. "Shall we say, underage? Others he farms out for housekeeping and, literally, farming jobs from Florida to Texas."

A shiver runs up my spine. "They force women and children to act in porn films?"

"Maybe boys, too." Francesco leans his forearms on his desk. "We also suspect Asia is where Geno gets his drugs. They come in along with the people. He deals mostly in heroin. Since Alfonso fell ill, Geno has made the family much richer and more vicious." He taps the paper I handed him earlier. "If this passes, Geno becomes even richer. Money is power."

"He has an insatiable appetite for everything," Matteo says. "With what you learned, it is clear now that Geno is taking steps to try and expand into our territory. Trying to muscle us out."

Francesco says, "If we let them squat for too long, they may claim they have rights. I have no doubt Geno was behind what happened to my son and our truck."

"What are you going to do about it?"

Neither man answers.

"Find out who's on board with this." Matteo holds up the bill. "Which representatives are most likely to support it, and which will oppose it. Where does it stand in the Senate?"

"Okay. But I don't understand. If Geno deals heroin, why isn't Viggo Johansen all over him?"

"Because no one is feeding Johansen information on the Gabiccis," Matteo replies.

I peer from Francesco to Matteo. "Do you want me to?"

"No." Matteo's brows twist tight. "Giving information to the police violates Omerta."

"Omerta?" I look from Matteo to his father. "Joey said he swore Omerta. What does that mean, exactly?"

"Omerta is our oath of loyalty," Francesco says. "It forbids us from working with law enforcement. Violating it is a capital offense. Even if Geno is violating it and working with Johansen to bring us down, no DeVecchio will ever ask law enforcement for help. Nor will we cooperate with them if we are wronged."

Matteo moves to lean on his father's desk, facing me. "The right to avenge wrongs is reserved for victims and their families."

My stomach does a quick turn-over. My conversation with Tina last night reverberates in my mind. Chris warned me to make sure.

"So, to be clear: In your world it's an eye for an eye."

"*Our* world, Sherry," Francesco says.

I don't know why this surprises me, but it does.

I turn my gaze back to Matteo. "You don't expect the cops to find who shot you and bring them to trial. You want to."

Those black eyes spark. His mouth is clamped shut.

I prod. "No trial?"

Still, Matteo says nothing.

Francesco does. "Oh, there will be a trial alright. I will be the judge and the jury."

I nod. "Okay. I get it now. But I didn't swear Omerta. I can give information to Viggo about the Gabiccis."

Matteo snaps. "Stay away from Johansen and the Gabiccis."

"Viggo would love that information. It would take his focus off of us and like I said—I didn't swear Omerta."

Matteo leans forward, his gaze bores into me as he lowers his voice to a dangerous whisper. "I said no."

Oh, my. Don't push him.

So, I do it just for sport. "Matteo—"

His tone is commanding as he holds up his index finger. "I don't want you near any of them. Now drop it."

"Okay. Will you tell me something?"

He rubs his hand over his mouth and chin, those dark eyes trying to see all the way inside of me as he takes his time to decide if he will or won't answer the coming question. "Maybe."

"Why do you and Geno hate each other so?"

"It goes back a lot of years."

I cross my legs and fold my hands in my lap. "I have time."

Matteo looks at his father before he walks to the window. He shoves his hands in his pocket and peers outside. "There was a girl, when we were young."

Dammit.

"I thought it might be about a girl."

He turns to face me. "Not the way you think. This girl was... slow. Retarded, people called her. She worked at the gym where Geno and I both trained. She was actually an attractive girl, but she struggled to put sentences together." He sighs. "Something was missing. Mentally. One day after sparring, Geno offered to walk her home. She let him, of course. That went on for a while until the girl disappeared. Her body has never been found."

"What did you do?"

"We all suspected he got her pregnant and killed her. One day, I came around a corner and caught Geno trying to force a girl in an alley, so I sucker-punched him. While he was down, that girl got away, and I broke his nose and some ribs."

I can see it in my head. Matteo pounding this Geno, who I've never seen.

"A while later, Geno and his buds caught me alone and delivered their payback." He hikes a shoulder. "Every few years, something happens, and Geno and I trade blows. We're both still standing."

"Enough." Francesco slaps his desk with his palms. "It's time for my Penicillin. Care to join me?"

Matteo shakes his head, answering his father with his eyes on me. "No thanks, Pop. I think Sherry and I will go for a walk."

I don't care what Tina or anyone thinks. I am all in. I want to know him.

Sherry
ALONE AT LAST

S tepping into the blazing August sun, Matteo immediately rolls up his long sleeves, and I notice that
the muscles in his forearms are so powerful that long
sleeves may be uncomfortably tight. "Do you own any
short-sleeved shirts?"

"Of course."

"It's so hot, why don't you put one on? And shorts. You
would be so much more comfortable."

His gaze is straight ahead. "My chest and legs are
scarred."

Him? Modest about his body? "Don't be vain. I don't care
about scars."

He flashes an absolutely disarming grin. "I am vain. And
I do care."

"Please, Matteo. We can sit in the sun, splash our toes in
the water. Wouldn't that be nice?"

His smile spreads as his gaze dips down to meet mine. "I
don't want to repulse you with bullet holes in my chest and
the scars on my legs."

"Nothing about you can possibly repulse me." An honest
answer, whether the man realizes it or not.

He scratches his jaw. "Well, you are in a sun dress. Okay,
but my shorts are in my house. We'll walk."

"Your house?"

"Yes." He points. "Down there. By the creek."

We stroll across a gently rolling pasture between his parents' house and his, blanketed in deep green grass dotted with spreading oaks and maples.

"This is so beautiful. You should raise horses. This property is perfect."

"Not a horse guy," Matteo replies. "I prefer boats."

"Really?" I'm not sure why that surprises me.

"I love to sail. I like deep sea fishing."

"Do you have a boat?" I like learning more and more about him.

His smile brightens my day, deep enough to expose a small dimple. "I do. I have a little catamaran and a thirty-foot Endeavor."

"Wow. A thirty-foot-long sailboat?" It wouldn't fit in my apartment. "So that's where you get the beautiful tan."

He cuts his eyes at me as we walk. "Do you like the sea?"

"Yes, I've just never been in it. On a boat."

He cocks he head. "Never?"

"Never."

The beautiful smile comes back as he nods. "I'll take you. Do you like seafood?"

"I love it, especially shrimp cocktail."

Matteo's hand finds mine, and we walk the rest of the way to his house, our fingers entwined. I feel like a schoolgirl, my heart drumming. I've dated plenty, but I've never felt... this. Tingly. Like I'm walking in a fairy tale.

Scott and I had a lot in common. We enjoyed sparring with each other across the aisle. He's handsome and athletic, and we shared a love for practicing law. We jogged together and played tennis. All was good. Sex was fine. Even satisfying. But I can't say it was ever passionate.

Just holding Matteo's hand sends a charge of electricity through me—as if my body anticipates... *him.*

Yes, passion is what my life—my body—has been missing.

"Welcome to my humble abode." He opens the front door, ushering me inside.

His home is not nearly as large as his parents'. It is modern, made of natural stone, with vaulted wood ceilings, lots of wood and glass, and sits maybe fifty yards above a tree-lined creek.

"It is beautiful, Matteo. Kind of Frank Lloyd Wright."

He smiles. "Thank you." He aims his arm. "The kitchen is there. Pour yourself something to drink while I change." He disappears down a hallway.

His home is one story with a massive fireplace in the living room. Soft leather couches are arranged to face the fire. His television is in the corner by the fireplace. A bar separates the living room from the kitchen, with a glass wall showcasing the tree-lined creek.

It is masculine but serene.

"What would you like to drink?" I call through the house.

"Not a Penicillin!" he responds. "Glen Livet on the rocks. I keep it in the freezer."

He likes it cold, like his father. Over ice.

I pour him a drink and set it in the refrigerator while I go on a wine hunt.

"Here." He reaches around me to a high cabinet, his body brushing against mine. It sends an even stronger surge of excitement through me. He doesn't seem to be affected as he asks, "Do you like Merlot?"

He could take me right now. I wouldn't stop him. "Yes."

Turning around, I see Matteo in casual clothes for the first time. Khaki shorts and a loose-fitting, short-sleeved tan shirt. Havana style. That beautiful black hair gently covers his muscular calves and forearms. Just enough. Not too much. If he takes off that shirt, I'm sure it will cover his chest. *Good God, he's sexy. My. Lord.*

His eyes lock onto mine, and for an instant, it feels like he's about to kiss me. Instead, he turns away, fishing in a drawer for a corkscrew. "I'm sorry. The wine isn't chilled."

"How about I have another baby girl Whiskey and Coke?" It tasted good yesterday.

"Consider it done."

"May I use the girl's room?"

He aims his arm. "Of course. Down the hall on the right."

It gives me a chance to explore his world. I want to inhale every part of this man. Recessed bookshelves line the hallway with overhead recessed lights. *The Iliad and the Odyssey, the Divine Comedy, Zane Grey, Hemingway, Steinbeck.* Oh, my Lord, *The Prophet.*

"I love *The Prophet!*" I call to him.

He is behind me. *"When love beckons to you, follow him, though his ways are hard and steep."* The man's voice is liquid sex.

I pick up where he left off, and our gazes join as I recite from memory. *"And when his wings enfold you, yield to him, though the sword hidden among his pinions may wound you."*

Matteo DeVecchio is not to be outdone.

He finishes the verse as he tucks my hair behind my ear with his fingertips. *"And when he speaks to you believe in him, though his voice may shatter your dreams as the north wind lays waste the garden."*

Looking into those alluring black eyes, I realize that passage is etched into his brain.

"Oh, Matteo. Your dreams were shattered, weren't they? You actually feel that verse."

He nudges his head. "Go to the girl's room. I'll meet you outside." He turns and leaves.

They call him a mob boss. Matteo DeVecchio is not what they think. He is so much more. I don't dare go into the master bedroom at the end of the long hall, but my gaze lingers on it. A big bed is against the back wall, facing the open door, with tables on either side. I can't help but envision Sophia in that bed.

No. I shove it aside.

He is waiting on the patio when I return, holding our drinks. "Walk?" he asks.

"Yes. I grabbed a sheet from your linen closet. We can sit on it by the creek."

Matteo

PICNIC

She is a painting that should be hanging in the Louvre in her pink sundress, flanked by the beauty of the woods.

Everything about Sherry Drakos is pure class.

She shakes out the sheet under the canopy of a water oak not far from the creek bank, letting the cotton fabric drift to the ground, and she crawls on it barefooted to spread it out smoothly.

She peers up at me over her shoulder and pats the sheet, indicating where she wants me to sit. I pass her drink, which she takes, and I slip off my boat shoes to join her.

I don't remember sitting on a sheet spread across soft grass in the shade of a tree, watching a creek flow past. I rarely pay attention to the creek. Not like this, anyway. I can't say I ever sat and listened to its clear water trickling over pebbles. Random fallen leaves bob on top of the water as they float by. Grass grows up to the water's edge.

Sherry leans back, resting her hands behind her, admiring the landscape and tilts her head back, eyes closed, soaking up the sun. Her long hair falls almost to the sheet. "This is heaven," she says.

"You don't hear any traffic. No horns or airplanes or people. Just the trees and the birds." She faces me. "If I lived here..." Her gaze roams the countryside.

I stretch out beside her, leaning on my elbow, admiring the view. Of her. "You should see the colors in the fall. And in early spring, these woods are full of rhododendrons. They are breathtaking in April."

It's false bravado. A little deceptive. I don't really know rhododendrons other than listening to Mother and others rave about them each spring for as long as I can remember.

I never thought it would be useful information to pass along—until now.

"I can only imagine." Sherry's voice is wistful. Soft. Her wavy hair glistens coppery in the sun. Her shapely legs are crossed at the ankles in front of her. Pink toenail polish. Dainty little feet.

You can't kiss her. She is your employee.

I shift my focus back to the creek. If I were to kiss her and it didn't work, we'd be miserable working together.

But it's hard not to. Speaking of hard...

It is all I can do not to reach over, lay Sherry down, and take her, to cup her perfect ass in my hands, draw her into me, and thrust inside. The image crowding my brain has my cock swelling.

I avert my eyes back to the little brook while I argue with myself. Touch. Don't touch.

I catch those beautiful eyes trained on the scars on my legs. From this angle, I see how long her lashes are.

"My right leg was broken above and below the knee. The left was gashed."

Now her eyes are on mine. "You've suffered so much in your life, Matteo. That horrible accident, now being shot not once but three times."

"Don't pity me, Sherry."

"I don't pity you. I admire you. You are so strong..." Her voice trails off as she melts into my eyes. "You are..."

I sit up straight. "Don't put me on a pedestal either. No one can live up to it."

She doesn't hesitate. "Don't look at me and see someone else. I can't compete with that."

"You're not competing with anything. We're just enjoying the afternoon sun." I stretch out on my back, rest my head on my folded arms, close my eyes, and feel the warmth of the afternoon sun on my face.

"Unbutton your shirt."

She has no idea what all I would unbutton. "Why?"

"So, you can feel the sun. It's good for healing."

I cut my eyes at her. "Are you going to unbutton yours?"

Her neck and cheeks flush deep pink. "No."

"I will if you will." It's such a high school thing to say, but it just comes out, along with a boisterous laugh, and she joins me. Both of us laughing.

She giggles and wiggles her shoulders like a high schooler. "It's different with men and women."

"Yes, I know."

Show me what is underneath that little sundress.

Her throat turns scarlet.

We embarrassed ourselves. We both go back to watching the water rush by.

She has no idea how close I am to ripping that pink cotton dress off of her to find out what is underneath, to feel her legs wrap around me.

A slight breeze wafts her scent over me. Fresh, like honeysuckle or roses, some soft blend of flowers.

Fuck. That damned hard-on. I have to sit up, or she'll see it.

"Matteo!" Tommy calls from my patio through cupped hands. "I've got something for you!"

I glance over my shoulder. Just in time. I am out of resistance. "Duty calls. Do you want to stay down here a while longer?"

As she smiles, I feel her eyes adoring me as gently as if she softly stroked my face. "I wish I could but it's almost quitting time and I need to wrap up and clean off my desk. I can walk back to your parents' house by myself."

I offer my hand to help her stand and pick up the sheet, folding it over my arm. "This was nice. Thank you."

"Tomorrow?" she asks.

"Seven o'clock sharp, sweetheart. I have your address."

"The building near ours, where they're listening—I think it's their film studio," Tommy tells me.

"Why do you think that?"

"The people coming and going. Most are young, twenties and under. I've seen men escorting in Asian men and women. I've seen some camera equipment and lights being carted in."

He hands me photographs. "Wouldn't surprise me if they don't warehouse some of their product there, too. I think they are positioning themselves near us to listen, hoping someday they will take us over, move into your family's warehouse and own the docks."

"And we are certain it belongs to Geno?"

"Apice Productions leased the building six months ago."

"Who from?"

"Working on it."

"Geno is one ambitious son of a bitch. We'll buy the building out from under him." The thought brings a laugh. "He can pay us rent."

We high-five as Tommy adds, "I like the idea of blowing it up. I don't like them so close."

"Have you pulled the bugs yet?"

"Not until you tell us to."

"Do it. I'm tired of all this. Pull everything."

"They'll know we're onto them."

"I don't give a fuck. Has Chris dribbled out false information about another shipment?"

"Can't say. You'll have to ask him."

"Anything else on what happened in Anne Arundel County?"

"Not a fucking clue."

"You saw the warrant. It doesn't have anything that identified our truck. How could they possibly have known which truck to stop if it wasn't Joey? Any chance the kid's a rat?"

"I don't know, boss. His old man's a good egg. I just... I don't know. Why would Joey Carbona do that to us? He was born into this family."

"True. But we're missing something."

"We don't know what we're missing 'til we find it. I'll keep trying."

I can remember when Tommy and I were the same size. Look at us now. He's got me by five inches. "Tommy, have a drink with me. It's been a long time." He's a family man. Married young. Always goes home to his wife, Regina.

He glances at his watch. "Sure."

Inside, I pour him an icy cold Glen Livet and refill my own, and we return to the patio to sit and watch the creek. The breeze has picked up, swaying the treetops.

"Are Regina and the kids doing well?" I ask.

"Yeah. We're all good." He tilts his head toward the creek. "You like the girl? I never saw you on a picnic blanket with anyone before."

I meet his questioning eyes. "A picnic sheet, and yes, I do."

He leans those enormous arms on the glass tabletop to level his gaze on me. "Does this mean you're through with Sophia?"

"I told you Sophia and I were over before I got shot."

Tommy studies me in a way he rarely does. "Sherry's eyes are the same. You can't replace Patsy, Matty."

"She's not a replacement. Sherry is her own person. I don't know what will happen, where it's going. She works for me so…"

Tommy chokes on his drink, sputtering. Wiping his mouth with the back of his hand, he says, "You and I both know exactly where it's going. I've seen the way she looks at you and the way you look at her."

My gaze travels back to the creek. "Patsy looked at me the same way."

"Patsy was already in love with another man when she met you, or she would have been yours. You can't change the past."

I lean back in my chair. "No, I've realized Patsy would never have been mine, even if she hadn't been in love with B.J. She was too disapproving of what we do for a living. Sherry seems to accept us for what we are." I run my fingers through my hair. "I don't know. Sometimes I feel like I don't know anything."

I peer at my friend as he takes in the countryside. "Do you really think Sophia set me up to be killed? Is she that cold-blooded?"

His huge shoulders shift. "She's the logical conclusion."

I finish my drink. "Are we set for tomorrow night?"

"Yep."

Sherry
THE WATERFRONT

It is August 31, 1978, and I am officially living the dream. Matteo is picking me up, and we are joining his parents for his birthday dinner.

While the men weren't listening, I asked Donna how to dress. She said I should, in her words, "doll up." Donna makes me laugh. She lights up the room.

Per her advice, I've done my best to dress up, choosing a low-cut but respectable black dress. Matteo isn't a flashy dresser. I think he will appreciate my attire reflecting his look: classic with a tasteful suggestion of sexiness: a little cleavage—not too much—and a little leg—not too much.

Makeup. Not too much, but with freshly manicured pink nails and toenails, which will show in my open-toe heels. I must have pink lips. I mean, come on.

I chose a single strand of pearls, pearl stud earrings, and nice, sling-back black heels—stilettos.

I like Donna so much, maybe in part because of what she shared with me while Francesco and Matteo took their turn mixing drinks. She leaned close and whispered, "My son has never taken a woman on a date with us. This is big. Don't break his heart."

I assured her, whispering back, "I won't break his heart. I have never been so impressed with any man."

Tina pulls me back to the moment, literally yanking on my hair.

"Ouch!" I squeal.

"Where is he taking you?" she asks.

"It's a surprise." I squirm as she brushes my hair a little too aggressively. We've already done the hot rollers. "I'm so excited. The first time I saw him, he took my breath."

She groans demonstratively. "Geez. Louise. You have told me that like, a million times."

"Well, it's never happened to me. Not like this." I'm afraid to ask, but I do. "What happened with you and Chris?"

"We'll talk about your gargantuan ass-wipe cousin another day."

"Did he take your breath?"

Watching her face in the mirror, I notice the quick shadow that passes across those garnet-colored eyes. Tina huffs out a deep sigh. "Yes. The son of a bitch."

"You really think Chris intentionally used you?"

Tina pauses her hairdo frenzy to meet my curious gaze. Her eyes leave mine to dart about the bathroom as she gathers her thoughts.

Our eyes meet again in the mirror. "Honestly, Sherry—I'd like to think that he got scared. I thought it was real at the time but... I guess that's what all women tell themselves when the guy they are crazy about just up and runs away."

"I'll ask him."

She gives the back of my head a hard shove. "Don't you dare."

That's not a look or a tone to mess with. She's little, but she's feisty.

"Okay," I lie.

As she brushes my hair back, she talks with a bobby pin in her mouth. "You know, I hear Matteo DeVecchio is like, the most sought-after bachelor in Baltimore… if you like mob guys."

I squint my disapproval at her in the bathroom mirror. "Quit calling him that."

Tina chuckles and pokes me with that bobby pin before she scrapes it against my scalp, which warrants her a serious scowl. "Dammit. Are you doing that on purpose? Quit."

"Sweetie, your man just got shot. He's been all over the news and that's what they call him." She mimics the newscasters. "Mob boss Matteo DeVecchio…"

"He's a businessman."

She giggles and slips in another bobby pin. "Keep telling yourself that."

I pull away to face my best friend. "His mother and father are wonderful. Matteo is a perfect gentleman."

She holds up her hands defensively. "Okay, okay," she giggles. "Just don't cross them. You might end up with a horse head in your bed."

"Tina, dammit. Stop!"

For the first time in all our years, I'm really irritated with her for her take on Matteo and his family. "You don't know them."

She can't help herself. She keeps giggling at her Godfather reference, which I find truly offensive. I cross my arms over my chest.

She holds up her hands in surrender. "I'm sorry. I'm sure he's wonderful. He's handsome as hell, I'll give him that, but you're right, I don't know him. And what I said the other night. I was just being pissy. I don't *know* that they have blood on their hands. But I assume, based on everything I hear, that they do. Hand me a bobby pin."

I offer her another little metal pin. "I don't believe half of what I hear."

She's working on the back of my head, intent on this updo she has going. I cringe, looking in the mirror. "What, exactly, are you doing with my hair?"

"It's a French roll."

"I'm mortified for him to see where I live."

"Bend your head over," she orders, as she slides several more bobby pins in my neckline. "He knows you're a public defender. Have they given you a raise since you changed positions? What are you doing for them, anyway?"

I remember Chris's warning. Even Tina gets nothing from me. "Yes, I got a nice raise. Enough for a better neighborhood soon. Right now, I'm just looking over contracts and stuff. All very boring legal stuff."

"Ta-da. What do you think?" With a proud smile, she aims her arms at her masterpiece.

Twisting my head to look at her handiwork, I grab the hand mirror, inspecting the back. I have to be honest. "I don't know... I think it's not me."

"You don't like it?" She's either going to stomp her foot or cry. Or slap me.

"Tina, I'm sorry. Just pull it back on one side and clip it and let everything else be long and curly. What do you think?"

"I think I just went to a hell of a lot of work for nothing." Her hands are on her hips. "Are you sure? This is really a very sophisticated look. You said he's sophisticated."

"But it's not *me*." I know. I sound a little whiny.

"Dammit. Alright. You have to be comfortable with how you look. You don't want to be worrying about your hair on your first date."

First date. I can only hope there will be more.

She pulls out her hairpins with a huff and starts over, brushing it out. Again, aggressively.

Finally, it's big and full and curly. "I like it. Much better. Thanks. Big hair is in."

Tina puts her hands on my shoulders, our gazes holding in the mirror as she leans near my ear. "At least, he's picking you up. He's not *meeting* you. That's in his favor." She gives me her warm Tina hug. "I want to hear all about it tomorrow."

"I promise." I kiss her cheek. "Wish me luck."

Yesterday, he said he hadn't been cleared to drive yet, so I don't know why I'm surprised when I peek out the window blinds and see a black limousine pull up in front of the apartments.

No doubt, all of my neighbors are gawking out their windows. They may line up in the street. This modest, predominantly Greek neighborhood is centered around St. Nicholas Greek Orthodox Church. I have never seen a limousine in this zip code.

I feel the familiar flush of my cheeks, something I rarely experienced before the night I met Matteo.

I was never embarrassed for Scott to come here. He started out as a public defender, too. But seeing Matteo step out of that black limousine and walk toward my door, I'm humiliated by my living conditions.

I'd chug a glass of wine, but I need my wits about me tonight.

My heart pumps wildly with anticipation.

One knock, and I open the door—and feel my jaw sag a smidge.

Matteo looks like he stepped out of GQ Magazine, wearing a tailored black suit and white dress shirt. His broad shoulders. His perfectly flat abdomen. Narrow hips.

But above all—his face. He could be wearing sackcloth. Nothing would tear my eyes away from those smoldering eyes, his not-too-thick and not-too-thin brows, and lashes any woman would envy. He has a small, tasteful dimple in his chin and a strong but tapered jawline.

He smiles beautifully, showing the little dimple in his cheek. "Are you ready?"

"As I'll ever be."

He offers me his arm, which I take after locking the door. I feel like Cinderella, doing my best to walk gracefully beside Prince Charming.

I bet Donna sent him to etiquette school when he was young.

Matteo senses my discomfort because he cuts his eyes at me as we walk, leans close, and says quietly in my ear, "You are stunning."

He's a gentleman. He wants to put me at ease.

Never have I ridden in a limousine. The driver, who I don't recognize, holds the door as I get in, and Matteo slides beside me.

I clutch my purse nervously, pressing it against my thighs to keep my knees from shaking.

He smells wonderful. You don't get the scent of Matteo's cologne unless you are right beside him, and even then, it's just a tantalizing woodsy, manly whiff with maybe a hint of anise, I think.

Whatever it is, it is like him. Tastefully sexy.

We ride with little conversation until I ask, "Where are we going?"

"The Waterfront on the Bay. Have you been?"

The Waterfront has been written up in national magazines and the Sunday paper. I fumble with my little black beaded purse. Only in my dreams. "No," I admit quietly.

I can't seem to meet his gaze. I'm afraid I might melt if I do.

In my periphery, I see him studying me. His gaze dips to my cleavage, lingers there for a beat, and he tilts his head with curiosity. "Are you nervous?"

My face burns. No answer. I'm too mortified.

But he keeps staring at me as if waiting for an answer that doesn't come. "Sherry." His voice is low and smooth as he touches my chin with his fingertips, turning my face to his. "Relax. It's just dinner with my parents. I'm not going to propose and I'm not going to bite."

I feel the heat of his eyes. "It's your birthday. I didn't know what to get. What could I possibly give you that you don't already have?" A birthday card seemed lame. Anything I thought of felt inadequate.

He smiles softly. "I don't need anything."

"Birthdays aren't about what you need. They're about what you want. What can I give you that you want but don't already have?"

An impish grin takes over his face, the little dimple on his cheek peeking through. His gaze is so intense that it is unnerving. Matteo glances away, staring out the window as we drive for a bit until his gaze slowly returns to me. "Your beautiful eyes, Sherry. They are all I need."

The air goes out of me. I want to cry. He still looks at me and sees her.

My focus dips to my purse, which I clutch tightly in my lap. It's my turn to peer out my window as he remains silent.

Finally, I find my words and turn back to face him. "I hope you have a nice evening, Matteo, but my eyes will never be hers. They just happen to be the same color."

I can never live up to his lost dream. After tonight, I need to get all thoughts of him out of my head. He is still in love with another woman.

Matteo reaches and tilts my chin, gently forcing me to meet his onyx eyes again. "You are a beautiful woman. I get lost in your eyes. What's wrong with that? I like you. Very much. Isn't that enough?"

"But you look at me and see someone else, don't you?"

He purses his beautiful lips, pauses a long beat, then whispers, "I don't know."

He does. He just won't admit it. There is nothing I can do to change what is, so I smile my acceptance of reality. "Happy birthday, Matteo."

He turns his body toward me, leans down, and takes my face in his hands. His lips touch mine, lingering on them, feather-soft, for a long, sweet, tantalizing moment.

I put my hand on his chest. "You can't kiss me. There's no such thing as smudge-proof lipstick. We will have pink smeared all over us when we walk into the restaurant."

He chuckles and draws back, runs his thumb over my lower lip, looks at the pink that transferred over and sucks his thumb into his mouth, swirling his tongue around it seductively, licking off the lipstick smudge. "If I can't have your lips, I will kiss what I can."

His eyes never leave mine as Matteo lifts my hand and brings it to his lips. He spreads open my palm and places my index finger on his lips, rolls his tongue around it, then sucks my finger into his mouth.

My head falls back with a moan.

"Delicious." He straightens my arm and trails the back of his hand... like a feather, from my elbow to my wrist and still, his eyes never leave mine.

Does he know what he's doing to my insides?

Of course, he does. He knows *exactly* what he is doing.

He reaches inside his jacket and pulls out a handkerchief. "Look what I found." Holding it up with a smug smile, he asks, "Did you happen to bring more lipstick?"

I nod and hold up my purse.

"Good girl. Let's get rid of that, just for right now." Matteo holds the soft cloth to my lips. "Open up."

I obey and fold my lips over the soft cloth, blotting off the pink lipstick and his eyes dance with anticipation. He places his fingertips under my chin and tilts my head back. "Now, give me your mouth, Sherry. Let me taste you."

My lips part obediently, and Matteo slants his mouth over mine—his tongue mastering mine hungrily as he brings his open hand to the back of my head. His tongue explores my mouth, slowly, sensuously, erasing every ounce of common sense I ever had. My body molds into his, my breasts pressed against him.

His satisfaction rumbles from his chest, making my bones liquefy along with everything else in me.

My heart races faster as Matteo bends his head, tracing his tongue from behind my ear to my collarbone while his free hand softly brushes across my décolletage. His index finger dips into my cleavage, tracing the curves. "Sherry," he groans. "You're killing me."

"And what do you think you're doing to me?"

His warm breath caresses my neck before he reclaims my mouth, his kiss more demanding than before, with both of his hands on my back, holding me against him. Pulling back, his eyes lock onto mine. "Sherry." His fingers trace the outline of my lips. "Do you have any idea how beautiful you are?"

Before I can answer, he has me in his arms again, his tongue demanding my submission, and again, I lose myself in the euphoria of his desire, the sheer strength of Matteo's big hand across the back of my head, pressing my mouth to his. *Oh, the intimacy.* With him. My core melts, for him.

I shouldn't let him do this. He is my boss. He's in love with another woman. There is every reason I should not do this, and only one reason I should: I absolutely, unequivocally crave this man. *Forget the Waterfront.*

Finally, his mouth leaves mine, and I feel his heartbeat drumming in my ear. "You are," he sighs, "Magnificent."

I knew he was capable of mind-numbing passion.

I gently kiss his jaw, leaving a tiny telltale trace of pink. "I think we both need that handkerchief now. And I need fresh lipstick."

He runs his fingers through my hair to smooth what he messed up. My heart and his heart—both pound furiously—as Matteo devours me with his black eyes. "Just so there is no misunderstanding, I intend to ruin you."

I grin tauntingly as I slide the pink tube from my purse. "You think you can?"

And here comes that salacious smile. He leans down to whisper in my ear. "Oh, sweetheart, I know I can. And I cannot wait."

Yes.

He wants me, not her. Matteo whispered my name—twice.

He wraps his arm around me and tucks me into his side. "We'll be there soon."

"Is it safe now for me to put on lipstick?" I ask as I blot his lips and face with the handkerchief.

He peers down at me with that boyish grin. "Yes. You are safe. For a while."

I hear Jim Croce in my head. *If I could save time in a bottle,* I would save this ride to the Waterfront.

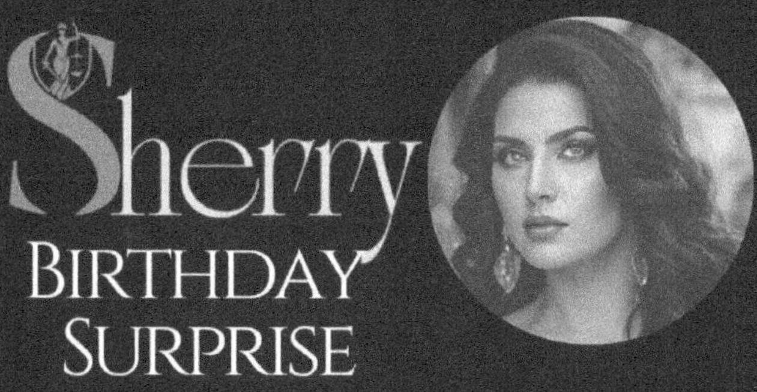

Sherry
BIRTHDAY
SURPRISE

I have never been prouder, not even on graduation day, than I am to walk into The Waterfront on Matteo De-Vecchio's arm. *The Waterfront. With Matteo.* It is ridiculous for me to feel this way—like a princess on the arm of Prince Charming.

I smile up at him. "Is my hair alright? My face?" I didn't bring a compact mirror.

His eyes sweep across me. "You are perfect." He leans close and whispers, "All eyes are on you."

"I think they're looking at you."

"Not hardly."

They can call him what they want. I adore this man. What he does for a living doesn't bother me one iota.

We look like a couple as we're seated at the table with his parents. Donna and Francesco see it, too, their heads together, whispering to each other as we approach.

"Oh, you two look wonderful together!" Donna claps her hands. She is a small woman, shorter than me, and a little thick in her age. I can only imagine how beautiful Donna DeVecchio was on her wedding day.

How handsome a young Francesco must have been.

Donna's salt-and-pepper hair is pulled up in a French roll like Tina tried to talk me into. Good thing I made Tina take it down. A beautiful diamond necklace graces Donna's generous cleavage in a black dress with short sleeves. A heavy diamond tennis bracelet is on her wrist.

Francesco, of course, is equally striking, obviously Matteo's father, in his black suit.

Glancing around the glass room that overlooks Chesapeake Bay, I see several men, all dressed in black suits, standing with their hands folded in front of them. DeVecchio guards scattered around the restaurant.

"Thirty-two years ago, today..." Donna lifts her glass.

Matteo groans. "Mother. Please. Are you going to do this when I'm fifty?"

She holds her drink high. "You're damned right I am."

He cuts his eyes at me with a smirk. "She does this every year."

She winks. "He was born at night. He was an easy delivery. A sweet baby—"

"Donna." Francesco interrupts, covering her hand with his, and their gazes join. "You're embarrassing your son."

She swishes her free hand with a smile, her eyes landing on me. "I'll tell you when we're alone then."

She gets a chuckle from all of us.

"What can I get you to drink?" the waiter asks Matteo.

He glances at me. "Merlot?"

"Yes, thank you."

"The lady will have your best Merlot. And I'd like Glen Livet on the rocks."

The waiter nods. "Are you ready to order?"

Matteo peers at me again. I'm beginning to read him. "Order for me. Please."

He turns to the waiter. "We will start with a dozen raw oysters for the table." He cuts his eyes my way. "Tomorrow is September, I think we're safe." He goes back to the waiter. "The lady will have shrimp cocktail. And for our entrée, the sea bass."

He looks at me for approval.

I smile and nod, noticing, out of my peripheral vision, that Donna is smiling at her son adoringly.

Francesco has his head turned, his gaze on the front door as the waiter takes our menus and says, "Your drinks will be right out."

Francesco covers his mouth with his fist and clears his throat loudly. Matteo's gaze darts to his father, who nods at the front door as Donna swears. "Dammit. Don't turn around. Don't look. Act like she's not here."

"Who's not here, Mother?"

"The Gabicci bitch."

Matteo stiffens. He draws a deep breath and exhales. "Sherry, no matter what she says, ignore her."

"Okay."

"I mean it." His eyes are on me, all dark and serious now.

"Okay."

Donna strikes up a conversation, "I heard on the news today that they are building a brand new—"

"Matteo." She is at our backs, her voice like silk.

My eyes are glued to Donna, who is glaring at the woman standing behind me.

Matteo answers without turning around. "Sophia."

"You never returned my calls."

His body is rigid. He says nothing.

She goes on. "I'm so sorry for what happened to—"

It's Donna who can't control herself. She slams down her napkin and starts to rise.

Francesco places his hand on her shoulder as he says, "Ms. Gabicci. Enjoy your evening while we enjoy ours."

I still haven't seen her. Matteo hasn't looked at her, either.

Sophia ignores Francesco. I can feel her eyes on my back. "Who are you banging now?" Sophia's tone has turned to ice.

Matteo puts his arm around my chair and turns in his seat to glare over his shoulder. If looks could kill Sophia would be a pile of ashes. "This woman is my date. Who she is, what our relationship is, is none of your business. Move along, Sophia."

I can see her reflection in the glass wall in front of me. Sophia's hands flounce to her hips, her elbows out. "Really? You're blaming me for what happened to you?"

Her escort says, "Sophia. Let's take our table."

I know that voice. Turning swiftly, I look into the eyes of Scott Buchanan.

We both freeze for a long moment.

"Sherry." His gaze moves from me to Matteo. "I see you moved on."

"As have you. Have a pleasant evening, Scott."

"You fucked her?" Sophia points at me like I'm a joke. Now, her voice is akin to fingernails on a chalkboard as she chuckles wickedly. "Well then, I guess we should get together and do a swap some night since we're all familia—"

Matteo shoves his chair back with his legs, stands, and turns. That is a murderous glare. "Leave, Sophia." His jaw flexes.

"Hold on there, buddy." Scott grabs Sophia around the waist, pulling her to him as she smirks.

Matteo shifts his intense glare to Scott. "Take your pet tarantula and move along."

Sophia's mouth falls open as the two men glare at each other.

The restaurant quietens. People sitting at surrounding tables stop their conversations to stare, and suddenly, several men merge to surround our table. Like synchronized swimmers, the circle tightens.

"The gentleman said for you to go." That's Tommaso's voice!

"Give Geno our regards." That's Chris!

Yes! My heart beats like a jackrabbit's as a smile spreads across my face. I am so proud. The calvary is here. Matteo was ambushed before. He doesn't have to fight this alone. But he is still a solo act, glaring at Scott, who nods, steps back, and says, "Sophia, let's eat somewhere else."

"Fuck them." She spits her words. "They aren't running us off." She cuts her eyes up and over at Scott. "As a matter of fact, I'm calling Geno. We'll get this pissing match over with once and for all."

Francesco chunks his napkin on the table and stands. "I'll be damned if I'll be in the same room as a low-life back-shooter. Son?"

Matteo looks at me, and I nod. "I go where you go."

Sophia snorts. "Give me a break."

"Enjoy your evening," Matteo says. "We'll take our party elsewhere."

Sophia tilts her head back to let a haughty laugh erupt from deep in her chest. "The DeVecchios are washed up. They tuck their tails and run."

Chris steps forward, invading Sophia's space. "DeVecchios don't shoot men in the back." He folds his hands in front of him as Tommaso takes his place beside him. Their shoulders shield us from Sophia and Scott.

Donna stands and spits to her side. "Sophia Gabicci, I know what you are. Hell will welcome you with open arms someday."

"Is that a threat? Did you just threaten my date?" Scott goes all prosecutor.

It is an instinctive move, something I don't think about. I shift on my feet, shielding Donna from Scott's accusing glare, and I meet Sophia's fiery eyes. She is several inches taller. My focus shifts back to Scott. "You know that doesn't meet the threshold of a threat."

Matteo grabs my shoulders, turns me, and walks us toward the door.

Francesco and Donna follow, while the guards face Scott and Sophia with their broad bodies. Each man has his hands folded in front of him, showing no aggression. They are have been schooled well. But no one in the room has a doubt—if Scott or Sophia try to follow and menace, they will be stopped.

As we pass the maître de, Matteo says, "I apologize for the disruption."

Francesco nods at the man. "We will make amends."

"No problem." He assures us. "We all saw what happened."

Matteo

PERFECT PRESENT

"**S**he is the absolute *worst*!" Mother fumes outside of the restaurant. "Now, where do we go? We can't get in anywhere this time of night."

"Home." Pop and I answer together.

"Francesco," Mother whines.

"Donna, we tried. We'll do it again another night. After that circus, I'm ready to go home."

Pop and I think alike.

Tommy and Chris join us in the parking lot, and we step away from the women, speaking quietly.

"Thank you for being here." Pop says it first.

"Of course. Matty's first night out since he was back-shot." Chris speaks barely above a whisper.

Tommy clears his throat. "Did you ever wonder how it is she shows up everywhere you go?"

"How could she know we'd be here?" I wonder aloud.

Tommy answers. "Simple. When your mother made reservations, someone gave Sophia a call. She's obviously stalking you."

Chris cuts his eyes at his cousin, who is comparing notes with Mother. They get along well. His gaze drifts back, settling on me. "So, you and Sherry?"

I knew this would be coming. "What about us?"

Chris tucks his chin, his gaze probing.

"Okay, yes. I like her. A lot."

"Not just as a replacement." It's not a question my friend asks. It's a demand.

"Fuck off, Chris. I'd never use her."

He hikes a suspicious brow.

Yes, I've used women. We all have. "Not *her*. She's... different."

"Good." He and Tommy exchange their fucking 'we're-thinking-the-same-thing' glances, and Chris folds his arms over his chest smugly. "I read it from the first night."

He gets nothing from me. "I think the show is over."

"You haven't had anything to eat, and you are beautiful. Would you like to stop somewhere for a drink or dinner?" I ask her in the car. I wouldn't mind showing her off, but secretly, I hope she declines the offer.

I have other plans.

A soft smile answers me back. "I'm not sure I could eat right now."

Good. Because I could.

"Home?"

"I guess." She tries to mask her disappointment with that gentle, polite smile.

I tap on the tinted window that shields us from the front seat. My driver opens it and I tell him, "Home. No disturbances."

"Yessir." The window closes.

I wrap my arm around Sherry, drawing her against me, and she rests her head on my shoulder as we ride in silence. It feels so natural. She smells of honeysuckle and spring. Her knees are pressed together, her ankles are crossed. Always the lady.

I've waited long enough for what I want. How long have I wanted her? From the first night. She is a magnet, and I am steel.

Nestled in the crook of my arm, she peers up at me with a timid but lustful look that whets my appetite. It's the way Cinderella looked at Prince Charming, with hopeful expectation. She's not the first woman to look at me that way, but she is the only one who ever made me want to be her Prince Charming.

I hook my hands under her arms and drag her into my lap. My mouth captures hers, and my tongue plunges inside as I unharness the desire I've throttled far too long.

As my tongue explores her mouth, as the blood rushes from my brain south, my hand finds its way to her thigh, slipping beneath her short little dress, moving higher and higher across her satin skin.

When she doesn't protest, my cock aches with anticipation.

Finding little lace panties, I finger them aside, and Sherry catches her breath.

"You want this," I mutter through the kiss. It's not a question. I feel her wet for me.

Her breath is quick and shallow as she answers. "Yes."

I slide my hand through her slit, press firmly against her, and she squirms against my hand, arching her back.

In response, I dip two fingers inside of her and she gasps as I curl my fingers, finding that sensitive spot deep inside. I am rewarded when a little whimper escapes her throat.

"You asked what I want. This is what I want."

"What's my name?"

"Sherry." My tongue toys with her neck. "Let me satisfy you."

Goosebumps pebble her skin. *Yes.*

"But it's your birthday."

"Give yourself to me, Sherry. *You* are all I want."

With a deep sigh, she softens in my hold, letting me have my way.

"Such a good girl."

"Oh, Matteo." Sherry lifts her hips instinctively as my two fingers work inside her. I pull out to spread her arousal between her legs and go back inside, fucking her with my fingers, finding that sensitive spot again, all the while watching her beautiful face.

When I pull out again, she wiggles her hips. "Oh, no, that's mean."

I lick my fingers. "Hmm, yes, but I wanted to taste."

I dip back inside, and she closes her eyes—but when I pull my fingers back out a minute later—her eyes open with a spark.

I smile as Sherry watches me bring my fingers to her lips. "Your turn."

With her gaze locked on mine, she opens her mouth, and I place my fingers on her lips. She twirls her tongue, sucking. *Oh, fuck*. My dick flexes. I'm getting blue balls, but what I want more than my own release is to make her feel like a queen. Not a princess. A queen. I want to take her where she has never been.

"You know what you're doing," she purrs.

"I said, I'll ruin you."

"Keep ruining me." She buries her face in my shoulder as her hips move with my hand.

"Lean forward."

She obeys, and I use my free hand to unzip her dress in the back, yanking it off her shoulders—the whole time, my fingers work inside as she becomes a soppy, silky mess. Unsnapping the black lace bra, her breasts fall free and she leans back to let me see her perfect little pink nipples.

"You are so fucking beautiful." Greedily, I take one breast in my mouth, suckling her already-hard nipple as my fingers continue to curl inside of her, bringing her to the brink. She gasps and stiffens. I still my movement. "Let it build..."

Her eyes widen, fixed on mine... she's right there... I gently rub her with my thumb as I hook my fingers inside—and cover her mouth with mine.

"Oh... Matteo!" She moans into my kiss as her hips thrust forward, her inner walls throbbing around my fingers. Her head tilts back as her muscular legs clench tightly around my hand, and I keep stroking ever so gently, helping her ride out this high. She takes in a deep breath. "Yes... yes..."

Gradually, her thighs ease their grip on my hand.

I yank the dress to her waist, fully exposing those beautiful tits.

She is a hot mess. I lay her on the seat and lift the skirt.

Putting my knees on the floor, I lift her hips and lick her clean. She runs her fingertips through my hair, her hips hunching into me. I never did this for another woman. I never even thought about it. But this feels natural.

I rise to kiss her mouth. "I love your taste." I plunge my tongue into her mouth.

Pleasing this woman is ecstasy.

She reaches for my belt, and I draw away. "Not yet. I want to satisfy you again before we get home."

She sits up, peering out the windows. "This isn't the way home."

"It's the way to my home." Her eyelids flutter with surprise. "Baby, you said I could have what I wanted for my birthday. I told you, you are what I want."

Sherry pulls me to her, kissing me hungrily, the way a man wants a woman to kiss him. Like she's starving for him. "Let me taste you now," she pleads.

"You have to wait." I smile against her kiss and go back to work, fondling one breast while kissing the other, sucking on her puckered nipple. She presses against the back of my head, holding my mouth to her breast as my tongue twirls and my lips tug on one, then the other.

Again, she arches her back, wiggling her hips, showing me what she wants.

My fingers slide into her again. I find the spot, and she groans, "Did you get a degree in this?"

I'm chuckling as I savor all of her that I can. When I hook my fingers inside of her, my tongue circling her clit—her walls tighten around me—again.

Sherry's body trembles as her head falls to the side. Her walls pulse around my fingers fiercely, and she groans, this time so quietly.

She is the perfect lady.

"I can't wait to get you home." I almost lost it watching her.

Matteo
Sweet Dreams

We leave a trail of clothes from the front door to the bedroom.

I tidied her back up and redressed her before we reached the estate. We were presentable when the driver dropped us off, and we'd been careful to keep the noise down. But unlocking my front door and stepping inside, we are both crazed with desire.

Sherry reaches for my belt and tugs hard, dropping it near the front door as I carry her to my bed. She unbuttons my shirt along the way as I slip out of my shoes, one here... one there...

In the bedroom, I set her feet on the floor, unzip that little black dress, pull it over her head, unsnap the bra again, and toss it into a nearby chair. "You don't need that anymore."

Finally, I slide her black lace bikini panties down, and she steps out of them. Sherry stands before me, letting me take in the sight of her. What a sight it is.

She is all I hoped she would be. Her abdomen and legs are toned from all of her running, yet her body is not athletically built; she is gently curved, with that long, wild, wavy espresso-colored hair falling onto her breasts.

Those sparkling eyes watch my every move.

Hooking my arms under her back and knees, I lay her across my bed and stand back to let her watch me undo my cufflinks and place them on the dresser.

I knew it. Underneath those perky dresses, a passionate woman smoldered. She bites her lower lip, watching. She wants me.

I take my time unbuttoning my white dress shirt. Our gazes are locked as I slip out of one sleeve and the other. Yes, I drag it out, watching her watch me, imagining what her body can do to me.

I want her to think about what I am about to do to her.

Her eyes trace over my bare torso—the new, ugly scars on my chest—and she licks her lips anyway.

I smile with anticipation as she sits to unbutton and unzip my pants. She's impatient, tucking her knees under her to sit straight. She yanks my pants down.

As they fall to the floor, she lowers my briefs. "Oh, Matteo."

She fists my engorged cock, taking it into her mouth eagerly as she massages my shaft with her thumb.

My head tilts back, and I hear my guttural groan as she runs that delicate tongue around my tip, sucks hard, and drags her tongue down my shaft.

"You are perfect Matteo. So hard," she whispers just before she slides me deep into her mouth. She grips tightly and strokes what she can't take as I thrust once, twice, into her mouth. I moan my pleasure. "Baby, slow down."

"You made me come twice before we got home. It's my turn to play." Somehow, she talks while her mouth does magical things to my cock.

"I can't do your fast turn-around. I want this to last."

"You'll come twice before I'm through with you."

It's like a dream, how she makes me feel.

But I've played long enough. I want to feel all of me inside of her. There is a hot, wet playground waiting for me.

I lift her, place her on her back in the middle of my king-size bed, and climb on top—grabbing both of her hands, holding them above her head, our fingers laced together—and I spend a moment hovering over her, appreciating the sight.

Long, graceful neck. Those perfect breasts, the trim waist, her hard, flat abdomen. That heart-stopping face. The mass of long, dark, curly hair. I savor the sight of her. All of her.

As I lower my hips, she lifts hers, fisting me to her entrance, and our gazes join. "I've been on birth control since college."

I can hardly concentrate as the head of my dick slides into place. She is wet and waiting, but I need to know. "What about Scott?"

"I always made him wear a rubber. I never trusted him."

"And you trust me?"

Her eyes glisten, and she nods breathlessly. "Yes. Do you trust me?"

"Yes." I push a little deeper, closing my eyes as I feel her soft heat around my tip. "I've always worn a rubber. I'm clean. I had myself checked after..."

She rolls her hips into me as she presses two fingers to my lips. "Don't talk about her when you're inside of me."

"You're sure? I have condoms."

My aching dick says, shut the fuck up, man.

"Matteo, just—"

Thank God.

I stop her mid-sentence, sliding all the way inside. Finally.

She gasps and shifts her hips. "Matteo." She widens her legs, adjusting.

Her fingernails dig into my ass, pressing me to her, and I grin, watching her face as I pull out and thrust again, as deep as she can take me. "That? You've wanted that?"

"Yes."

I move slowly, knowing if I don't force self-control, I will come inside of her in a heartbeat. I want this to last for both of us. I want to make this memorable. So, I set my pace, moving smoothly, pushing deep each time. Pulling out slowly.

I stop, holding my tip at her entrance. Teasing her. I fist my cock, teasing her with my tip.

"Matteo. Please."

"You want my cock?"

"Yes."

I hold still, continuing to deny her what she wants.

"Matteo!" Her demand is lustful and throaty, and I love it. I swell with satisfaction, sliding back inside, driving hard, losing myself in this. In her. I know now how Mars felt when he took Venus, the goddess of love. No, Sherry is Greek. Helen of Troy had nothing on this woman in my arms.

As I pump into her—slow and deep—I whisper, "I want all of you, Sherry."

With her fingertips exploring my shoulders, trailing down the curve of my back to my hips, her eyes searching mine all the while, she answers, "You have all of me, Matteo."

We move together slowly, languidly. She is heaven. This is heaven. Gripping her ass cheek, I lift with one hand.

As our gazes remain locked and at my cock's insistence, I begin to move faster... and she meets each thrust, using her muscles to clench the hot walls of her pussy around my cock each time I pull out. We move together in a rhythm.

"Goddamn, Sherry...." I thrust hard. Harder. Faster.

She gasps as a gush of warmth pours from her, soaking me. She groans as her walls tighten and ripple around me—this time involuntarily—the orgasm rolling through her in waves.

I can't hold back any longer. My cock erupts, and I hold still, buried deep inside of her... my chest heaving, my breath hot on her neck as my release... keeps... coming. "Sherry..." I exhale deeply. "Oh, shit." My cum still pulses into her.

She was more than I ever dreamed.

"Happy birthday, Matteo." Sherry whispers, dragging her tongue along my sweaty neck.

"I bet I taste salty."

She smiles against my skin. "Yes, you do."

I pull her against my chest and roll us to our sides. "That was... you are... wonderful. You made me come too fast." I confess. "Next time I'll do better."

She giggles against me. "Matteo, honey. I have you three to one."

Lying on my back with her pressed against my side, her head resting on my shoulder, Sherry trails her fingernails through the hair on my chest.

My dick takes notice. If she keeps that up...

I tuck my chin to ask, "Now, are you hungry?"

She tilts her head back to meet my eyes. "I think I could eat now. What do you have to cook?"

"We'll have to check. I had Bettina restock, but I'm not sure what I have. Coffee, I know."

Sherry props up on one elbow with a little grin. "You expected I would spend the night?"

I play with a strand of her hair. "Hoped, baby. Hoped."

"No regrets?" she asks.

A laugh erupts from deep in my chest. "Me? No. Hell, no. You?"

"No." Sherry strokes my cheek with the back of her hand. "Do you want the truth?"

Our gazes hold. "Always."

She rises to her knees beside me, and I can't take my eyes off her beautiful breasts right there in front of my face. I want them in my mouth.

She lifts my chin so our gazes catch again, and she shifts her shoulders. "Matteo, I think I fell in love with you at first sight. At the warehouse."

The words bring a pang to my chest, and I smile sadly. "Love at first sight. We call that colpo di fulmine. It means the thunderbolt."

"You understand the thunderbolt?" she asks.

"Yes. I do." I pull her to me and hold her tightly, understanding too well the overwhelming feelings she speaks of.

She nuzzles her nose in my neck. "I broke up with Scott the night I met you."

"Speaking of Scott..."

"Let's not. I wish now I'd never dated him."

"Why?"

"Because he wanted me to wear a dog collar and handcuffs. I declined."

I tilt my head to let a roar of laughter explode from my chest.

"What?" she asks. "Oh, no. Please don't tell me that you like..."

"No, sweetheart." I will spare Sherry the details. Sophia is... I would say adventurous sexually. "It sounds like he and Sophia make a perfect pair. It would seem she was doing Kerrigan and Scott at the same time she was doing me."

Sherry slaps my stomach playfully. "Ugh, Matteo. Does that mean he was doing me and her at the same time? Yuk! Gross! Thank the Lord for condoms."

She is so much fun.

Sherry tilts her head with cautious curiosity. "So... we are... equally old-fashioned? Just regular... sex?"

I tuck a stray strand of hair behind her ear. "Sweetheart, I don't see how it gets any better than what we just shared."

"Agreed. " She bounds out of bed, buck naked, cute as she can be. "Now we need to clean up. Then I'll see what I can find to fix for us."

"Scrambled eggs and bacon?" She's wearing one of my white undershirts that hits mid-thigh, and I can see the curves of her body through the thin fabric.

Sherry has no idea how sexy she is.

I slipped on briefs after cleaning up. "Do you really want to go to the trouble to cook? At this hour?"

"I will for you. Would you prefer a BLT?"

"See if there's not sandwich meat we don't have to cook."

She bends over, prowling in the refrigerator with that cute ass wiggling in my face. "Yep. Ham or turkey?"

"Ham."

She goes to work gathering the makings for sandwiches while I get bread and plates.

We sit at the kitchen bar, devouring our midnight snack.

Sherry peers at the clock on the stove. "A few more minutes and it's not your birthday anymore."

"It's the best birthday I've ever had. Thank you."

"Even with what happened?" Her eyes search mine.

"You gave me the perfect present." I kiss her pretty mouth, slip my arms under her, and carry her back to bed. It's a new day, and I am hungry for dessert.

We're lying in bed together, me on my back, her on her side against me, with her hand softly exploring my chest and abdomen. She's reading my body with her fingertips as if I am her personal Braille book.

"You are absolutely perfectly ripped," she says.

I angle my eyes to see her tucked into my side. "Boxing. They say swimming is the ultimate exercise but I'm pretty sure boxing is right there with it. Cardio, skipping rope, endurance running, strength training..."

She tilts her head back to ask, "Why didn't you pursue a career in boxing? Chris said you were very good."

"Pops was dead set against it. Said it was too corrupt." I shrug a shoulder. "And it is. People have no idea how many professional fights are fixed one way or another. It's just something I enjoy. Getting to fight legally."

She sighs. "I don't want to give you a big head, but you really are the perfect male physical specimen."

I kiss her forehead, smiling to myself. "Lots of scars now, baby."

"Scars are proof of life." She licks my nipple, rubs her nose in my chest hair, and snuggles back into my shoulder. "I like your hairy chest. I especially like this." She runs her fingers through the thin line of dark hair that grows down the center of my abdomen.

Fuck. My cock can't help itself.

She feels my dick thickening, rising to the occasion.

"Easy, boy." She moves her hand. "If we don't get some sleep..."

She's right. I change the subject. "I'm thinking about getting us out of the drug business."

She draws up on her elbow, her eyes full of surprise. "Seriously?"

I meet her curious gaze. "Yes. My gut tells me it's time to find something else to do."

"What would you do instead? I mean, to replace that revenue?"

"I have some ideas. I'm not ready to share."

She accepts that and snuggles back into me, nesting her head into the pillow. "Good night, Matteo."

"Sweet dreams, sweetheart."

As I'm drifting to sleep, she asks—out of nowhere—"Matteo, did you have Sophia in this bed?"

Women.

I squeeze her to me. "Sherry, you're the only woman I have ever had in my house. Go to sleep."

Matteo stirs beside me. His tossing and mumbling awakens me. My eyes open to darkness.

A single sliver of light streams across the foot of the bed—the moon shining through a break in the drapes that protect his bedroom from the nighttime exposure of an all-glass wall.

Matteo rolls from his back to his side, facing me, and he groans, "No! Pio, no!"

I reach to pet away this nightmare of losing his childhood friend.

As my eyes adjust to the darkness, he rolls onto his back, and I peer at this beautiful man who makes me feel all woman, saddened by his pain. He still mumbles, shaking his head as I stroke his powerful chest, running my fingers through the soft hair covering it.

Then he mutters wistfully, "Patsy."

My ears begin to ring. *Breathe.*

My insides crumble as my hand stops moving, and I stare in disbelief. I have been living inside a beautiful snow globe—a fairy tale land with a prince and princess—that just dropped onto a cold tile floor and shattered—the magical world and its figurines obliterated. Glass shards splinter my insides.

Rolling away from Matteo, I curl into a ball, close my eyes, pressing my fingertips against my eyelids. My chest aches.

He called out her name in his sleep after making love to me—even as my hand stroked his chest.

No one ever made such passionate love to me. Ever. It felt like love. But I was just a replacement. A body double.

My eyes dart about the dark room. Sweat beads on my neck and face as I fight to breathe.

Dammit, breathe.

I have to stop this insanity. It's not his fault. I was a willing participant. He said he loved my eyes, and he liked me, and he even asked, wasn't that enough?

Matteo made no false promises.

When I told him I was in love with him, he didn't respond the same.

This is on me. I didn't listen to what he said. I heard what I wanted to hear. I heard what I felt, not what he said.

Slipping out from under the covers, trying not to wake him, I search the blackness for my clothes.

Maybe if I turn on the bathroom light with the door open slightly, I can see.

Yes, a wider, brighter streak of light falls across the bedroom.

My panties are still on the floor beside the bed, where he dropped them. I slip them on. My bra is in the chair. I get it on. My dress. I slip it over my head. My shoes. Where are my shoes?

"What are you doing?"

"Go back to sleep. I'm gathering my clothes."

Matteo sits up in the bed and turns on the lamp beside him. "Why?"

"I need to go home."

"Why?"

I don't want to go there. Matteo doesn't know he said it. But I know. "I just want to go home."

He's out of the bed and on his feet. "What happened?"

I stop looking for my shoes to face him. "What happened? I was a fool."

His brows scrunch. "What are you talking about?"

Tears burn the back of my eyes but I deny them freedom. "Matteo, you called out her name in your sleep."

His powerful arms swing wide. "Whose name?"

"Really? Patsy."

His face morphs to stone. It is a long beat before he answers. "If I did, it was a dream. It means nothing."

I laugh in his face. "It means everything. Your body makes love to me, but your heart is making love to her. You don't want *me*, Matteo. You want her."

He stands still, staring. His jaw flexes, and he finally shakes his head. "That's... just not true. I'm a grown man, Patsy, I know what I—" His mouth freezes open.

He heard himself call me Patsy.

Is it shock or remorse or regret that overtakes his expression? He knows he can't take back what we both heard him say.

"Call someone to take me home." My heart isn't broken anymore. It is a hard fucking rock. Cold as Arctic ice. Any tears that had threatened dried to dust, hearing her name come out of his mouth for a second time.

"I just woke up. You said her name. I guess it was on my mind because—you know I didn't mean—"

"Fine. I'll call a cab. I'll meet it at the gate." I head for the living room. I know there's a phone in there.

Matteo yells after me, "You're not going home!"

"I can go home if I want to."

He's beside me in the hallway, his arm barring my way. "No, you can't. We just had that run-in with Sophia and your ex. He knows where you live. He can tell her. You're not going home."

"Fuck you, Matteo. I don't want to be here."

I try to duck under his arm, but he blocks the hall with his body, now both arms out. "You told me I was your thunderbolt."

"*You are!*" I scream at him, giving vent to the misery. "Why can't you see, Matteo? I'm in love with you already. *Dammit!* I know it doesn't make sense but you take my breath. But you... you... don't love me. Do you know how that feels, Matteo? To love someone who's in love with someone else?"

He clutches his heart with both hands and closes his eyes.

A beat later he shakes his head softly. "Sherry, you are wonderful. Beautiful, sexy, smart, funny—"

"But you can't say it, can you? You can't say you love me because you don't. Just let me go. Please."

Without warning, Matteo roars and smashes his fist into the bathroom door, burying his hand in splintered wood. Pulling his bloodied fist free, he aims his arm toward the living room. "Get out!" As I race to grab my purse in the kitchen, he has me by the wrist. His knuckles are bloody.

"Wait. Let me get dressed. I'll drive you home." His voice is calm.

Mine is not. "Matteo, you can't drive!"

He erupts again, shouting, this time with his arm pointing toward the bedroom. "I just fucked you, didn't I? I can drive."

My breathing stops. My heart stills as we glare at each other. "Yes. You fucked me."

A river of lava runs between us.

"Don't move. If you do, I will drag you back. Give me time to get my clothes on."

"Can I make coffee?"

"Help yourself."

The coffee is brewed, and he hasn't come back to the living room or kitchen. Maybe his hand is hurt worse than I know. Maybe he's trying to bandage it one-handed.

I down the rest of my second cup of coffee. God knows I needed it. Resting my head in my hands, I wait with a black hole in my chest where my heart once was. I have no right to be mad. He didn't lie. He never said he loved me. He never made a promise. I cannot blame him. Hearts have minds of their own. Maybe his head wants me. Maybe he *wants* to want me. But his heart still wants someone who broke it a long time ago.

Some things we never get over. I don't see me ever getting over this.

I glance toward the bedroom. No noise. What is he doing?

He was crazy mad. I'd never seen this side of Matteo. It helps me understand why people fear him. If that rage was unleashed on a true enemy.

I know he would never hit me. I don't believe Matteo would hit any woman or a child. But another man? I can only imagine what that temper inside that body could do.

Cautiously, I make my way down the hall. Stepping into the open bedroom doorway, I see Matteo dressed, sitting at the foot of the bed with a rag wrapped around his hand, staring at the curtained window facing the creek.

"I'm ready."

My voice startles him.

As he turns to face me, I recognize the agony in his beautiful eyes. His voice is hushed. "I don't want you to go."

I sink against the door frame. "I... I can't keep myself from loving you, Matteo. People don't choose who they love. Their hearts choose. The human mind does not rule the heart. I can't be angry that your heart loves someone else. I just can't endure the pain of wanting you this way, knowing you want her."

His black eyes plead with mine. "You said, I was your thunderbolt. So, you understand how that feels?"

"Yes."

"She was my thunderbolt. Yes, she broke my heart a long time ago." His eyes close slowly as he takes in a deep breath. "When I saw you in Chris's office, it felt like that all over again."

I clasp my hand over my heart. I didn't know.

His gaze finds its way back to mine. "Maybe the thunderbolt does hit twice in a life. I don't know. I just know that when I felt it with her, I wasn't afraid of it. When I felt it with you, I ran like a frightened little boy. But the more I was around you, the more of you I wanted. You, Sherry. Not *her*. I don't know why I had a dream and said her name. I don't remember it. You say people can't control their hearts and it's true, I know. But neither can they control their dreams. I swear to you, I didn't just *fuck* you. I made love to you."

"Me or her?"

He closes his eyes and shakes his head softly. "It wasn't her. It was you. I'm really sorry I said that."

His pain breaks my heart. It's real, on his face, in his eyes and voice. It takes all the air out of the room. But my pain is real, too. "Just let me go home and re-group."

I walk to him and sit beside him on the bed, my head on his shoulder, speaking quietly. "The way you make me feel, Matteo. What I feel in your arms. I have never felt anything like it. I fell asleep feeling so safe. Waking up, hearing you call another woman's name... it felt like a knife in my chest."

His arm wraps around me and his hand grips the side of my neck, under my ear as his thumb runs along my jaw, gently forcing my eyes to meet his. "I never felt with any woman what I felt with you earlier."

I whisper into his hand. "Then maybe there's hope for us, when I can get the sound out of my head of you saying her name. Please, give me space to get my head on straight."

"Kiss me first."

I reach, placing my hand on his neck—on the neck of this man whose touch I crave, this man whose heart is breaking, this man who broke my heart—and I kiss his perfect lips softly.

He won't settle for that. Matteo digs his fingers into my arms and pulls me to him with the passion that only he has, and I yield to his desperate kiss as he lays back on the bed, pulling me on top of him, his hands roaming every part of me, gripping my ass cheeks, pressing me into him.

Yes, I feel him hard against me again. Yes, I'm wet again. I ache for him inside. But I have to leave.

Matteo feels my body tense. "Okay."

Turning on his garage lights, Matteo stops in the doorway, staring at his car, a white Porsche 911 with a bullet hole in the hood.

"Are you okay?" I ask behind him.

His voice is wistful, as if meeting a dear friend who has been wounded. "I don't even know if it runs. I hope the bullet didn't ruin the engine."

Opening the passenger door for me, he presses a button for the garage door to open and climbs into the driver's seat. The engine turns over and purrs.

I've never been in the car with him driving. When we pull up to the gate of the DeVecchio estate, the men know his car. Matteo rolls down his window, telling them, "I'll be back before long."

Both trucks move, and we pull onto the road.

Sherry
TRASHED

We ride in agonizing silence as the sun rises in the east. It's September first, and the air is fresh. The sky glows in hues of pink and peach, but I can't enjoy its beauty. My heart has never been heavier. To soar so high and fall so far. I think he speaks the truth. He wants to want me. But his heart still wants her.

The Sunday morning sidewalk is still as Matteo parks in front of my apartment building. People aren't out yet. A few lights are on in apartment windows, but for the most part, this blue-collar neighborhood rests peacefully. Quietly.

When Matteo opens his console and pulls out a pistol, I place my hand on his forearm. "You don't have to walk me inside."

He scoffs dismissively. "You don't seem to comprehend what you're dealing with. You are on her radar now." Nearing the top of the stairs, he holds out his arm, blocking me. "Wait," Matteo whispers.

I fist his shirt. "What is it?"

"I watched you lock your door when we left. It's open."

"No." My heart begins racing.

"Shh!" He presses his finger to his lips with a scowl and mouths, "Stay here and be quiet."

When I start to follow, he's irritated, whispering. "Dammit, Sherry. Stay put."

I nod and stand still as Matteo walks softly to the front door and eases it open with one hand, the other aiming his gun straight ahead. He steps inside.

Moments later, he ushers me in. "It's been trashed. At least I think it's been trashed. I don't think you keep your clothes and silverware on the floor."

Stepping inside, I am stunned at the disarray of my little apartment. Kitchen drawers were pulled out and dumped. The coffee table turned over with its legs stretched toward the ceiling. My sheets are stripped off the bed and clumped on the floor. Dresses have been torn off hangars, some of them ripped. The word BITCH is smudged on the bathroom mirror in lipstick.

I peer from the mess to Matteo. "Sophia?"

His lips scrunch up as he shakes his head. "Probably. What Sophia wants, Sophia gets. She couldn't have me. Seeing me with you was like a slap in her face. I guess. Who the hell knows?" Matteo glances around the disheveled room. "She probably didn't do this herself. She got one of her minions to do her dirty work."

Turning in a circle, I try to figure out where to begin to clean up my apartment. My eyes meet his, and I feel the tug of a sad smile crack my face. A smile of goodbye, at least for a while. "Thank you, Matteo, for bringing me home."

He draws back in angry surprise. "You're not staying here."

"We're not going through—"

"*Shh.*" He claps his hand over my mouth as his head tilts to the living room.

Stepping me backward into the bathroom, Matteo slips back into the living room, his back pressed to the front wall, gun in hand.

The opening door will shield him.

A man the size of Tommaso swings the door open, strides in, and Matteo slams the butt of his gun into the man's head.

The big guy crumbles to the floor.

Quickly, Matteo hits him again, I guess for good measure. He walks to the front door, closes and tries to lock it. But the lock has been jimmied, so he slides the couch in front of it. "Call Chris. Tell him to get over here with troops."

Staring at the figure on my floor, I don't act fast enough. Matteo barks his orders again. "Sherry! Call Chris now! Tell him to get over here and bring backup."

I dial the phone as Matteo removes the man's shoes. He strips out the shoelaces, using them to tie the man's hands behind his back.

As I finish relaying his message to Chris, Matteo asks, "Do you have any scarves?"

I scrounge through the chaos of my bedroom, coming out with a pink scarf.

Matteo ties the man's ankles together, and I stifle a chuckle. "He'll love the color."

He cuts his eyes at me, failing to appreciate my humor, and holds out his hand. "I've got to have more to hold this guy. See if you have more scarves or take the shoelaces out of your tennis shoes."

He strips off his belt, looping and buckling it around the man's ankles.

I run into the room with two more scarves. One, Matteo stuffs into the man's mouth.

And another, which he uses to re-enforce the wrists.

He stands, studying his handiwork. "He's not going any-where."

The big guy stirs, and Matteo hits him again with the butt of the gun in another spot on his head.

"Don't kill him." It just slips out. He peers at me with murderous eyes, and I realize it was a stupid thing to say. "What are you going to do with him?"

"Make him talk. Maybe I'll finally get some answers." He steps over the man toward me. "They came after you. I don't walk away from this."

He peers out the window blinds, cuts his eyes at the man on the floor, and takes me by the shoulders, walking me backward to the wall. Matteo presses his body into mine. "I'm not losing you. Do you hear me?" He pins my hands against the wall by my head and pushes his leg between mine, pressing himself into me. His eyes glisten. "I don't know what this is, but I know the past is the past. We are the present and I will not lose you."

Maybe I get it. "You'll do anything to keep from saying I love you."

Matteo pulls me to him, his big hand pressing my face to his chest. "I'll figure it out. I just know, I won't let you go."

"That sounds suspiciously like love."

His hungry mouth captures mine, his hand holding my chin in place as his tongue overpowers mine, again kissing the sense out of me.

When we are like this, nothing exists—not the chaos in the room, or the man on the floor, or the girl from his past. I lose myself in Matteo's overpowering passion—until someone's fist pounds the door. "Hey!" Chris bellows.

Matteo sighs and shoves the couch aside to open the door, and as Chris comes inside, Matteo points to the man on the floor. "You know him?"

Chris squats to study the man, who has olive skin and short, dark, curly hair. He is Tommaso's size but older. Heavier. "One of Geno's. I've seen him but I can't recall the name."

He glances over his shoulder and around the room, then flashes a sarcastic grin. "Like what you've done with the place, Sherry Baby." He frisks the man's pockets and pulls out his billfold. "Here's what you need."

Chris hands it to Matteo and stands as a horde of men take the stairs two at a time, crowding into my tiny apartment.

Matteo looks at his troops and points to the unconscious man. "I want him alive. Get him into Chris's truck. I need someone to take Sherry back to my place." He peers at me. "Get your stuff. You're not coming back here."

I open my mouth to protest, but he holds up his hand. "No."

With the door closed, in the privacy of my bedroom, I strip off last night's clothing. No time for a shower, so I slip into fresh panties and bra, pull on a clean T-shirt and jeans, and slide into loafers.

I find my suitcase undamaged in the back of the closet and start throwing things in. Panties, bras, pajamas, jeans and tops. Oh, yeah. Toothbrush, hairbrush, and makeup. There's no room for dresses or shoes.

As I stare at an overstuffed suitcase, he says, "I'll send someone to pack this place up for you." He is standing behind me, the bedroom door closed. "Joey said he'll take you home."

"Joey? I thought he was a truck driver."

"Chris told him to. Since he's a good driver, Leo's son who swore Omerta, I'm trusting my girl and my car with him."

"You know, I drive a Volkswagen stick shift. I don't need a driver."

"I feel safer if you have a man with you. I can't be worried about you and do what I have to do."

I can't hide my smile. "Are you always going to be over-protective?"

Matteo draws me close as he slides his fingertips through my hair. His other hand grips my ass, yanking me hard against him, and finishes the kiss he started earlier. His erection is rock-hard against me.

I melt in his arms, my hands resting on his thick chest.

My passionate lover knows he has me as I let his tongue trail down my neck, and he slips his hand beneath the T-shirt to grip my breast. Matteo slides his fingers into my bra, jerking it down. Taking my breast into his mouth, he uses his magical tongue while he slides his hand down the front of my jeans into my panties. "Oh, damn. You are wet again," he mumbles.

"Yes."

He puts my bra back in place and pulls my T-shirt down as he grins devilishly. "Go home and wait for me to come to you, and finish what I started. If you think last night was good, baby girl, tonight I will make you forget all about it."

Oh, please, yes.

He plants a quick kiss—makes an adjustment—and turns to leave, but I grip his forearm. "Matteo, be careful. I can't lose you, either."

He smiles. "Hurry. I won't leave until you are safe in my car with Joey."

Matteo
SEEKING TRUTH

"Put him in a cell." It took three men to haul Paul Bunyon's dead weight out of Sherry's apartment, down the stairs, and hoist him into the back of Chris's truck.

It's not the kind of neighborhood where we have to worry about people calling the cops. Everyone minds their own business, which is another reason Sherry doesn't need to live there any longer.

I've claimed her. I will not let her go back. She will live safely with me.

"He's coming to," Chris observes as the men carry the monster into the freight elevator.

"Use the chloroform. This son of a bitch is going to give us some answers."

The capos can quickly gather information, which will aid in an effective interrogation.

I hand Chris the driver's license back.

He's Enzo Accardi from Trenton. Six foot six inches tall. Two-hundred forty-five pounds. Born January 3, 1930. Forty-seven years old. That means his kids are teenagers.

"We need everything about Enzo that we can use for leverage. Wife, kids, house—anything." They take off. "Wait."

My capos turn around. "You pulled the bugs, right?"

"Suckers are locked in a box. I thought we might find a use for them ourselves," Chris answers.

"Tommy? You're sure there aren't any more?"

"Checked and re-checked. We're clean."

Taking this fight to Sherry is too far. "If I have to threaten his wife and kids, stuff his balls down his throat—neither one of us leaves here until I know what Geno Gabicci has up his sleeve."

The capos high-five each other as Chris croons. "About fucking time."

Our third floor is like a hotel. Every man has a clean place to sleep with fresh linens and bedding. Most rooms have multiple beds, but my capos and I have private rooms and baths. We keep clothing here.

The second floor houses weapons and munitions. It has an employee kitchen with refrigerators, freezers, and a walk-in pantry with staples. And holding cells.

During interrogations, this floor is off-limits to everyone but me and the capos.

I change into warehouse overalls to greet Enzo Accardi as he awakens.

Waiting in a chair, I sip a fresh cup of coffee. I woke up before I wanted to this morning, but I'm wide awake for this. "I'm tired of waiting."

Tommy holds smelling salts under Enzo's nose.

I'm the only person Enzo Accardi will be allowed to see. Chris and Tommaso are at his back, watching. They can come and go through a door behind him. Enzo might hear their footsteps or even their voices, but mine is the only face he will see until he draws his last breath. If this guy escapes under some bizarre circumstances, he will not know their faces.

I take responsibility for what happens to Enzo.

Enzo shakes his enormous head, regaining consciousness. First, his gaze darts around the dimly lit room. He turns his head left and right. He's realizing his situation.

I don't say anything. I sit directly in front of Enzo, out of his reach, staring at him.

His hands are cuffed, the handcuffs locked to a chain hanging from the ceiling. He is stretched high and sitting in a straight-back chair. A thick leather strap over his lap, attached to the floor on both sides, prevents him from standing. The scarves around his ankles have been replaced by steel shackles embedded into the floor.

Enzo fucking Accardi isn't going anywhere.

The wait begins.

I'm impatient, but I won't let him know that. This room has no windows, just long fluorescent lights in the ceiling.

A sole wall sconce illuminates an ominous clock that reminds men how long they have been our guests. The big, round clock on the wall at my back—the wall Enzo faces—is *tick... tick... ticking.*

A door on either end of the room opens to the corridor. Both are kept locked. Only Pop, the capos, and I have keys.

A deep janitorial sink is between the two doors. It comes in handy sometimes. In the center of the tile floor is a drain.

On either side of the drain, a wooden chair, like the one Enzo sits in, is anchored to the floor.

I check my watch. Ten minutes have passed since he woke up.

Tick, tick, tick.

Enzo blinks, still gathering his wits from the blows to his head and the chloroform.

His black hair is short and wiry, beginning to gray. He has a wide forehead and a bulbous nose. Heavy jowls drag his thin, hard mouth into a permanent frown. "I need to piss," he finally growls out.

"So, piss. You will sooner or later. You might as well get it over with."

Nothing.

Tick, tick, tick.

I check my watch, noting the time, and walk out of the cinderblock room, leaving Enzo alone in his chair, fighting his urge to urinate.

In the men's room I relieve myself, since he made me think about it.

When I walk back in the room with another cup of coffee—just to intensify his urge to piss—Enzo barks. "What do you want, DeVecchio?"

My gaze meets his over my cup of coffee. "You know who I am?"

"Yeah." He hocks a big old nasty loogie my way. He's lucky it didn't reach me.

"You know what I will do to you?"

His upper lip curls. "Yeah."

Our gazes are locked. "Just so we're clear."

Enzo spits at me again. He is a big dog on a short chain. "I said, what do you want, motherfucker?"

Tommy takes a step and backhands Enzo, whipping his head around.

Enzo can't see the face of the gloved hand that hit him. Blood dribbles from his mouth. "Fuck you, De—Vecch—i—o."

I nod at Tommy. This time he slams the butt of his gun against Enzo's jaw.

"Goddammit!" Blood oozes from his mouth as Enzo wipes fragments of teeth onto his shoulder.

"Respect, Enzo. Think about it."

We leave the room and meet in the kitchen.

"How much time do you give King Kong in there?" Chris asks as he rips open a bag of potato chips.

Tommy rubs his chin, his pencil poised over his crossword puzzle on the table. "A few hours. Who was the 15th First Lady?"

Chris reaches into his pocket and places a bill on the table. "I've got fifty bucks says he caves in... two."

Tommy does the same. "You're on. Now who was the 15th First Lady?"

"Who the hell cares?"

"The crossword. It's 15 down. I've been stuck here for the past day."

"It's a trick question," I tell them. "James Buchanan was the 15th President dend he never married."

Tommy scoffs. "My frigging crossword begs to differ."

"Try Harriet. Harriet Lane was his niece. Maybe that's who they're talking about."

"H.A.R.R..." The big guy bends over this folded paper, penciling as he calls out each letter. "I.E.T. It fits!" He high-fives me. "Fuck, Matty, how do you know this shit?"

"I listened in school."

"Hey!" Enzo's voice travels down the hall. "Get back in here!"

I check my watch. Paul Bunyan's dark doppelganger has been alone for going on twenty minutes. He still needs to whiz. I'm not getting in on their bet, but Enzo is hardcore. Let him sit awhile longer.

His shoulders are starting to ache in that position.

"What have we got to eat?" Tommy sticks his head in the refrigerator.

"Do either of us look like a fucking waitress?" Chris answers, chomping on his chips.

"DeVecchio!" Enzo shouts.

I check my watch again.

Not even five minutes since Enzo's last bellow.

"He must really need to piss," Chris says.

"He'll have to piss himself. I'm not about to uncuff him," I reply.

"We got any pizza?" Tommy's stomach growls so loud we hear it and chuckle.

"In the freezer, but you'll have to warm the oven," Chris says.

Tommy growls and snatches his own sack of chips from the pantry.

Enzo's chain rattles. "Goddammit, you motherfucking prick! What do you want?"

He is one defiant, noisy fucker. This is going to take a while.

"I'm going to make sure Sherry got home alright." I insulated her from what is going on here, as Pop would Mother.

Taking the freight elevator to the first floor, I walk into the office and call the house.

No answer.

Maybe she's in the shower. Who knows. She could be up at my parents' or down by the creek, knowing her.

I call the big house. Bettina answers.

"Bettina, it's Matty. Can I speak to Mother?"

"Yessir, one second."

A minute passes before Mother answers. "Will you go down to my house and check on Sherry?"

"Are you two official now?" She sounds like a kid expecting a big birthday present. Mother likes Sherry, and she's wanted to marry me off since I turned twenty.

"Jesus, Mother."

"You love her?"

I groan. "Mother, just go check on her, will you? One of the men was driving her home in my car. I'm checking to make sure she's back, and so is my car. But she doesn't answer. Maybe she's in the shower or outside. Someone broke into her apartment overnight. We went to get her clothes." I lie.

"Oh, goodness. Alright. I'll call you back."

It will take my mother at least fifteen minutes to get herself into her car, drive to my house, and get back. Probably closer to thirty, knowing her.

I head back upstairs and hear Enzo hollering as the freight elevator opens. "Somebody, get in here!"

I walk to his room, stand at the door, and reply, "When you can ask nicely, Enzo, someone will be here."

I leave.

Enzo shrieks at my back. "Motherfucker!"

Nobody is winning this bet. Enzo's a crusty bastard. He has not pissed himself. He will refuse to break for a while.

But he will, eventually.

"The older the oak, the harder the bark." Tommy talks with his mouth full of chips. "Is Sherry home?"

"No answer. I asked Mother to go down and check on her."

I feel a nagging worry. Where is she?

"Who took her home?" Chris asks.

I meet his questioning gaze as my throat tightens. "Joey."

Chris's brows pinch tight. "Joey? What the fuck was Joey doing there?" His voice is full of alarm.

My stomach twists. "Joey told me that you told him to drive her home."

"Oh, fuck, man." All color washes from Chris's face. "I haven't seen Joey."

Sherry
SWEET RIDE

"**T**hanks for running me home," I tell Joey as I buckle my seat belt. This car is low to the ground. Lower than my little Beetle. Matteo's Porsche is the epitome of luxury. Red leather interior, bucket seats, automatic windows and doors, tinted glass. It is pristine.

Except for the bullet hole in the hood.

Joey grins at me. "Thanks for getting me out of jail, Miss Drakos. I can't believe he's letting me drive this thing. Do you have any idea what a car like this costs?"

I run my fingers through my hair. I should have used the brush before I packed it. "Actually, I don't."

"More than people like you and me make in a year."

"What can I say? Matteo makes good money."

Joey snickers. "No shit."

I peer at my young driver who wants to be a lawyer. "How is school going, Joey?"

He hikes his shoulder. "Okay."

It's clear Joey is too busy admiring Matteo's car to want conversation, and my mind digresses to my apartment. I never imagined something like that could happen to me. Why dump my kitchen drawers on the floor? Rip my clothes?

Scott must have told Sophia where I live. He'll get a piece of my mind when I see him.

It's like Joey reads my mind as he cuts his eyes at me. "So, someone messed with your place?"

"You could say that."

He glances over his shoulder into the back seat, where Matteo placed my bulging suitcase. "You moving in with Mr. DeVecchio?"

"He just wants me out of that apartment right now, after what happened."

"But you said you were going home, so..."

I'm not comfortable talking to Joey about my relationship with Matteo, so I don't answer. My relationship with Matteo. He wants me out of my apartment. So what? What am I doing?

I close my eyes and shake my head. Before I met him, I'd never dreamed of letting a man tell me what to do, much less order me to move out of my apartment... and here I am, obeying like a Stepford wife. Why?

I was sick of defending remorseless creeps, so I went along with the order to quit the public defender's office. I've wanted a better apartment all along. It's the ordering and obedience I'm trying to wrap my head around. It's not me.

And yet with Matteo, it's me. Maybe I don't like the new me. I really have gone off the rails.

I let my head fall against the headrest, staring at the headliner. If I didn't work for Matteo—if I wasn't involved with him—I wouldn't need protection.

But how can I give him up now that I've gone there?

"If you don't mind, I need to run by my place." Joey's voice jerks me off the ledge. "It won't take but a second. I need to check on my mom."

"Of course."

He stops in front of an older home in a neighborhood, not unlike the one I grew up in. My parents still live there.

Joey looks at me apologetically. "Mom's been sick, so if you don't mind, wait in the car. I won't be long." When he exits, he takes the keys.

That's odd. It's not like I'm going to steal Matteo's car. Maybe he wants to show them off to his mother.

This neighborhood takes me back to my childhood. Two-story houses are crowded onto small lots. Big, old trees shade the yards. I'm playing hopscotch with friends on a sidewalk exactly like the one leading to Joey's front door—balancing on one foot, bending over to move my rock forward, and hopping around it.

I check my watch. He's taking longer than I expected. I hope his mother isn't terribly ill. What if she has cancer or something, and he has to tend to her? Poor thing.

When he finally gets back into the car, Joey smiles wide, like he's relieved. I feel a wave of relief for him. "Your mother's better?"

"Yeah, thanks for asking. She's fine."

He turns on the radio, and we ride in silence while I stay locked in thoughts—between my childhood and wondering about this new life Matteo's dragging me into—until I become aware of my surroundings.

This is wrong. "Joey, this isn't the way to Matteo's house."

Joey cuts his eyes at me. "It isn't?"

"No. Haven't you been there before?" I peer out the window. "This isn't the right way at all." I know where we are. "He didn't say go to the warehouse."

"We aren't. Relax."

I turn in the seat to face him. "Joey, where are we going?"

He ignores my question, absorbed in the car. "Man, this is a sweet ride." At the stop sign, Joey puts the Porsche in neutral and revs the powerful engine, both hands on the wheel, a silly grin plastered across his face.

Something about that grin... the hair on my arms prickle. This isn't right. Get out.

As I grab the door handle, Joey slams the car into gear and lurches the Porsche forward, forcing the door to slam shut. He clicks the automatic door locks. "Relax, Sherry Baby, we're taking a detour."

My scalp tingles. Panic claws inside my throat. "What are you doing, Joey?"

Nothing. He says nothing.

My heart pounds furiously, climbing from my chest into my throat. Think.

His gaze is on the road. I don't know where his mind is, but I hope he's too focused to notice me quietly unbuckling my seat belt, holding it in place. "Matteo trusted you, Joey. I trusted you. We all trusted you."

He twists his neck to leer at me with a nasty snarl. "You know what you get when you trust? Fucked."

"Who are you?"

"I'm Joey Carbona." His gaze narrows with malice. "Carbona with a B, as you say."

"Are you even studying at community college?"

He tilts his head back to emit a wicked cackle. "If you were as good a lawyer as you think you are, you wouldn't believe everything your clients tell you, Miss Drakos." He cuts his eyes at me. "Or should I call you Mrs. DeVecchio? How about just DeVecchio's fuck?"

That doesn't deserve a response. "Your father has been with the DeVecchio family for years. Why would you do this?"

"Because he has been with them for years. And what's it gotten him? He's still a foot soldier while Tommaso and Christos, younger than he is, are capos. Dumbasses make capo because they're your boyfriend's buddies, while men like my father put their lives on the line for him every day and get paid barely enough to get by. Look where we live."

"There's nothing wrong with your neighborhood, Joey. I grew up in one just like it. My parents still live there." Asshole.

"Bet your sweetheart doesn't live in a house like ours."

I twist in the seat to see him better. "So what? Do you think life owes you something?"

He takes his eyes off the road for a second, his glare overflowing with hatred. "No, life doesn't owe me a damned thing and I'm not sitting around waiting for breaks to fall my way. I'm going to take what I want from life."

"And what do you want, Joey?"

He scoffs. "I want to topple his uppity ass." He thumps his chest with his thumb. "I want to sit in the cat bird's seat."

I'm watching *To Tell the Truth: "Will the real Joey Carbona please stand up?"*

"You sabotaged that run, didn't you? How much did Geno pay you?"

"Wouldn't you like to know."

"You think Geno's a better man than Matteo or Francesco? Are you trusting him to deliver on his promises? Remember what you just said about trust, Joey. Geno will throw you to the wolves."

"Shut up or I'll shut you up." He raises his hand like he's going to hit me, but he doesn't. That's learned behavior. He's been smacked around by his father or mother all his life.

"Where are you taking me?" I hear fear in the rising tenor of my voice. I'm sure he does, too.

"Relax. We'll be there in a minute." He fishes in his pocket and holds handcuffs, displaying them for me. "Put those on."

"Screw you."

He tosses the handcuffs in my lap. "Put them on, if you know what's good for you."

I punch the automatic window button on the door and sling the cuffs out.

"You fucking bitch!" Joey's right arm swings out. The back of his hand strikes my face, splitting my lips. Sharp, stinging pain dulls my mind, blurring my vision. My ears ring. I taste the blood in my mouth. "You'll pay for that."

I blink to regain focus. The ringing in my ears is so loud it drowns out everything. Blood dribbles down my chin. I use my left hand to wipe it. "You low-life bastard." I slur with my busted, swelling lips. "It was you. You trashed my apartment."

He doesn't reply. But I know it's so. The way he called me bitch.

He keeps his fuming gaze straight ahead, gripping the steering wheel so hard his knuckles are white. "Why would you do that?"

"Because you think your shit doesn't stink. You, getting ahead by screwing the boss. Nothing but a slut." He tries to backhand me again, but this time, I see it coming and dodge.

He misses my mouth, barely catching my jaw.

We ride in silence with my back pressed against the door to keep as far away from Joey as possible as panic silently creeps through me.

My heart leaps into my throat as I see the red brick of the DeVecchio warehouse rising above the surrounding single-story metal buildings. It rises in the sky, a symbol of hope.

Joey isn't much taller than I am, but he is powerfully built. I can't fight him and win—but I can outrun him.

I can't let Joey get me into some building where he could do God knows what, where there's probably someone waiting to kill or torture me—maybe Geno, maybe even Sophia.

As we pull into a parking spot in front of a sprawling metal building with several parked cars, I take my chance—punching the automatic window control on my door. It lowers swiftly and silently.

Before Joey realizes what's happening, I scramble through the window with the Porsche still moving.

He grabs my ankle, but I kick free from his grasp and fall through the window, grateful the car is so low to the ground.

Kicking off my shoes, I run—not for a trophy or a medal. This is a run for my life, fueled by sheer terror. I race for Matteo's warehouse as if a bear is on my heels, the balls of my bare feet scraping raw on asphalt.

The Porsche appears beside me as Joey yells, "Get in, bitch!"

I keep running.

He swerves the car, trying to hit me, but I veer, picking up speed.

As the warehouse comes into view, the Porsche and Joey are no longer beside me. He won't follow me here. He knows Matteo will kill him.

Matteo
HEAD OVER HEELS

The alarm in my mother's voice is palpable. "Matteo, Sherry isn't at your place, and the men at the gate told your father no one has been here since you left early this morning."

"I'll call you back." I peer at my capos, my gaze shifting between them. "Joey. He's taking her to Geno."

"That warehouse is one block away," Tommy says.

"Have someone guard Enzo. Let's go."

Chris passed out automatic rifles when we realized what Joey was up to.

Stepping out of the warehouse into the glaring morning sun—I stop, frozen by what I see. Sherry is racing toward me—panic in her face—her long dark hair flying behind her. *She got away. Smart girl.*

"No!" I yell as the Porsche comes into sight. She thinks she's safe. She doesn't glance over her shoulder. "No!" I wave my arms trying to get her to look behind her or veer sideways.

Her eyes are on me as the car slams into her, sending her body flying into the air.

"NO!"

She flips upside down, tumbling over the Porsche, as my men unload automatic weapons into the tires and windshield. The car careens and I flinch, hearing the ungodly thud of her body striking something. Like a rag-doll, she skids across the asphalt.

As I race for her, men run for the car. I hear their shouts and the screams of the driver as I near Sherry, who lies motionless. Over my shoulder, I holler, "Keep him alive!" Reaching her, I see clearly what my car did. "Oh, God, baby." I pull her to me, and she cries out in pain, so I ease her back to the ground. My heart sinks as my eyes take in her battered body. "Someone, call an ambulance!"

I study her raw, bleeding face. "Can you move your head?"

Her eyes are wide as she nods softly.

"Can you turn your head from side to side?"

Her head moves back and forth.

"Yes, you can move it. Good. Now, be still." I kiss her hand. "An ambulance is coming. They'll have a neck brace." I'm afraid to touch her. "Baby, I'm so sorry. I know the pain of a broken leg."

She blinks and croaks, "I don't feel anything."

A sickness seizes my stomach, seeing her on her back, blinking as she stares at the empty September sky. She doesn't try to move.

"Can you wiggle your toes?" I watch her bare feet.

Nothing happens.

"Wiggle your toes."

Nothing. She can't move her feet.

Chris looms over us. "Sherry Baby, I'm so fucking sorry." He reaches for her, and I shake my head. He stops, instinctively knowing.

I glance over my shoulder to see the men drag a kicking-and-screaming Joey into the warehouse. "Stay with her."

Running for Joey, I hear my visceral roar—as if it's coming from something or someone else—like it's not from me—as I jerk him from the men, pick him up, and body-slam him into the parking lot.

He squeals. I pick him up by his shirt and drive my fist into his face as hard as I can, trying to shove his nose out the back of his head. The motherfucker flails and whimpers as I pound his jaw again... and again to make his face as bloody as hers. My hands seize his throat, and I squeeze the life out of the filthy fucker, watching his eyes bulge when big hands grab me from behind, yanking to pull me off of Joey. They can't. I will take the life out of this miserable—

"Don't kill him, Matty!" It's Tommy's voice. "We need his answers."

Tommy. My voice of reason. Answers. My hands ease the grip on his neck.

"She can't feel anything!" I fist Tommy's shirt, pointing at the beautiful woman lying motionless on the asphalt. "The motherfucker paralyzed her!"

And I lean my head back and roar at the sky. I roar loud enough and long enough to wake up everyone in heaven and hell.

Tommy grips my shoulders, shaking me, his voice quiet but seething. "Stop it, Matty. You're no good to her this way. Now get it together and go to her. We've got him."

"Keep that fucker alive."

"Matteo?" She peers up at me, still motionless, her voice weak and raspy.

"What is it, baby?"

"Was that you yelling?"

I stroke her hair, wincing at the sight. What he did to her. How she must hurt. Dry blood is caked on her lips and in the corner of her mouth. That didn't just happen. "He hit you, didn't he?" Her lips are busted, swollen, and blue.

"Yes." She blinks through tears. "Joey sabotaged your run. He ransacked my apartment."

"I can't believe I put you in the car with him."

"He tricked us all." Her hand grips my forearm. Relief washes over me feeling the strength in her hands. "He stopped. I think he called someone."

"Probably Geno."

"He took me to a metal building not far from here. I could see the warehouse so I got out of the window and ran before he could stop."

"I'm so proud of how smart you are. How brave you are." I want to hold her and pet her, but I can't. Her body is too broken and raw.

Sherry pauses a moment as she takes me in. "What on earth are you wearing?"

I glance down at the overalls I changed into earlier, which she has never seen. "Work clothes."

Sirens.

I look over my shoulder. "The ambulance is here. They'll take care of you."

"What will I tell the police?"

"The truth. A man tried to steal my car, and you tried to stop him, and he ran you down in the process. It's a hit and run. The cops will never find Joey."

She smiles softly. "Do you have him?"

"I have him."

Again, she blinks, tears pooling in her eyes. "Matteo, I don't care if you kill him. Make him tell you why."

I have to touch her. I softly stroke her hair, wet with blood. "Baby, I won't leave your side until they patch you up. Then I'll deal with Joey. He's not going anywhere."

She nods and shifts her eyes to her cousin, our fingers locked together. "Chris, will you call Mom and Dad?"

"Yes," he says, "I am so fucking sorry."

They won't let me ride with her in the ambulance. My men shot out the tires on my car. It's bullet-riddled, so I have to use a company truck to follow the ambulance, leaving Tommy and Chris to get Joey settled in his cell. They'll meet me at the hospital.

There, I ask to be at her side in the emergency room. The desk attendant checks, telling me Sherry's already been taken to surgery. The woman smiles sympathetically. "You can wait here."

Wait. I'm not good at waiting.

I use the payphone to call my parents and fill them in. The capos already did. Bettina says Mother and Pop are on their way here.

It isn't long before a frantic couple hurries through the automatic doors. I know they are her parents before I hear them ask for Sherry Drakos. She is a blend of these two people. She asked Chris to call them.

I approach and introduce myself.

Her father is about my size, with light hair like Chris's, but he's graying at his temples. "What happened?" he demands. This man is as furious as he is afraid for his daughter.

How do I even begin?

"They hurt her to get to me." I can't be more honest than that.

I see on his face that her father wants to pound me the way I did Joey.

I can't blame him.

"A man tried to kidnap her. She got away and ran. He ran the car into her while she was running from him. She never saw it coming."

Her mother shakes her head and covers her face with her hands, speaking into them. "Chris said he saw it."

I will never forget the pain I experienced when I broke my leg. It was mind-numbing. Something you cannot put words to and something you can never forget. Sherry should be in agony. Instead, she feels nothing. I cannot bring myself to tell them. "Her leg is broken. She could have a concussion. I don't know what is damaged inside."

Her father arches his brow and extends a calloused hand. "My name is Joseph Drakos. Chris tells us you and Sherry are—"

I take his hand and shake it. "Together, yessir."

"This is my wife, Charlene," Joseph says.

Charlene looks at me through teary, ice-blue eyes that bring a smile to my face. "Your beautiful daughter takes after you."

"Thank you." She wipes tears from her cheeks as her husband wraps a protective arm around his wife.

"Forgive me. I'm going to step outside and smoke a cigarette."

They nod.

Standing outside the emergency room, I fish for my pack of cigarettes. I don't smoke a lot, but at times like this, I do.

I could use a drink, too.

Chris's truck screeches into the parking lot. A small woman exits with him, and they rush to me. "How is she?" he asks.

I show him my palms. "Already in surgery. I haven't been able to see her."

"Matty, this is Sherry's best friend, Tina."

The small woman, with light blonde hair and crystal-green eyes, peers from Chris to me with a guarded smile. "Nice to meet you," she says.

I tilt my head toward the ER. "They're all inside."

Tina peers up at Chris—he is at least a foot taller—and whispers, "Thank you, Christos." She stands on tiptoes, kisses his cheek, and rushes inside.

We stare at each other, neither knowing what to say. "Isn't that the girl you were crazy about back—?"

"Yeah."

"What happened with that?"

"She married someone else." He nods at my cigarette. "Let me have one of those."

I hand him my pack and lighter, finally confessing, "I put her in the car with Joey." I'm not sure I'm even speaking to Chris. I just finally get the filthy words out of my mouth. "I put her in the fucking car with him. Goddammit!" I turn in a circle, my rage erupting. I want to hit something. Anything. "I fucking gave her to him! Fuck!" I yell at the top of my lungs.

Someone walking in the ER turns to glare at me.

Fuck off, buddy. You don't want a piece of me right now.

Chris takes a deep drag on his cigarette and exhales. "I was the first idiot, Matty. I administered the oath to the son of a bitch. He took it. He fooled us all. But he fooled me first. I want my shot at him."

"You'll have it. Where is he?"

"Pissing and shitting himself in his cell. He's trussed up just like Enzo, only I blindfolded him, too. Nothing scarier than being blindfolded. I stationed two men on the first floor and two on the second to make sure they don't get out and none of Geno's men get in. I'm through taking chances."

Chris draws on the cigarette again, pinching it between his thumb and forefinger. He tilts his head back and takes his time to blow out the smoke. "We got complacent, Matty. We didn't think something like this could happen. We should have hit back when they shot you."

"I should have killed Geno when he stepped foot inside my parents' house."

Tommy steps up to us. I hadn't seen him arrive. "I'm still not convinced it's all on Geno. I'm telling you, Matty. Open your eyes. Sophia's hands are dirty, too. You can't let yourself admit it because you fucked around with her, but I'm telling you—she is a black widow."

"The bitch wanted you to marry her, so she'd be queen of two families. When you didn't give her what she wanted—your name and your seed—she set out to burn your house down. And after she saw you with Sherry the other night? Shit. Hell hath no fury..."

Before I take the last hit from my cigarette, I use it to light another, noticing my hands. They are steady, but not my insides. "Either one of you have a flask?"

They both shake their heads.

"I'd kill for a drink." She may never be the same. She loves to run. Now, her legs may be ruined. Forever.

"I'll run to the liquor store," Chris volunteers.

"I'll get by without it." I take a deep drag off my cigarette and catch Tommy studying me. "Okay. You may be right about Sophia." Checking my watch, I glance behind me. "That kind of surgery takes a long time."

"You said Joe and Charlene are inside?" Chris asks.

"Yes, I met them."

"I'll be back."

As the automatic doors close behind Chris, Tommy asks quietly, "You really think she's paralyzed?"

"You didn't say anything to Chris?"

"Not my place."

"Good."

I feel dead inside.

Visions of Sherry fill my mind. Her in my arms in the back seat of my limousine, my mouth on her breast. Her in my bed, her fingertips trailing across my chest, the way she crosses her ankles so ladylike—our fighting, our last kiss. Sometimes...

Tommy shakes my shoulder, pulling me from my trance.

His voice is loud and demanding. "She's going to be alright, brother." His grip on my shoulder is firm. "Look what we came through. Who the fuck would have thought either one of us would have lived through that crane falling?"

"You're right."

My friend smiles at me, but I know him well. I see the concern in his dark eyes as he goes on. "As Regina says, you've got to keep the faith."

Faith. What a foreign concept. Faith in what? The myth of a higher power? For people like me, there is no happily ever after.

Chris returns to the parking lot. "I told them to let me know when she wakes up. We have too much to do to sit here."

I rub my hand over my face, feeling the stubble. I didn't shave. "You're right. If he doesn't already, Geno will know shortly that we have two of his men, and he knows we can make them talk, so he's getting ready to strike."

I ask Chris, "Remind me. Who are his capos?"

"Guiseppe Pugliese and Fernando Piccirillo."

"Can you find them?"

Chris twists his neck with a lopsided grin. "Matty, we keep tabs on everyone."

"Have Benji and Sal eliminate those two. As soon as they can. Geno can't fight without them."

I shift my gaze to Tommy. "Blow that fucking warehouse off the map. Late tonight, or in the morning to minimize damage to civilians. I want to see a hole to China there in the morning. You two take care of that."

I butt out my second cigarette. "Have someone else get Joey and Enzo in a frame of mind to answer questions. I'm staying here until she's out of surgery and I talk to the doctors."

"Joey's mine," Chris says.

"Help yourself."

Matteo

PEEL THE ONION

Her surgery lasted—I don't know how many hours. Almost a pack full of cigarettes' worth. If anyone was keeping track, I probably paced half the distance to California waiting to hear if she would be alright. Waiting to get my hands on Joey. Hating myself for putting her in that car.

The sun was setting on the first of September when a doctor finally came down, saying she came through surgery fine. She was taken to recovery and would be there for quite a while. From recovery, she would be taken to intensive care. Since we aren't married, as long as she's in recovery or intensive care, I can't see her.

I learned from experience that patients with broken bones are moved into their rooms much sooner than victims of gunshot wounds, but the bottom line is—I can't see her for hours.

I am a wild animal in a small cage. Pacing. Smoking. Pacing.

As the sun fades, I tell the parents I have pressing business.

At the warehouse, I'm greeted with a surprise from Chris. "Giuseppe and Fernando. Not a problem anymore."

The announcement stops me dead in my tracks. I check my watch. "Already?" Chris and Tommy beam like proud fathers. "I didn't expect it that fast."

"Geno's people got complacent, too," Chris says. "They stopped bothering to vary their routines. We knew those two made happy hour every single day at the same joint in Trenton, so I sent Sal and Benji. Giuseppe and Fernando never made it inside."

Tommy offers me a drink, which I scull and I hold out the glass for another.

"The men are hot," he says as he refills my glass. "What they did to Sherry. Your men are ready for war."

My mind is still stuck in Trenton. "No family ever took out two competing capos at the same time. You may have made history."

Chris slaps my back. "You made the call. It was a good one."

A family is like an army.

No general is successful without proficient field commanders who depend on skilled soldiers. In reverse, fighting men rely on field commanders who take strategic directives from generals. We rise and fall together.

I shudder to think what I would do if I lost Chris and Tommy together. It would be... unrecoverable. Now Geno goes to war crippled.

After he loses his building tonight, my hope is he will tuck his tail and crawl back to Jersey. But I will follow that son of a bitch, and I will kill him. "Time to extract the truth from our guests."

As I step into the freight elevator, I realize, for the first time, that I wore these overalls all day. I'm dressed as a dockworker, which probably made Sherry's father more comfortable than he would have been otherwise.

I can't remember wearing overalls outside the warehouse before.

"Have either of you worked on our guests?"

"Just Joey," Chris says. "I couldn't help myself."

"Has he said anything?"

"Other than calling us all names? Not yet. But I didn't get serious. Just a few love taps, waiting on you."

I swallow my anger when I think my instinct about that kid was right all along.

This is my fault. I should have trusted my gut. Everything pointed to the driver from day one, but we cut him slack because of his father. Even Pops.

"What about Leo?" Tommy asks quietly.

"What about Leo? For all I know he's as dirty as his son."

Tommy scratches his jaw. "I don't think so." His shoulders rise. "But I didn't think that about Joey, either. You know by now he's heard about Joey, but he hasn't contacted me or Chris."

"Leo knows what his son did, so he knows what will happen."

"The man has been a good soldier for years."

I won't argue, but I'll follow my gut from now on. "I want to hear what Joey has to say before I think about Leo."

In the restroom, I splash water on my face and take a long look at myself.

The beautiful girl who loves to run may never walk again.

Staring into my own eyes, I tell myself, "You're the idiot who put her in the car with him."

Entering Joey's windowless room, I am hit by the stench of piss. Already. He'll soil himself soon. His arms are cuffed to the chain over his head, the same as Enzo, and as Chris forewarned, Joey is blindfolded.

I want to look into the little viper's eyes.

Stripping away his blindfold, I see Joey's nose is smashed and swollen, which means he can't breathe through it, so his mouth hangs open for air. His eyes are red and swollen from the broken nose, and knowing how men react in this situation, I am certain he's also been crying.

Joey doesn't know pain yet.

His gaze follows me as I pace in front of him, trying to control the rage. All I want to do is snuff the life out of him. But I need to know what he knows first. "I guess you're proud of yourself, hitting a woman with your fist. Running her down with a car. That makes you quite a man."

Joey says nothing as terror crawls across his face, settling in his dark eyes.

I bend to study this miserable, soulless piece of shit up close. "What are you afraid of, Joey? Big Man Joey."

"I didn't hit her with my fist."

I backhand him fiercely as I straighten, feeling his teeth scrape my knuckles. "That's how you hit her."

Joey was in the driver's seat. That's exactly the way he hit her. As blood oozes from his lips, I let him feel the sting of my hand across his face again... and again. I bend my knees so our eyes are even. "Now, Joey. Do you want me to run my car up your ass?"

"Please, Mr. DeVecchio."

I straighten as a cynical laugh rattles from my chest. "Did you hear that, Chris? I'm Mr. DeVecchio now. That's not what I heard you called me earlier."

"Please." Joey struggles against the shackles on his wrists and ankles.

"I think I was motherfucker earlier, wasn't I, Chris?"

"Among other things."

As a member of our family who swore Omerta, Joey knows everyone's face and voice. He'll never leave the warehouse alive, so I don't care who he sees.

"What should we do with you, Joey? The capos could turn you over to the men and let them have some fun. The men love toying with a rat. Especially a rat who hits women."

Chris grabs Joey by a fist full of hair, jerking his head back. "Remember? She's my family."

Joey's eyes widen more with visions of God knows what.

"Here's what's going to happen. You're going to lose one finger for every lie. When we run out of fingers, we will go to your toes. If I don't have all my answers by then, I will cut off your feet, your ears and your hands. One. By. One."

Piss runs down his leg as he cries like a child.

"You wanted to play in the big leagues. Now here you are, in bed with the Gabiccis."

"I'm not in bed with them."

"Who are you in bed with?"

Joey turns his head away from me.

I nod at Tommaso, who grips Joey's wrist as I move forward, reaching into my pocket to pull out bone shears.

Seeing me thumb the sharp tip of the stainless-steel rongeurs, Joey screams, "Sophia," as he tries unsuccessfully to yank his hand free from Tommy's iron grip.

My gaze snaps to the capos. "Sophia?"

Joey sobs. "Yessir, yessir."

"You're sure?"

Joey shakes his head. "No. Maybe. I don't know."

This gutless prick is so scared he's addled. He's lost his mental facilities. Useless. I take a deep breath of annoyance and blow it out. "I'm out of patience, Joey." Playing with the bone shears, I run my thumb along the razor-sharp blade. "It's fast."

He shrieks. "Put that up. I'll tell you the truth."

I wait, clasping the shears in my right hand. I've had to use them before.

Joey swallows. "A friend of mine from school... he works for Geno. I guess maybe I was complaining one day about how you've treated my dad, so he introduced me to Geno.

Geno said I should keep working for you, and he'd pay me, too, for information."

My eyes meet Chris's.

"So, you accepted Geno's money while we paid you?"

Joey's gaze hits the floor, and he nods.

I step closer, fisting Joey's hair with one hand while jabbing the point of the rongeurs beneath his chin. The sharp tip is at his windpipe. "Clarify for me, how badly have we treated your father?"

I twist the tip of the shears into his chin. Deep enough to draw blood that trickles down his neck.

Joey snarls, his eyes meeting mine. He knows I could begin his journey to hell with a soft shove, but his gaze flames. "You don't pay him shit for as long as he's worked for your family. You promoted your stupid fuck friends over him."

I push and twist the shears dangerously near Joey's windpipe, his blood sliding down the blade, as my mind shifts to her busted lip and swollen jaw.

"Matty!"

Tommy again.

I ease back. I won't end him. Yet.

I shove his head back, stepping away.

"These two men, your capos, have proven they are the best and smartest. Your father may be a good soldier, but not all men are commander material. Is he part of this?"

Leo may not be complicit in his son's actions, but if Joey thinks his old man is mistreated, that means Leo has complained about his treatment in front of his family. Who else did he complain to?

"No, no," Joey stutters. "Leave him alone. I swear."

Chris scoffs. "You swear? You expect us to believe anything you say? Your word is worth nothing. You raised your hand and swore Omerta, too."

I drag a chair to sit in front of Joey, get a whiff and pull it back. He stinks. "Start at the beginning. How did you sabotage our shipment?"

"I told Geno when I was picked to make the run to Florida."

"How did the cops know to pull you over?"

"I gave Geno the truck's make and license number. I called him after I made the pickup and again about thirty minutes before I got there. They were waiting."

Either Viggo or his snitch was in direct contact with Geno that night. "Who is the cop on Geno's payroll? This fed who was in Ann Arundel?"

He shakes his head. "I never saw that dude before. Or heard of him."

"I want Geno's phone number."

"It's private."

Chris grabs Joey by the throat, squeezing, lifting, and stretching his body against the leather restraints. Joey's face reddens as his eyes protrude. "Give me the fucking phone number."

Joey closes his eyes and squeaks out a string of numbers.

Chris shoves Joey's neck, releasing his grip, and leaves the room.

"Do you actually meet with Geno, one-on-one? Or is it a phone thing only?" I ask.

"I've met him."

"Where?"

"A building on Market Street."

Tommy and I exchange glances. "We need the address."

"I don't know. It's near Broadway." Joey snivels and wipes his face on his shoulder.

"And why is Geno spending so much time in Baltimore? His turf is north."

"I swear I don't know. Visiting Sophia, I guess, since she lives here. And he has a girlfriend here."

"What's her name?"

"I don't know." His gaze darts from me to Tommy. "I mean, really. I don't know."

"Describe her," Tommy demands.

"I only saw her once. She's about Sophia's size only a redhead."

Chris speaks as he reenters the room. "That's the one who came to the warehouse with her." He peers at me and speaks quietly. "Running the number."

I nod at Chris and ask Joey, "Did you help plant the listening devices inside our building?"

"I didn't know there were any."

I open and snap the rongeurs. "Truth, Joey."

"I swear, I swear." He shakes his head, sobbing.

"And what about Sophia? What do you know about her?"

Joey sniffs his tears and swallows. "She's like a model or actress. She's in films."

That's the first I've heard that Sophia has an acting career. Then, it strikes me. "What kind of films?"

He shrugs. "I don't know." He stares at me. "Really, I don't. Must be B films or something because I never heard of her in big movies."

"Do you know where Sophia lives?"

He averts his eyes.

"Joey!" I yell. He is trying my patience. I don't want to have to cut off his fucking appendages because it's messy as hell, and they scream and cry and flail and piss and shit. But I will. "Where does Sophia live?"

He turns his face away. "Downtown."

It's in the way he squirms and averts his eyes. I tilt my head with suspicion. "What do you know about what happened to me downtown?" I saw him for the first time a few hours before I was shot.

Joey Carbona sobs silently, his body shaking.

Trussed up the way he is, Joey can't wipe the tears that roll down his face and neck, so he weeps into his shoulder, and I know: *It was you.* You shot me." My gaze moves from Joey to the capos. "That's why I lived. Geno sent an amateur." I point at Joey. "He was nervous, shaky."

We all laugh.

"Now I'm actually glad it was you. How did you know I was there?"

Joey nods at Chris. "Blame him. When he couldn't find you to tell you about the DEA agent, he called someone and then he told Miss Drakos maybe you went to Sophia's. So, when I left, I called Geno and told him, and it was like he already knew. He gave me the address and said I should go there and stay out of sight and let him know when you arrived. So, I did."

I peer at the capos. "I knew I wasn't followed." Looking back at Joey, I ask, "You waited all that time?"

He hesitates before he confesses. "Geno promised a bonus."

I fish for a cigarette, light it, take a deep hit, and toss the pack of cigarettes and lighter to Chris. He never buys. He just bums on the rare occasions he smokes.

I aim my cigarette at Joey. "Don't guess you got your bonus when I didn't die."

Joey shakes his head.

"How much?" Just curious what I'm worth to Geno dead.

"He didn't say. He just said bonus."

Tommy steps to loom over Joey. "Was Sophia in on this?"

Joey peers up at the towering Tommaso. "She called Geno sometime, because when I checked in to ask if I should keep waiting, he said yes, that Mr. DeVecchio would be coming out soon."

Tommy rivets me with his eyes before he and Chris exchange smug glances.

This means Sophia talked to Geno before she woke me up sucking my dick. Fuck me one last time before I send you off to be killed. Jesus, she's one hell of an actress.

I'll be hearing I told you so for the rest of my life. I'll have to be man enough to take it. But I'm not fool enough to take Joey's word at face value. "We'll be back."

"What about me?" he pleads.

"What about you?"

Matteo
ONE LAYER
AT A TIME

"Anything on the phone number yet?" I ask Chris in the second floor kitchen.

"It's the Market Street building where Joey said he met Geno, near Broadway."

"What has Enzo said about Geno or Sophia?"

"Enzo hasn't said shit. I won the bet." Tommy reaches for the money on the table.

Chris slaps his bear paw over it. "You didn't win shit. He's lasted a hell of a lot longer than two or three hours."

Sometimes, they tire me. Other times, they're amusing, like watching bear cubs wrestle. "Both of you take your money back, and let's see if we can't coax Enzo into cooperating."

Entering Enzo's room, he is still in the same position, but he has fallen asleep. The unventilated room wreaks. He finally gave up and pissed himself. He is probably two of Joey, which means a lot more piss. I am sure it happened in his sleep.

The janitorial sink is equipped with a hose. I turn on the water and aim a stream at Enzo to wake him and help wash away the stench.

He jolts and shakes his head.

"I don't play games Enzo. What is your youngest son's name? Robert, I believe. You call him Bobby. He goes to school—"

"Leave my family alone!" It is the sound of a roaring lion. But Enzo is a chained lion.

I make a point to look him in the eyes as I slowly draw a pack of cigarettes from my pocket and pack them on my palm. "You didn't leave mine alone. So talk, or they will die while you sit here in chains protecting Geno."

I get nothing back but a raging stare as I light a cigarette, my eyes locked on his. I inhale and blow the smoke his way. "I said I don't play games. Your daughter is Rebecca."

He's lasted longer than any before him. Enzo has been held in that ungodly position for twelve hours and hasn't yet soiled himself. But hearing his children's names, tears fall from big Enzo's eyes, sliding down his cheeks. He begins to weep, and as he sobs, after all this time in that excruciating position, he can't stop. He loses control of his sphincter.

It almost makes me feel sorry for him, seeing him defecate on himself, shit running down his leg. The humiliation. The degradation.

But there is no room for sympathy now.

"Do you want a drink of water?"

He nods.

"Then talk. Who do you work for?"

"Gabicci."

I nod. "Good. Now, which one?"

"What do you mean which one?" He blinks at me through a veil of tears, this giant of a man.

"Sophia or Geno?"

"Alfonzo is the head of the family. Sophia is his only heir. Geno is his nephew."

I let my head tip back as a snicker escapes. "The world knows that Enzo. Who actually runs the family with Alfonzo so ill?"

"They kind of both do."

I pull up a chair and sit a few feet in front of him so our gazes are somewhat level. "What is your position?"

At his back, the capos listen, arms crossed over their chests, legs braced.

"Enforcer."

"You shot me?"

"If I shot you, we wouldn't be here."

My gaze darts to the capos. We know Enzo speaks the truth. It was Joey.

"I accept that. Now educate me on the Gabicci family, its operations, Geno and Sophia. By the way—so you know—Giuseppe and Fernando died this afternoon."

I watch the color drain from Enzo's face.

"Natural causes," Chris says from behind Enzo. He elbows Tommy. "Natural in their line of business."

"They were my friends, you fucker!" Enzo yells, glancing over his shoulder into the darkness. "You coward. Won't show me your face. I hope Geno skins you alive."

I stand and step closer despite the stink surrounding the giant. "He would be glad to show you his face. He doesn't at my request." I lean in, feeling the fire in my eyes. "This is the face you will remember when you enter hell."

Enzo spits to the side. "I'll meet you there."

"Someday. But you're going to beat me. Now, you earned yourself a slice of bread and a drink of water."

I step outside the room to reconvene with Chris and Tommy. "It's late. You need to sleep. I can finish Enzo alone."

"No one needs to be alone with Enzo, even trussed up the way he is. He is as dangerous as they come," Chris says, then looks at Tommy. "You go first. When Matty and I finish with Enzo, I'll wake you to prep for the building."

Tommy nods. "I'll blow it a couple of hours before sunrise."

"When we finish with Enzo, I'm going back to the hospital."

Chris presses his thumb and forefinger against his eyelids, shaking his head. "You have a bed here. You need to sleep, too. "

"I'll sleep there." I grab both of my friends by a bicep. "Don't get caught by those people. I lost Pio. I'm not losing either of you."

They each give my shoulder a brotherly squeeze before Tommy heads to his room upstairs.

Chris and I return to Enzo with a piece of bread and a glass of water, which I feed him because I will not unchain Enzo Accardi.

I'm fortunate I brought him down with a blow from the butt of my gun. I caught him just right because Enzo is a monster. If he got ahold of a man, he could squeeze the life out of him like a python. This is the last man I'd ever want to fight.

He eats the bread and drinks the water in silence, and I dampen a washcloth to clean and mop his face.

Chris stands behind him.

We all three have to deal with the foul odor of his shit.

"Enzo, you know you can't save yourself."

He turns his head away from me.

"But you can save your family."

Still staring at the wall, he swallows. "How?"

"More information."

His dark eyes meet mine. "What will you do for me?"

He's not in a bargaining position, but hoping to speed this along, I tell him, "I will see that your wife and your children have a comfortable widow's pension to live on."

"You can do that?"

"I can do that."

He knows there's no point in asking me to spare his life. But no man faces death easily, so he tries. It's human nature. "Can we make some kind of deal?"

"If Geno had one of my men, would he make a deal? You just said it. You hoped he'd skin my man alive, so you know what Geno Gabicci is, and you still work for him. You don't have to worry about being skinned alive, Enzo. We aren't animals like Geno."

"You swear to me on the lives of your children, you will honor our deal? You will provide for my wife and children."

Maybe this man has a soul.

"I will provide for your wife as long as she lives or until she remarries. Your children until they leave high school."

Enzo nods, pauses, and says, "She handles the X-rated film business. He handles everything else."

Son of a bitch.

"Go on."

"Sophia started Apice Productions when Geno started smuggling in refugees from the war in Asia. She realized some of the women were beautiful, so she started using the pretty ones in her porn films."

"Are some of the so-called actresses children?"

"Girls and boys."

"What does Sophia do, exactly?"

"I just know she is the powerhouse behind Apice Productions, which makes a ton of money worldwide. Sex sells."

Why did I never connect the dots before? I guess I was blinded by her beauty and her pussy, but in truth, I never suspected Sophia was smart enough to be behind their porn business.

Never underestimate your enemies, Pop has said many times.

What an incompetent I have been.

Chris and I exchange glances as Enzo goes on. "Geno set up the business of smuggling migrants and profiting from their labor. Sophia hand-picks the boys and girls for her movies. Geno sells others for farm labor. Others process the heroin he brings in."

Enzo pauses to wag his head, his gaze on the floor. "Those poor fuckers sell themselves as indentured servants to do whatever is demanded of them for years in return for safe passage to America." Our eyes meet. "They're drowning in overcrowded boats trying to get out of that hellhole, so what Geno offers sounds pretty damned good to lots of them."

"Where are Geno's drugs processed and held?"

"Jersey."

"Where?"

"He has a place on the docks."

"How does Geno get information to the police? Who does he use?"

"I think it's Sophia who does that, but I'm not sure."

"And you know all of this how?"

He shrugs. "The same way your men know you."

"I need the address of the building where the drugs are processed and held, the address where the migrants are held when they first come here, and I want to know where I would put my hands on Geno Gabicci. Give me that, and we will put you in a cell. You can sleep. You'll have a toilet and a sink, and I will provide a washcloth and towel so you can clean yourself. If I can find anything large enough, we will put clean clothes in your room."

He sobs, his chest and shoulders heaving. I don't know whether it is from gratitude or relief, shame or fear or hatred.

There is nothing pleasant about breaking a man like Enzo. He has served a family loyally for twenty years. A dutiful soldier. He meets the same fate as any prisoner of war.

As I start to leave, I have one more question. "Why were you at Sherry's apartment?"

"To get her."

"You didn't do that to her apartment?"

His ugly face squinches. "Do what? He sent me to bring your woman to him."

Chris's eyes widen. His nostrils flare as he does everything he can not to shoot Enzo where he sits. To his credit, all he does is grind his jaw.

"Bring her where?" I ask.

"I was supposed to call him when I got her, and he'd tell me where. I didn't get that far."

"Why did Geno want Sherry?"

Enzo surprises us both. Letting his head tip back, he laughs like he just heard a good joke from one of his buddies at the bar.

We stand silently, letting him laugh.

Waiting.

When he stops, he peers at me with his brow arched. "Why do you think? To fuck her. When he had enough, he'd sell her."

Rage makes the foul-smelling room spin.

"How did he know about Sherry?"

"No idea. Ask him."

My birthday was the only day I left the protection of the estate since I was shot, the only time I'd ever been anywhere with Sherry—and Sophia just happened to waltz in and see us together.

Scott told her where Sherry lived. Sophia told Geno.

He tried to take his vengeance out on me by stealing and using Sherry.

But she would never submit to Geno. He'd have to beat her unconscious first.

"I know what you're thinking," Enzo says.

I meet his gaze, which is laser-focused, studying me as he says, "She wouldn't have any choice if she's full of smack. You think those little chinks free fuck in front of cameras voluntarily? He gets them hooked, so they do what they have to do to stay high. The more they do it, the easier it gets."

Chris steps toward Enzo, and I shake my head. "Not yet." My gaze goes back to Enzo. "Who would Geno sell Sherry to?"

Enzo maintains his steady stare as all levity drains from him. "You people are clueless. How many females disappear along the East Coast every year? Geno doesn't just import people, DeVecchio. He exports them. Women. Girls. Boys."

My scalp tightens, and as I absorb it—the hair on my arms stands on end.

A moment earlier, I thought I might respect Enzo as he bargained for the lives of his family.

Now I'm tempted to leave him hanging in chains, in his own piss and shit.

I step closer, bending so our eyes are even. "You would deliver my woman to him, knowing what he would do to her?"

"It's a job."

I'm going to kill them all.

"Put this son of a bitch to sleep. But don't kill him."

Chris wraps his arm around Enzo's neck, choking him as Enzo's eyes bulge. He finally passes out from lack of oxygen.

In the kitchen, I clench my pounding forehead. This day started out bad and went downhill from there. "Have the men get Enzo in a cell and chloroform him. Leave him a toilet and towels and have someone find clean clothes for when he wakes up."

I made Enzo a promise. I'll keep it. It's not all altruistic. I don't want to have to smell his shit again tomorrow.

"Leave Joey hanging just like he is for right now, but have them hose down both rooms. I'm sick of smelling their shit. When I leave Sherry, I'll come back to finish up with Joey."

"Why not just eliminate their sorry asses now?" With one twist, Chris could have killed Enzo. Snapped his neck. He used restraint only because I asked him to.

"Christos, if I was certain they didn't have more information that we need, I would gladly let you kill him. I never suspected Geno's export operations or that Sophia was behind the porn business. What else is there? I think Joey has given us all he has, but not Enzo. He knows a lot more."

My friend looks as tired as I feel, his eyes dead, so I have to ask, "Are you okay?"

Chris runs his fingers through his hair, grips his head, and lets it fall back, his eyes closed. He takes a deep breath and shakes his head as if trying to ward off everything he saw and heard this day. "She is like my little sister, Matty. I feel responsible."

"I understand, brother. But this doesn't fall on you. I'm the one responsible. I'll call from the hospital."

Sherry
PARALYZED

"Stretch forth Your arm which is full of healing and health, and raise my daughter from this bed..." It is the soft sound of a familiar voice.

"Mom?"

My mother, a devout Greek Orthodox Christian, smiles down at me, tears glistening through her lashes. "Oh, angel. You're going to be fine now. Everything will heal." She wipes a tear sliding down her cheek.

Fear chokes me as I try to roll over to see her. "I can't move. Am I paralyzed?"

She strokes my hair. My mother's voice is reassuring. "No, dear, they don't want you to move until they have all the X-rays back."

My gaze drifts to my chest and follows my body down. My leg is in a full cast, raised high by some contraption. "But I can't move my head."

"Because you're in a neck brace. They don't want you to move."

She emphasizes *want.* That means I can move. This immobilization is precautionary.

"For how long?" *Tell me this won't last. This is miserable.*

"They'll do X-rays in the morning to decide if you can lose the neck brace. The rest, I don't know. They said you have a lot of swelling from your waist down."

"What all is broken?" A panic creeps over me again into my voice.

"Your thigh, obviously. Your hip and your neck are cracked, and you have a mild concussion. But they say, if you follow doctor's orders, you will heal."

My mind replays the shocking blow. I thought Joey had given up, that he would be afraid to follow me to the warehouse knowing Matteo was there. *Matteo.* He was watching with horror on his face. Then he was over me. I cut my eyes to see my mother. "Did you meet Matteo?"

"Yes, dear. He was here when we got here. He loves you, Sherry."

"Did he tell you that?"

She smiles with a reassurance only my mother can deliver. "He didn't have to."

Donna appears at her side, leaning over the bed so I can see her.

The two women are almost the same height, but Donna is thicker. They both have salt-and-pepper hair, but Mom's is shorter. She's worn her hair in a chin-length bob for as long as I can remember.

"Trust me, he loves you." Donna's gaze scans my body. "I expect shit like this from my son but not you. You're not allowed to scare us to death like he does."

She makes me smile, which makes my face hurt. "Do I want to look in a mirror?" I remember my head hitting the back of the car, my face scraping on asphalt.

Donna and Mother exchange knowing looks. "I wouldn't. Not right now, anyway." Mom says.

"How bad is it? Will my face scar?"

Mother's eyes are misty-sad. "I don't know, angel. You're so bruised from the blow I can't tell. I think mostly it's just scraped. You have no skin on the right side of your face."

Donna waves her hand dismissively. "Consider it a face peel. You will be as beautiful as ever soon." She turns to someone behind her. "I'm going to kill someone myself for this."

I mouth to Mom. "Who is she talking to?"

"Francesco." She mouths back.

"Francesco?" I lift my hand, and he is on the other side of my bed, smiling down at me.

"Sweet girl. Matteo asked us to stay with you when he had to leave. He had pressing business."

I smile through the pain. I know he knows about Matteo's pressing business, and Francesco knows that I know. I don't want to say anything to Mom or Donna. "Where's Daddy?"

Mom groans. "Getting coffee. You know your father. He can drink black coffee at midnight and still be able to sleep."

"So, you all know each other?"

My gaze bounces between Mom and Donna, who wraps her arm around my mother, drawing her close. "We're already fast friends. She's going to learn to drink Penicillin."

"Quit making me laugh. It hurts."

"Laughter is the best medicine, dear. Next to Penicillin." Donna winks. "Both kinds."

I can't turn my head to look outside or see a clock. "What time is it?"

Mom squeezes my hand. "It's late, angel. Get some sleep." She leans over to kiss my forehead, and I wince. "Ouch."

She squeezes my hand again and whispers, "Sweet dreams."

Yes. I rest my eyes.

"Thank you all for coming," I mumble.

I'm running with everything in me. I can't let him catch me. I don't feel tired, just desperate. Faster. Run faster.

I see Joey laughing in the car, tossing the handcuffs into my lap. His hand clenches my ankle as I climb out of the window, but I kick him. I think I kick his face, and he loses his grip on me.

The front of the DeVecchio warehouse comes into view. I'm in the parking lot as Matteo comes out of the building. He is carrying a rifle surrounded by men. All carrying rifles.

Matteo sees me. I see him. He looks relieved, and then he yells, "No!" just as I feel the impact of the bumper.

I'm flying through the air—it feels like I move in slow motion as I flip upside down. Everything happens at once. My head hits something. I'm skidding across the asphalt. Matteo is over me, calling my name. The look on his face. He is terrified. He grabs me, and I squeal. He lets me go.

Chris is over me. I hear Matteo yelling. Hollering. He is back. He wants to ride with me, but they won't let him.

The room is dark and empty when I wake up. My eyes seem to pop open. I don't know why. Maybe that horrible dream. I understand Matteo crying out, 'Pio!' He still relives that moment in his dreams, and it's been years. How long will this haunt me?

The incident with Joey plays like a horror movie on a loop in the darkness above me, over and over and over.

What could I have done differently?

I know I'm laid up for now, but I'd rather be in this hospital bed than for Joey to have gotten me inside that metal warehouse. I'm afraid to imagine what might have happened inside. Would men have raped me? Tortured me? Killed me? I had to run. I'm thankful that I could.

I'm so glad the automatic windows on the Porsche work so swiftly, allowing me to get rid of the handcuffs. I'm thankful now that Joey backhanded me. I remember listening for the dreaded click of him locking the windows as I badgered him with hateful questions. Anything to keep his mind off the windows. That would have doomed me.

I would climb out the window and run for my life all over again, even knowing he would run me down. Knowing I would end up here. Anything is better than where he was taking me.

Matteo and the men were all carrying rifles. Somehow, he'd found out. He was coming for me just as I reached the warehouse.

My gaze drifts down, and even though I can't move, I see the back of his head near my hand. He is resting his head on the mattress. I reach to touch his beautiful black hair with my fingers. I think he's deep asleep, so I rest my hand on his shoulder.

"Sherry?" He raises his head.

"I'm awake."

Matteo stands over me. In the darkness, through the dim lights of the machines, I see his eyes. "Have you been crying?"

He blinks. "Nonsense."

"You sound like your father."

"I've been with him thirty-two years. I guess I should." Matteo pulls my hand to his lips and kisses it softly. "How do you feel?"

I hadn't thought about it until he asked. I guess I'm lucky that I feel no pain. Just the discomfort of being unable to move. "I think they must have me over-drugged because I don't feel anything."

My words echo in my head. *I don't feel anything.*

The terror takes hold of me—I'm choking—and I see it move through him. His eyes instantly fill with pity.

What if Mom was lying to protect me from the truth? Tears well in my eyes. "Matteo, am I paralyzed?"

"No, baby. No." He smiles weakly.

I begin to sob silently. "Tell me the truth, Matteo. I can't feel anything."

He squeezes my hand tightly, holding it to his chest. He takes a long beat to answer, our gazes locked together. "It's too early to know, baby."

He turns his head, and I know he's been crying.

I'm paralyzed. Oh, God, no. I can't move.

Sherry
BURDENS

I jolt awake from a dream—another nightmare to see Matteo standing at my side with alarm written on his face.

"Baby, it's going to be alright." His voice is as soothing as warm skin lotion. I cut my eyes to see him. "You cried out that you are paralyzed. Don't dwell on that. I swear honesty. It's too early to know anything." He clutches his forehead with one hand, squeezes his temples, and runs his hand down his face.

"Your head hurts?"

Matteo nods. "A little."

"You haven't slept at all have you?"

"Some."

"I'm sorry, Matteo."

He smiles so sadly. "You're sorry? You have nothing to be sorry about." He kisses my hand. "I am the one who is sorry. But as Mother says, this, too, shall pass."

"Will it? Why don't I feel something, Matteo? Anything? Pain is better than nothing."

"I'm not a doctor and I haven't talked to a doctor, but logic tells me that swelling can block a nerve, and your body is badly swollen." He lifts my hand and squeezes. "You feel that, don't you?"

With this contraption around my head and neck, I can't even nod. I answer, "Yes."

He runs his warm hand under the sheet, slips it beneath the hospital gown, and strokes my stomach. "You feel that?"

I blink. I hate that all I can do is stare at the ceiling. "Yes."

His hand slides to my breast, squeezes gently, and he brushes his thumb over my nipple. "And this?" He leans over me with one brow raised and an impish grin. His little cheek dimple shows.

"Yes," I answer with a pained smile.

He removes his hand.

Dammit.

"We will get beyond this, whatever it is." He kisses my hand sweetly, looks at his watch, and says, "I need to make a phone call."

"Is Joey alive?"

My question is met with a terse shake of his head. His Cupid lips press into a straight line. "I can't talk to you about what I'm doing."

Our gazes hold. "Why not?"

"Baby, I can't. I'll use the phone over here." He disappears from my view.

I hear him talking to someone. Chris or Tommy, I feel sure. He asks, "Is everything taken care of?" A long pause. "Good... Okay. Get some rest."

He is back at my bedside.

I don't like being left out of the loop now that I've been in the loop. "Matteo, you've talked business in front of me and with me. Why—?"

He cuts me off with a frown and a head shake. "No, sweetheart. I have never discussed this kind of business with you. I never will."

As I open my mouth to protest, he shows me his palm. "My father does not burden my mother with details. I will not discuss these things, Sherry. Don't ask."

I take a heavy breath, our gazes latched together.

"It is for your own good. Do you mind if I rest here a little?"

"Of course not."

He sits in the chair beside the bed, resuming the position he was in before I woke him, with his arms folded on the mattress, only this time, he holds my hand.

"Matteo, why don't you go home and stretch out in your bed and get a good, deep sleep?"

"Because I'd rather be here."

"Then get closer, so I can touch you."

He scoots his chair closer and rests his head again, and I run my fingers through his hair, stroking his head like petting a baby to sleep. It isn't long before I hear his even breathing. Yes, he's asleep.

I can use my hands. I felt his touch. Like he said, we will get past this.

The door swings open, and the room comes to life with people whispering and mechanical noise, enough to wake me and stir Matteo, who straightens and looks over his shoulder.

He stands, and I hear him demand, "What are you doing?"

"Bringing in a patient," a man replies.

"Not into this room," Matteo barks, his protective instinct kicking in.

"This isn't a private room."

"Well, I want her in a private room." His determination is palpable.

Someone else, a woman, says, "You'll have to talk to the business office about that. This patient is assigned to this room."

A curtain swishes beside me, and I hear their noises, attending to my new roommate.

Matteo's glowers at the curtain. He looms over me, his irritation evident in his posture. "I'll be right back."

I have nothing to do but stare at the ceiling, so I rest my eyes again.

Maybe I'm still drugged...

The movement of my bed jostles me awake. Still, I see nothing but the damned ceiling.

I pass through the door frame and stare as the long fluorescent lights of the corridor pass by, one by one. I don't have words to describe how much I hate this. "What's happening?"

"Moving you to a private room," a male voice says.

"My insurance plan doesn't cover a private room," I say to no one there. I know they're there, pushing my bed and guiding me into the elevator, but I see no one. Just the damned ceiling lights.

Given my age, good health, and salary, I opted for the least expensive insurance plan the public defender's office offered.

Matteo huffed out of the room before I could explain. He doesn't understand that not everyone can afford the best.

I say again, "My insurance doesn't cover a private room."

"Well, somebody's covering it, because the charge nurse told us to move you."

After a ride in an elevator, traveling up, I could tell, I am rolled along another corridor into a new room. One that must have a window because it is much brighter here.

The nurse is young and perky, and she peers over me with a smile. "Your doctors should be on rounds shortly. They called in a specialist, Dr. Billingsly. He's the best on the East Coast."

"What kind of specialist?"

My insurance doesn't cover specialists, either.

She answers over her shoulder as she leaves the room. "A neurosurgeon."

That fear claws back. Matteo did this. He thinks I am paralyzed. He just can't say it.

When Matteo enters, he holds a vase of red roses high over my bed with a smile. "You can't enjoy them yet, but I wanted you to have them."

As he disappears from view, I guess setting down the vase, I ask, "Matteo, did you put me in here?"

"You're not staying in a room with someone else."

"Did you hire a neurosurgeon?"

He's standing over me, and I watch him draw in a heavy breath and blow it out before he answers. "Yes."

"Why?"

"To put your mind at ease. I want you to have the best."

"Matteo, please. Tell me the truth. Do you think I'm paralyzed?"

His gaze darts above me. I have never known him to lie. When his eyes come back to meet mine, he says, "Sherry, I don't know. But I will get answers. And we will fix whatever is wrong."

"If my spinal cord is severed, it can't be fixed." I cringe, hearing the bite in my voice.

He heard it, too.

"I'm sorry, Matteo."

For the first time, anger crawls all over me. I want to choke Joey. I'm mad at life. Mad at God for letting this happen. Maybe even a little mad at him. Yes, he did insist I get in that car. But my heart and my brain know Matteo thought he was protecting me.

I'm just, I don't know what to call this feeling.

Anger? Frustration? Desperation? Fear? Is there one word for all of that?

How can life change so much so fast? I'm a living yo-yo. Up. Down. Up. Down.

Matteo says, "I've spoken with the hospital. Your spine is not severed. They believe it's just all the swelling. Dr. Billingsley is here to make sure."

"Matteo, why are you doing all this? My insurance doesn't cover a private room or specialists. It will cost a fortune that I don't have."

"You're on our insurance now and what insurance doesn't cover, I will."

"I don't like imposing on you this way. It makes me feel uncomfortable."

He flashes his cunning grin. "I told you yesterday, Sherry, I'm not letting you go. I will take care of you."

Flattering, in a way. But I'm not his property. He can't not let me go if I want to go.

Before I can mount an argument, he says, "I'm sorry, but I really have to go back to work."

"Did you sleep?" I ask.

"Some."

"And you won't tell me what's going on?"

"I'm taking care of business. Now, I have a man posted outside this door. I can't spare Chris or Tommy, but unlike Joey, I know Angelo very well. We can trust him to take care of you." His eyes are still sad. "I wish I could kiss your lips, but they are swollen. Your beautiful face is raw. I can't stroke your cheek, and your neck is covered with that brace, which I hope they get off today." He kisses my hand for the umpteenth time. "This is all I can do right now. When you get out of this hospital, I will still keep my promise."

"What promise?"

"The one I made you right before we left your apartment."

It takes me a second. Oh, that one.

"Don't make me laugh. It will be a long time before you can keep that promise.

Even mad at him, I succumb to his delicious grin. "Sweetheart, I might surprise you. I'll be back."

Mom and Dad come into the new room at midday, probably during their lunch hours, each with bewildered faces. "Why are you on this floor?" she asks.

"Matteo wanted me in a private room."

"And he's paying for it?" Dad's tone is disapproving.

"Apparently. He called in a neurosurgeon, too."

"Why?" Mom asks.

If I cut my eyes, I can see them standing side by side at my bed. "He said he wants me to have the best doctors."

"That boy must love you," Dad says, standing over me with his fatherly concern.

I wish.

"Dad, Matteo would do the same for any member of the DeVecchio family if he thought his mistake caused their injury."

"I find that hard to believe." Dad snaps. "How do you feel?"

"Nothing."

Mom's temper erupts. I know the tone. "I don't know why he's called a neurosurgeon. The doctors didn't say anything yesterday about paralysis. They said you have horrible swelling from your waist down. Your pelvis is bruised, and you have a hairline fracture. Your femur is broken. They put a steel rod in it—but no one ever said the word paralysis. I promise you that."

Thank you, Lord.

She glances around. "I guess the roses are from Matteo. Where is he? We keep missing each other."

"He went back to work."

Dad's gaze narrows to a squint. "He was here in the night?"

"He stayed with me in my first room, yes. When they rolled in another patient, being Matteo DeVecchio, he got mad, huffed out and the next thing I know I'm being rolled into this private room. He just left. Why?"

Nothing. They're looking at each other.

"Dad? Why did you ask?"

"Because we heard on the radio driving over that a building not far from their warehouse blew up before daylight. The news said it looked like a natural gas explosion. Obliterated the building and everything around it. It registered like a mild earthquake."

"Wow." I force myself to keep a straight face. "Did anyone die?"

"Apparently it was empty."

"Knock! Knock!" I guess they're all trained to knock and announce before entering a patient's room.

A man walks to my bed, peers at the cast on my leg, and says, "I'm Dr. Denison. I patched you up yesterday. Checking out my handiwork."

He bends over my leg, I guess examining the cast.

Dammit, I wish I could see what is going on around me.

The doctor straightens and looms over my face. "We can take the cast off before too long. It just makes sure nothing shifts." He smiles. "You have a steel pin in your femur. No shifting."

Doctor Denison turns to Dad and extends his hand. "Brad Denison. I'm Sherry's orthopedic surgeon."

I hear Dad clasp the doctor's hand. "Joseph Drakos. This is my wife, Charlene."

"You are definitely my patient's mother." Dr. Denison says. "She has your eyes."

"Thank you." My mother is already fawning over this apparently good-looking surgeon. "Will Sherry be able to run again?"

He turns to me. "You run?"

"Sprinter. Yes."

"I run cross-country. I see no reason you won't run again. Just not anytime soon." His eyes are, like, really gray. Not pale blue. Frosty gray. And they're studying my hideous face. "Tell you what, when you can run again, I'll race you."

"I can beat you in a sprint."

He grins. "The bet is on." He turns to my parents. "Okay. Here's the deal. I've looked at her X-rays. That neck brace can come off. No break, no crack there. She has a hairline fracture in the pelvis. The femur took the brunt of the blow. I had to implant a metal rod in the marrow canal to align the two pieces. Her leg has to stay immobilized for at least a month then it will be three to six months before she can put her weight on it."

"Why can't I feel anything in my legs?" I interrupt.

"Well..." He seems to hesitate. "I'd say there is a ninety-nine-point nine percent chance your lack of sensation is because of the swelling throughout your lower extremities. You can't see, but everything from your pelvis down is swollen. As the swelling subsides, you'll regain more and more feeling."

"But you can't guarantee that, can you?"

Matteo is worried, which makes me worry.

Dr. Denison rakes his fingers through sandy brown hair, which likes to fall into his brows. "I'm sorry. There are no guarantees in injuries like this." A slow smile moves across his face and into his eyes as my heart tries to tread water so I don't drown in panic. "I just made you a bet that I can out-run you, didn't I? I'll hold you to it when the time comes."

"What do you want to bet?" I ask.

He smiles. "Hum. Good question. I'll think about it."

Matteo
ENZO'S REDEMPTION

Pop is in the den, watching the noon news, when I walk in. The news people are showing pictures of the fire as some reporter says, "Authorities say this morning's massive explosion in the Port of Baltimore was caused by a natural gas leak."

Pop's eyes leave the television and land on me. "Good work."

"Thank Tommy." I pour myself a drink, toss it back, savor its warmth, and tilt my head back to rest my eyes.

After getting Sherry into a private room, I went back and took care of Joey, then drove home to shower and change. She wasn't there—and yet she was in every room. In the hall reciting Kahlil Gibran, her little moans as we brought each other to the edge of ecstasy, her anger, our passion—another blue-eyed girl has rocked my world, twisting me around her little finger.

Somehow, I don't mind. Sherry is not Patsy. She said I am her thunderbolt. But as for the L-word? I expunged the word from my vocabulary years ago, and once removed, I can't seem to drag it back in. I prefer to show her how I feel. Love is a four-letter word that jinxes things. It is the ultimate vulnerability. I prefer to feel in control, even with her.

"You need to sleep, son," Pop says.

"I will."

"What are they saying about Sherry?"

"Nothing definitive." Belting back another drink, I make a confession. "She didn't want to go with Joey. I made her. I thought she needed a driver. A man."

"You didn't know, son."

"That's the point. I *should* have known." Resting my head in my hands, I rub the palms of my hands against my closed eyelids. "Sometimes, my failures overwhelm me. I made a fool out of myself over Patsy. I let Sophia play me. I let Joey—"

"Damn, son. Look what you just did." Pop stands, loud and animated. "You cut Geno off at the knees before the war began. He's lost his capos and his place of operation. He's done. And Joey? The little prick proved himself to be a sociopathic conman. He played everyone, including your men and your capos. Everyone who knew Joey liked and trusted him."

He walks to the windows, crams his hands into his pants pockets, and peers outside for a long moment.

Pop makes a slow turn to face me. "I need to tell you." Our gazes catch. "Leo Carbona killed his wife and himself this morning, in their home."

"Shit."

"When Leo learned what his son did, he couldn't live with it. Is the boy alive?"

I join him, peering through the window. A few days earlier, Sherry and I walked through that tall grass field under a promising summer sun. It was the first time I took her hand in mine. The world seemed so bright at that moment. "You never know what the next day holds, do you, Pop?"

"Nobody does, son."

I turn to face him. "To answer your question, Joey rests with his parents. I took care of it myself a while ago." I let the silence linger before I tell him everything. "I... kept his right hand. The hand he hit Sherry with. The hand he raised to swear Omerta. It's in the freezer. When I find out where Geno is, I'm sending it to him in a box."

Pop nods his approval. "Sometimes you have to make a point."

"Geno has to know what happens to anyone who touches one of us. I'll do the same with Enzo's hand when I finish with him, and I will not feel any remorse. He would have taken her to Geno to be raped and sold."

My father tilts his head as a small smile lifts the corners of his mouth. "You're saying she is one of us?"

Inhaling deeply, I take only a second to ponder. "You know the answer to that. Now, I need to tell you something important. I'm getting us out of the drug business."

He absorbs it with no expression. "I never wanted to be in the drug business in the first place, but we were outvoted. How will you replace the revenue?

"Our interest in the Colosimo casino, even though it is small, is... surprisingly lucrative."

"Yes. I'm aware."

A genuine grin hacks into my face despite the situation. "Allesandro is finally earning his keep."

"Do tell." With a smile, my father heads for the bar.

"Your nephew is a born politician. I've used him to make friends with, shall we say, people in high places. He heard whispers and did a deep dive on his own. Did you know, more than a hundred years ago, the Supreme Court ruled that Indian tribes are sovereign nations?"

"No." Pop sits behind his desk, his focus on me.

"Cherokee Nation versus the State of Georgia, 1830. The very next year, the high court ruled state law does not apply within Indian territories."

"What's this got to do with us? Where are you going?"

"The Seminoles are breaking ground in Florida on a high stake's bingo parlor. Pop, it is the first step toward legalized gambling on Native American reservations nationwide. I want in on the ground floor."

"What makes you think this will ever be big? It's an Indian reservation for God's sake."

"Think about it. It's one step from big stakes bingo to slots. One more tiny step to craps and blackjack. This is the beginning of legalized gambling a day's drive from home, Pop. These tribes don't know how to run casinos. We already do. And we can build them as grand as Las Vegas. Draw in entertainment.

"They're going to need advisors and partners. We get in the door before anyone else, establish relationships now, so that when the bill is passed—and make no mistake it will eventually pass—we are the family that builds and operates casinos on Native American land across the country, sharing revenue with them. Legally."

I take a seat in front of my father's desk. "Sherry and I will cultivate the relationships. You and I will negotiate the financial agreements for the partnerships while Allesandro makes sure the bill gets through Congress. We won't have to look over our shoulders for DEA agents any longer."

Pop raises his glass high. "Brilliant." He beams like a proud father, which warms my heart. This feels like a victory—a load lifted.

Fuck Viggo Johansen.

Pop leans back in his chair. "Now, what about Geno? I want to know everything you learned from Joey and this other guy. You say Enzo Accardi is still alive?"

"For a while."

It is satisfying to see the smoldering remains of Geno's warehouse. Where Joey tried to take Sherry.

Tommy obliterated it. I should have had him do that as soon as I learned about the bugs and the Gabiccis listening to us from inside. But I didn't.

Like I didn't act on my gut about Joey.

"Where's Tommy?" I ask, entering Chris's office. "I want to congratulate him. Damn good job."

Chris chuckles. "Man, you should've heard it. I'm surprised it didn't knock out our windows—I mean, the earth shook."

"Where is he?"

"He went home to see Regina and the kids and sleep. After I told him what Enzo said, Tommy said he wanted to go hug his kids."

"He deserves the rest. So do you. You two made history yesterday. Pop said to congratulate you."

"Thanks. How's Sherry?"

"Not much change," I tell him. But the more I think about her words and her expression, the more my gut tells me there is a change. She's beginning to blame me. I saw it in her face. Heard it in her tone.

Okay, blame me, but I don't understand her resistance to letting me help her.

"Hey," Chris draws me back, squinting like he's studying me. "About Sophia. Tommy and I were talking. Snake that she is, she's still female. Like your dad warned once, taking a woman out may not play well."

"Do you think I care how anything plays with anybody after what they did? What Enzo revealed? Sophia gets no immunity just because she has a pussy."

Chris leans his forearms on his desk. "Are we going after their territory?"

I hadn't thought about it, but now that I do? "No. First, we don't have the manpower to control Jersey. It would be a constant fight with one family or another. I don't want anything Gabicci has. I just want to live in peace with what is ours. And by the way—that was our last drug shipment."

Chris has SHOCKED stamped on his forehead—or what's left of it, with his blonde brows crowding his hairline.

I chuckle and repeat. "We're out of the drug business."

"Why? It's pretty fucking profitable." Chris plops into his desk chair, looking like I just kicked a kitten.

"Some things aren't worth the risk, no matter the profit. Geno sicced Johansen onto us and you know what that means. He's a bloodhound that never lets up. I can't speak for you, but I don't ever want to see the inside of a prison."

Taking a seat, I remember the first night the highway patrol pulled over our truck. That night changed everything.

"I haven't spent the past few weeks sitting around the house playing gin rummy. There are other means of supporting this family that won't send us all to the pen. I'll go into detail later. In the meantime, Geno's underground. What are we doing to find him?"

"I told you. We've got button men on the streets in three states. No one has seen him. Word is, he's out of the country."

My gut says no. This time, I'm listening to it. "Let's pay Enzo another visit."

Enzo Accardi is a sad sight, back on his chains, but he is clean and in fresh clothing—rested. He is a doomed man, and his dull eyes show that he knows it. "I have something else to offer," he says when he sees me.

"In exchange for what?"

"Forgiveness, maybe."

"I'm not the forgiving type." I pull up a chair and take a seat in front of him.

"Not you. God," he says.

"That's between you and Him. Why drag me into it?"

"I can tell you who owns the property I heard blow up this morning. I don't think you'll ever learn names without my help. With what I give you, you can end it all."

"What does their landlord have to do with anything?"

"Maybe everything."

Involuntarily, my head tilts as I try to discern his meaning.

He sees he piqued my interest.

"What do you want in exchange?"

"Double the pension for my wife."

I roll that around in my mind. There are more layers to this onion than I knew. How many more? If I don't play, I won't find out.

"I'll match your current salary. That's all I am willing to do."

Enzo nods. "That's a hell of a lot more than double the widow's pension."

"Okay. Who owns that property? What is the connection to Geno?"

"It's owned by a company called Horizon Enterprises."

Chris snarks. "We established that already."

"But you don't know who that is, do you?" Enzo smirks with his new sense of power. "You will find too many layers of paperwork to ever learn the names of the owners."

"Shoot," I say.

"Horizon Enterprise is a silent partnership that exists to protect the Gabiccis and enrich three men."

I nod, prompting.

"You will find the warehouse in Jersey is also owned by Horizon. And the building on Market Street and all the holding houses."

"Keep talking."

"Why do you think the DEA is suddenly on your ass? Because Geno wants your territory."

"Cut to the chase. Who's helping him?"

"He has friends in high places. Friends who share..." Enzo tilts his head with a nasty grin. "The same tastes, if you get my meaning."

"I do."

"Among other things, they selectively funnel information about everyone but Geno to law enforcement. In return, the Gabiccis rent all of their properties from Horizon exclusively. You take care of my needs. I'll take care of yours."

"Johansen?"

"He eliminated Colosimo, didn't he? He gave Geno one less competitor."

"Viggo Johansen is Horizon?" I ask.

Enzo scoffs. "Johansen is a stooge. Someone in Horizon gets information to him under the guise of being a 'confidential informant,' leaving a trail of evidentiary breadcrumbs that lead the hapless Johansen, like Hanzel and Gretel, straight to Geno's competitors. Colosimo being a perfect example."

"Spit it out. Who are the people in Horizon Enterprises?"

Enzo squints. "You swear you will take care of my family."

"My word is good."

"Scott Buchanan, a Baltimore prosecutor."

My skin crawls. "And?"

"Richard Kerrigan. An aide..."

"I know who he is. And?"

"Congressman Don Mulholland."

My heart drums inside my ears. Sherry made that connection—she just didn't know what she had. None of us did.

"So, Geno and Sophia make sure these guys have all the fresh, free tail they want, they rent their properties exclusively from Horizon and in return Horizon funnels information to Geno's competitors to eliminate them one by one?"

"Exactly. And they're all getting rich along the way."

"How are they connected to each other?"

Enzo's eyes flash as if an idea takes form. He thinks he might have another bargaining chip.

I shake my head. "I've given all I'm giving, Enzo."

He shrugs. "Guess I have to draw you a picture. Any idea where Robert Kerrigan grew up?"

I shake my head.

"Donald Mulholland?"

"No. And I don't like guessing games."

"Mulholland and Kerrigan. Dumbass. Irish. Both of their fathers were part of the Westies."

"New York. Hell's Kitchen." Tommy says.

When I was young, Pop and Antonio talked about how the Westies worked closely with the Gambino and Genovese families.

"Alfonso Gabicci grew up with Donald Mulholland's father, Conor," Enzo says.

"Which means Donald and Geno kind of grew up together," I finish.

"Bingo. Think about it, DeVecchio. How do you know your capos?"

"We grew up together."

"Exactly. Alfonso and Conor figured out a way to groom and install a mob member in Congress: Donald Mulholland. Kerrigan's old man, Liam Kerrigan, was also part of the Westies. May he rest in peace."

Enzo snickers, his arms still stretched high, cuffed to the chain, knowing he will soon meet his maker. "It has never ceased to amaze me, DeVecchio, how people put such blind faith in their elected officials. The public thinks we're corrupt? Most of the fuckers running this country are more depraved than any of us ever thought about being. They just manage to hide behind the law."

Sherry
UNEXPECTED VISIT

I wish they would hurry up and take this neck brace off me. It is so miserable to lay here, wide awake, staring at the ceiling, unable to move my neck.

I hear a quick, loud rap of knuckles at my hospital door, and a second later, who looms over me but Viggo Johansen, holding out a vase of flowers. Flowers and Viggo. Incongruous, like a cactus rose. I've never understood why God put such a pretty flower on such an unfriendly plant. He says, "Sorry you're laid up," and the man of many words disappears, I assume, to set the vase of big orange and yellow blossoms somewhere.

He is the last person on Earth I expected to see, and he spoils his surprise of fresh flowers as only he can, jerking his thumb over his shoulder toward my door. "Nice guard dog. Who does he belong to?"

"What are you doing here, Viggo?"

"I heard about your accident." His blue eyes roam across my battered face and drift to my leg. I am sure now that Viggo is a descendant of Leif Ericson as he hovers over me, obviously recognizing that all I can do is stare straight up. "Thought I'd offer my condolences."

Even though my eyebrows are embedded in the warehouse parking lot, the skin where they once were pulls tight. "You? Condolences? Really?"

He grins. "I'm not a total dick. How are you?" With his imposing size, blue eyes, and fair skin, Viggo could not look more different than Matteo.

"Look at me, Viggo."

The smile widens. He releases an apologetic sigh. "Yeah, stupid question. I heard you left the public defender's office."

"They won't miss me. Public defenders are a dime a dozen."

"Private practice?"

"You could say that."

Slowly, his smile dissolves like Kool-Aid powder in water, his face becoming a deep shade of raspberry. Viggo shuts his eyes, tips his head back, and mutters, "Fuck me. The guard on the door. You didn't. You didn't go to work for DeVecchio."

Hum. How do I say this? "I... represent one client."

Viggo's eyes narrow. "He'll drag you down with him."

"I don't know who you're talking about."

He clamps his mouth together and looks away from me, blows out a huff, and takes in an equally big breath, his gaze meeting mine. "I went to your office a while back. Thought I'd take a chance and ask you out. They said you didn't work there anymore. Then, out of the blue, in the courthouse today, I hear you were the victim of a hit and run. So, I called the hospital, and they said you were a patient. I brought flowers—idiot that I am."

"Well, thank you, for the thought, Viggo. I'm sorry I don't live up to your standards."

"I'm Matteo DeVecchio. You are?" That was a little louder than normal.

I still can't turn my head. *Dammit!* I can't see—but Matteo's anger is unmistakable in his voice.

I cut my eyes. He's near enough that I can see him glaring at Viggo's six-foot-some-odd-inch frame standing beside me.

Viggo stiffens, his face turning as cold as a February night before he turns to face Matteo. "I'm Viggo Johansen."

After an uncomfortable silence with the two of them staring—rather glaring—at each other, Viggo adds, "I stopped by to check on the lady. I heard about her accident."

Noticeably, neither man offers the other his hand. Matteo steps farther into the room, but Viggo doesn't leave my bedside.

Matteo says, "What happened to Sherry wasn't on the news."

"I hear things."

"Do you." That wasn't a question.

Neither man breaks his stare until Matteo asks with icy politeness, "Anything more we can do for you, Viggo Johansen?"

Matteo knows Viggo wants to send him to prison, and Viggo is finally getting his first long look at the man he's after. Neither is ceding ground, and my stomach is in a twist, wondering who is going to hurl who out the window and how far it is to the ground.

Neither moves until Viggo gives his head the tiniest shake with his chin jutted. "Nope. Just came by to extend my condolences."

"With flowers." *Oh, Lord. The bite to his words.*

"Yeah. With flowers." Slowly, Viggo turns from Matteo to me. "See you, Sherry. Hope you get well soon."

When Viggo leaves, Matteo closes the door and stalks to glower down at me. "I thought you two hated each other."

"I was as surprised as you were."

"I don't like it."

"Matteo, I don't think he came here about you. He didn't know about us. He said he went to the public defender's office to ask me out—"

"I'm sure he did."

I know jealousy when I see it. I can't resist the urge to gig him, just to keep him on his toes. "You don't like other men being my friend?"

"No."

"Are you jealous?"

"Yes."

It makes me smile.

Matteo changes subjects. "Can I kiss you now?" He asks it like he's still mad.

If I could laugh, I would. My face hurts less than it did yesterday, so I don't try to stop the smile from spreading like wildfire. "Please. Gently."

He ventures closer. "Forehead or lips?"

"Lips."

Matteo plants a feather-soft kiss on my mouth, holds it, pulls away, and whispers, "I'm so sorry."

I'm not sure why that infuriates me. But it does.

"Stop saying that, Matteo. It's not your fault."

"But it is."

"I don't want to hear it." The chill in my voice makes me shiver. It surprises me—and him.

That bad feeling from earlier shifts into overdrive. The anger revs in my chest. "Are you doing all of this—the private room, specialists, flowers because you feel guilty? Because you feel responsible?"

"I don't *feel* responsible, Sherry. I *am* responsible. You didn't want to get in the car with..."

I cut my eyes away from him as my heart drums furiously. "I don't want your pity or your charity."

He drags his fingers through his thick, wavy black hair. "You can blame me, Sherry. I accept it. But I don't understand your anger at me for trying to take care of you." He squeezes my hand with a little shake. "Look at me."

Reluctantly, a little angry and hurt, I obey and meet his gaze. I wish he would just say he's doing it because he loves me.

Why is that so important to you, Sherry? I don't know. Maybe it's because I can accept kindness out of love, but kindness out of guilt or pity feels very different. *Why can't he say it?*

My logic answers. Simple, stupid. Because he doesn't feel it. Why is that so hard to believe? You told him you loved him. He never said it back.

Maybe because I fell in love with him at first sight. He already did that with Patsy. He admitted he ran from the feeling like a frightened child when our eyes met. Even if he thought he loved me, Matteo would fight it. I don't know. It's... everything.

Those damned tears sting the back of my eyes.

This time, Matteo softly runs his fingertips across my eyelashes, wiping away the moisture. "Shh. Why do you think I'd rather sleep in a chair beside you than at home? Because your presence soothes me. I go home, and it's empty. You aren't there, and yet you're everywhere. Why is it so bad for me to want to take care of you?"

Dammit to hell! Just leave it alone. I blink through tears. "They're taking off my neck brace. I'll be able to sit up and move my head freely soon."

"When?" His relief is contagious.

"I thought they'd be here by now. What time is it?"

He checks his watch. "Six-thirty." He freezes. "Where's your Rolex, Sherry?"

I hadn't thought about it. "I have no idea." My Rolex. My parents scrimped to give me that watch when I got my law degree. "Oh, Matteo, my Rolex."

"I'll find it. Have you seen Dr. Billingsley yet?"

"How will you find it?"

"I'll ask around. The ambulance, emergency room, hospital. Our parking lot. If I can't find it, I'll replace it."

"It's too much. And I want the one they gave me. My parents saved to give me that."

"I'll move heaven and hell to find it for you. Now, what about Billingsley?"

"He ordered X-rays. They're supposed to send them to him."

"Still no feeling in the legs?" His eyes are hopeful.

"No, but Dr. Denison said there's a ninety-nine-point nine percent chance I will get the feeling back and run again. He said he runs cross-country. He said he'd race me when I can run, which made me want to laugh because I could kill him in a sprint. Cross country guys jog. They're in it for the long haul."

Matteo's brows shift high on his forehead. "Another suitor?"

"Don't be silly. He's the orthopedic surgeon who put the pin in my leg."

"Sherry. Baby. Doctors don't race their patients. Men do. He's hitting on you. Like Viggo."

Before I can ask him if he's jealous again, a nurse raps on the door and sings out her call, "Knock! Knock! We're here to get that neck brace off. Are you ready?"

"Oh, please, yes."

"I'll wait outside." Matteo kisses my lips again. "I'll be back."

"Better. Much better." He smiles when he returns.

My bed is raised so I can sit somewhat straight, turning my neck from side to side because I can. I am so relieved. If I could, I would skip.

I never knew what a simple pleasure it is to be able to turn your head, roll your neck, and shift your shoulders.

I will never again take my mobility for granted. Now, I'm just waiting on the legs. Praying, actually, about the legs.

Matteo holds up my overstuffed suitcase like a trophy. "I didn't know if you wanted or could wear anything you crammed in here, but I thought it was of better use with you than in the back of the truck I'm driving." He places it against the wall. "I had your apartment packed up and cleaned out. Everything has been moved to storage. You'll decide what to do with everything on your own time."

"Thank you, Matteo."

"Sherry, we've slept together in more ways than one." He slides his hand under the sheet, finding my stomach again, grinning devilishly. "Don't you think it's about time you called me Matty, like everyone else in the family?"

"I don't know. I've called you Matteo for so long, it seems natural."

He grins. "Well, I'll answer to whatever you call me."

"Will you do me a favor?"

He twists his neck and tilts his head cautiously, waiting.

"My purse was in the Porsche. Did you find it?"

"I tucked it inside your suitcase. For some strange reason, I didn't feel like walking through the hospital with your flowery purse slung over my shoulder." He heads that way.

"It has all my identification the hospital needs. And I need my hairbrush, please. I'd like to brush my hair. And my teeth. And wash my face. All of that is in the suitcase."

He winces. "I don't know about the face. It's... kind of raw. It might hurt to rub a washcloth over it."

"Mirror, please." I hold out my hand.

He digs in the suitcase and holds my hand mirror just out of reach. "Remember, you are beautiful, and it will heal." It all feels perfectly domestic.

After one glance, I drop the mirror like a hot frying pan and groan. "Oh, no." I want to cry. I am disfigured. My forehead is big and blue, and my skin is removed from the right side of my face. "Mom was right. She told me to wait."

"Baby, it will all heal." He glances at the door. "Where is your mother?"

"She and Dad came at lunchtime but they both have to work. Everybody has to work. It's not like I'm going anywhere."

"I don't like you being alone."

"Matteo, Angelo is still at my door. Viggo noticed."

"If Johansen wasn't a cop, I'd have shoved Angelo up his fucking ass."

I want to ask him what he's learned and how things are going, but he said he won't talk to me about what he's doing. It's all over the news; I heard nurses talking about the warehouse explosion, but he hasn't said a word about it.

That anxiety washes over me again. The feeling of being shut out. Stuck in this bed. And I still don't know if I will ever walk again. But he is right here, doting on me. He soothes my soul.

Matteo
WIGGLE ROOM

Summer has bowed to fall. As surely as the changing of the season and the falling of summer leaves, Sherry has steadily... changed. She has grown more and more irritable. Short-tempered. I tell myself it is understandable.

She is trapped in the hospital bed, chafing at not knowing her future. Not knowing if she will ever walk again. Entering her room each day, I never know if I will be greeted by the Sherry I adore or the cryptic Sherry who is growing increasingly discontent and distant.

"Matteo, guess what!"

She is wearing the biggest smile I have seen since the day she was so excited about tracking Sophia. *Thank fuck.*

She wants to squeal and jump up and down, but she can't. "Look!" She points at the foot of her bed as I approach. "Now watch." The sheet moves over her feet. "I can wiggle my toes!" Sherry spreads her arms wide. "Oh, Matteo, I can wiggle my toes!"

Tears flow down her face as I grab her and press her face to my chest, breathing my own sigh of relief. "Thank you, Mother Mary," I whisper with my gaze to heaven.

If I feel this relief, think what she must feel.

The skin on her face has healed nicely, so I plant a triumphant kiss on those beautiful lips and take in that gorgeous face. "Congratulations, sweetheart. You *will* run again."

"Yes!" She beams. "And when I do, I will leave Brad Denison in the dust."

"Brad Denison?"

"The doctor. Remember? My surgeon, who said he'd race me."

My pulse quickens. "Forget him."

Her cheeks flush as she straightens her shoulders. "Matteo, I can race him if I want to."

"No, sweetheart. You cannot."

Lightning flashes inside those crystal blue eyes. "Matteo DeVecchio, you don't possess me. You can't control me."

The hell I can't.

"He has no place coming onto a patient. It's unprofessional. Besides, you said I'm your thunderbolt. You shouldn't want to race him."

She tilts her chin high and twists her head with defiance, a bite in her voice. "Racing him and fucking him are two different things."

My eyes flare wide, stunned by the bitterness in her voice. It is so unlike her.

"If you are my woman, you don't cavort with other men."

"Cavort?" She snickers. "You mean I can't have male friends?"

Denison doesn't want to be your friend, sweetheart. But I didn't come here to argue. I redirect. "Look what I found." I dangle her Rolex watch in front of her face.

"Oh, Matteo!" She snatches it from my hand with a glorious smile. "Where did you find it?"

"They took it off of you in the emergency room but somehow it didn't make it to your room. It languished and was forgotten in the business office until I rattled their cage."

She hugs my neck tightly. "Thank you so much." She slips the watch on her wrist with a grand smile.

She will return to her old self now that she knows she will walk again.

"When can you go home?" I want her back in my bed. We can hold each other again, even if we can't make love. Sleep together. She will be there when I wake in the morning and get home from work.

"They want me to do one week of rehab before I go home. Then I think I'll be released."

"I can't wait."

I drive from the hospital to my parents to spread the good news.

"Sherry has regained feeling in her legs and feet! She will be home in a week. When I get a hard date, what do you say we throw her a welcome home party?"

If there is one thing my mother loves, it's a party.

"Oh yes! Of course!" She claps her hands together. "Shall I plan it?"

"No, I want to this time."

Unless you count college and kegs, I've never thrown a party. This isn't that kind of party.

"Who do you want to invite?" Mother asks.

"Her friends. I'll get a list from her parents and Chris. Plus, all of us, of course."

"Decorations?" Mother's eyes twinkle.

"Okay, Mother, you can handle decorations. But I want it to be a surprise. And I want it to be festive and feminine, like her. Pink and peach flowers and balloons and a pretty welcome home sign. Even if it's fall, Sherry embodies spring to me."

Since my birthday, every day has felt like walking barefoot on nails. We woke up to our fight and found her apartment trashed; Joey kidnapped her and crippled her. She was in the hospital, none of us knowing if she would ever walk again.

What a huge relief this day has been. It feels like the first day of the rest of my life. Finally, we can put the past behind us and move forward.

She will recuperate at my house and use my office to do her work. When she is well, we will begin working together, establishing relationships with the Native American tribes, and traveling the country together.

I see a future for us.

"What's the latest on the Gabiccis?" Pop's question yanks my thoughts away from Sherry.

"Chris hears Geno may have retreated overseas—sought refuge with family in Europe or even be in Asia." I run my hand over my face, squeezing the bridge of my nose with my thumb and forefinger. "I'm not convinced."

"Why?"

The corners of my mouth drag down with a mind of their own. "It's just not Geno's style. No. He's skulking around here somewhere, waiting to strike back."

"With what? He lost his capos and local warehouse."

"Pop, you taught me not to underestimate my enemies. Geno hasn't given up. I feel it in my bones."

"What about the woman?"

"Sophia?" I shift my shoulders. "When it comes to her, obviously my gut doesn't work. I mis-judged her every step of the way. I thought she really wanted to get married. I never could fully accept what you and Chris and Tommy kept saying, that she set me up. But she did."

Pops leans on his forearms. "You know where they're processing the heroin and where they hold the immigrants. Why haven't you hit them?"

"Hit them and do what?"

Pop clomps his glass of sherry on his side table. "Destroy his drug labs and set the enslaved migrants free."

"That's all on Geno's turf. And he has cops on his payroll. No, too risky." I rub my hands over my tired eyes. I haven't slept well all this time. "When a cohesive plan comes to me, I'll act."

"You're distracted. With Sherry."

I scull a drink and concede, "Yes." My gaze meets my father's. "I have been mentally paralyzed by the fear that by putting her in my fucking car with Joey, I rendered her physically paralyzed for life." I have to glance away. "Shit, this has been the hardest fucking month of my life."

"No, son. You lived through that crane accident."

"That was me, Pop. This is different, worrying that my actions ruined someone I care so much about."

"But you know now, that didn't happen. She will walk and run again. Soon, she will walk through that door, right into this house to a welcome home party."

 Matteo
A BIG GAMBLE

In the weeks since Joey hit her with my car, Sherry's face has healed. She is unscarred, as beautiful as before.

She has been pushing herself, like she does, working out in the hospital rehab every day since she regained feeling in her feet.

Today, she is coming home, albeit on crutches.

But my girl will recover completely.

I look forward to telling her about my plans to work with Native American tribes and how she can help our family establish a lucrative new legal revenue stream.

Still, the capos have nothing to report on Geno or Sophia. Everyone seems to believe they are out of the country.

Somehow, I don't think so. I have not released the gate guards to return to regular duty.

Pop convened an early meeting in his office to brief everyone on our new direction.

Allesandro is in attendance, and I let him lay the groundwork.

Antonio asks the first question. "Do we have any data, any reason to believe casinos on native American land will draw people? Will Americans be willing to travel to these reservations to gamble? How long until we recoup our initial investments?"

I let Allesandro answer. "If these casinos are advertised effectively, and they will be, we believe people will come in droves. Think about it. Americans have never been able to sit at a table, drink scotch, and legally play blackjack without buying a plane ticket to Vegas or Jersey and spending their savings on high-end hotels. This way, they'll be able to drive from home, gamble, and go home."

Antonio squirms in his seat. "What you described the Seminoles building is nothing more than a glorified bingo parlor."

Pop and I exchange glances. Time for me to speak up.

I stand. "Allesandro and I have done the homework. It will be evolutionary, yes. But we have confidence, as other nations see how bingo profits the Seminoles—how they're able to improve their roads, build schools, even hospitals because of what you call a glorified bingo parlor, one by one they will want in. Then they'll want slot machines. Who owns the slot machines? We do."

Pop ventures in. "They'll want everything Vegas has." I've kept him up to date on everything Allesandro and I learned. Pop tells them, "This is a long-term investment. It is the future. Within a decade native American casinos will be spread coast to coast."

He peers around the room, gauging the expressions, and stands. "Think of Coca-Cola. No soft drink company has ever been able to top them because they were the first one in. If we start now, the DeVecchio family can secure the rights to run the gaming in native American casinos nationwide. And we can all sleep peacefully at night."

Chris and Tommy exchange their customary glances, smile wide, and high-five each other. "Hell, yeah," they say together.

"Where do we start?" Chris asks.

I feel a relief I haven't felt in a long time. This feels right. Everybody is in.

Illegal drugs are the past. Gaming is the future.

Viggo Johansen will disappear because there is nothing for him to find anymore.

Geno and Sophia don't pose an immediate threat.

And Sherry is coming home. At last, all is right with the world.

Arriving at the hospital, my throat tightens. Her room is empty. The bed is empty. Her suitcase is gone.

At the charge nurse's station, I ask, "Where is Sherry Drakos?"

"Doctor Denison took her down to rehab while her parents are checking her out," the woman says.

Denison. The fucker who wants to 'race' her. Race. I'll bet. "Where's rehab?"

"Second floor."

Punching the down button on the elevator, when the door opens—who stands there but Viggo-fucking-Johansen. We each stare, stunned until he steps off the elevator, and I get in.

Neither of us wastes our breath.

Has he been coming here to visit her, and she never told me?

My heart drubs. This isn't what I expected.

The elevator opens, and a sign on the corridor wall aims an arrow to the right, pointing to Rehab Services.

Marching through the glass doors—there she is, sitting in a wheelchair, giggling with some man with sandy brown hair who is too fucking close—*to her.*

He puts his hand on her forearm.

I walk up to them.

"Matteo!" She smiles, seeing me. "This is Doctor Denison."

The doctor and I shake hands, maybe a little too hard and too long.

She notices.

Releasing my hand, Denison nods at Sherry. "She's excited about the next phase of her recovery. I've arranged for her to go into a facility in Raleigh that specializes in getting athletes back to full performance after traumatic injuries like hers."

My gaze moves from the asshole to Sherry. "You didn't tell me about this."

"He's just telling me about it." She is as happy as a puppy getting its first biscuit.

I shake my head, trying to control the anger. "You're not going to Raleigh. You're coming home with me."

Her face scrunches into a question.

"Baby, I've made arrangements, too." She doesn't know—the welcome home party awaits her at my parents' house.

Everyone will be there, including her parents, who I didn't know were checking her out. Her friend Tina is there with Chris. Her aunts and uncles and people from her former work. I can't tell her. It's a surprise.

"If you want specialized rehabilitation, I'll have the specialists come to you. You don't have to go to Raleigh."

"But Matteo—"

I hold up my palm. "No."

"Matteo," she insists.

"No. I'm here to take my girl home." I lock eyes with this doctor who wants to steal my woman. "A word, Doctor Denison." I step away, lowering my voice. "If you're as wise as a surgeon should be, you won't put your hands on her again."

He replies in an equally hushed tone. "I don't see a ring on her finger. Who the hell do you think you are?"

I lean closer. "I don't think. I know. I'm Matteo DeVecchio. You touch her again and you will never perform another surgery. Unless you can grow new hands." Our gazes hold, and I can tell no one has ever spoken to him so bluntly.

Before he can speak and say something stupid, I tell him, "I'm a man of my word."

Denison looks from me to her. "Sherry, we'll talk later." He turns his back and stalks away.

The fuck you will. I want to shove my fist into his upturned nose.

Instead, I maintain control, telling Sherry, "Your room is empty. Are you ready? Your parents have checked you out."

Her eyes are angry as she nods.

She's fuming.

She'll get over it when she sees the party waiting.

I thought she would be so excited to get out of the hospital and come home. To sleep beside me tonight. I've wanted her back in my bed every night since we were together. My birthday feels so long ago.

Instead, in the car, she broods and finally unleashes. "What did you say to Doctor Denison?"

I cut my eyes at her. "I told him not to touch you again."

She covers her face with her hands and shakes her head. "Matteo! How embarrassing. He's my doctor. He didn't do anything wrong."

"He's trying to seduce you. You're not his to touch."

She closes her eyes. "You don't own me."

"You said you love me. If you love me, you don't want other men to touch you."

"Matteo—do you think because you have done all of these things for me that I'm your possession? You can't dictate to me where I can go or what I can do or who can be my friend." Her beautiful face is contorted with anger.

"He doesn't want to be your friend, Sherry." And neither does that fucking cop.

She purses her mouth and clams up, staring out her passenger window.

I won't lose my temper.

She's just frazzled after her injuries and being in the hospital for so long.

A minute later, she asks, "Where are you going?"

"I'm taking you home, sweetheart."

"I don't live with you, Matteo. My parents are expecting me to stay with them."

"We discussed it."

Her brows shoot high as her eyes become blue frisbees. I think they are about to spin. "You discussed where I'm going to live—with my parents? Not me?" She's shrieking.

She keeps surprising me.

I take my eyes off the road to meet hers. "I thought you loved me, Sherry. I thought you wanted to be with me."

"Dammit, Matteo, I do love you. But you don't love me. And I'm not about to live with a man who wants to own me. Possess me. But doesn't love me. I'm not chattel."

"Actions speak louder than words. I've shown you how I feel."

"Oh, yes," she sneers. "Your sense of responsibility and your guilt is abundantly clear. But I'm not your burden or responsibility. I never was." Her body trembles with rage. "I didn't ask you to do all those things for me. I didn't have to have a private room. Guards at my door."

I can't drive and have this conversation.

I wheel the new Mercedes into a parking lot and put it in park. "What has changed?"

I'm not sure I know this woman beside me.

The waters of Lake Bolsena boil as her lips pinch together tightly. Finally, she looks away and says, "I want to go to my parents' house."

Stunned would be an understatement as I feel the muscles in the back of my neck and shoulders tighten. "Your parents are waiting for us at my parents' house."

She whips her head around, facing me. "Why?"

I reach for her, but she pulls back, her shoulder pressing against the passenger door—she wants as far away from me as she can get.

My fuse ignites.

Haven't I been here for her every step of the way?

She doesn't care what I've done, how I've become a contortionist trying to take care of her. How I dream about her at night, reach over wanting to touch her, pull her to me, but she's not there.

Who has she become?

With my hands clenching the steering wheel, I answer her question. "Why are your parents at my parents' house? Because I have a fucking surprise party waiting for you."

I slam the Mercedes into gear and look over my shoulder before getting back on the road. "Just get through the party. When everyone leaves, I will take you wherever the fuck you want to go. I'll take you back to Denison if that's what you want."

He can have you.

We drive in silence, my heart pounding like a marching band, until she places her hand on mine. "I'm sorry, Matteo."

Right now, I don't care. She'd rather be with her parents than me? Have at it.

She whispers, "I'm sorry, Matteo. Please, look at me." Inhaling deeply, I cut my eyes at her as she says, "I said, I'm sorry. I just... don't like being dictated to."

"So noted, sweetheart. I'm sure your parents won't dictate to you."

I never dreamed this was how we would end.

Like an idiot, I let myself believe. Again.

What. A. Fucking. Fool. I didn't see this coming.

She doesn't have to draw me a picture.

She's got Viggo-fucking-Johansen stalking the halls of the hospital for her and an orthopedic surgeon drooling. Suddenly, I don't shine much anymore.

"Colpo di fulmine," she whispers, stroking my hand.

And that does it. I jerk my hand away.

I would pound the steering wheel until it bent—but I will not give her that pleasure.

I won't look into those blue eyes again.

With my gaze on the road and both hands on the wheel, I tell her, "You don't know what it means."

Sherry

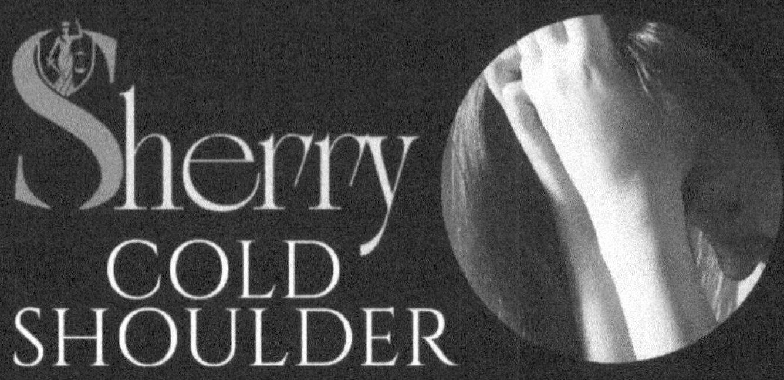

COLD SHOULDER

He won't look at me. I wounded him more deeply than I imagined. I didn't mean to. I try one last time as we pull up to the gate. "Matteo, I wish you would look at me."

He doesn't.

"I'm... *sorry.*"

"You have made that abundantly clear." The ice in his voice as he throws my words back at me makes me shiver.

We drive through the gate, and Matteo stops the car where my feet will step onto the sidewalk leading to his family's front door. Even in his anger, he is considerate of my needs. Matteo walks around the back of the car, gets my crutches from the back seat, opens my door, and holds them out for me, stepping aside as I get them under my arms.

I don't attempt conversation again. I have experienced his passion, withered under his fire, and now he is freezing me out. There is no lukewarm with this man.

I make my way to the front door, with him walking beside me. Escorting me, good gentleman that he is.

Finally arriving at the oversized front door—the long walk being more of a struggle than I anticipated—Matteo rings the doorbell, opens the front door, and steps aside as everyone yells, "Surprise!"

I'm overwhelmed by all the people. The foyer over-flows with pastel-colored balloons, pink and peach-colored roses, and carnations. Streamers flow from a big sign welcoming me home.

I am stunned. Speechless.

Mother grabs me. Donna grabs me… Tina is beaming.

Chris bends low to hug me. Tommaso is here, introducing his wife, Regina. Lovely woman with kind black eyes and black hair that falls almost to her waist.

Antonio, the consigliere, and his wife.

Marguerite, from the defender's office, is here along with several others.

Allesandro is with a woman he doesn't name. Matteo's sisters, Lia and Ophelia, are here with their husbands.

It is a DeVecchio-Drakos extended family get-together.

"Let's get our girl to the den so she can sit down," Donna tells the crowd as she ushers me further inside. The house has twisted pink crepe paper and ribbons and pink flowers everywhere. Breathtaking.

Matteo has disappeared. He's off fuming.

Everyone asks their questions about my recovery, telling me how much better I look.

"Thank you. I feel better," I tell each.

On… and on… and on. An hour passes. Continuously, I glance over my shoulder, around the room, out the windows.

He's not here.

"Where's Matteo?" Donna demands, standing over me with a drink in her hand.

I meet her gaze. "I haven't seen him."

A shadow crosses her eyes as Donna levels an odd stare. "What happened?" It is her demanding tone.

"Nothing." My voice is quiet.

"Don't try to blow smoke up my skirt." She sits herself beside me, wiggling her butt for more room. "My son has been planning this party since he learned you were coming home." Donna waves her hand across the room of visitors. "He did this. For you. *He* did it, not me."

My head sinks into my hands. "I don't know, Donna. We... quarreled."

"About what?" I've heard him call her a momma bear. Now I understand.

I draw a deep breath. "It was my fault." I meet her probing gaze. "I'll tell you later. This isn't the place."

Donna tilts her head back, her gaze narrow. "Was he a jerk? Or were you?"

"Both of us. Mostly me, I think. I didn't mean to. I just..." I let it trail off.

Donna studies me another long bit and leaves without another word.

I feel unwelcome.

Mom watches Donna storm off and sits where she had been. "What's wrong?" Mom asks.

"I'm ready to go home."

"Oh. Okay, I'll call Matteo."

I grab her arm. "No, Mom. I mean your home."

"He said you would recover at his house."

I shake my head. "I don't think so. Not now."

"Sherry, I know you're disappointed that he doesn't say it, but the man is obviously in love with you. What happened?"

"Oh, Mom. I can't talk about it. Let's just... go. Tell them I'm tired. It's not a lie."

Her eyes wander the room, finding Dad.

Maybe I took him for granted. I scoff at myself. There's no *maybe* to it. He was my Prince Charming, and I took him for granted. I was mad at him, yes. He tries to control me.

But I never dreamed Matteo would just walk away from me. He has.

I left the hospital two long weeks ago. It has been an eternity. I'd like to say the nights are the longest, but I can't. Every hour of the twenty-four-hour day, my heart aches. I wait, expecting, hoping maybe he'll call. Maybe I'll see headlights shine through the living room windows, and he will knock on the door.

He'll surprise me, like he has so many times, walking into my hospital room with a smile. With flowers. He came in one day with my watch. The watch.

"Where did you find it?" I'd asked him.

"They took it off of you in the emergency room."

He found it. He'd promised, 'I'll move heaven and hell, and I'll find it for you.' And he did. He'd said it so matter-of-factly. Because Matteo knew he wouldn't stop until he found what I wanted.

And all I did, day after day, week after week, was harp about how he was only doing everything out of guilt.

Why was it so hard to believe he loved me? Because he wouldn't say the words.

Oh, God, my pride.

I ruined everything because he wouldn't say what I wanted to hear. The one thing I wanted the most, he wouldn't give me.

I am not his property.

He cannot rule my life, especially if he cannot say he loves me.

I want to cry. But I can't. I'm too empty for tears.

"Angel, are you not sleeping?" Mom asked at breakfast this morning.

"I'm resting." I lied.

"You don't look rested," she'd said, her forehead furrowed with worry. "And I haven't seen you eat hardly anything since you came home. You are skin and bones."

"I eat." *Haven't I?*

She kissed me goodbye on top of my head and left.

That was two hours ago.

When the hour hand reaches nine, I call Francesco's office.

Francesco answers his own line at his desk on the first ring.

"Francesco?" My voice is meek as I squinch my eyes, fearful he will take my head off. Or hang up on me.

Instead, he purrs, "Hello, sweet girl. How are you?"

"Okay. I've waited to hear what work you or Matteo have for me. Since he hasn't called, I felt like I should. Do you want me to work there, or do you want me to work from my parents or the warehouse? And what assignments do you have?"

"Let me speak with Matteo and I'll call you back."

"Is he there?" I ask.

I close my eyes again, waiting for the answer.

"No... he's... dealing with business. I'll call you back."

Francesco doesn't.

About an hour later, I grab the phone on my bedside table on the first ring. "Hello?"

"Sherry."

It's Matteo. My stomach twists, hearing his voice.

"I need for you to find out as much as you can about all of the native American tribes between the Atlantic Ocean and the Mississippi River. Population, location, land mass, demographics, infrastructure, if there's anything on it. Get the names and contact information for the tribal leaders and mostly, I need to know about their governance. Report back when you get it."

I open my mouth to ask a question—but he's gone.

My heart crashes to the floor.

I hang my head.

I want to cry, but still, I can't.

I have pride.

If he cannot say he loves me, he cannot possess me. Make demands.

But God, I miss him.

I suck in a deep, deep breath.

Okay. Native American tribes.

This will require a trip to the library.

Nope. My parents still have a set of Encyclopedia Brittannica. I'll start there until I can get a ride to the library.

While I search the bookshelves in the hallway for the right encyclopedia, my parents' phone rings again. I hobble on my crutches as fast as I can, reaching the telephone on its third ring, hoping Matteo thought of something else.

Hoping maybe he just wants to reach out.

"Hello."

"Sherry Drakos?" It is a deep voice.

"Yes."

"Hey, how are you?"

I peer into the receiver. "Who is this?"

"Sorry. I thought you'd know the voice. It's Viggo."

My hand finds my hip, resting there. "How did you find me here?"

A low laugh rumbles from his throat. "Sherry, I'm a federal agent. I investigate. For a living."

"Oh," I giggle nervously.

"So, how are you?" he asks.

"Better than the last time you saw me." I sink into the couch. Not really.

Viggo hesitates. "I wanted to ask you a few questions... nothing about your boss, I promise, something else. And buy you a cup of coffee. Or a meal."

"I won't talk to you about Matteo."

"I get it. This isn't about him." He lets out another throaty chuckle. "I got the message from our last meeting; you don't just work for him, Sherry."

I don't respond because first, my relationship with Matteo is none of his business, and secondly, as of right now, all I am to Matteo is an employee.

But I won't tell Viggo that.

Instead, I answer with a question. "Okay. So, what's it about?"

"Can I come see you or meet you or pick you up and take you somewhere? To talk. Privately."

"Since I can't drive, either we visit here at my parents, or you pick me up. It will be a while before I can drive."

"But you'll talk to me?"

I have to chuckle. "It depends, Agent Johansen."

"On what?" he asks.

"On what you want to talk about."

Viggo shows up at my parents' house a little over an hour later carrying a big, greasy sack, which he holds up proudly. Almost boyishly. "Thought you might be hungry, since I'm hitting here at lunchtime."

"I have coffee and tea." I hold the door back and usher him inside. "I have no idea what you drink. I think we have some soft drinks, too, if you prefer."

"Whatever you have is fine," he says as he follows me to the kitchen, which hasn't been updated since, I don't know, maybe the early 60s.

We sit at the Formica table I grew up eating on.

I sat at this very table when my feet wouldn't reach the floor. Chrome legs curve from a swirly red Formica top. The set has six matching chairs. Miraculously, the plastic-like fabric is not split on any of them. "My mom refuses to get a new table. She says this one holds too many memories."

"We had a table just like it when I was a kid," Viggo says. "Only ours was yellow."

"Where?" I ask.

His gaze meets mine. He really has gorgeous blue eyes. They are crystal light with a deep blue rim, which makes the light blue even more noticeable.

Such a curmudgeon to be so handsome.

"Texas," he answers and dips his monster-sized claw into the bag, withdrawing a wrapped burger, which he places in front of me.

He nudges his head at the burger before me. "I got everything on it. Figured you could take off what you don't like easier than finding something that it doesn't have and you want."

"Thank you, Viggo. Texas. Wow. I understand that drawl now. Calling me darlin'. Are you a cowboy?" I can see it.

"I grew up in the Panhandle. Yeah, I can ride but I'm no cowboy. Guess I watched too much Lone Ranger and Roy Rogers when I was little. All I ever wanted to do was catch the bad guys."

We share an extended blank stare before Viggo shrugs. "Not talkin' about your boss, darlin'. I told you, that's not why I'm here."

"Is your family still there? In Texas?"

"My parents passed. Both of them." He takes a swallow of his drink. "Anyway, I've got some questions, not for me, but for a friend, another law enforcement officer, who brought up a name and it was a name I know you're familiar with."

"Dammit, Viggo." I show him my palm, with my mouth full of hamburger. "I told you, I won't—"

"Scott Buchanan. I understand you dated for a while."

I swallow hard and wash the burger bite down with a sip of iced tea. "Scott? Yes. We did. What about him?"

Viggo drags his French fry through Catsup, swallows it whole, and wipes his mouth with his napkin, those blue eyes studying mine. "What can you tell me about him?"

"Not a lot. He's a prosecutor..."

He angles his head and flashes me a no duh look.

"Scott's a good prosecutor. Athlete. Loves to golf and run and—"

"What else?"

"Really, Viggo? We dated for about six months. I don't know that much about Scott outside of our work across the aisle and going out. We ran together. Played tennis. We liked sparring with each other."

He snickers. "Didn't talk a lot, obviously."

"You just have to get your jabs in, don't you?"

"Let me cut to the chase." He leans his thick, hairy forearms on the table. "Was the man kinky?"

That's not a question you expect. At least I didn't. "In what way?"

"Geez. Fuck. Do I have to spell it out? In bed."

I draw back, feeling my eyes double in size. "A little personal. Why are you asking me these things?"

"Look, it's not my case. I'm helping a friend. They have a runaway, an Asian girl, who claims she was held captive and used for sex, and she picked Scott Buchanan's picture out of a book as one of the men who sexually abused her."

My gut churns, and I push my burger aside. "Why was his photo in a book of suspects?"

"We jam lots of pictures into books like that, to see if our victims know who they're talking about. Hell, mine's probably in somebody's book."

"So maybe it's a mistake."

"My guy says no. The girl wasn't prompted. She drew back in fright when she saw his picture. Said he handcuffed her to a bed and... did some pretty sickening things."

My heart glitches with the vision, and I groan as Viggo goes on. "If Buchanan did this, he could be key to breaking the people who held her. She says she only saw handlers, has no idea who pulls the strings. And she says there are lots of others like her. She just managed to get away."

"Oh, Lord." I sink my head onto my hands, resting my elbows on the table. "Scott..." I had no idea.

"The girl said she was brought here from Viet Nam with a promise of work, but she says she thought she was going to be a maid or a cook or a farm worker. Maybe work in a meat processing plant or something like that. She says she didn't know she was going to be making films and servicing men."

"Whose case is it?" I ask.

He shakes his head. "Can't say. I'll take your information to him. He doesn't know your name either."

My mind is spinning like a top. Matteo told me last summer he suspected Geno Gabicci of smuggling Asians. He surmised some ended up basically as sex slaves. I can't share that with Viggo.

"I will tell you this: I quit seeing Scott when he asked me to wear a dog collar and handcuffs, if that means anything. How old is the Asian girl?"

"Fifteen. But she does look older." I suddenly see Johnathan James Jenkins sitting in front of me. Scott Buchanan is no better than him.

Worse—he handcuffed her and did horrible things.

"Oh, my God. Scott? It's hard to believe. But maybe it's not." My eyes meet Viggo's intense stare. "I saw him at the Waterfront last summer, with Sophia Gabicci."

He doesn't seem surprised. "Yeah, they go way back. As a federal agent, I think it's hinky as hell that the District Attorney lets an assistant DA date a Mafia princess."

"Maybe he doesn't know."

Viggo scoffs loudly. "In this world? He knows."

"You think the D.A. is questionable?"

"That alone makes me wonder. But like I said, I work drug investigations, which is why my friend called me. The girl is addicted to heroin. He has her in a treatment facility."

I stew for a minute. "Mafia princess, you called her. Sophia Gabicci is a fucking bitch."

His brows shift high. "And you know that because?"

"I just know. Leave it at that."

Matteo
STALEMATE

Pop's gaze catches mine seconds after he answers the phone at his desk. "Hello, sweet girl. How are you?"

Her. Great.

I start to leave, but he ushers me to sit back down, waving his hand as he says, "Let me ask Matteo, and I'll call you back." He listens and replies, "No, he's dealing with business. I'll call you back."

He hangs up the phone and snaps at me. "It's been two damned weeks. You can't keep avoiding her."

"Who says?"

Pop points angrily at the phone. "I'm not going to tell Sherry what to do. That's your job. Now out with it. What happened between you two? You were so excited to get her home. You get her here and leave, for Christ's sake." His arm flails over his head as his volume rises. "You didn't even attend the party you threw for her."

I haven't heard the end of that.

I couldn't deal with her doubts and accusations any longer. I did everything I knew to do. No one, not even Sherry, can force me to say something I cannot say. Do I love her? I don't fucking know.

I needed her. I wanted her—the way she was. The way we were. But not the way she acted recently. Especially those last few days. I don't need that or want that. I won't subject myself to that badgering.

My mother plops herself into the chair beside me, facing Pop across his desk, and chimes in. "I want to hear this, too."

"Are you eavesdropping?"

"It's a mother's right. Now explain yourself."

"No, goddammit. I will not discuss what is between me and Sherry with my parents. For God's sake."

She leans in, about to peck. "Matteo Dante DeVecchio, I will not take no for an answer. Not on this." Mother wags her finger at me. "I have never seen you love anyone but her. Now why? I want to know why?"

Fuck. Fine.

"She doesn't love me."

"Bullshit!" Pops slaps his desk openhanded.

It's nine o'clock in the morning. He shoves his chair back with his legs and stomps to the bar. "Have a drink, son. It lubricates the tongue." He pours two glasses and hands me one, going back to his chair. "Now spill it."

I groan. Anything but this.

I throw back the bourbon, close my eyes, inhale a chest full of air, and blow it out. "I took responsibility for what happened to her. Putting her in the car with Joey when she didn't want to go with him."

"She blamed you?" Mother's bear claws are out. I see it on her face and hear it in her shriek.

"She never said that, Mother. But I think she felt it. It seemed anything I did for her in the hospital, she'd say I was only doing it because I felt guilty. Responsible. She didn't want charity."

Pop looks at Mother and narrows his gaze at her. "What are they fighting about?"

She lifts her hands in confusion. "I need a drink, too." She goes to the bar.

"This doctor wanted her to go to Raleigh for rehab and I said no. She was coming home with me. If she needed specialists for her rehab, I'd have them come to the house. Anyway, she said she won't live with me if I can't say I love her."

Pops leans in on his forearms. "You never told her you love her?"

I shake my head.

"Why the hell not? You do love her!" I see his incredulity.

Pop doesn't understand. "I... just... can't say it."

Mother stands, hovering over me, drink in hand. "So let me get this straight." She sets the drink on Pop's desk. "You do all of this. You want her to move in with you, and you want to take care of her, and you have never once said, Sherry, darling, I love you?"

I head back to the bar. "Correct."

In my periphery, I see them share bewildered stares. "Son! What the hell?" Mom is yelling.

That is why I didn't want this conversation.

"Why can't you say it? I see it in you. You do love her. Just tell her," Mother orders, as only my mother can order.

She should have been a fucking general.

"Right now, I'm not sure I do. Besides, even if I did, I'm not sure she'd accept it. She's got two men at the hospital fawning over her. The Matteo star doesn't shine as brightly as it once did."

Mother tilts her head. "Did you threaten either or both of those men?"

"No."

They do the eye exchange.

"Of course he did," Pop says. "This is the most absurd thing I've ever heard. Two people love each other, and they are apart because of—"

"It's not that simple. She thinks I dictate to her."

"I'm sure you do!"

My Mother.

"Your father and I butted heads over that when we were young. It's natural. What you see as protective, she sees as controlling. You are possessive, Matteo. You are controlling and she could probably accept all of that, because Sherry loves you—but son, it's all got to be predicated on love. Without love, it is just control. And no woman worth her salt wants to be controlled. So, tell her. She needs to hear it."

"Dammit, what more can I do to show her how I feel?"

"Say it!" They sound like a fucking choir.

"Actions are more important than words."

Mother glares at Pop and points. "It's your fault. He has your hard head." She tromps demonstratively out of the office.

"If I tell her I love her, and everything's fine, what's next?" I ask my father. "One day she says, 'Well, if you really love me, you'll do this... or that.' Am I supposed to jump through a fucking hoop because my woman needs proof that I love her when everything I do shows her? What's the point?"

My father takes a deep breath, shuts his eyes, wags his head, and exhales heavily. "She wants to know where she is to work from and what you want her to do. Call her at her parents' house." He leaves the room, too. Probably joining Mother for a morning Penicillin.

I pour a short drink, sit in the chair, and lean my head back.

I planned on traveling together and developing relationships with the tribal leaders. She would be so good at that. She can charm the scales of a snake—not seductively or manipulatively charming like Sophia. No, Sherry is genuinely happy, likable, fucking adorable. Which is why men are flocking to her feet.

It is impossible not to like Sherry Drakos. We would have had our own private adventure away from everything else.

I know what I felt for her. Now, I'm not even sure of that.

My chest is empty. *Colpo del fulmine,* she said. She told me over and over I was her thunderbolt. She loved me, she loved me, she loved me.

I believed her.

Sherry really doesn't know what it means. When you feel something that strongly, you don't walk away.

My heart sinks to my stomach. I closed the door, too. I don't guess it was the thunderbolt for either one of us.

Fine.

I'll give her enough work to keep her out of my hair for a while.

When I pull in for my daily check, the warehouse is bustling. The men are unloading a cargo ship anchored at the dock. Skid loaders are shuffling products around, organizing.

Chris has already found several new products to import from Turkey and Israel, and he's looking for more. He needs to find room to store them as we expand our import operations around the Mediterranean to replace the revenue we will lose while we change directions.

"Hey." Chris looks up from his books when I walk into the office. "Joe just told me Sherry's recouping at their house."

"Yes."

His forehead furrows. "What's going on? I thought you wanted her to stay with you."

"I did." I sit in the chair in front of his desk.

Another fucking inquisition. Just what I need.

"What happened?" Not an ask. A demand.

"Not discussing it."

"You've been one fucking sad sack for two weeks. You need to discuss it, my friend. With someone." Tommy is behind me. He is quiet for a big guy. I didn't hear him open the door, and Chris's gaze didn't betray his entrance.

Ambushed.

"Fuck off, both of you."

"I told Tina I love her," Chris announces with the widest smile I've seen him wear in a long time, as if he's proud. As if he's achieved something.

"I thought she was married," Tommy says.

"They split."

I can't suppress a chuckle. "That's fast."

"Not really. We dated, split up, she married fuck-budget. Anyway, I got up the nerve last night and told her how I really feel." He cuts his eyes at me. "I have to thank Sherry for rattling my brain about that. When she got hurt, I called Tina. I knew she'd want to know. I picked her up to take her to see Sherry. That's when we started talking."

"I'm surrounded by fucking pussies!" Tommy roars. "Damn, you two cowards. Love isn't something you run from. It's something you run to. Love is everything."

Who knew Tommaso Ricci was a romantic?

Now Chris and I lock eyes while Tommy lectures. "Love makes you want to get up in the morning. I can't imagine my life without Regina and our kids. What would be the point?"

Fuck this shit.

"I'll see you two later."

My mind isn't right.

Yes, I guess... maybe I love her.

Okay, I fucking love her. But I won't jump through hoops every time pretty little blue-eyed Sherry Elisabet Drakos wants me to prove my love.

She has to understand that.

I told her—before Joey took her—I'm not going to lose her.

I'm not.

My car steers itself to her parents' house, an old, well-maintained two-story house on a narrow street with overhanging trees.

This is the right address, but her parents should be at work.

Why is a pickup truck parked in the driveway?

I walk the sidewalk and ring the bell.

It will take a while for her to answer at the speed she made it into my parents' house. But that's been two weeks. She'll be nimbler now.

When the door finally opens, my heart flies out of my chest.

Our eyes meet and latch. Frozen for a long moment. I clench my jaw, turn, and walk back to my car.

"Matteo, wait!" She calls. "Please! He just stopped by to...."

Fuck it. Fuck it all.

H is initial shock erupted into a scorching inferno. Those black eyes flashed lightning first at Viggo, then at me. I was speechless watching him storm away.

It was innocent enough. Viggo didn't come onto me. He came here on business.

But Matteo is so possessive, so jealous—even though he's the one who walked away from me—he will never understand.

"Go, Viggo. I'm sorry. Just... go."

"Didn't mean to cause problems." The big guy's voice is unusually gentle. I didn't know he had it in him.

I offer a pathetic smile. "I know." I take his hand. "Thank you, Viggo, for turning out to be such a truly good guy. Let me know what you find out about Scott. But the truth is, I love that man. And now he thinks I'm—"

"You don't have to say it."

It hurts my neck, craning it back so far to meet Viggo's gaze, standing so close. "Viggo, he's not what you think he is."

My declaration is met by a flat expression and a hesitant response. "I hope he proves me wrong, for your sake." Viggo's eyes linger on mine, and he twists his neck a bit. "But if he disappoints, I'll be around."

After watching Viggo drive away, I call Chris.

He picks up after several rings. I wasn't about to hang up because it's the warehouse. I know somebody is there.

"Yeah, Baka." He's out of breath. He must have run through the warehouse to catch the telephone.

"Chris, will you come pick me up and take me to Matteo?"

"What's up?" he asks.

"Oh, God, Chris. He just came over here and Viggo—"

"Johansen? What the fuck, Sherry!" He can be so loud.

I rest my head in my hands. "It's not how it sounds or what you think. But he left mad, and I want to find him."

"Shit. Better not."

"If you won't take me, I'll call a cab."

"They won't let you through the gate if he just saw Viggo Johansen at your house." Again. Loud.

"Dammit, Chris. We're family." I choke on my words. My prayers were answered. Matteo came to see me—and Viggo was here. "Please, I can't drive. Take me to him."

It takes him a moment, but finally, my cousin lets out a noisy huff to demonstrate his displeasure. "Fine. But shit, I can't guarantee either of us will be safe when I do. Not if he saw Johansen... with you... inside your house."

I wish I could pace. Maybe waiting would be easier if I could.

My stomach twists tighter and tighter with each passing minute.

Is Matteo done with me for good this time?

I thought his heart was ice—then I opened the door. He came here on his own.

My shock was as great as his.

I wait, watching from the front windows of my parent's home as time moves at a glacier pace.

When I finally see Chris's truck approaching, I exit the house and lock the door, arriving at the sidewalk before he stops.

"What the hell was that narc doing here?" He asks before I get my seatbelt on.

Viggo didn't swear me to secrecy or anything, although, in all fairness, I think he probably expected it.

But Chris came to save me. I owe him. "Viggo said a friend of his, another law enforcement officer, found a runaway, a young Asian girl, who identified Scott as one of several men who sexually abused her. He knew I went out with Scott. That's why he came. To ask me questions about Scott, not Matteo."

His surprise is evident in his unusually high pitch. "Buchanan? The assistant DA?"

"Yeah."

When the shock wears off, Chris shakes his head as he runs his hand over his mouth. "I'm not buying it. Viggo's been after Matteo. It's a ruse."

"I didn't tell him anything about Matteo. As a matter of fact, when Matteo saw him and stormed off, I told Viggo to leave. I told him, I love Matteo and that Matteo's not what he thinks."

Chris tilts his head back and lets out a loud, ridiculing laugh.

"Really?"

"Sherry, Sherry, Sherry. Matty is *exactly* what Viggo thinks he is. We all are. Or were. We're out of the drug business now."

"Matteo DeVecchio is a good man."

Chris cuts his eyes at me. "Matteo DeVecchio doesn't turn the other cheek."

I bury my face in my hands.

How can everything go so terribly wrong all of a sudden? I have to find him and explain. I have to make him understand how much I love him. Still.

I cannot imagine ever letting another man make love to me. He did exactly what he said he would do. He ruined me for any other man.

Chris clears his throat loudly. "Johansen is a pit bull. Once he sinks his teeth into you, he doesn't let go. Matty said he weighed the risks, and with Johansen on our asses, the stakes were too high. He's developing a new revenue stream."

"Has it got anything to do with Indian reservations?"

"He'll tell you when he's ready. When I get you to Matty's—"

"Leave."

My cousin casts a questioning stare. "You sure?"

"Matteo would never physically hurt me. If I'm there and I have no way to go anywhere, he'll have to listen to me."

He snickers. "After he goes through how many doors?"

"You've seen him hit a door?"

"More than once." He cuts his eyes at me as he drives. "He was in the office earlier. Tommy called us cowards for being afraid of love. Matteo told us to fuck off and left."

I plunk my head against the passenger window. "He leaves you, comes to me, and sees me with another man." I groan.

"Not just any other man. Viggo."

My chest aches. "Do you think he will listen to me?"

"Hell, I don't know. He's got to be pretty raw."

"I didn't mean to hurt him."

My cousin scoffs wickedly. "For someone who didn't mean to, you apparently did a damn good job."

We ride in silence a bit before he glances at me again. "By the way. Tina and I... I told her I love her."

I backhand his shoulder. "I didn't know you two were seeing each other, much less professing love."

"It just... kind of happened. After you got hurt, I called her, picked her up and took her to see you that first day." He glances my way. "You were in surgery."

Wow. Another Chris and Tina secret I never knew about. "Why hasn't she said anything to me?"

He shrugs. "It's... complicated."

My jaw sags a bit. "You think? Tina's *married*, Chris."

He cuts his eyes at me and answers flatly, "Not for long."

"What do you mean?"

"I mean they're separated. Talk to her. With all you've had going on, I don't think she wanted to dump on you."

"She told me you broke her heart when I was in college."

"Yeah, biggest mistake I ever made. When I found out I had a chance, I made up my mind not to fuck it up twice."

A realization hits me like a punch in the gut. "You already told Tina you love her. Matteo has never said it to me. And yet, he wants to rule my life."

His glance is fiery. "First of all, it took me a long time to say it. Secondly, Matty doesn't want to rule your life. He wants to take care of you. There's a difference."

"I'm not so sure."

We ride in silence for a long time before Chris reaches over and shakes my shoulder. "Listen, kid. Words are just words. Some men use the word love too easily. When they wake up and realize what they felt is gone, they end up breaking the girl's heart. Other men are more comfortable showing it than saying it. What have Matty's actions shown you?"

"I don't know, Chris. I started feeling like everything he did was because he felt guilty about putting me in the car with Joey. I mean—would he saddle himself with an invalid for the rest of his life just because he had Joey drive me? I didn't want him hovering over me out of guilt or sympathy or pity. I don't want to be anybody's burden."

"Sherry. You're not an invalid—"

"But he didn't know that."

My cousin shows me his palm. His gaze bounces between me and the road. "Get this straight: Some people drag guilt around like a ball and chain, thinking if they make themselves miserable enough, maybe they can earn forgiveness. That's not Matty or me or Tommy—because we all know—there is no forgiveness for what we do. Whatever Matty did for you, he did it because he wanted to. Not out of guilt. We don't waste our time on fucking guilt. It wreaks of self-pity."

Internally, I groan again and remember something Viggo said one time.

I face him and ask, "Chris, do you *off* people?"

His face hardens, the same way Matteo's face had once before when I asked him to tell me about his business. "Sherry, I do what's necessary to protect our family and I don't apologize to anyone. We don't talk about what we do, try to justify it or explain it to anyone. We take care of family. Period."

Raw, chilling truth.

In my periphery, I see my cousin watch my face as I absorb stark reality.

Sometimes, when Chris speaks with such an absence of emotion, it feels like he plunges me into ice water. It takes time to get the feeling back.

He lets off the accelerator. "You still want to go to Matty's?"

I nod, turning to face his direct gaze. "Yes."

I reach across the console and grip his bicep. "I accept you Chris, and Matteo and Tommy. I accept this family as it is. No family's perfect. Did you hear what I just told you about Scott Buchanan? The high and mighty D.A. sexually abusing young girls? At least we aren't hypocrites."

Chris reaches across, squeezes my neck, pulls me to him, and kisses the top of my head like I'm still ten years old. "Thank you, Sherry Baby."

Sherry
CONFRONTATION

S eeing Chris's truck, the guards at the DeVecchio gate move both barricade trucks without him getting out. The long driveway forks, and we turn right onto the lane that leads to Matteo's house.

The car he used to drive me home from the hospital is parked in the garage. It's a deep, dark blue sedan.

Chris nods at it as we approach the house. "He bought that Mercedes for you. You think he did that out of guilt?"

My jaw falls slack. "It's a Mercedes Benz?"

"Yeah."

"For me? When?"

"While you were in the hospital. He ordered a new 911 for himself."

How badly can one person screw up a relationship? I guess I'm about to find out.

Reaching for the door handle, I ask, "Do you think the garage door into the kitchen is open?"

"I wouldn't walk into his house unannounced. You might get shot."

He catches the surprise that washes over my face.

"Matty's got guns stashed all over his house. Just in case. We all do. You never know when you might need to put your hands on one." As I exit the car, Chris leans over, yelling through the window, "Call me if you need me."

I nod. I hope I don't have to.

Making my way clumsily on my crutches from the driveway to Matteo's front door, I knock.

Nothing.

I ring the doorbell and wait.

No one.

I hobble my way around to the garage door and knock.

Still, nothing.

I head around to the back of the house.

In the distance, at the foot of the hill, Matteo lies on a sheet near the creek with a bottle at his hand.

He is on his back, his face to the sun, with one arm shading his eyes.

I maneuver on my crutches down the slope to him. Carefully. I cannot slip and fall. You'd think I'd have mastered these damn crutches by now, but in my parents' house, I don't use them a lot.

Approaching, it appears Matteo is sound asleep. The bottle isn't empty, but it's low.

With great difficulty, I manage to sit beside him. He is so still. So handsome. He takes my breath, just looking at him.

I'm too close. I can't resist. I reach out and stroke his wavy black hair.

Matteo jumps to his feet and whirls around, crouched like a panther about to pounce.

He's drunk.

I've seen him drink. I've never seen the man drunk.

He's wobbly.

He blinks and seethes when he realizes it's me. "What are you doing here?"

"It's not what it looked like—"

"I don't care." He aims his arm at the house. "Leave."

"He came to ask me about Scott Buchanan."

"I said—I don't care!" Yes, *that's* the voice I know. The raging roar.

"I would never lie to you, Matteo."

"Why would that fucker be in your house?"

"It's not that. He knows I dated Scott. He thinks… Viggo thinks Scott is involved with sex trafficking."

Matteo shakes his head softly with a look on his face like he just bit into a lemon. "It doesn't make any difference."

"Matteo, please."

He looks at me with—repulsion—and closes his eyes, almost whispering, "Why, Sherry? Why?" When he opens them, those beautiful eyes are filled with hurt as he demands to know, "WHY?"

Tears sting my eyes.

I can see that I have lost him.

"Because I'm stupid. I thought you just felt sorry for me. I didn't want your pity or sympathy. I wanted your love."

"Do I look like a sympathetic son of a bitch to you? Leave! Get the fuck out!"

He stands motionless. As motionless as he can be, woozy from the alcohol, staring at me. Staring like he's trying to understand.

Like he's waiting for me to go.

Okay. I'll call Chris.

I try to get to my feet. He reaches to help me. We fall together onto the sheet, and Matteo clutches me to his chest. "Oh, God, did I hurt you? I didn't mean to hurt you."

He crushes me with his arms.

"I wasn't far enough up for that little fall to hurt me."

His mouth hovers over mine, his eyes searching my face. I feel it. He wants to kiss me.

He turns away. "No."

I take his face in my hands and force him to see me. "Matteo, I never meant to hurt you. I love you."

"You don't know what it means."

"And you do?"

Ice overtakes his voice. "That's the problem. I do know what it means." He pauses, looking away from me to peer at the sky. "Do you think I ever slept in a chair next to a hospital bed just to be close to a woman? And don't say I did it out of guilt or sympathy. It wasn't fucking guilt."

"I know that now. I'm sorry."

"I wanted to be near you. I wanted you. What do I have to do to prove my feelings, Sherry, when every day, every single fucking day, everything I did, I did for you? Why couldn't you see that?"

"I... thought at first it was because I looked like her. And then I thought—"

Matteo swipes his arm wide with disgust. "Just go." He turns away, sitting motionless with his back to me, and I watch as he stares into oblivion.

I touch his shoulder and whisper, "You made me feel loved. That's enough."

"Go. Away. I said I want to be alone." He shifts his shoulders, rebuffing my touch. "It won't work."

"I'm not leaving."

"I don't want you here." He looks over his shoulder at me. "Sooner or later, you will rip my fucking heart out of my goddamned chest, and I already know what that feels like." He turns to face me, glaring. "You think bullet holes hurt? You think broken legs hurt? *Nothing* hurts like a broken heart. *Goddammit! Leave!*"

He turns his back to me again.

My mind shifts into idle. Not reverse. I'm not leaving. Not drive. I'm not pushing him anymore.

I will just wait. Yes, I'll idle until his frozen heart thaws.

Gathering my crutches, I make my way up the slope to the patio.

Matteo doesn't offer to help. Doesn't watch me.

It's a haul. One step on the good leg. Pull up the bad.

I open the sliding glass door and enter the kitchen, collapsing into the nearest chair.

He's still sitting with his back to me.

A bit later, I flinch as I hear the beast inside of him demanding to be set free, and hearing that painful roar, suddenly, I know—he does love me. If he didn't, he wouldn't be so hurt.

If Matteo didn't love me, he would have left my house, picked up some girl in a bar, and fucked her for a distraction like he did Sophia that time.

Now I know, whether he can say it or not, Matteo Dante DeVecchio loves me, Sherry Elizabet Drakos. Not the girl from his past.

The new question is, can he get past this hurt to let us move on?

I find the coffee and brew a fresh pot. He'll need a stiff cup to help sober up.

Periodically, I peer out the sliding glass door. Just checking. He's still sitting down there. He's not drinking. Just sitting with his back to the house.

Killing time, I scrounge through his refrigerator. He must have had Bettina restock, thinking I would be here with him because the fridge is full, but the lettuce is beginning to wither.

I pull out the makings for sandwiches, make two, and cover them with paper towels.

I sip fresh coffee and wait. For him.

I have experienced the passion that is that man.

I will not let it go.

I will fight... for him.

Matteo
COMMAND

She shows up here? What does she expect? Tilting my head back, facing the late afternoon sky, I roar at whatever is above. I want my voice to shake the trees. "Goddammit!"

It's too much. My heart throbs in my throat. I don't want this. This is what caring too much does to a man. I shake my head and mutter to myself. "Son of a bitch."

I let time pass as my mind goes void.

Wind.

The wind stirs the trees. The canopy over my head shudders, and I tilt my head back to watch golden leaves rain over me. Some drift through the air, skip across the grass and tumble into the creek, where they float away. Others rest on the sheet around me. I finger the sheet. The one she and I sat on so long ago.

Empty.

My mind, my body, my soul. All of me. Empty.

If you give someone your heart, they have the power to crush it. That's why you don't give it.

I didn't give it. She stole it like a little thief.

I feel her at my back.

She's up there. I know her. I told her to leave, but she didn't.

Shit, she can't leave. She's waiting for me to drive her home. Fuck.

I cut my gaze to the whiskey bottle.

All it did was weaken me. It didn't wash away pain or anger. I sat here and let whiskey rob me of my wits. I drank myself to sleep. And when I opened my eyes, seeing her, I had to blink to see straight.

Did I cry in my sleep? Is that what I've been reduced to? Crying?

With a new burst of rage, I sling the bottle halfway up the hill and see Enzo's face. That giant of a man wept.

A man can only take so much.

You're pathetic. Enzo was stronger than you. He didn't break until after he'd been in chains for days—until he defecated on himself. Enzo knew there was no way out. And I threatened his family.

I sat here and wallowed in my own self-pity and apparently cried in my damned sleep.

Why? Over a woman? They're a dime a dozen.

No. Not women like her. Sherry is as rare as a blue diamond.

I pound the sheet. Seeing that son of a bitch standing next to her inside her house... I shake my head at the vision. I wanted to kill the motherfucker.

But I can't. He's a fucking fed. That bastard could drive himself off a damn cliff, and they'd come looking for me, the last man he was investigating.

She let him in her house. And she has the gall to show up here?

"Fuck," I tell the tree.

That doctor. Denison. He wants to get in her pants. He doesn't think I know that?

I swear under my breath and glance up the hill again.

She's got some balls; I'll give her that.

Twice I've been like this. Both women had those eyes. If I ever see a woman with those eyes again, I will run for the motherfucking hills. Hide in the Sahara. I moved past the agony that was Patsy. That was never real. But Sherry? We were real. I thought she accepted me for what I am. She swore she fell in love with me at first sight.

But I can't please her. She demands more than I can give. And I thought I gave it all.

I fist the sheet. Why does the world have to revolve around three little words? I will not surrender to it. Words are cheap. I could say them and not mean them.

Why is saying something so important? Have I asked her to say anything?

I turn to watch up the hill. I see her sitting at the bar. Drinking coffee. Waiting. For me.

Hard-headed woman.

I suck in a long, slow breath and blow it out.

Run my hand over my face.

Okay. Let's get this over with.

Gathering the sheet and the half-empty bottle I pick up on my way, I deposit both in a chair on the patio, open the sliding glass door, and walk into the kitchen.

Like a magnet and steel, our gazes lock and hold.

Her eyes are bright and wide, full of expectation.

I shake my head. "Not now."

She pleads with her eyes and voice. "I made sandwiches."

"I'll drive you home after I shower." I head for the solitude of my bedroom.

A shower. I need a hot shower.

Turning on the steaming stream full blast, I shuck off my clothes to stand beneath it. Resting my folded arms on the tile wall, I lower my head and let the hot water flow over me, begging it to wash this unending agony away.

We had a few glorious moments—the best I ever had—then Joey happened. Nothing I did was right, even after we learned she would walk and run again. We ceased to be.

I tilt my head back, enjoying the hot water streaming across my face and my shoulders, easing the tension, dripping off my ass.

I flinch as the shower door opens and peer over my shoulder.

She is naked, her weight on her good leg, gripping the shower doorframe.

"What are you doing?"

Her gaze is locked with mine. No answer.

I turn my back to her. "Go away, Sherry. I said not now."

"I'm not leaving you, Matteo." Her voice caresses my skin.

I turn to face her, my heart about to rip through my ribs as I yell, "You can't get in here. It's wet. You could fall."

She's unshaken, determined as she steps inside, her eyes on mine, not her footing. "You won't let me fall."

My eyes are glued on hers—then glide down her body.

Her years of running sculpted Sherry's abdomen and ass—and those legs. Her body is chiseled perfection, with water pouring over her as if she was standing under a waterfall—dripping from her perky tits, streaming to her tiny waist. My dick takes notice.

My gaze drops to follow the water sliding... beyond.

Oh, God.

She bobbles.

"Dammit, Sherry." I clutch my arm around her waist and draw her to me.

Sherry slides her arms up my pecs and around my neck, pressing her breasts into my chest. Her taut nipples tease me, and my dick throbs.

The curves of her body are slick and warm and wet as all of her rubs against all of me, and from somewhere deep inside comes a rumbling, animalistic growl as I tug on her hair, tilting her head back, demanding access to her mouth.

She parts her lips with her hungry little whimper, and I take command.

A man can only take so much.

Gripping her ass cheeks with both hands, I pull her into me, and like a starving man, I slip my hand between her legs, tease her clit and feel the wetness, before thrusting two fingers inside.

My cock aches.

She moans into my mouth as I delve deeper, two fingers working inside of her.

It's not enough.

I hook my hands under her arms and lift her, the shower water streaming over us both. "Can you wrap your legs around me?"

She nods, her eyes almost childlike.

I lift her higher, and her wet knees slip around my hips.

Higher, I lift.

She hooks her ankles at the small of my back, and I cup her ass in my hands, pressing her against my throbbing erection.

Her.

I position her so my cock glides just inside her entrance, and she catches her breath in anticipation.

Gripping her waist, I lift her and bring her down as I thrust up.

"Oh, fuck..." So tight. So wet. So hot. It's been so long...

Her head falls back as she moans and rolls her hips into me.

I do it again, lifting her and pulling her down as I pump into her... Yes... again... and again.

There is nothing gentle about... this.

She meets each thrust with an urgency of her own.

Her tongue traces up my neck—I tilt my head back and let her have her way, surprised by the feral sounds coming out of me. They erupt from my chest and gurgle past my throat.

This.

It's been too... fucking... long.

My dick seeps into her.

I turn around and shove the shower door open with my back.

Gripping her ass in my hands, her ankles still locked at my back, I carry Sherry across the bathroom, into the bedroom—both of us dripping water along the way.

I lower her onto my bed and stand over her—we each devour the other with our eyes.

Yes, she is back in my bed, where she belongs. The bed I haven't been able to fall asleep in since she was last in it.

Nothing exists but her, looking up at me with such desire.

She touches herself.

Fuck, yes.

I slide my hands under that sweet ass and lift her high. Her knees drape around my shoulders, and I bury my face between her legs, dipping my tongue inside of her.

I'm fucking her with my tongue. I am claiming what belongs to me.

"Matteo, please, yes, please." Her voice is needy as she rolls her hips. Every word out of her mouth, every movement of her body, makes my cock pulse.

She whimpers, "Let me feel you, Matteo. I want to feel you inside of me."

"Not yet." I lap her slick heat and move higher. "Taste." I plunge my tongue into her mouth, and she takes it with little cries of pleasure. "Am I hurting you?" I ask.

"No. No. No."

While she's breathless, I take her nipple into my mouth, tugging and nibbling while I knead the other breast, circling that waiting nipple with my thumb. With my hand under her shoulder blades, I move to the other tit, sucking. "Say it."

Her nails dig into my shoulders as her hips rise with desire. "I love you."

My hand teases the sensitive skin between her legs. "I said, say it."

"I said it. I love you."

"More."

With my tongue trailing down her abdomen, I stroke between her legs, and I command, "Say it, Sherry. You... belong... to me."

"Please, Matteo, I ache for you inside."

"Say. It."

"I'm yours." She wiggles her hips with unbridled desire.

My fingers plunge inside of her as my thumb owns her silky, swollen clit, and I watch her beautiful face in agonized ecstasy. "We aren't going through this again. Say it."

She says nothing.

I spread her legs, fist my dick to her entrance, and drive my shaft as deep inside of her as she can take me, and she moans her pleasure. Twice more, my stroke is powerful and commanding.

Her body can't take any more of me.

"We aren't going through this again." I thrust hard. *"Say it."*

When she doesn't respond—I pull out and thrust viciously, demanding, "Goddammit, Sherry. Fucking say it."

Her body stiffens in my hold.

I grip her shoulders tightly, pulling her upright. Our faces are inches apart, with my dick still buried deep inside of her. "Say it!"

Her blue eyes are stretched wide, her mouth gaped, her body rigid.

My breathing halts as my heart hitches seeing, she is terrified. *Of me.*

I lower her onto the bed and pull out of her, then slide my cock into her again—gently, slowly—holding there as the words erupt from my aching chest and tumble out of my mouth. "Ti amo," I whisper.

Her face is still frozen with fear. She doesn't understand.

"Sherry, I do love you."

She blinks in disbelief as her fear is slowly replaced by confusion.

The words come out again, feeling like sweet relief as I hold my cock buried to the hilt inside of her, finally confessing, "Dammit, Sherry, I love you so fucking much I cannot breathe."

With the admission, I'm in control.

She buries her face in my neck. "Oh, Matteo, I love you. So much. Say it again. Please."

I pull out of her and thrust again, slow but deep, with each word. "I... love... you."

I watch bliss overtake her face. She softens and submits fully to me as I plunder her body.

My movements are strategic now. Our gazes are cemented together as I take her... and tease her... savoring each sensation that her body has to offer: the fragrance of her hair, the taste of her skin, her slick heat around my cock—which swells every... single... time I pull out and drive back in.

Each time, Sherry meets my thrust. We move in perfect harmony.

I slide my tongue around one sweet, taut nipple and suck it into my mouth. Then my tongue trails up her long, slender neck to behind her ear, and I whisper, "Sherry, we are one."

Her body shudders. *"Matteo!"* she wails, digging her fingernails into my ass as she lifts her hips high, pressing into me as her body continues to tremble and her walls throb around my shaft—and I groan her name as my cock erupts like Vesuvius, spewing hot inside of her... again... and again.

I've never had anything like this.

Her breaths are shallow as she whispers. "Matteo, I've loved you from the first moment our eyes met."

She has no breath left.

I have very little.

After a moment of our hearts pounding, pressed together, I cradle her injured leg and roll off of her onto my side, bringing her with me.

We're still joined as one, our bodies sloppy and wet from the shower, our sweat, and our releases. We'll deal with the sheets later. Right now, I feel vindicated, and I don't fully understand why. "We aren't going through this again." It's not a question.

"This?" She giggles, rubs her nose against my neck, and tilts her head back to peer at my face. "Oh, yes, Matteo, we *will* do this again and again and again. But not the part that led up to it."

I cut my eyes to meet her gaze. "No other men in your life."

"No."

"No man is allowed to touch you but me."

"Yessir."

"You'll live with me."

"Yes."

"You'll marry me, you'll be with me for the rest of my life. *I* will die before you do, Sherry. *That* is a command. I'm not going through this again."

She nods through tears. "Yes, Matteo."

She arches up and kisses me, dragging those perfect tits across my chest. And my cock throbs again.

Sated and exhausted, we drift to sleep in each other's arms. So much tension for so long, suddenly gone. It has been so long since I slept well.

My eyes open as the sky dims in hues of pink and purple.

My bed is empty. Dammit.

Throwing back the covers, I stride down the hall to hear her humming in the kitchen.

"Your sandwich was getting stale." She wraps it in cellophane.

"Come here," I command. Remembering her injured leg, I say, "Never mind."

I walk to her, lift her off her feet, and set her on the bar. I rub my thumb across her lips and take her chin in my hand, tilting her head back so her gaze meets mine. "So that you don't think it was a fluke or something—I love you, Sherry. Completely."

She brushes her lips across mine. "I know you do. I can't believe you're actually saying it, though. It feels like Christmas."

"When do you want to get married?"

"Whenever you do."

I twirl her long locks around my finger. "Do you want a traditional Greek wedding?"

She shifts her shoulders in a question. "I'm sure that's what my parents will want but your parents will want a traditional Catholic wedding. We could make them all mad and get married somewhere else. Anywhere else."

I ponder aloud. "A beach wedding might be nice. Sail away together for a long getaway?"

"You really want to get married." It is in her voice and in her eyes—she is still in disbelief. "I'm going to be Sherry DeVecchio?"

"You did agree."

Her sweet dimple shows with her smile as her ice-blue eyes twinkle. "You've made me the happiest woman on earth, Matteo."

"I guess it wasn't the most romantic proposal, was it?"

"It was the most romantic proposal ever." She pauses. "I have an idea. Let's go back to bed—yes, you can have your way with me again—or I can have my way with you—then I want to prop up on pillows and read Kahlil Gibran to you."

I scoop her into my arms and carry her back to bed.

Our next round of lovemaking is slower and lasts longer as we take our time to explore, learn, tempt, and satisfy each other's bodies.

We shower together, me washing Sherry's hair, her slathering frothy soap all over me. All the touching—neither of us can resist the temptation to satisfy each other one more time before she props herself against the bed pillows, the evening heavy upon us.

"Put your head in my lap," she orders.

"What about your leg?"

She giggles. "You have a big head but it's not particularly heavy."

I do as I am commanded since she has accepted each order that I barked at her.

She opens the book. "Now, close your eyes. I'll pet on you and read."

A smile cracks my face as I lay on my back, peering up at her. "You're serious?"

"As a heart attack. Close your eyes and listen."

So, done.

With one hand, she holds her book and reads; with the other, Sherry softly trails her nails through the hair on my chest. Heavenly.

"I'll pick up where we left off..." she says.

Her touch is soothing as she reads... For even as love crowns you, so shall he crucify you. Even as he is for your growth, so he is for your pruning.

I interrupt, reciting the book from memory... Even as he ascends to your height and caresses your tenderest branches that quiver in the sun, so shall he descend to your roots and shake them in their clinging to the earth.

Our gazes meet. "We just lived it," she whispers.

"Yes, I am aware." I hook my hand on the back of her neck and pull her to me. I feel so free to say it. Liberated even. "I'm going to marry you."

Matteo
COFFEE TIME

"**M**y parents!" Sherry exclaims at first light. "They'll be worried!"

Her squeal rousts me from the deepest sleep. "I'm sure Chris told them."

She asks with wonder in her voice, "How did you know Chris brought me here?"

I tuck my chin to see her back nestled against my side. "Who else would have the balls?"

She chuckles quietly. "You're right. Even he said he was afraid neither of us would be safe."

"Sweetheart, he is lucky I really do love you."

She rolls to face me and smiles sweetly. Proudly. Smugly, as she wiggles her shoulders. "He said you did."

Proof the capos, and I know each other better than we know ourselves. I throw back the covers and pad to the bathroom, slip on briefs, and trudge to the kitchen as Sherry takes her turn.

I don't remember leaving the kitchen lights on. The coffee is brewed. "Did you do this?" I call down the hall. "Or do we have a phantom housekeeper?"

Sherry has made her way into the kitchen. "Do what?"

"This." I point to the coffee pot, which is almost full and hot.

Stopping at the bar, peering at the coffee pot on the kitchen counter, my love's face pales as her gaze lifts to meet mine. She whispers, "Matteo, I didn't make coffee."

Opening the drawer beneath the coffee pot—the Glock is missing.

My chest tightens.

"Looking for this, Matteo, darling?" Sophia steps into the kitchen, my Glock aimed at Sherry's forehead.

Sophia wags the weapon. "So, you'll marry this mousy little tramp but not me."

I whip my head, peering left and right. "How did you get in here?"

Sophia tilts her head toward the garage, where a Goliath of a man steps inside with his gun pressed to Bettina's temple, his other hand gripping her meaty shoulder.

Bettina's eyes are red and swollen. "I'm sorry, Mr. Matteo. They have my family. They are at my house."

I'm... stunned... speechless for a long second.

Peering at Sophia, I ask with wonder, "And you made coffee?"

A terrified Bettina answers. "She made me."

Sophia hikes a smart-ass shoulder. "I needed some caffeine. Didn't think you'd mind."

So why is the coffee pot still full?

With her eyes on me, Sophia rolls her wrist with the gun barrel aimed at Sherry menacingly. "I always did love that body of yours, Matteo. But you might want to cover up."

"I wasn't expecting company. Excuse me and I'll get dressed."

She laughs haughtily. "Nice try."

My gaze goes to Sherry, standing like a statue by the bar, dressed in one of my T-shirts.

They could have killed us in our sleep. She wants us alive.

The bitch pulls two listening devices from her purse, takes a step, dangles, and shakes them in Sherry's face.

Her gaze narrows as she leans into Sherry. "Wish I'd had cameras rolling last night. That would have made one hell of a film." She mimics, sneering, "I love you, I love you, I love." She slings the listening devices viciously at Sherry, who dodges.

They smash against the wall, shattering.

"I thought I'd puke," Sophia says as she levels the gun between Sherry's eyes.

"What do you want Sophia?" I demand loudly, stepping toward the two women.

Staring into the gun barrel, Sherry's eyes are unreadable. I cannot tell if she is frozen in fear or if her mind is whirring, calculating, analyzing the woman holding a gun in her face.

I recall her saying she kept Joey talking so he wouldn't lock her automatic window. Maybe...

Sophia sniffs. "What do I want, Matteo? Eventually, I want both of you dead." She levels the gun at Sherry tauntingly. "Her first."

I move to put myself between them, but Sophia swings the gun at me. "Stay where you are."

I aim my arm at Sherry. "She has done nothing to you! Neither have I, for that matter."

She twists her neck and sneers. "You killed Geno."

"News to me."

"He was in the warehouse."

"I can only hope."

"I hate you, Matteo. You hurt me."

I snicker. "You tried to kill me, Sophia."

Something human crosses her eyes and her tone changes. Softens. Quietens. "I loved you, Matteo. But you treated me like garbage. Coming to me late at night, never taking me out. I wanted you to fall in love with me. Show me off on your arm." She inhales deeply. "But Geno lost patience." She hikes that insolent shoulder again. "And eventually, so did I."

I stare in mute disbelief as Sophia steps closer to me.

If she gets close enough, I can snatch that gun out of her hand.

"I hoped if I laid it out that morning, that you would realize you loved me." Her face and voice harden again. "It became painfully clear you didn't."

I step toward her, seeing her chocolate-colored eyes are actually misty. "You already had Joey waiting downstairs to kill me."

She lifts her chin high. "If you had said, yes, Matteo—I would've called it off."

I scoff. "How long do you think Geno would've let me live once you had my name?"

A snide chuckle escapes from her chest. "Long enough to give me an heir to two families."

I close my eyes, finally seeing the whole truth.

"So, you were Geno's pawn. His first move. Use your beauty and charm to get me to marry you. He would kill me, and you two would run two families."

Again, she offers her dismissive shoulder shrug. "I've said enough."

I will feel no remorse when I kill her.

Sherry takes the opportunity to draw Sophia's attention. "I'm curious, Ms. Gabicci, did you send Joey to trash my apartment and kidnap me? Or was that your cousin Geno?"

With Sophia's gaze on Sherry, I slide farther down the kitchen counter, still facing Sophia.

Sherry notices. The gunman around the counter doesn't.

"Answer me!" Sherry demands. She moves toward Sophia with no fear in her eyes. "I'd like to slap you. Do you have any idea what Joey Carbona did to me?"

Sophia clamps her free palm to her cheek dramatically. Sarcastically. "Oh, poor dear. I feel so sorry for you."

She is not nearly as pretty as I thought she was—not standing by Sherry, who asks, "Why are you here, Sophia?"

Before Sophia can answer, I do. "If she was going to kill us, she would have done it already." Sophia whirls to face me as I go on. "You plan to take us somewhere for the sheer pleasure of torturing us, don't you? Your warehouse is gone. Where are we going?"

Sophia's eyes shoot fire as she hisses, "You. Killed. Geno."

"Like I said. News. To. Me."

"Idiot. Maybe you didn't know. He was humping a little chink when you blew the place. Apparently, their remains will never be found."

Cautiously, glancing from me to Sherry, Sophia steps closer.

One step closer, sweetheart. Just one step.

But she won't. She knows I can take that gun away and kill her in less than a second. She knows I will.

She taunts. "A natural gas explosion? Bribing the fire investigators? Ingenious, Matteo. I'll give you that."

She turns back to glare at Sherry, and I take my opportunity to slide slowly down the cabinet to my destination.

Seeing me move, Sherry fearlessly aims her index finger at Sophia. "You bitch."

Sophia eyes widen, this time with surprise. "I can kill you right here, cunt. But I won't. It will be so much more fun to force Matteo to watch my men fuck you every way from Sunday and force you to watch me fuck your lover in front of you. I promise you I can fuck him better than you can."

"Why did you have Joey kidnap me?"

"I didn't."

The two women glare at each other while I reach my destination. I cut my eyes at Sherry and nod.

Sherry pipes up. "I need some coffee if no one minds." She limps to the coffee pot.

"Yes. You should drink some coffee," Sophia says. "I really made it for you two."

Her back to Sophia, Sherry cuts her eyes at me as she reaches for cups from the overhead counter. "Nice of you to have coffee ready—" She twirls, slinging the almost-full pot of scalding coffee in Sophia's face.

As Sophia screams, I fire one bullet center chest.

Her gunman fires at me, misses—and I plant a bullet between his eyes.

Bettina is on her knees, screaming hysterically as I walk to Sophia, who is bleeding out on my kitchen floor.

Our gazes lock as Sophia groans with pleading eyes, "Matteo."

I fire a bullet between her eyes.

I walk to her henchman and put another round in his chest, for good measure, and cut my eyes at Sherry, who is as calm as bath water. "Good work, sweetheart."

She seems unshaken by my killing two people in front of her. "We make a good team."

I grip her shoulders. "Her plan was for us to drink the coffee. It would knock us out so they could take us to be tortured."

"I know."

"Don't let your guard down."

Sherry's face scrunches. "Why?"

"Because Geno isn't dead. Take care of Bettina while I call the capos."

Matteo
GROUND RULES

It's not an ideal way to announce an engagement, but Sherry rolls with the circumstances. While crews work at my house, the family huddles in Pop's office, briefed on what happened with Sophia. Seeing Sherry and me together—I know a million questions are about to be hurled our way. I have neither the time nor inclination to answer. "Sherry and I are getting married," I tell them without ceremony.

Mother does something I don't remember seeing before—she runs her fingers under her eyes, wiping tears—and Pop smiles at Sherry adoringly as I tell them, "It's not that we have more important things to discuss than our wedding—but something more immediate." I focus on Pop and the capos. "Sophia said Geno died in the warehouse explosion."

Tommy scoffs. "If Geno was dead, the fire investigators would've sucked us dry."

"*Exactly*. They would've demanded more money to keep quiet."

Chris snickers, "Especially if two people died inside. Shit."

Tommy twists his neck. "Besides, I didn't see any vehicles around the warehouse. Trust me. I was there."

Sherry interjects. "I didn't read her as lying. Could it be that Geno *wanted* her to think he was dead?"

"That's my guess," Chris says. "But we've got two men in the cells who can tell us."

"One from Bettina's. One from the van," Tommy adds.

"Where's the van?" I ask.

"In the warehouse. We'll tear it apart."

Sherry peers at me with surprise. "The *cells?*"

I have to draw the line.

"Excuse us," I tell the people in the office, taking Sherry into the adjoining room and speaking quietly. "This is where you have to step back, baby. These are the things you *cannot* know about."

Her brows furrow as she fires back, pointing in the direction of my house. "Matteo, she held a gun to my head. I have a right to know everything."

This moment was always coming. "Are you going to be my wife and the mother of my children, or my business partner?"

She twists her neck. "All three, I'd hoped."

Our gazes are locked as I shake my head gently. "No, sweetheart. It doesn't work that way. There are things you'll never know. Things You Can. Not. Know. As my wife, trust me, please, the way my mother trusts my father."

Her jaw sags as Sherry takes a step back. "Dammit, Matteo. I'm not your mother."

Fuck.

"I know that. I didn't mean it that way."

How can she not understand I'm trying to protect her from the ugliness? The answer washes over me: *Because she has no idea what the ugliness looks like. Not. A. Clue.*

But Sherry's a lawyer. She'll understand this: "Listen to me." I bend so our faces are inches apart. "You can help take our family into the next phase of our existence, operating legal casinos." I tuck my chin. "I can't have you exposed you to... certain legalities."

She narrows her gaze, staring for a long beat. I see her wheels turning, trying to crawl inside my mind. Sorry, beautiful girl. Some parts of me you will never see. You might not love me if you did. I lift my brow, waiting for her answer.

Finally, she nods. "Alright, Matteo. For you."

I release a sigh. "Don't you have a wedding to plan?"

Two men, handcuffed to overhead chains, sit side by side. Normally, we don't allow two men to be interrogated together, but I have a reason for this arrangement.

"State your names," I tell them.

They're both young. The man on my left spits at my feet. His face has been pummeled by fists. I don't know whose.

The other says, "Fuck yourself." His face fared no better than the first. His nose is broken, the swelling spread across both eyes.

"Where's Geno?" I keep my voice quiet, addressing both as I tuck my cufflinks in my pocket and roll up my sleeves.

The one who spit at me earlier says, "Dead."

"Wrong answer." I aim my Glock at his friend's face, my eyes on the spitter. "I'll ask again, where is Geno?"

The spitter sneers. "Shoot him, I don't give a shit."

I put him about Joey's age. Taller, thinner. Fair skin and hair. I don't like his disregard for his fellow soldier. I fire the Glock, putting a bullet in the spitter's kneecap, and he screams like a wildcat. I aim the Glock at the other man, who heaves onto the cement floor. "Where's Geno?"

With his arms stretched straight over his head, he wipes the vomit from his lips onto his shoulder. "I don't know."

His companion is dying. Blood seeps toward the floor drain between them as the spitter groans in agony. I don't care.

My eyes are on the second man, the one on my right. "What's your name?"

"Massimo."

I aim the gun at his chest. "I won't ask again, Massimo. Where's Geno Gabicci?"

"Jersey."

I lower the barrel to aim at the floor. "And you know this how?"

"It's what he told me."

"When?"

"Couple of days ago."

"What was Sophia's plan, breaking into my house?"

"Take you and the girl to Geno."

My brows rise high. "Sophia knew Geno was alive?"

"Yeah."

She really missed her calling. Sophia Gabicci was one hell of an actress. Those misty eyes in the kitchen. She manufactured them, too.

"Where were you going to take us?"

"They didn't tell me. That was between her and Geno. We just do what we're told."

"What were you told to do?"

"Use the housekeeper to get into your house."

"Then?"

"Dispose of her and her family. Get you and the girl to wherever Sophia said."

"And she never told you where you'd be going? Think hard."

He wags his head. "No. I swear."

I scratch my cheek. I didn't get a chance to shave, the stubble is itchy. "If you had to get in touch with Geno, how would you?"

Fear. It's a hard thing to miss in a man's eyes. "I have a phone number."

Tommy steps out of the shadows. "Give it to me."

These two aren't getting out of here alive, so there's no need for my capos to hide.

The man recites a phone number, which Tommy scribbles on a notepad. As he's writing, he says to Massimo, "Tell me everything about what they're doing in Maryland. The more you talk, the easier I'll make it on you."

I see hope flit across the young man's face. "You'll let me live?"

Tommy's lips press into a tight line. "I didn't say that. I said I'd make it easier."

Fear overtakes the young man's face, his gaze darting from Tommy to me. "I don't want to die."

I step toward him. "No one wants to die but we all do. It's a matter of when. And how." I watch tears well in his eyes and roll down his face. "Massimo, your time has come earlier than it should because you made bad choices. Tommaso can make your death painless... or painful. Make the right choice." I peer at my friend, who holds up the phone number and hands it to me. "I'll give this to Chris. I'll check back in."

After everything that happened last night and this morning—I want to see Sherry. Alone.

Sherry
THE BEGINNING

"I'm taking my wife-to-be home," Matteo announces as he walks into the sunroom of his parent's house. He shifts his gaze to me. "We're clear to go back in."

I've been visiting Francesco and Donna since Matteo left with Tommy and Chris, waiting while what happened in Matteo's kitchen this morning was... being taken care of.

I'm good with our new ground rules.

My part of the business will be getting us totally out of the drug trade. *Yay.* Francesco took the time to fill me in. He says Matteo's plan should eventually be more profitable than drugs, with no more worries about law enforcement.

I ask no questions about how Matteo handles his end of the business. I've witnessed how he handles business. After the way Matteo took care of me this morning—his quick precision with a gun—he validated everything Chris said. He. Is. Lethal. People should fear him.

But not me. Matteo loves me. And I love him.

Donna is so excited about the prospect of her son finally settling down. He was telling the truth when he said his mother had been pushing him to get married since he was twenty-five. Further proof the man can't be pushed. Something inside of me loves that, too. He is such a force to be reckoned with.

Francesco's been listening to Donna and I talk about wedding plans, feigning interest as he sips iced tea and peruses the TV.

Seeing Matteo enter the room, Donna pops from her chair to wrap her arms around her son's waist, and he wraps his arms around her. "I'm so glad you came to your senses," she purrs. She hooks her arm around his and beams at me. "I couldn't be happier." Her gaze moves from me to Matteo. "Now, I want grandchildren."

Francesco chokes on his tea, and I feel my cheeks flush.

Matteo cracks a lopsided grin. "Mother, give us a minute or two before you expect grandkids."

"When's the wedding?" Donna demands.

"Ask Sherry."

Our eyes meet. "Matteo, when and where do *you* want to get married?"

"Sweetheart we can do it this afternoon, as far as I'm concerned. The frou-frous of marriage have always been a female thing. I do have one request, though." He moves close.

"Anything," I whisper. Will he always take my breath?

He stands close, peering down at me with those piercing black eyes, and flashes his grin that shows his little dimple. The one that makes me quiver deep inside. As he twirls my hair around his finger, Matteo says, "I want to honeymoon on Lake Bolsena."

"Where?"

"The Italian Alps. I want you to see what I see when I look into your eyes."

Italy. My hand clasps over my heart. "I don't see any reason to wait. I want a small, intimate wedding. We can do it wherever your mother and my mother agree." I turn to my soon-to-be-mother-in-law. "How does that sound to you, Donna?"

She claps her hands together. "Perfect. When?"

I lift my shoulder. "One month from today?"

"Not enough time!" Donna protests.

Francesco speaks for the first time in a while. "Donna. She said she wants a small, intimate wedding. We're not filling the cathedral."

Matteo draws me to his side. "Six weeks, Mother. That's all you've got. And I want a small wedding, too."

"Matteo, just how insatiable is your sexual appetite?" I laugh as he carries me to his bedroom. He started taking my clothes off of me in the car. I've lost count of how many times we've made love since I climbed into the shower with him yesterday.

I am so glad I did.

I almost didn't. I almost shrank away from his icy anger.

But watching Matteo from the kitchen that afternoon, I had heard Chris's words when he drove me there: *Some men say it too quickly. Some men can't say it at all. That doesn't mean they don't feel love.*

I wasn't going to let him push me away. I was determined to make it right. Thank God.

Matteo carries me bridal-style down the long hallway, my arms around his neck. "We lost a lot of time, sweetheart."

Setting me beside the bed, he pulls my sweater over my head, chunks it into the nearby chair, and unbuttons my jeans, sliding them to the floor.

I stand before him in nothing but a lacy white bra and white bikini panties. He removes my bra greedily.

His eyes drift from my face to my feet and back up.

As our gazes lock—like they always seem to do—I tug hard on his belt, unbuckling it.

"You were amazing this morning," Matteo says as his pants fall to the floor. "Throwing that hot coffee on her was genius. And fearless."

"I trusted you." I unbutton his shirt.

It's my turn to take him.

Before he can remove the cufflinks, I drag my fingernails across his thick chest, raking them through the soft, black hair. Rigid muscles ripple beneath his warm skin. Not one ounce of fat is on this man.

I kiss and run my tongue over one little nipple. He leans his head back with a soft moan.

"You were awesome this morning Matteo. So cool. So calm. So... deadly."

He grips my face in one hand and tilts my jaw so our gazes can catch. "That doesn't scare you?"

"The opposite. You make me feel safe."

Matteo's beautiful black eyes leave mine as he gives all his attention to my breasts. His lips close over a sensitive nipple and he begins to suck, taking my breast into his mouth. When he does, he pulls all the sense out of my head. As always, all I can do is feel. Him.

He's an expert at many things, not the least of which is this.

I lower his briefs to cup his erection and squeeze tightly.

Matteo thrusts against me with a grunt, grips me under my arms, and places me on the bed, yanking off my panties impatiently. He tosses them aside. "How can I want you so much, again and again and again? Will I ever get my fill?"

"I hope not."

"On your knees, sweetheart."

I hold up my index finger. "Give me one minute."

I grip his thick shaft, swirl my tongue around his tip, then take him into my mouth, sucking hard, massaging the base that I can't take.

Matteo runs his fingers in my hair with a growl of pleasure.

Sucking as I pull up and out, I pause to tease his tip with my tongue again.

"Sherry... you..."

I keep sucking and pumping him with my fist.

"Oh, fuck. On your knees. Now."

This time, I comply.

He grips my hips, pulls me to the edge of the bed, and slides his fingers through my folds. "You're ready."

I wiggle my hips impatiently. "I know."

Standing by the bed, he moves his cock to my entrance. "Oh, my God, Sherry. You are so fucking wet." He grips my waist tightly and pulls me into him as he thrusts.

I shudder and groan, arching my back and hiking my hips, giving him full access. He draws out and pushes back in, filling me up again.

It is all I can do to take all of him.

Matteo strokes one palm down the curve of my back as he begins to pump rhythmically, slowly at first, and I roll my hips to meet each thrust.

He pulls out, running his cock through my folds, teasing my sensitive skin.

Matteo leans over, kneading my breast, and whispers in my ear, "I'll pleasure you like this for the rest of your life."

His voice is so fucking sexy. I feel my juices running down my thigh.

He pulls me upright on my knees, draws my back to his chest, and thrusts into me again and again, moving deliberately.

Matteo takes his pleasure as if he were playing a musical instrument thrusting... pulling out... long strokes. I have never been this wet. My body is on the brink of bursting as my walls begin to pulse.

Such a sensuous man.

Maybe it's *not* his words that make my insides quiver. Maybe it's his hand squeezing my breast, his thumb teasing my nipple as he works inside of me. Or maybe I'm so wet because he slides that hand from my breast, down my abdomen to stroke me where we join—as he continuously, rhythmically thrusts in... and pulls out.

I turn my head to kiss the taut skin over the sculpted muscle that is his bicep, tasting the salt of his sweat. "*Oh, Matteo.*"

I luxuriate in every... inch... of him. He takes my breath. He is so... hard... so strong...

I feel the orgasm building inside of me.

He senses it, too. My heart drums wildly as Matteo begins to move faster and harder, driving me to the edge... My body is...

His hot breath brushes my neck as he whispers his command. "Come for me, Sherry. Let me feel you come... on me... now."

An electrical charge courses through me, rippling from my head to my toes as my muscles contract around him and my body shudders. "Oh... God!" My nipples draw tight and stand erect as my walls ripple around him again and again. I come on his command.

He thrusts hard and deep once... twice... spilling inside of me with a loud groan. "Sherry." His face drips sweat as he buries it in my neck, sucking on my shoulder.

It feels so right, us coming as one.

"What about a ring?" Matteo asks as I lay in his arms, our legs wrapped around each other.

With my cheek resting on his pecs, I trace my finger down that sexy line of black hair that disappears at his V-line. It must tickle. His abdomen flexes.

"Boxing was so good for your body."

He chuckles. "The same way running has been good for yours."

"You have a gym. I've never seen you work out."

He twirls my hair around his finger. I can see it will become a habit. "Not since I got shot. I'll go back to it soon. Now quit changing the subject, sweetheart. What kind of wedding ring do you want? White gold? Yellow gold? Platinum? A wide band? A thin band?"

His question warms my heart. "Matteo, I have never thought about a wedding ring. I want you to choose it. Surprise me."

"I'll give you a diamond so big you won't be able to hold your hand up."

I can't help but giggle, which prompts his warm laughter.

"Not that overboard." I trace the outline of his beautiful mouth, telling him. "Your lips are perfect."

He takes my finger into his mouth and sucks sensuously, circling it with his tongue. "What about the stone? Square? Round? This is important. I have to get this right."

"Matty, you have impeccable taste. Whatever you choose, I'll love."

He smiles slowly, raking his fingers through my hair to comb it off my forehead. "That's the first time you ever called me Matty."

"It just came out."

He kisses my forehead and squeezes me tenderly. "Finally. We're family."

 Matteo
RAT TRAP

The temperatures plummeted overnight. An early Arctic blast had taken aim at the Mid-Atlantic.

We have enough windows to keep the place comfortable in summer, but this ancient building is like a refrigerator when the wind whistles off the water with the temperature hovering around freezing.

In the comfortably warm office, I pour my capos drinks, deliver them, and hold my glass high. "To my best men."

Tommy laughs. "You can't have two best men."

"Says who?" I down my drink. "I can't pick between the two of you—so you're both best men."

"Salute, brother." Chris lifts his glass high and throws it back. "As soon as Tina's divorce is final, I hope to do the same."

"Congratulations." I pull him into a brotherly hug.

In a rare daytime event, Tommy tosses his bourbon back and clomps the glass on the desk. "About time you two dumbasses grew up."

I chuckle and ignore the jab, asking Chris, "Did we have an address on the phone number Massimo gave us?"

With a nod, he passes a sheet of paper from his desk to me. I k now that address. "I'll be damned. He ran home to Alfonso."

"I've never cared enough to ask. Why doesn't Geno have a father?" Chris asks.

"His father, Alfonso's younger brother, was killed in the war. Geno was a baby. His mother lost her mind and abandoned her only son. If I didn't hate him so much, I'd feel sorry for Geno. Alfonso stepped up and raised him. He might as well be Alfonso's son, Sophia's brother."

"Alfonso can't protect Geno," Chris says.

"I don't know," Tommy says. "He's got a fortress and an army. Massimo had some valuable intel."

Our eyes meet. "I'm all ears."

"He says Geno has a hundred men. And he's put a bounty on your head and Sherry's. Wants you both delivered alive."

I cringe, remembering what Enzo said Geno wants to do to Sherry. I stroke my hand over my face and pinch the bridge of my nose. "How much?"

"A million."

I choke and have trouble clearing my windpipe. "It's hard to start a life when my wife and I have a million-dollar bounty on our heads."

"A million each. That's what the kid said."

"The kid, Massimo. Is he still...?"

"Yeah, we gave him a bunk cell for the night. Thought he might be useful. The other guy?" Chris clears his throat. "Expired."

I wonder aloud, my gaze moving from Chris to Tommy, "Do you trust this Massimo kid?"

The capos glance at each other, and Chris shrugs his broad shoulders. "I'd like to. But after Joey, I'm afraid to trust my gut."

"I know the feeling." I stand, shoving my fists into my pants pockets to keep myself from hitting something. "Fuck." The trash can suffers the brunt of my frustration, clanging across the floor. *"Dammit!"*

"We know Geno'll take Massimo's call," Tommy says. "Might be worth a try. We don't take our eyes off of him. We don't give him a chance to betray us."

Chris says, "We can make him an offer: if he helps us bring down Geno, he gets his life."

"I don't know." My gaze roams the room. "We don't know anything about him." I tilt my head back, staring at the ceiling.

Enzo. He struggled and died right above where I am now.

I've been thinking. "Do you remember what Enzo told us? About the company working with Geno? Horizon? It consists of Mulholland, Kerrigan, and Buchanan?"

They both nod. "Sherry told me Johansen thinks Buchanan is part of Geno's sex trafficking ring."

Chris spits into the trash can he just picked up and set down. "Hypocritical fuckers."

The two capos watch me.

I'm not successfully connecting the dots for them yet. "Remember the afternoon Geno lost both of his capos? You two ended a war before it started."

They nod again, both all eyes.

"Time to do it again."

Chris's brows draw together. "Are you talking about taking all three of them out at once?" His words drip with disbelief.

I nod with a sideways smile.

"Damn." He looks at Tommy with wide eyes. "If we kill a congressman, his aide, and a prosecutor at the same time, we'll have every fucking fed from here to California up our asses."

"Who said anything about killing anyone? I can, however, foresee that a congressman and his aide might have a tragic accident somewhere on the interstate. Some cars have been known to burst into flames when the turn signal is used."

Chris snaps his fingers, pointing at me. "I think that's the Pinto." He perks up. "A lady in California was rear-ended with her turn signal on and her Pinto exploded. Killed everyone in the car."

I lift my hands in wonder. "Who's to say other cars don't have the same fatal mechanical problem? Brakes fail. Eighteen wheelers cross the median into oncoming traffic. People die all different ways on the interstates. And Buchanan? I'm sure there are ex-cons out the ass who would love to take him out. As payback." I raise my fresh two-fingers of whiskey. "*We* aren't killing anyone."

I show them my index finger for emphasis. "But I want Genovese Gabicci alive."

"Boss?" Massimo whispers into the telephone, his hand curled around the mouthpiece. "Need to see you."

"Where are you?" the gravelly voice asks.

"Port of Baltimore."

A long silence is followed by a threatening whisper. "What are you doing there? The warehouse is gone."

"They got me and Eddy. I've convinced them they can trust me. I can get you inside this warehouse. DeVecchio and his two capos are downstairs. They're dumbasses. You can deliver some payback."

"You're shitting me." Geno is skeptical.

"No sir." Massimo pauses before adding, "You know... they killed Sophia... and Big Tony."

"Fuckers!" Geno roars so loudly that Massimo pulls the receiver away from his ear. We can all hear him. "What did they do with her body?"

"No idea, sir."

If Sophia's death doesn't drive Geno into a murderous rage, I've given Massimo one more carrot to dangle.

He says, "I overheard. They've got a shipment coming in tonight. You can kill them and take their shipment. Payback for killing Sophia."

"What time?" Geno snaps.

"I think they said around ten."

A long pause as Geno ponders. "They'll have too many men there to unload," he says. "Too much risk."

"Unless your crew sneaks in early and hides. It's a big place," Massimo says. "Fuckin' penguins are shivering in here."

Another stretch of silence. Geno's wheels are turning. Greed and revenge are powerful motivators.

"You said a million dollars for DeVecchio alive. I trust you meant it," the kid says.

"I meant it," Geno replies. "But how do I know I can trust you, Massimo?"

"With a million dollars on the line? And a chance to help you take down the high and mighty DeVecchio? You think I'd fuck that up?"

Nothing from Geno.

"Whatever," Massimo says. "I'm going to sneak down and leave the back dock door unlocked. Gotta go." He hangs up the phone and looks at me through steel-gray eyes. "Is that what you wanted?"

I nod, rubbing my thumb along my lower lip, studying Massimo. A gangly kid with buzzed brown hair. My gaze narrows. "You're a good actor, Massimo. How do I know I can trust you?"

He shrugs. "I guess you don't. I'm learning, sir. In this business, nobody really knows who they can trust."

I head from the warehouse to Sherry, finding her going through boxes in the garage. When I drive up, she looks up and smiles. I picked up my new 911 while I was out. It's black. She puts her hands on her hips and beams. "Pretty car."

That, sweetheart, is an understatement.

"Your men delivered my clothes and things." She turns in a circle with her arms extended wide. "Where will I put all this stuff? It's everything I have."

I kiss her hello. "I'll hire a housekeep to help you. In the meantime, I'm sure Mother will let you use Bettina. This is your home now. Our closet has plenty of room. There are two guest rooms. I have an office off of our bedroom. And remember. We have a gym. Arrange things the way you want. You can tell me where to find what I need."

That earns me a million-dollar smile and a come-hither kiss. But we don't have time for more. "Right now, though, I need for you to pack a bag and come with me."

She tilts her head curiously. "Where?"

"I'll show you."

She flashes a dangerous look. "Why?" I see her mind ticking. Sherry has good intuition.

I pull her to me and, in spite of myself, slide my hand down the front of her jeans, teasing her. "Do you trust me?" *God, I can't help myself.*

She doesn't blink as she cups my erection, smiling. "With my life."

"That's what I'm doing: protecting you so we can have a life."

We gather in my father's office: Mother, Sherry, the capos, and Antonio. Tommy tells them of Geno's million-dollar bounty on bringing me and Sherry in alive.

My eyes are on Sherry as Tommy lays it out.

Her face drains of all color—so does Mother's. The two women stare at each other in silence.

I draw Sherry tightly to my side. "You'll stay here, in this house, until we end this."

Sherry whips around, facing me with fear on her face, her hands on my chest. "Oh, Matteo."

I saw no fear in her eyes when Sophia was pointing a gun at her head, but now I see it. Holding my fingers to her lips, I don't let her finish. "I'll be alright. I have Christos and Tommaso. We're posting two men inside this house and two outside, in addition to the men on the gate."

"Bullshit!" Pop erupts. "I'm going with you men to end Geno. This has gone far enough."

"Pop, if by some chance Geno's men got past the guards, I need to know you're here to protect Mother and Sherry as only you can."

I see his flash of recognition. He draws in a deep breath and exhales. "You're right."

I glance from the capos to the group. "We feel certain Geno will show up tonight, with a force. He wants to take me alive and take our shipment."

Pop peers at Mother and Sherry. "Let us talk."

The women leave.

"What is your plan?" Pop asks.

We lay it out step by step.

Pop rubs his chin. "Sounds solid. But plan what you're going to do when something goes wrong. Because it always does."

Matteo

BAITING THE RAT

Out of the mouth of babes... I keep thinking about what Massimo said this morning. In this business, you don't know who to trust.

The trap is set. Waiting for the rat to take the bait, my mind races.

I trust Tommy and Chris. My father. Sherry and Mother. Benji and Sal.

A lot of these men, though, I don't know. I have to trust my capos. They vetted them all.

But since Joey... I can't.

Massimo is locked in his cell. I refuse to trust him.

Trust is a treasure that cannot be bought. You earn trust with time.

"The wind is howling!" Tommy yells. "It's going to be hell up here if it starts raining."

He's posted on the roof with night goggles, waiting for Geno's men to show. I can only imagine how cold it is up there.

This is the first freeze of the year. Sleet is predicted before morning. I have a flash vision of sitting in front of the fireplace with Sherry's head nestled against my neck. Get your shit together, man.

Chris and I are in the office, talking to Tommy over his two-way. He'll tell us when he sees headlights or movement.

"What time did you say the truck is coming?"

"Ten o'clock," Chris answers.

Tommy knows what time the truck is coming. He just needs to talk to someone to help him endure the misery of being on the tall roof of this old building, right at the water's edge, in freezing, biting wind.

"Who guarded the warehouse while we were at Pop's?" I ask.

"Benji," Chris answers and clicks his two-way. "Benji, check in."

"Nothing here." Benji's posted on the second floor, watching out the front windows.

A fear slaps my chest. "You sure they aren't already inside?"

Chris nods. "As sure as I can be, but I'll have a couple of men double-check." He keys the radio. "Sal, you and Nico start on the third floor. Check each room moving down. Make sure no Gabicci men already snuck in."

Sal answers his radio. "Ten-four."

"Key twice if you see anything suspicious."

"Ten-four."

Chris studies me. "You're worried."

"Yeah."

"It's a good plan."

Our gazes meet. "Ever since what happened with Joey... I worry about her. What if they skip the warehouse and go to Pop's?"

Chris leans his elbows on his desk. "He has a safe room, right?"

"Of course."

"He'll get them in there. We need your head here."

I nod. Chris is right. He's level-headed. Pragmatic about all things business.

I'm worrying like an old woman. I stand. "I'm going to walk the first floor." I can't sit still any longer.

Bundling my coat around me, I check my weapons. Two Glocks and a Steyr AUG with four spare magazines. If they don't kill me first, I've got plenty of firepower.

We all do.

Walking around, I realize how long it's been since I spent much of any time inside the warehouse. I worked here through high school and college. Loading and unloading pallets. Pop's requirement. Nobody works for the company without coming through the ranks, like he did.

That included his son.

Pop worked in this warehouse before he bought it.

Massimo was right. This old building is unbearably cold. We have gloves, but I hate to use them and handle weapons. But if your hands are freezing...

This old heating system cannot keep up with weather like this. I hold my hand over a vent. It's blowing, and it's warm. The warehouse is just so big. We need to upgrade.

Pallets of goods are stacked high around the perimeter of the first floor.

The freezer. I key my radio, speaking quietly. "Who checked the freezer?"

"I did," Benji answers. "Herring and sprat."

"That new room?"

"Clear."

Calm down. Your men have it covered. We've been over everything with everybody.

"Incoming. Dock side." Tommy says into his two-way, the wind howling around him. "Two squads. One north, one south."

He pauses, lowering his voice as much as possible and still be heard over the wind. "I count ten in each group. Rifled-up. Get ready."

I check my watch. It's ten minutes until ten.

"How far out?" Chris asks.

"Guessing fifty yards." Tommy pauses again. "They've taken a knee. Waiting."

"Sal, do you see anything?" Chris asks.

Sal answers, "Nico and I are still on the third floor. It's clean inside but we count another twenty men out front. Two squads twenty feet apart. They've taken a knee like the guys in back."

So, Geno's men have two-way radios, too. "Looks like everyone is waiting on the truck," Tommy says.

Four squads of ten. More men than we anticipated.

"Anyone see who's in command?" I ask.

Tommy. "Negative."

Sal. "Negative."

Benji. "Negative."

I squat behind a pallet near the big dock doors. The driver will pull the truck in front and flash his lights. Our men will open the front sliding doors to let the eighteen-wheeler will pull in, then our men will close the front doors behind him.

But before they can shut it completely, Geno's twenty men in front will rush inside.

As instructed, the dock doors are unlocked. Twenty men will rush this door.

"All men in position?" I ask.

One man after another answers, "Affirmative."

"Truck's coming." I hear the urgency in Tommy's voice. "Get ready."

Chris keys his two-way. "When the driver gives the signal, open the door like business as usual."

We wait. My heart drums. This is it. We live or die on this battlefield.

Sherry
SAFE PLACE

My stomach's been a washing machine since I learned Matteo and I each have a one-million-dollar bounty on our heads.

Geno wants to torture and kill him. He wants to rape and sell me.

Matteo's doing the only thing he can do. He's gone to kill Geno.

They call him a killer. I've experienced his world. What Joey did to me. What Sophia tried to do to us. Outsiders don't understand—this is a kill-or-be-killed world.

It's new to me but it's all Matteo knows.

Sitting here waiting, wringing my hands, not knowing if...

No. I won't think it. He's alive. He'll defeat Geno Gabicci and end this campaign of terror.

Closing my eyes, I rest my head in my hands, envisioning him. Us.

I couldn't breathe without Matteo. His ice melted. He loves me. He wants to marry me. Matteo has to come back to me. Safe.

"Sherry."

I look up and blink. I think Francesco's been talking to me. "Sir?"

"Come with me." He holds out his hand. "I want to show you something."

I get up from the couch and follow.

Donna's at his side, scolding him. "We should've already showed her this."

"Hasn't been a reason. Donna. I haven't thought about it in—I don't know when."

I follow them into the formal dining room, which has heavy, floor-to-ceiling drapes drawn. A large mahogany China cabinet is along one wall, and a sprawling mahogany bookcase filled with dishes, framed pictures and, of course books, stretches across another.

Francesco slides a large vase on one of the shelves and the wall begins to move.

My jaw sags a bit watching it swing open, bookshelf, dishes and all.

Francesco ushers us inside a hidden room, flipping a switch. Overhead fluorescent lights illuminate the space. Francesco pulls the door shut and threads a wide steel bar through metal U-shaped fasteners embedded in the block wall. Two fasteners are embedded in the bookshelf door itself.

"Even if they find the door latch, if we have it dead bolted like this inside, with the bar running through the fasteners on either side and across the door, they can't get in. The bar and the bolts are steel—even this side of the door—all steel. They can't shoot it off." Francesco looks at his wife. "You know what to do if anything happens."

Donna nods, and for the first time since I've known them, I watch her stand on tiptoes to kiss Francesco, and his lips meet hers. He pulls her to him in a tight embrace as she nuzzles her head in his chest.

I don't know why it surprises me—they have three children—I've just never seen it.

The way she looks at him, with adoration and complete trust. It's sweet.

I hope we look at each other that way in thirty or forty years.

Francesco opens a cabinet on the back wall, showing me the DeVecchio firepower. It's lined with all kinds of rifles, guns, and boxes of ammunition. "Do you know how to use these?" he asks.

"Never touched one."

"Matteo will teach you. I taught Donna. She's never had to use one, but I make sure she can. I make her take a refresher course every year."

She twerks her mouth and nods. "You do what you've got to do."

"Thank you for showing me. Is there food in here, too?"

"Staples and water. You could stay here a long time, but you won't have to." Francesco walks to the far end of the room and points to the floor. He bends down and pulls up a trap door that exposes a black tunnel. "If you ever have to, you can escape this way. It leads to a pumphouse near Matteo's house."

He pulls the door open wide, ushers me closer, and points again. "Look. It has the same deadbolt system inside as the big door. If you ever have to go down there to hide, you slide that deadbolt bar through the loops on the underside of the trap door, and they won't be able to follow you."

I peer at Donna. "I never imagined such a system."

"Our husbands' work is dangerous, dear. We have to be prepared to guard our children."

I nod. "What now?"

"We go back and wait," Francesco says. "I wanted you to know where it is, how to get inside and how to lock yourself in."

I guess I look frightened because his thick white eyebrows draw together. "Unless you want to wait in here."

I look at Donna, who shakes her head. "No TV. And we've got men on the gates, outside and inside. I say, let's have a drink."

I'm terrified—for Matteo. For Chris and Tommy. I catch myself biting my lower lip.

I. Will. Not. Cry.

I can't. I'll be Matteo DeVecchio's wife. And I *will* be strong. "Francesco, what's happening?"

My father-in-law-to-be looks at his watch. "About now, I'd say all hell is breaking loose."

Matteo
SPRINGING THE TRAP

"**O**pen the doors," Chris commands over his two-way. "Prepare for engagement. Radio silence."

As he speaks, he turns his office lights out and moves to the open office door. He's armed with the same Steyr AUG we all have. And a Glock.

With the high ceilings and old fixtures, the warehouse is dimly lit. The truck headlights beam through the cavernous space onto the back dock doors as the truck pulls inside, driving deeper than normal.

Tommy says quietly, "They're moving. Front and back."

I chamber a round as the driver stops the truck and turns off the engine.

As our men start to slide the front doors shut, rifle fire sprays into the warehouse.

Our men on the doors were prepared, wearing bulletproof vests.

They drop and roll, firing their weapons as a line of men rush the front.

At the same time, the dock doors open wide, and another line of Gabicci soldiers storm the warehouse, along with rifle fire and a blast of icy air.

I fire, dropping the first three men through the door before drawing fire.

Chris is doing the same, taking out the first few through the front door.

I dive and roll behind the nearest pallet, hunkering down as men stationed high in the warehouse loft open fire on Geno's men.

They are like fish in a barrel. The problem is that this barrel has plenty of pallets that offer protection to us and our enemy.

Chris and I have to worry about being caught in the crossfire. I'm sure he's tucked behind the office wall as I crouch behind this pallet.

I drop a man sneaking up from the side. That's four down that I can count. He started with forty.

Checking left, right, and behind me, there is no sign of Geno.

With the main action in the center of the warehouse, I move to close the dock doors. No one seems to notice as I move swiftly—bullets are spraying everywhere.

I slide, close, and lock the dock doors. Fuckers aren't going to escape this way.

Back behind a pallet, I crouch low and move forward, my rifle ready, my gaze roaming. The front doors are closed now, too.

We are all trapped inside our warehouse.

Motionless bodies litter the center aisle, blood pooling around each. Geno has lost several men, but that still leaves him plenty.

I don't know how many of us are injured.

The cargo doors of the eighteen-wheeler swing open, and fresh reinforcements jump out, firing on Geno's men.

All DeVecchio soldiers are in uniform, wearing Army green overalls with the eagle emblem.

Not dressed in green overalls? You are a fair target.

While the truck crew fires on Geno's men, our soldiers in the loft reload.

I take down a man creeping between pallets across from me.

The echo of rifle fire, high and low, is deafening.

I'm close enough now to see the windows to the office are gone. Shattered.

A shrill whistle pierces our ears. "Cease fire! Cease fire!"

That is fucking Geno Gabicci.

The warehouse silences as Gabicci yells, "DeVecchio! Come out. We'll settle this, you and me!"

I'm not answering. It will give away my position. Instead, I creep toward Geno's voice.

He's on the far side of the warehouse, somewhere near the front of the building.

"DeVecchio! You gutless dick! Get out here and fight me like a man!"

Chris snipes toward Gabicci's voice, and the crossfire erupts again.

I crouch low and dart across the warehouse to Geno's side of the building. I'll meet you, motherfucker. But not on your terms.

We've got a lot of ammunition. But we've used a lot already. If this keeps up for much longer, the cops will be on top of us.

It's after ten o'clock on the docks. Not many people are in this remote stretch at this hour, but this kind of firepower is bound to be reported if it keeps up.

Geno didn't expect our Trojan horse. We didn't expect him to bring this many men.

A shrill whistle pierces the warehouse again, and Geno yells, "Cease fire!"

It doesn't sound like he's moved. "DeVecchio, you sniveling coward! You'll pay for what you did to Soph—!"

Pop!

Someone shuts him up. Maybe they hit him. Maybe Geno will learn to keep his mouth shut or get shot.

I'm making my way to him. He won't see me until it's too late, if I don't have to shoot someone between here and there.

Fire shoots through my left arm. *Dammit.* I hit the floor as another bullet zips past my temple. Too close. Shit. I'm in their territory.

I roll onto my back between two pallets to load another magazine, draw a deep breath, and stand, opening fire in the direction of that last bullet.

When I do, someone fires a continuous stream in Geno's direction, and he is joined up by others.

I'm looking for the fucker who shot me.

Sal and Tommy emerge from the stairwell, back-to-back, unloading in Geno's direction.

Silence.

Half of my men should have reloaded while this half was firing. Our men are trained.

My eyes dart about the room. I don't know who is dead and who is alive.

How many Gabicci men are still standing?

If I call out, I give away my position like Geno did.

Silence envelopes the warehouse. Geno doesn't call out.

That doesn't mean anything. He may be trying to lure us into a trap.

"Joey!"

I don't know that voice.

"Geno's hurt!"

I'm not falling for that.

"Geno needs help!" the man calls.

I want to laugh, but I can't.

"Joey—" *Pop!*

Somebody puts an end to that idiot. Make any noise, and you give up your location.

Silence.

I check behind me and overhead. Nobody knows where anybody is. And in this warehouse, there are many places to hide.

I fire twice. A body drops from a pallet stacked almost to the ceiling, landing several feet in front of me.

His aim was on my head when I happened to glance up.

I stay on my back, checking high. While all the shooting has been going on, Geno's men have climbed to get vantage points.

I drop another man high over the freezer.

"Psst!"

I flinch and turn to see Tommy squatting low—as low as a man his size can get. He motions for me to come to him.

I roll and belly crawl.

"Get in here." Tommy grabs me and pulls me into the hidden room. I forgot it was here.

Outside the room, *Pop! Pop! Pop! Bap! Bap!* Sporadic gunfire echoes in the warehouse as soldiers on both sides spot targets.

"You're bleeding."

I look at my left arm. I've been so focused on fighting I didn't feel it. "It's a nick."

"Damn, Matty. Look at your arm. It's soaked. I've got to get a tourniquet on it."

"I'm okay. Do you have any idea where Geno is?"

"Somewhere on this side near the front."

"Are you good? Benji?"

"Yeah, we're good. Benji is guarding the stairwell so they can't go up."

"Do you think Geno's shot? Hurt?"

"Naw. That was a stupid schoolyard trick."

"He's near the freight elevator. If he gets on it, he can reach a fire escape. I can't let that happen. It ends tonight. I'm going for Geno."

Tommy clutches my shoulder. "No, man. They are all over this side of the building. They can pick you off between here and there."

"Then cover me. I'm going low. If we don't end this soon, the cops are going to be all over us."

"I wondered about that."

"It ends now. Cover me."

Opening the door, glancing left, right, and above, I hunker low and make it toward the front of the building, stopping at each pallet to check left, right, and high. One pallet at a time.

Men are firing from near Chris's office.

That truck is parked in the middle of the warehouse. *The truck.* If a stray bullet hits the diesel tank, it could cause an explosion that will kill all of us and burn down the warehouse.

I have to end this.

I glance over my shoulder and see Tommy as he aims high and fires. Another Gabicci man falls.

I peek around the pallet beside me. Every time I do it, I know I could get my head blown off. But it's the only way.

There he is.

Geno is squatting, rifle in hand, facing Chris's office. His back is to me.

I won't backshoot him. First, because I don't backshoot. Secondly, it might give away my position to the Gabicci soldiers who surround me. So, I stand, step, and swing my rifle, full force.

Geno senses me and turns, eyes wide with alarm, as he raises his rifle to fire. He's a half-second late. My rifle stock catches him in the temple before he can take his shot. Geno Gabicci crumbles like a sandcastle struck by a wave.

Zipping out of my overalls, I yank off my belt, and wrap it around his feet, buckling it.

He's wearing Gucci loafers. So am I.

He stirs, and I hit him in the head again with the butt of the rifle, roll him over, unbuckle his belt, and pull it free. I use his own belt to bind his hands behind his back, pull off one of his loafers, slip off the sock, and stuff it into his mouth.

Moving to the end of the pallet, seeing Tommy, I motion for him to join me.

Together, we roll Geno toward the center of the warehouse, where his men can see him bound and gagged.

"Look at your boss by the truck!" I yell. "Put your hands up and come out!"

Rifle fire in my direction answers as Tommy and I both hit the floor.

"Shoot at me again and your boss is dead! Look at the fucking truck!" I glance at Tommy and then my watch. "If you surrender you will not be shot."

Tick, tick, tick.

Fifteen seconds later, I yell again. "If you don't, we kill Geno and you. No one leaves here alive tonight unless you surrender!"

"They're afraid to," Tommy whispers. "Afraid their own men will shoot them if they surrender."

"Throw your weapons down and come out!" I command again. "You will not be shot by DeVecchio men!"

I check my watch. I'll give them another fifteen seconds.

Tick, tick, tick.

Nothing. Fuck. My patience is done. "You've got thirty fucking seconds to surrender your weapons, or we open fire. We will not stop until every Gabicci soldier is dead, starting with your boss! Twenty-nine seconds!"

Ten long seconds pass before a gun is shoved into the middle of the floor. Five seconds later, another slides into view. One at a time, Gabicci soldiers shove their weapons across the concrete floor toward the truck, their hands held high as DeVecchio soldiers step forward with their weapons trained on them.

"What are we going to do with them?" Tommy asks.

"There are too many of them to kill. Take them to the cells for the time being."

"What about Geno?" Chris asks.

"He gets a cell of his own. In the meantime, get the dead in the freezer."

"How many DeVecchio men are injured?" I ask, sipping a cup of coffee in the second-floor kitchen.

"We've got four wounded, including you. No one is going to die." Chris says.

I glance at my arm again. "It's a flesh wound."

"Back to the question at hand: What are we going to do with the Gabicci prisoners?" Tommy asks over his cup of coffee.

I drag my fingers through my hair. "I'm not executing twenty-some-odd men. A firefight is one thing, but that would be... unacceptable."

"Agreed." The capos speak in unison.

"They're soldiers, same as ours. Just doing a job. What would you want done if it was our men?" Chris asks.

"Let them go, and tell them to hightail it back to Jersey *after* we clean up the mess downstairs. Everyone works, either on clean-up or carrying bodies to the freezer."

"I say we load them in the truck and give them a ride back to Trenton, minus their weapons," Chris says. "I'll make it clear if they come back, it's at their own peril."

"Fine. *After* we clean up. You oversee that." I turn to Tommy, "You take everyone in the freezer deep sea fishing. Make sure they all have proper weights on their lines. What about the vehicles they came in?"

Tommy says, "They came in Gabicci trucks. The Gabiccis won't exist after tomorrow."

"Is our truck driver unharmed?"

Chris snickers. "Yeah. Little chickenshit never got out of the cab."

"So give him a mop and tell him to be ready to drive tomorrow."

Matteo
VELVET BOX

"**I** haven't made up my mind about what do I do with Geno."

Pop eyes me over his breakfast coffee, white-knuckling his cup with both hands. "You know what you do with him."

Our gazes hold as Pop unleashes. "If you let him go—even if you exile him to Europe, he'll come back and he'll try to kill you again."

I scoff as I pour my coffee. "I wasn't thinking of letting him go, Pop. I want to fight him. He called me a coward in front of my men and his—and I didn't do a fucking thing."

"You couldn't. It would've been exactly what Geno wanted—for you to give away your position." My father's bushy, white brows knit together as he stands from the breakfast table. "You won. You caught the son of a bitch, that's what counts. Now end him."

I grumble to myself. "I want to feel my fist in his face one last time. I can kill him afterward."

Pops erupts, pounding his fist on the kitchen counter so hard his coffee sloshes. "Don't be an idiot!"

He swings his arm wide as if pointing at the warehouse. "Had Geno won last night, he would've skinned you alive, probably in front of Sherry. Probably would've made you watch him rape her before he killed you. He does not deserve a chance to touch my son!"

Pop's as mad as I've ever seen him. His eyes are on fire as he bellows. "End him, son! End him! Today!"

I rub my hand over my face and feel the stubble as my mind takes a left turn. Some people are connected by blood. Family.

Some are connected by love, the way Sherry and I are connected. Like Tommy and Regina. Chris and Tina.

Others, like me and Geno, are bound by a hatred embedded in the core of our souls.

It's almost as if the gods pre-ordained us eternal enemies at birth with a vengeful lightning strike—Colpo d'odio. The strike of hate.

Yes. I realize, from the day we were born, one of us was destined to kill the other. So, why do I hesitate?

Because I am selfish. I want the satisfaction of killing Geno with my hands. The same way he wanted to settle it. Eye to eye. Man to man.

And, maybe to a degree, it's because his death will mark the end of an era. For half of my life, I've fought Genovese Gabicci. Who will take his place? *The enemy you know...*

"Matty?" Sherry's soft voice startles me from thought. She touches my arm gently. "Does it hurt?"

I glance at the wound. One bullet passed through my bicep. "I'm fine."

Her aqua eyes are focused on mine as she whispers, "Sweetheart, as long as that man lives, we'll constantly be looking over our shoulders. Think of our children growing up with the threat of Geno Gabicci looming over them."

"None of you seem to understand. It's not that I don't want to kill Geno. I want the satisfaction of killing him with my hands. In a fair fight."

"You did last night!" Pop is about to have a stroke. It's a rare occasion when Donna DeVecchio remains silent, her gaze bouncing between her husband and son, but she recognizes my father's rage. "There is no such thing as a fair fight with Genovese. He brought forty men to our warehouse and you still beat him. You out-planned him, out-thought him and out-fought him. Now take your victory. Leave well enough alone."

Sherry peers up, stroking my cheek. "Matty, you killed Sophia because she tried to kill me. I'll kill Geno. He tried to kill you."

Somehow, I know she would. "I can't let you do that."

She whispers, "But I would."

"Wake up, Geno."

He's bound in the same way Enzo was. The same as all of them, handcuffed to the chain that hangs from the ceiling of the dimly lit second-floor cell. His ankles are shackled to the floor.

He pissed himself in the night.

No man's piss smells any better than another's. No matter how good or bad you think you are, the human body is the human body. It can only take so much.

I nod at Tommy, who holds smelling salts under Geno's nose.

He stirs, blinks, and shakes his head. Gaining his senses, seeing me, Geno snarls. "Coward."

"Always a pleasure, Geno. But you're my prisoner now."

He viciously jerks on his cuffs, testing the strength of the chain. When it doesn't yield, Geno bellows. "What do you want, fucking butcher?"

It brings a grin to my face. "You got my gift?"

As soon as we knew Geno was hiding at Alfonso's house, we had the box with Joey and Enzo's hands couriered over. Further incentive to lure him to our warehouse. "I guess you know who they belonged to?"

Geno spits. "That worthless weasel, Joey, who couldn't do anything right. But Enzo Accardi was a fine man."

"You sent Enzo to kidnap my woman. He would've done it, if I hadn't happened to have been there to stop him. The world needs to know what happens to anyone who touches her. Word will spread. You never could keep your mouth shut."

If looks could kill... but they can't. All Geno can do is growl like the dog he is. "Finally living up to your nickname? Butcher of Baltimore? Fucking pussy. You going to cut off my hands, too?"

I shake my head with a satisfied smile. "There's no one left to send your hands to, Geno."

"Is it true you killed Sophia?"

I step toward him, studying this man who's done everything in his power to ruin me and mine, and I realize, peering into his shark eyes, that Geno and I are Neptune and Mars. Water and fire, each capable of destroying the other. In this lifetime, I triumph. "You killed Sophia when you sent her to deliver Sherry to you. Just like Enzo and Joey. You're lucky I didn't have her hands sent to you, too."

He spits. "You worthless piece of shit. You used her. Fucked her. Killed her." He roars. "Just kill me, too."

"I will."

Geno and I were born into this life. There's nothing either of us can say or do to change anything, and I know, were I the one in cuffs before him, he would take his time to torture and torment me. But I don't have to drag it out the way he would. "Look at me, Geno."

His eyes meet mine for the last time as his upper lip curls. "I'll see you in hell, DeVecchio."

"I'm sure you will."

I pull the trigger, embedding a bullet into his brain.

"Matty! Did you see the news?" Sherry asks through a mist of steam as she enters the bathroom.

"Sweetheart, I just got out of the shower. I haven't seen anything. Why?"

She peers up from the newspaper in her hands. Her blue eyes are wide as they bore into me. "Remember that Congressman Mulholland and his aide Richard Kerrigan?"

"Yes. Of course."

"Well... they died in the night."

"Really? How?"

"It says their car was rear-ended by an 18-wheeler at a red light—and it just burst into flames." Her forehead furrows as her eyes dart across the broadsheet, absorbing the morning news. "It says they both died in the fire."

I dab shaving cream on my face. "Where were they?"

"In D.C.," she answers.

Sherry watches me with suspicious eyes as I begin to shave. "Matty?"

Our gazes meet in the steamy bathroom mirror. "What, sweetheart?"

"That doesn't surprise you?"

I shake my head softly and go back to shaving. "Were they in a Pinto? I hear that's happened before, out in California."

She scans the newspaper. "It doesn't say."

"Hum."

Her gaze narrows as she tilts her head, watching my every move as if I were a fly creeping along the counter. I fight to suppress a grin when she says, "And you know, Scott was shot to death yesterday, too."

I stop shaving and turn to face her. "Buchanan? Your ex? Good riddance. Who did it?"

"They don't know. It says Scott was hit by a sniper's bullet, coming out of the courthouse."

I finish shaving and rinse my face. "What do you want me to say, sweetheart? Life is dangerous." I pat my face dry.

I'm showered and shaved and naked except for the towel around my waist, and looking at her, my dick stands at attention. "Come here," I command. "I have something for you."

She sets the paper on the counter and moves to me, wearing nothing but the silky black nightie she slept in. Her long, curly hair cascades wildly. Sherry is one hell of a woman: beautiful, intelligent, and brave.

Her perfect brows rise high with surprise as I place a velvet box in her hand.

As she opens it, she draws in a quick rasp of air, her hand clamping over her heart. "Oh, Matty, it is beautiful!"

"Try it on." I take the ring from its nesting place and slip it on her finger. It is a perfect fit.

She stares at her hand. "Matty! A blue diamond. I never dreamed. Oh, my Lord, how beautiful!"

She peers from the ring to me with wonder, and my heart sings.

"It was the only choice. Big and blue, like your eyes. Sempre, amore mio." I pull her to me and brush my lips across hers as I grow rock hard. "Il mio colpo di fulmine."

Those eyes tell me she doesn't understand. It's time I teach her the old language. An Italian honeymoon will help. "Forever my love. The first time was false lightning. *You* are my thunderbolt."

Afterward

DeVecchio: Colpo di Fulmine was inspired by two literary works of art.

First, the passage, 'On Love,' from *The Prophet*, published in 1923 by Lebanese-born philosopher Kahlil Gibran. The book is, in my opinion, a must-read.

Secondly, by *The Godfather*, (the book, not the movie), written by Mario Puzo and published in 1969.

Matteo DeVecchio is a blend of Santino Corleone's quick temper and his youngest brother Michael's cold, intellectual reserve - two passionate men who were willing to face the fires of hell in order to protect their loved ones, as is Matteo.

Hope you enjoyed reading!